A Kiss from Mr Fitzgerald

NATASHA LESTER

hachette
AUSTRALIA

hachette
AUSTRALIA

First published in Australia and New Zealand in 2016
by Hachette Australia
(an imprint of Hachette Australia Pty Limited)
Level 17, 207 Kent Street, Sydney NSW 2000
www.hachette.com.au

This edition published in 2017.

10 9 8 7 6 5 4 3 2 1

National Library of Australia
Cataloguing-in-Publication data

Lester, Natasha, author.
A kiss from Mr Fitzgerald/Natasha Lester.

ISBN: 978 0 7336 3800 8 (paperback)

Nineteen twenties – Fiction.
Women – Social conditions – Fiction.
Man-woman relationships – Fiction.
Love stories.
New York (N.Y.) – Fiction

A823.4

Cover design by Ingrid Kwong
Cover images courtesy of Shutterstock and Sarah Tröster/ ImageBrief
Text design by Bookhouse, Sydney
Typeset in 14/16.75 pt Centaur by Bookhouse, Sydney
Printed in Australia by Griffin Press, Adelaide, an Accredited ISO AS/NZS 4001:2004
Environmental Management Systems printer

To my family, for always understanding my need to spend time with imaginary people.

Prologue

How did I get here? How did I get here? The words reverberated between each click of Evie's heels as she stepped off the moon and executed a perfect Ziegfeld strut. Her arms were extended as if to lift the skirt of a dress she wasn't wearing, and her head was pulled back by the halo of a hundred silver-dipped stars. She smiled at the audience, who thought that what she did was, at the least, entertaining and, at the most, foreplay. Her neck ached but she concentrated on the sound of the dollar bills that Ziegfeld would flick into her hand at the end of the night, like a baccarat dealer at a high-stakes table.

The music changed to the big, belting fanfare of the finale and Evie curtseyed, then took her place near the centre of the line of showgirls. She knew what she had to do: join arms, scissor-kick the legs, emphasise the breasts, and damn well make herself look so delicious that no one in the crowd remembered the New York that existed beyond the doors of the theatre. That was a place of discreet money and manners and hidden mistresses, where a woman called Evie Lockhart fought a battalion of men every day for permission to become a doctor. Inside the theatre, the men had no manners, the mistresses were out on show, the money was splashed around like whiskey, and Evie Lockhart was once again fighting, this time to remember that an exchange of dignity for college fees would be worth it.

Where did it all go? Evie thought as she spun around. All my joy, all my wonder. New York used to knock the breath right out of her. Now it was a daily struggle just to get enough air. But she slapped her smile back on, because Florenz Ziegfeld was glaring at her, and Evie needed to be a Ziegfeld Girl more than Ziegfeld needed her. She'd better give someone in the audience a sultry wink to show she was still playing the game. As she looked for a man to dazzle, she got a feeling like an itch at the corner of her eye; she blinked once, twice, but the irritation was still there, narrowing her focus to the man in the fourth row from the front – centre seat so he must be important.

When she saw who he was she got what she wanted – the breath knocked right out of her.

It was Thomas Whitman. Tommy. Back from London.

Would he recognise the girl from Concord, Massachusetts, who used to live next door – oh, such a long time ago? He'd never expect to see Evelyn Lockhart dancing a cancan with a line of beautiful girls whose long legs shimmered from toe to thigh in a way you'd never see in a drawing room on the Upper East Side.

Evie knew she should look away. But two and a half years in London had transformed Thomas into the cat's whiskers. He'd been handsome before, but now he was heart-stopping, and he looked all the better for not slicking back his hair like the rest of the Valentino imitators in the crowd. His eyes were like black marble, and unlike those of most of the men around him, they were studying her face, not roaming her body.

Then he stood up and began to step past the people seated beside him. He strode towards the exit, even though the show wasn't over. It could only mean that beneath the thick kohl lining Evie's eyes, the red lips, the leotard and the stars, Thomas had seen someone he used to know.

Luckily it was the last number of the night. The curtain was about to come down and Ziegfeld's Girls would be officially off duty, unless they wanted to don a sheer, lacy robe and go up to the bar and pout because the cigarette dangling so elegantly from their quellazaire was unlit. Evie never joined them and she certainly wouldn't tonight. Instead she'd lie awake, remembering how often she'd dreamed of kissing Thomas Whitman. And she'd try not to think about the fact that now he knew she worked for Ziegfeld, he'd never want to see her again.

PART
One

Chapter One

'"None of the Victorian mothers – and most of the mothers were Victorian – had any idea how casually their daughters were accustomed to be kissed"', Evelyn Lockhart read aloud from the book hidden inside the covers of *Ladies' Home Journal.*

'I don't believe it says that,' said Viola, looking up from her embroidery.

Evelyn carried the book over to her older sister and pointed at the page. 'There. Kissing is the bee's knees.'

'Mr Scott Fitzgerald isn't a reliable source of information.'

Evelyn groaned. 'You sound like Mother. Don't you want to know what it's like?'

'Curiosity killed the cat.'

'Why should only bad things happen to a girl who is casually kissed?' Evelyn dropped the book and the magazine on the sofa and walked over to the Victrola, which was droning 'Sweet Adeline' at her like a dirge. She began to dance to a song in her head which had decidedly more brass.

'I'm not going to read it,' said Viola. 'So you needn't leave it there. And did you know that *Ladies' Home Journal* disagrees with you?' She put down her beloved embroidery and picked up the magazine. '"Anyone who says that youths of both sexes can mingle in close embrace – with limbs intertwined and torso in contact – without suffering harm lies. Add to this position the wriggling movement and sensuous stimulation of the abominable jazz orchestra . . ."'

Evelyn wriggled her hips as hard as she could and extended a hand to her sister. 'Dance with me, Vi. Have some fun.'

Viola stood up and Evelyn thought they might dance around the room together, talking about the things that mattered, like kissing and life in the city and women who did things besides sew coloured thread into pieces of fabric.

But Viola walked past Evelyn to the window and gasped. 'Charles is coming up the path,' she said. 'If he sees you dancing like that he'll never get around to proposing.'

'And I suppose he'll marry you instead,' Evelyn retorted.

'I'm the oldest.'

'It doesn't matter. He . . .' *He likes me better*, Evelyn started to say. She stopped herself. But her unspoken words hung in the air anyway, causing Viola to study her stitches, which were straighter and smaller than Evelyn could ever manage, and Evelyn wished for a moment that Viola would be able to find a man to whom sewing mattered more than beauty.

She heard the maid answer the door and Charlie's footsteps in the hall. She stilled her hips but couldn't help whispering, before he came into the room, 'I wonder if Charlie is accustomed to casually kissing the daughters of Victorian mothers?'

'Evie!' Viola bleated.

The door opened.

'Ladies,' said Charles Whitman, bowing with a flourish. 'What a picture you look, sewing so contentedly.'

'I can't remember the last time I saw Evie sew anything,' Viola said smugly.

Evelyn laughed. 'You win, Vi.'

'She stitched a crooked C on a hanky for me to take to Harvard,' Charlie said.

'That's right! I did,' said Evelyn triumphantly, although she couldn't help wondering why such a minor accomplishment should matter so much.

'It's the one I always carry with me.' Charlie tapped the left side of his chest and looked at Evelyn in a way that made her wonder what it would be like to touch his cheek, to run her hand through the waves of his blond hair. To casually kiss. To think of him as Charles the man, not Charlie the boy who'd been her great friend.

'I'm glad you're back,' Evelyn said. 'But aren't you supposed to be studying for your examinations?'

'I've been asked to take a week off,' Charlie replied, grinning unrepentantly. 'Somehow Harvard's taxidermied animals escaped from their cases and were found lurking around campus and I've taken the blame. I'll return with downcast eyes next week, be forgiven, and I can get back to learning to be a banker.'

'You get away with everything,' Evelyn said. 'If you're rich, charming and a man, you can steal a stuffed cougar, call it a prank, make a donation to the college and then become a banker in the time it takes me to embroider a hanky.'

'Not that long, surely?' Charlie smiled.

'Evie's just annoyed because she can't do whatever she wants,' Viola broke in, always eager to highlight Evie's flaws in front of Charlie. 'She wants to stay on at Radcliffe but Papa won't let her.'

Evelyn tried to defend herself against Viola's accusation, at the same time noting that Charlie's hand was still resting over the pocket that kept her hanky safe. 'I've taken literature at Radcliffe and am qualified for nothing,' she said. 'So I thought about continuing on. I thought doing more study would . . .' Her voice trailed off. Would what? Keep her amused as if she was a lapdog yapping for a bone?

'Surely literature's more than enough?' Charlie asked.

'That's what Papa says,' Viola agreed.

'Maybe I'd like to do more than sit in the parlour and compose pretty sonnets while I wait for my true love to sweep me off my feet.'

'What lady wants more than that?' Charlie said.

'I don't,' said Viola.

Her mother's arrival in the room stopped Evelyn from saying the words that nobody — her mother, her father, Viola and possibly Charlie — wanted to hear: *I think I do.*

'Charles!' Mrs Lockhart exclaimed, kissing his cheek. 'Lovely to see you. It's been so long. I was hoping you'd escape Harvard and come to your parents' party this evening.'

'I wouldn't miss it,' Charlie replied, not mentioning the prank that was the real reason he was in Concord. 'Thomas is bringing along a lady from Boston whom everyone expects him to marry. My parents want to introduce her to Concord society.'

'Oh,' breathed Mrs Lockhart. 'I didn't know. How marvellous. An engagement is exactly what we need.' She looked pointedly at Evelyn, who pretended not to notice. 'Well,' she continued, 'it's such a fine day, why don't you go for a walk together. I'm sure your mother will be glad to keep you out of the house while she prepares for the party.'

Charlie nodded. 'A walk sounds capital. Ladies?' He held out his arms for Evelyn and Viola.

'Go on ahead, Charles,' Mrs Lockhart said. 'I need a word with my daughters first.'

Charlie left the room to collect his hat and Mrs Lockhart turned on Evelyn. 'With a bit of effort, you could find yourself with a ring on your finger, or at least the promise of one, by the end of the night. Be pleasant on your walk and again tonight and anything could happen. You're quite the belle when you want to be.'

'Mother,' sighed Evelyn.

'Marrying Charles is what you want, isn't it?'

It's what *you* want, thought Evelyn. And it was something Evelyn used to think she wanted from the moment she was old enough to understand that certain things were expected of her. She'd begun to look forward, with more than her usual enthusiasm, to summer, when the Whitmans left New York and came to Concord, to Mrs Whitman's grand and gracious family home, to escape the sticky heat.

Having Charlie next door filled Evelyn's days with fun and adventure, especially as Charlie did anything Evelyn dared him to do, even dive off the North Bridge outside the Old Manse in a ridiculous attempt to disturb the peace of the town. Evie and Charlie went together like roses and sunshine, which Evelyn's mother thought was splendid, because it would have been impossible for the Lockharts to ever mix with the likes of the Whitmans if they weren't summertime neighbours. Mrs Lockhart might consider her family to be upper-middle class, but the distance to upper-upper class, where the Whitmans resided, was like flying to the moon. And the moon could be conquered if Evelyn married Charlie. Even her mother had had to relinquish her hopes for her favourite child, Viola, the one who was most like her, when Charlie's preference for Evelyn was so obvious to all. There was the older brother, of course, but as Thomas came to Concord so rarely, busy as he was at the Whitman Bank, Mrs Lockhart had accepted he was beyond their reach. Whereas handsome young Charlie would make the perfect husband for a Lockhart girl. And the Lockhart girl he seemed to adore was Evelyn. But Evelyn couldn't help the thoughts that had begun to nag at her lately, now she'd finished college and had nothing to do: what if marriage meant she became like her mother, napping in the afternoon from the exertion of coming downstairs to breakfast, content to organise parties of ladies to sew useless whatnots for the hospital fair?

'Do you really like sewing?' Evelyn asked her mother and sister before she stepped into the hall.

'Of course.' Her mother shook her head, as did Viola, puzzled by the question.

'I hate it. It's not something I want to spend the rest of my life doing.'

'What other choice do you have?' Evelyn's mother said.

And that was the problem. Here in Concord she had none.

Evelyn followed Viola out of the room. 'What if it doesn't work out the way it's supposed to?' she whispered to her sister.

'Of course it will,' said Viola, clearly unable to imagine anything other than what was expected of them. 'Charles will propose tonight and you'll be married and be the lady of the house next door. And I'll marry one of his friends,' she added determinedly, her plain face momentarily brightened by the thought.

Evelyn smiled. So Viola had dreams too. But she had to ask, 'What comes after that? After I'm married?'

Viola looked surprised. 'Does it matter?'

They'd reached Charlie, so Evelyn couldn't answer. As they walked down the front path to the road, Evelyn glanced at the house next door, the Whitman house. She was unable to picture herself there, waiting for Charlie to come home from work, embroidery hoop laid in her lap like a noose ready to squeeze the life out of her.

⁓

Early summer in Concord was glorious. The blossom trees extended their jewelled fingers into the sky and petals drifted down to wreath Evelyn's hair. Rabbits hopped out of the way, their cottony tails bobbing like bits of fallen cloud. Robins twittered a tune that reminded Evelyn of 'April Showers' and all its optimism about blooms that follow the rain and the hidden bluebirds that could be found if only one listened hard enough. She wished the birds would sing something more spirited and less sentimental. At the same time, she looked around and realised that she was alone with Charlie and that Viola was nowhere in sight.

'Viola's bootlace came undone. She'll catch up,' Charlie said, taking Evelyn's hand and stopping in front of her. 'You're so beautiful, Evie,' he continued. 'If I took you to Harvard my pals would burn with jealousy.'

Evelyn knew she was blushing; it was nice to be complimented rather than criticised or ordered around as was her parents' way. 'Thank you,' she whispered, but somehow, even in the midst of all the glorious summer colour and Charlie's admiration, she couldn't shake the word *noose* from her mind.

Charlie put his finger under her chin and lifted her head so he could see her face. 'With you beside me, everyone would know I was the successful one,' he said.

Evelyn had thought he might be about to kiss her. She certainly hadn't expected him to say that. 'But you *are* successful,' she said.

Charlie took his hand away from her face and began to walk on. 'My father doesn't think so. Not compared to Thomas.'

Perhaps you should study more and play with stuffed animals less, Evelyn wanted to say. If her parents let her go on to university, she wouldn't waste the chance on stupid pranks. But she knew Charlie wanted petting rather than scolding, so she kept her thoughts to herself as she walked beside him.

'Thomas is announcing his engagement tonight,' Charlie said. 'Why else would he invite a girl out here for a party? I could make it a night for engagements. Beat Tommy at his own game.'

'I don't think Thomas is getting engaged just to show your father he's more successful.' Why were they talking about Charlie's older brother? Charlie had practically just told her he would propose. They should be strolling hand in hand at the very least, savouring the moment. But did he want to marry her because he loved her, or only because he thought she was pretty and it would help him prove a point? And did she really love him, or did she just want to know what it would be like to kiss someone?

Evelyn had never been so glad to see her sister reappear, lank hair stuck to her cheeks and her face flushed red with the exertion of hurrying after them. It saved Evelyn from her confusion. But she had to work out an answer to her question – did she want to marry Charlie? – before tonight.

She needed to be by herself so she could think. Her mood suited a brisk pace, whereas Viola needed to catch her breath and Charlie was lost in the art of strolling, clearly preoccupied with his idea of trumping his brother at the party. She soon found herself well ahead of the others, and the further she tramped, violently crushing swathes of white lilies beneath her feet as if they were embroidery hoops, the more she knew embroidery was not the issue. There was so much she had not yet done, so much she could do — go to university, or work like women in the big cities did. If she married Charlie, the only life she would ever know was the one she lived right now, the one that chafed her like a tightly laced corset.

'Aaaarrgh!'

A sudden wail made Evelyn glance back; Charlie and Viola weren't in sight and, in any case, the cry was coming from somewhere ahead, closer to the river. The sound came again, the guttural, animal cry of someone in pain.

Evelyn scrambled down the bank. When she reached the river's edge she could see nothing, but she heard a rustle of movement in a copse of reeds. She bent down, pushed the stems aside and gasped at the sight of a woman crouched on all fours like a cat, her skirts rucked up around her waist and her backside bared — two hanks of thick white flesh and between them a rush of blood, pouring onto the soil below. But there was something else there, something emerging from that place Evelyn knew existed but had never really seen, that space of secret monthly bleeding and other things she had heard whispered of, and which she knew could somehow produce a result such as this. A baby. This woman, screaming in terror, was giving birth to a baby right here and right now. Evelyn's skin began to prickle because she felt as if the baby was looking straight at her, pleading with her. Was that even possible? Could a half-born baby open its eyes?

Evelyn blinked and the sensation vanished. 'Let me help,' she said, crawling into the reeds, heedless of the blood. She gasped again when she saw the woman's face. 'Rose!'

The woman was a fellow student from Radcliffe. She and Evelyn had collided one day while crossing the quadrangle with their heads down to avoid the pouring rain. They'd laughed and taken refuge in the main hall. After they'd introduced themselves, Rose had told Evelyn that she was one of the few women going across to Harvard to take courses at the medical school, even though Harvard wouldn't allow women to graduate with a degree in medicine. Evelyn had been fascinated by the idea, so Rose had smuggled her into one of the lectures.

It was like stepping off this world and into another. No decorous recitations of Shakespearean sonnets. Instead, the inner workings of the human body were exposed. Evelyn had since crept into a few more lectures with Rose, who welcomed the female company and urged her to come along whenever she could. But Evelyn knew her parents would banish her to a cornfield in Iowa if they ever found out. As it was, it had set off a restlessness inside her, a longing to know more. College had finished a week ago, leaving Evelyn with only a taste of the possibilities that existed beyond literature and marriage, and she hadn't seen Rose for some time because Rose had simply vanished after Easter. Now here she was, her face as white as if it had been laundered to Evelyn's mother's exacting standards. Her arms were sinking into the ground; she was no longer able to bear her own weight and she clearly didn't recognise Evelyn. Her eyes were glazed with pain and fear.

'Lean against me.' Evelyn said. She sat on the ground with her legs extended, helping Rose to turn over and lean back on her. 'It'll be all right,' she said. 'My father used to be a doctor. I'll call for the others to get him. You shouldn't be out here on your own. You should be in Boston with your family. You should be . . .' She realised she was babbling, because this was beyond anything she'd ever imagined. How could Rose be having a baby? And why was she on a riverside in Concord, far from home?

She cradled Rose's head against her shoulder, wiped the hair off her clammy brow and hugged her. Rose's body sagged. Was she simply tired? Unconscious? Dear God, she couldn't be dead, could she? And what was happening with the baby? 'Charlie!' she shouted, as loudly as she could. 'Charlie!'

Evelyn heard footsteps. Viola and Charlie were getting closer. She needed to check on the baby. She eased herself out from behind Rose, propped her against the reeds, lifted her skirts and found the baby's head, still exactly where she'd first seen it. It hadn't moved, it was blue and Evelyn didn't know if this was normal. 'Help!' she screamed.

Kneeling between Rose's legs, she put her hands on the baby's head.

'Evie! What is it? Are you hurt?' Charlie's voice sounded panicked and Evelyn was glad he was there: he would help her while Viola fetched Father.

The baby's shoulders began to move into Evelyn's hands and she forgot about feeling scared. If she could get the child out, perhaps Rose would wake up. She pulled gently and felt a surge of wonder as more of the baby appeared.

Then Evelyn found herself cradling a child. 'Oh,' she said. 'Look at you.'

She wanted to hug the baby, hold it close, but some instinct told her to wrap it in her skirts and rub it. It was so blue and it hadn't made a sound. 'Cry,' Evelyn whispered. 'Please cry.'

Charlie's face appeared above the reeds, followed by Viola's.

Viola's hands flew to her mouth and she said, 'Oh. Oh,' before turning away and holding onto a tree.

'She had a baby,' Evelyn said, needlessly, but what else was there to say? *Help us, we need help, I don't know what to do. What if I hurt the baby?*

Charlie grabbed Evelyn's arm and pulled her, heedless of the child.

'Careful,' Evelyn said. 'Hold the baby while I check on Rose.' As she spoke, the baby began to cry. Thank God. 'Get Father,' she called to Viola. 'Tell him to bring his medical bag. He still has it somewhere.'

But Charlie didn't take the baby from her. 'You need to leave. Now. Take Viola with you,' he said.

'I can't leave. I have to help. Viola can go by herself.' Evelyn realised that her sister was still standing there, her back turned to them. 'Viola!' she called again. 'Hurry up!' She cradled the baby in one arm so she could help Rose with the other.

'This woman doesn't deserve your help,' Charlie said. He tightened his grip on her arm and tried to force her to stand.

Evelyn dug her shoes into the soil. 'Stop it!' she cried. 'You'll hurt the baby. Let me go!' She tugged her arm away but Charlie was strong, stronger than she'd realised. The baby was wailing now, as if it sensed danger, and Evelyn wanted nothing more than to soothe it, to see if Rose had revived, but Charlie would not let go. She tried pleading. 'You can't expect me to leave them here. If you've ever felt anything for me you'll let me help. Please!'

Her last word was a frantic scream. She could no longer hear the baby crying, had no idea where Viola was. All she could see was Charlie's face, so close to her own that she could not mistake the hard flash of anger in his eyes, and the curl of disgust on his lip at Rose's plight. *Damn you!* she wanted to shout. Damn everybody and their stuffy rules that said she couldn't help someone who might be dying, just because there was a whiff of scandal. She would not move. She would not stand up. And short of dragging her up the riverbank, she knew there was nothing Charlie could do.

He let go of her arm suddenly and Evelyn tipped backwards onto her elbow, desperate to keep the child safe. Charlie stormed up the riverbank, not bothering to help Viola, who stumbled after him, crying.

Evelyn could only hope that he would be back soon with her father and that her father's long-retired skills as a doctor would somehow revive Rose, whose eyes were closed, her face devoid of colour, her limbs lifeless. What should Evelyn do? She had no idea. Nothing she had ever learned at Concord's Ladies' Academy or at Radcliffe had taught her anything about saving someone's life. What good were French and dancing to her now?

'I'm sorry,' she whispered to Rose as the tears ran down her cheeks. 'I'm so sorry.'

Her father and Charlie found her like that, sobbing, the baby held close to her chest, her body curved around Rose as if she could will life into her.

'Evelyn!' her father snapped. 'Stand up at once!' Mr Lockhart's face showed the same look of horror as Charlie's had.

'You'll help her?' she asked, unwilling to move until she had secured his promise.

'Go straight back to the house,' her father bellowed. 'Only then will I help her.'

Evelyn scrambled to her feet and gave the baby to her father. He glared at her and she reluctantly walked away.

The climb up the riverbank was like a hallucination. The woods were still awash with peach blossoms and buttercups. And she was in Concord, home of girlish delights and *Little Women*, not death and scandal and secrets. There was no longer any blood, except that covering Evelyn's hands and soaking her skirt. There was no crying or screaming, just the rustle of Evelyn's feet and the constant drip of tears from her face. The sense of stupor intensified when she reached the house. As she stood in the doorway of the sitting room, surrounded by the warmth of mahogany wood, gilt lamp stands and the ochre velvet of the chaise longue, what she had witnessed seemed unreal. Had it really happened?

'Viola?' Evelyn said.

Viola, who was collapsed on the lounge, uttered a groan that Evelyn knew came from no real affliction, so she said it aloud, trying to make it real again. 'She had a baby.'

'Evelyn!' It was the nutcracker snap of her mother's voice. 'Your dress!'

Evelyn stepped aside to let her mother pass. 'There was a woman by the river,' she said. 'I tried to help her.'

Mrs Lockhart held up her hand. 'I know what happened. I heard Charles tell your father. This is the last time it will be discussed. A woman like that has fallen in the eyes of God and in the eyes of man and her fate is not a subject for young ladies.'

'But –'

'No. Besides being filthy, your skirts are pulled up so high I can almost see your knees. Go and change now.'

'They're just knees, Mother.'

'And that attitude is how women end up in disgrace by the river.' Mrs Lockhart moved over to Viola, to smooth her brow and murmur consolation in her ear, as if Viola, not Rose, had been the wretched one.

Evelyn understood that the incident had been swept away like breakfast crumbs, discarded and forgotten. Nobody would speak of it again. All of Evelyn's questions would remain unanswered. But they clamoured in her mind nonetheless: was Rose alive? Was the baby? Had Evelyn helped it or hurt it?

She took off her hat and laid it on the hall stand. She suddenly realised she hated that stand, with its gold Minton tiles and gold-plated drip trays. Who really needed their umbrella to drip into a gold tray? Society did. A society that thought Evelyn was not supposed to sit in the dirt and let a labouring mother bleed all over her. She was supposed to run away, aghast, and then faint like a lady. Because an unmarried woman having a baby alone by the river was a position never to be recovered from; it guaranteed invisibility and revulsion, so that every time hereafter, when Rose went to the grocer's store and was ignored, she would know she was also being mocked and judged and declared repugnant, like the cow's feet the butcher threw away because even the poor wouldn't eat them.

Evelyn remembered the baby's eyes, how they'd stared at her. It was helpless and trusting, yet she'd abandoned it. For its whole life, everyone would treat that baby the way Evelyn had, turning their backs. How could she have left Rose and her baby to the mercies of Charlie and her father? And would she ever be able to make amends?

Chapter Two

'Evie!'

As the Lockharts stepped inside the ballroom of the Whitmans' enormous home that evening, Charlie rushed over to greet them. He took Evelyn's hand eagerly and kissed it, eyes fixed on her face, but the ache in her arm where he'd gripped it that morning and the memory of his concern for decorum over compassion made her look away.

'I hope you'll dance every dance with me,' Charlie said. When Evelyn didn't reply, he turned to her mother. 'You won't mind if I monopolise Evelyn tonight?'

'Not at all,' Mrs Lockhart replied, staring at her daughter, trying with the power of her eyebrows to make her respond to Charlie with gratitude and a smile.

Charlie held out his arm. Evelyn was aware that people were watching them, having heard Charlie call out her name and kiss her hand, noting that he'd singled her out above all the other ladies in the room. She had no choice but to take his arm. But she held back her smile.

As Charlie led the family through the room, Evelyn began to feel hot. Her dress was one that suited her mother's idea of modesty: the full skirt fell to her ankles and the sleeves finished below her elbows. Her hair was up, the long, blonde length of it sitting heavily on her head, pressing down on her like the imperious hand of God. The room was crammed with the important families of Concord, men from Harvard, and couples from New York, where the Whitman bank was located. Thomas, Charlie's brother, moved through the crowd, introducing Alberta, the prim-looking girl on his arm who Evelyn assumed was his intended fiancée. It was all very elegant, from the lovely turquoise gown that Mrs Whitman wore – which Mrs Lockhart, with her preference for the drabness of the peahen, whispered was shockingly bold – to the six-piece band playing on the terrace outside, to the abundance of cut crystal glasses filled with impossible-to-get French champagne, handed out by waiters who pretended never to have heard of Prohibition. But it was also stiff and constrained; everyone smiled and said how lovely Alberta was, even though Evelyn thought she looked wintry, as if chatter and spontaneity were unknown to her. She longed for someone to dance the Breakaway across the room to relieve the monotony of it all, but that would be almost as scandalous as what had happened this morning.

'Excuse me,' she whispered to Charlie, retrieving her arm and moving away.

Before she could escape, her mother squeezed Evelyn's left ring finger and hissed, 'Remember why you're here.'

But Evelyn wasn't in the mood to smile until she got the engagement ring her mother wanted for her. She needed some air. As she walked out onto the terrace, she heard her name; it had been spoken by one of a group of men who were clouding the air with cigarette smoke just inside the door. She quickly moved against the wall, hidden from their view, and listened.

'Yes, she's a looker,' said another man. 'Charlie isn't all brag and no substance this time.'

'He'd better get her down the middle aisle before somebody else does,' said the first man. 'I wouldn't make a girl who looked like that wait too long.'

'But Charlie isn't renowned for his smarts,' sniggered another. 'Besides, a pretty girl like that wouldn't be marrying him for anything other than the dollar bills lining his pockets.'

Evelyn's cheeks burned brighter than the full moon shining outside. She couldn't bear to hear any more, so she hurried down the steps of the terrace and crossed the lawn, then stopped in front of a tree. She remembered herself as a child sitting astride a branch of this old apple tree in the Whitmans' garden, bouncing up and down, riding a pretend horse. Life was so uncomplicated then. Charlie was her friend. Nobody knew anything about marrying well or how babies were born, and nobody boasted about anything other than how many spots they had had when they caught the measles. Back then, Charlie would sit on the branch opposite, racing Evelyn across the fields of their imaginations. If her mother saw her, she would send Viola to tell Evelyn to get down at once as it wasn't ladylike, but Evelyn ignored her, knowing that nobody would climb up and fetch her, knowing she had the power because she was up high and out of reach. She'd be sent to her room later for her disobedience, but she didn't care; the fun was worth every bit of her mother's scolding.

Now Evelyn pulled up her skirt, feeling the breeze rub against her stockinged legs. She slipped off her shoes and tossed them onto the ground, grabbed hold of the tree, gaining a foothold on the lowest branch and then the next. Being tall, she quickly reached the branch that had always been her horse, Sunny. To sit astride it she had to hitch her dress higher, so she looked like a girl from a Fitzgerald novel – except then she would have been sitting in the back seat of an automobile, not on the limb of a tree. The ground seemed so much closer than it had when she was a child. In her memory, the distance between Sunny and the lawn was celestial; the fields she'd traversed were the vast plains of the sky, splashing through cloud lakes and jumping over rainbow bridges. She pulled an apple off a branch and bit into it; it tasted like summer and devil-may-care. The apple was gone in a minute and she threw the core down with satisfaction, just as she used to, imagining that Viola was beneath, never expecting a direct hit even though one got her every time she came to take Evelyn home.

'Ouch!'

Shocked, Evelyn peeped through the branches and saw Thomas Whitman staring up at her. 'Oh no!' She blushed. 'I'm sorry.' She hurriedly swung her leg around so that she was balancing side-saddle on the branch, and tugged down her skirt.

'I thought everyone was inside,' Thomas said. 'May I ask what you're doing?'

'Riding a pretend horse like I used to with Charlie, and stealing your apples,' Evelyn said quietly. Her mother would be mortified: young ladies who were meant to be pursuing engagement rings didn't climb trees and attack men with apple cores. She blushed again and sought to explain. 'Trying to steal back a moment I'm probably too old for.'

The last thing she expected was that Thomas Whitman would reach out to one of the lower branches and pull himself up, with a grace that suggested he'd been climbing trees since long before she could walk. She barely knew Thomas; he was five years older than Charlie, and when the family came to Concord he'd always been away at school, or off on holidays with friends, and, lately, in New York helping his father run the bank. He sat down on the branch that had once been the horse Charlie rode.

'Shouldn't you be inside?' Evelyn asked.

He nodded. 'I should. But I haven't climbed this tree in years. I taught Charlie.'

'No, you didn't. I dared him to climb it one day and we raced to see who won.'

'Who won?'

'Charlie.'

'Of course.' But she could tell he didn't mean that of course Charlie won because he was a boy, he meant of course Charlie won because he'd known what he was doing all along.

She shook her head and turned the conversation to something more conventional. 'Alberta seems lovely.'

'She is lovely.' His voice was lacklustre and Evelyn hoped that if ever a man called her lovely, he'd say it with more passion than Thomas had mustered.

They were both quiet a moment. The sounds of laughter and conversation waltzed demurely out of the house and away with the breeze, along with the strains of 'Let Me Call You Sweetheart', a song to whose dated schmaltz Evelyn had a particular aversion. She leaned her cheek against the tree trunk, remembering Rose and the baby among the reeds. The garden was dark. She couldn't see Thomas's face. All day she'd held back what she wanted to say. She was tired of holding her tongue, and there was nobody else to ask. 'Did you hear about . . . what happened this morning?' she said.

Thomas didn't reply straight away. He probably had more pressing things to think about, like proposing to Alberta. Evelyn was about to climb down from the tree when he moved and sat on the branch beside her.

'At the river?' he asked.

'Did Charlie tell you?'

'Yes.'

'What did he say?'

'Charles was concerned about your clothes. He said he'd helped your father with a woman in trouble.'

'You mean he was cross with me for not fainting like Viola. And that's a very polite way of putting it. *In trouble*. It's like the woman's a haunting or a curse, the way everybody avoids speaking about her.'

'Perhaps they think they're protecting you.'

'Perhaps I'm old enough to look after myself.'

'I didn't say you weren't. I said they might *think* they're protecting you.'

'Do you know what happened to the woman? And the baby?'

'My mother went to the hospital this afternoon with a box of things for the baby. Apparently the woman died. But the baby survived. I expect it'll go to an orphanage, because nobody will take in an illegitimate child. It'll probably be dead too, within five years.'

Evelyn closed her eyes. She'd always thought she knew what kind of world she lived in. But this world of death and disgrace, of a woman she knew dying by the river, was not a place where one galloped on a tree-horse through sunshine and sky. She could still hear Rose's groans, still feel the moment when her body went limp. She wondered if she should say any more; her mother would send her to a convent if she knew what they were discussing. But Thomas was listening to her, apparently without outrage; he actually seemed nice, not the stuffy older brother Charlie had always made him out to be.

She opened her eyes. 'I held the baby. I helped it out. It was ... incredible.' And then the question she needed to say aloud even though she knew the answer. 'Why wasn't she at home? Or in a hospital? Why was she out there alone?'

'I expect nobody knew she was carrying a child. Perhaps she thought if she went to the river she could make the child disappear.'

Disappear. Vanish – drown, perhaps. What would it be like to think you had to kill your own child in order to survive? 'She could have gone to New York, or another city far away, to a hospital where nobody knew her, and had the baby and pretended she had a husband.'

'Who would she ask for the money to travel? Would you go to an unfamiliar city and expose your predicament to a doctor who'd probably scorn you for it?' Thomas didn't ask the questions in an interrogating manner, the way her father spoke to her when he was doubting her judgement about something like college. Thomas asked the questions as if they deserved thought rather than anger, and at the same time he was provoking her to take her mind to places it had never been before.

'No,' Evelyn whispered. Now that she'd seen what childbirth looked like, it was hard to imagine doing it in front of anyone. But that was the point. Rose had literally been brought to her knees by bodily function and shame, and everybody was too polite and well bred to help her. 'I knew her. She was a Radcliffe girl. And now she's dead.'

'Did you know she was ...'

'No, we weren't close friends. She was taking science classes and I . . .' Evelyn hesitated before confessing. 'I went to a couple of anatomy classes with her. But please don't tell anyone that. My parents would be horrified if they knew I'd been to a science class.'

'Which do you prefer, science or literature?'

'Science.' Evelyn waited for the snort of disapproval but it didn't come. 'You're very different to Charlie,' she said.

'I'm the reserved one and Charles is the fun one. Right?' He looked across at her and she could just see, with the help of the moonlight, that he was smiling.

She laughed. 'I meant it as a compliment. But you're right, Charles had led me to believe you were the pompous one.'

'Pompous! That's worse than reserved.'

'It is. Charlie used to tell me stories about you and I'd tell him stories about Viola, how she was always so niminy-piminy, always doing everything Mother asked her to do and telling Mother when I invariably didn't. Apparently you're the model of your father,' Evelyn teased.

'My father taught me to study hard and to work hard and that the rewards would follow. It's not such a bad thing to believe in.'

Evelyn remembered what she'd wanted to say to Charlie earlier that day: *Don't waste your time at university.* 'It's not a bad thing at all,' she agreed.

Thomas removed a cigarette case from his pocket and offered it to Evelyn. She took one. He then produced a lift-arm lighter, which Evelyn was too embarrassed to admit was the first she'd ever seen. All the men she knew used matches, as did the Radcliffe girls she'd smoked with on occasion. In the flame, she looked at him properly for the first time in her life. Dark hair, dark eyes. Handsome. Alberta would be happy.

'All we need is gin,' she said as she leaned back against the tree again and blew smoke into the night air.

'I came prepared,' he said and pulled out a small silver flask. 'It's whiskey though.'

'I was joking.'

'I know, but it's that kind of night.' He offered her the flask.

'Well, whiskey it is.'

In spite of the uproar she knew there'd be if anyone found her smoking and drinking whiskey, she took a sip and felt her throat blaze as she swallowed. She coughed. 'That must be an acquired taste.'

'I would have brought gin if I'd known I was going to be sitting in a tree having a conversation like this.' Thomas smiled at Evelyn again and she smiled back, feeling more exhilarated by talking to Thomas than she had by anything since she'd left Radcliffe.

'If that's all we have I'd better start acquiring the taste.' She took another sip, managed not to cough and found herself saying, 'That's not the first birth I've seen. When I was about ten, I remember my mother labouring over a birth that went on for more than a day. She would groan every now and again and that's how I knew there was a problem; I'd never before heard Mother make a sound so loud. When the midwife left the room, I went in and held my mother's hand, thinking she'd tell me to leave, but she didn't. She clenched my hand every time the pains came. I think it was the only time in my life when I helped her rather than annoyed her. Of course the baby died, like all the others that came after me. We've never spoken about it though.' She returned the flask to Thomas.

'It was good of you to help. Both times.'

'I didn't even think about *not* helping. Or that it was an improper thing to do until Charlie tried to drag me away.'

Thomas studied her face. 'Charles mentioned something about an engagement announcement tonight.'

'Yes, but did he say it was because he loved me or because he didn't want you to be the first to get engaged?' Evelyn bit her lip as she saw Thomas's expression cloud over. But in the semi-darkness and with his face turned slightly from hers, it was hard to tell.

He didn't reply immediately and Evelyn thought she'd ruined the moment – that he'd climb down from the tree and return to Alberta, that he'd tell Charlie what Evelyn had said. But instead he shifted a little so that he was sitting closer to her. 'I'm sorry you think Charles might do that,' he said.

I'm sorry too, Evelyn thought. 'Perhaps we shouldn't talk about Charlie any more. Then we can't betray any confidences.'

'That's probably a good idea.' Thomas sipped from the flask and held it out to her again. 'What shall we talk about instead?'

Evelyn took a large swallow this time, because she wanted to loosen her tongue, to say something she'd never said to anybody. 'I've heard some of the universities in New York are starting to accept women into their medical degrees.' She said it lightly, as if she was just making conversation and the answer didn't matter a great deal.

'Columbia has. Unlike Harvard.'

'If more women were doctors, perhaps they could help women like Rose.'

'Perhaps *you* could help women like Rose.'

Neither spoke for a moment. Evelyn stared at Thomas. He'd read her mind. And he'd said it as though it was actually possible. 'I helped a baby into the world today,' Evelyn said. 'I'll never forget it.'

'Thomas!' It was a woman's voice, probably Alberta, calling from the top of the terrace.

'I think dinner is about to be served.' Thomas's words, bringing them back to the world they'd briefly forgotten, made Evelyn laugh, a gush of released tension.

Thomas jumped down from the tree. 'I won't offer you a hand,' he said from the ground, 'because I know you're more than capable of making your own way down.'

And then he was gone, leaving her to think about what he'd said: *You could help women like Rose.* Which would mean becoming a doctor who delivered babies, feeling the same surge of wonder she'd felt when she held Rose's baby. But if she decided to pursue that path, her parents and Viola would never speak to her again. Would Charlie? After this morning, she doubted it. And even if she *could* do it, did she have the strength to go against everyone's wishes, to create a life for herself that was so different to what everybody expected of her?

By the time Evelyn appeared, Thomas and Alberta were sitting in pride of place at the head of the long table, with Thomas's parents on either side. Charlie sat alongside his mother, with an empty space on his right for Evelyn. Viola had been placed beside their father, and the expression on her face showed her disappointment at her lack of prospects.

Even though the oysters on the half-shell and the soft-shell crabs on toast had already been served on delicate Delft porcelain plates and Evelyn knew she should sit down, she stood behind her sister and whispered, 'Why don't you take my place?'

Viola stared at her. 'Why?'

'Would you like to sit there?'

'Yes. But don't you?'

'Not tonight.'

Viola stood up, clearly excited by the prospect.

'Viola, where are you going?' Mrs Lockhart had seen them. 'That is Evelyn's place.'

Evelyn saw her sister's face crumple. She sat in her allotted place and shook her head. Why was today so determined to show her that nothing and nobody was the way she had thought? Viola was never scolded. She was their mother's preferred child. It had always suited Evelyn to think so. But perhaps Mrs Lockhart could be just as hard on Viola as she was on Evelyn, caring more for social advantage than her daughters' feelings.

'Evelyn, my dear, I wondered where you were. I haven't even said hello to you.' Mabel Whitman leaned across her younger son to give Evelyn a kiss on the cheek, and Evelyn smiled back warmly. Mrs Whitman had always been one of her favourite people, turning a blind eye to tree climbing and Mrs Lockhart's calls from next door.

'I was outside. It's a beautiful evening.'

'Fresh air seems to be in demand tonight,' Mrs Whitman said. 'I almost had to send out the hounds to find Thomas.'

Thomas caught Evelyn's eye and they shared the briefest of smiles, which reassured her that he wouldn't mention their rendezvous in the apple tree, and certainly neither would she.

'I thought you'd taught him better than to leave a lady to look after herself, Mother,' Charlie said.

'I think Alberta managed perfectly well on her own.'

'How does your mother like Alberta?' Evelyn whispered to Charlie once Mrs Whitman's attention was elsewhere.

'Honestly?' Charlie sipped his wine. 'She thinks Alberta is more interested in Tommy's money than in him. Mother is ever the romantic; she's the only person in the world who thinks money shouldn't matter. Surely you've heard the story about how she and my father met?'

'I haven't.'

'Their eyes locked across a crowded ballroom and she knew, from that moment, that she loved him and would marry him. Without first finding out about his income, his prospects, his family or his profession. Luckily he more than passed on each of those measures.'

'Charles.' Mrs Whitman overheard the last part of the conversation. 'You're teasing me. And being cynical. I hope both my sons marry for love. That's not such an awful thing to wish for.'

'But love and money would be a better thing to wish for,' Charlie said, smiling.

'Your father has worked hard for everything we have,' Mrs Whitman said. 'Did I ever tell you,' she turned to Evelyn, 'that we did quite the scandalous thing when we were married?'

'No,' Evelyn said. 'What did you do?'

Charlie rolled his eyes. 'Here comes her other favourite story.'

Mrs Whitman ignored him and continued. 'I lent George my entire dowry so he could set up the bank. It wasn't at all the done thing, a man borrowing money off his wife, but he was the sort of man who put securing a future ahead of his pride.'

'That's a wonderful story,' Evelyn said. And it explained something of her revised view of Thomas. If he really did take after his father, then he had probably never been pompous to begin with.'

'Mother likes to do the unexpected and not fall into line with others,' Charlie said indulgently. 'We let her because she says it keeps her young.'

Evelyn didn't hear Mrs Whitman's response; her attention had been caught by her mother.

'Did you hear that Nancy Totten went to see Alice Paul speak?' Mrs Lockhart was saying to the woman beside her. 'The *suffragette*.'

Please stop, Evelyn urged her mother silently. *Please don't say anything more.* After what had happened that morning, after seeing her family's lack of charity, after watching a woman die before her because she knew nothing other than how to read quatrains, Evelyn didn't know if she would be able to sit in silence and listen to her mother's closed-mind opinions.

'I don't think I'll be hurrying along to use the voting machine any time soon,' Mrs Lockhart continued. 'I'd much rather use one of those new washing machines I've been hearing so much about.' Several of the ladies nearby tittered in agreement.

It was the fault of the whiskey, most likely. But it was also because Evelyn needed to know: did Charlie's behaviour at the river mean that he felt the same way as her mother did about everything? She spoke up distinctly. 'At school, Miss Forbes said that the opportunities the suffragettes had won for women would only be understood by history, as we're all too satisfied with our comfortable lives to understand the benefits of their work.'

'Evelyn.' Her mother gave the smallest shake of her head and flicked her eyes towards Charlie, who certainly wasn't stepping in to defend Evelyn's views. 'Miss Forbes is clearly something of a revolutionary who won't retain her position at the Academy if she continues to express views like that.'

'Surely you're not going to complain about a woman championing the intelligence of other women?' Evelyn said.

'Alberta and I were talking earlier,' Mrs Lockhart said quietly, and Evelyn knew that the subtext was that she should take note of Alberta's opinions and reshape her own to match. 'She agrees with me that it's only middle-class girls who harbour aspirations for intellectual accomplishment. It's unfortunate really; some middle-class girls have enough money to give them aspirations, but not enough money to become ladies. Luckily, we are not in that position. Henry,' she turned to her husband, 'didn't you say that Harvard had allowed some Radcliffe girls to come over for science classes? And that they were . . . fast? Henry is occasionally invited down to lecture as a distinguished alumni.' This last was directed to the wider group around the table, presumably lest anyone think Mr Lockhart made his living from being a middle-class professor.

Evelyn realised that following her outburst, Alberta and some of the other ladies within earshot were looking at her with amusement, as if she was a whimsical attraction at Coney Island. She wanted to change the subject, but Mrs Lockhart was determined to drive her point home. 'Charles,' she said, 'what do you think of the girls who come across to Harvard for the sciences?'

'They're not the sort one thinks about,' Charlie replied.

Evelyn felt a sting of pain.

Mrs Lockhart smiled triumphantly. 'Suffragettes and sciences. One wonders what some women will dream up next. Besides, the word "suffragettes" speaks for itself. Now we all have to suffer the boredom of politics. If they really knew what they were about, they'd have chosen a more pleasing name.'

More titters. Evelyn stared at her plate to hide the flush on her cheeks and to stop the tears from falling. She perfectly understood what her mother meant. Talk of university would not be tolerated. By her mother. Or by Charlie. She should be more like Viola and Alberta. Docile. Unambitious. Happy to marry. She nodded gratefully at the waiter who was offering to refill her champagne glass.

'I'm looking forward to casting my vote. Women have to live under the laws passed by Congress. We might as well have a say in who passes those laws,' Mrs Whitman said, and Evelyn felt a small spark of hope. But then she heard Charlie snort derisively and the feeling passed. Mrs Whitman's views might be less conservative than those of most women in her position, but her son's obviously weren't.

Charlie's mirth had caught his father's attention.

'And I would prefer Charles to think more about his studies than the women who attend Harvard,' Mr Whitman said. 'Then he would spend less time on enforced breaks from university.' Mr Whitman frowned at his son and Evelyn could see that Thomas really did look just like him, although less grave and also more open, warmer.

'Oh, Charles can't help that he has a mischievous side.' Mrs Lockhart reached across and patted Charlie's hand.

Charlie cleared his throat. 'I'll give my full attention to my studies when I return.'

'I've heard that many times before, Charles.' Mr Whitman turned to Evelyn and said, affectionately, 'You know why he's here, don't you? Too busy pranking to study. Perhaps if I hand him over to your care this evening I can hope to find him improved by the end of the night.'

'Oh, I don't know about that –' Evelyn began, but broke off when she saw Charlie's face. He looked mortified to have his lack of studiousness brought to everyone's attention, just as Evelyn had been humiliated when her mother launched her veiled attack earlier. She felt her heart soften a little. Perhaps Charlie hadn't been himself today. His father had most likely upbraided him when he'd arrived back from Harvard, and he'd probably still been upset when they'd encountered Rose and the baby. That must have been what had made him seem so unfeeling.

Before main course was served, Mr Whitman stood up and tapped on his glass. Evelyn expected the announcement of Thomas and Alberta's engagement. Mr Whitman began to talk about Thomas, praising his hard work and Midas touch, which she didn't think was all that relevant to marriage, and she only understood where the speech was going when Mr Whitman finally said, 'I'd like you all to congratulate the bank's new vice-president.'

Thomas smiled at his father and received the combined congratulations of almost everyone at the table. But not his brother's. Charlie stared at his wine glass with the same expression he'd worn when his father had admonished him. The evening hadn't gone the way Charlie had planned; he'd been well and truly trumped by Thomas, in a way he clearly hadn't anticipated, and now Evelyn felt sorry for him. She reached out her hand to touch his, to say, *I understand*, but he brushed it away and looked past her.

'Richie!' he called down the table to one of the men Evelyn had heard talking about her earlier. 'Have I introduced you to Evelyn yet?'

'You haven't.' Richie smiled, and Evelyn nodded at him uncomfortably.

'She's quite a girl, isn't she?' Charlie added.

'She is,' Richie agreed.

This time, Charlie reached out for Evelyn's hand. She let him take it, because Richie was watching and because she understood that Charlie didn't want her pity, that he was trying to regain the dignity he'd lost in the conversation with his father and in Thomas's promotion. She said no more at dinner. She smiled at Charlie. She received approving looks from her mother for her compliance. And she kept the restlessness that had been building inside her since the walk by the river and her conversation with Thomas tightly reined in.

Once the plates were cleared away, Mrs Lockhart grasped the opportunity to show Evelyn off to her best advantage. 'Why don't you play for us? Charles, you always like to hear Evelyn play, don't you?'

'It's one of my greatest pleasures,' Charlie said, leading the way into the drawing room and taking Evelyn over to the piano. He took out the music for 'I Love You Truly'. 'My favourite,' he said. 'Especially when you sing it.' Then he leaned on the piano and waited for her to begin the serenade.

People gathered to watch the performance, and Evelyn heard someone whisper, 'It seems that both brothers have found their match.'

Evelyn started to play and she could see both her mother and Charlie basking in the reflected glory of her voice singing that the rest of life faded in the face of love. But it didn't. No, as of tonight, life had suddenly become more vivid, a beautiful fan unfurling fold after fold of brightly coloured possibilities that she could pursue, if only she dared.

The whiskey, combined with the champagne from dinner, had made her head spin and her vision blur. Suddenly, everything she'd been holding in, all the fears about Charlie and the ridiculous idea she'd discussed with Thomas, threatened to spill over. She stopped singing, recklessly shifted her hands and tried to pick out the tune to 'Hot Lips', a jazz recording she'd covertly purchased and only listened to at low volume when her mother was out of the house. It took her a couple of bars to get it right, and then she started to play it louder, the rhythm completely unlike anything usually played in a Concord drawing room. Her mother rushed over, as the guests stared at Evelyn's musical outburst, and hissed, 'What are you doing?'

Charlie had stopped smiling too. His friends were laughing, probably at her, the provincial girl who didn't know how to give a decorous after-dinner recital. Evelyn remembered what Viola had read to her that morning from the *Ladies' Home Journal*, about the sensuous stimulation of the abominable jazz orchestra. Everyone in the room could do with a bit of sensuous stimulation. But Charlie's hand was moving down to close the lid of the piano and cut off Evelyn's song.

'You're right. We could do with something livelier now that dinner's over. Would you help me choose something for the phonograph?' It was Thomas. He'd stepped in front of Charlie and her mother and was offering to sweep her away from their censure.

'Thank you,' she whispered as she joined him at the phonograph. 'I don't know what's wrong with me tonight. I'm upsetting everyone, having conversations I shouldn't, drinking whiskey, playing jazz.'

'Is that really so bad?' Thomas asked, but before she could reply he left her speechless by saying, 'Besides, your voice is beautiful, Evie.'

Chapter Three

*H*er parents castigated her as soon as they arrived home. Her performance had been a disgrace — a rebuke that made Evelyn giggle although she knew she shouldn't.

'What's so disgraceful about music with a bit of tempo?' she asked.

'If you put as much effort into securing Charles as you do into behaving inappropriately, then we'd all be celebrating an engagement right now,' her mother said.

'Papa?' Evelyn looked across at her father, who could sometimes be more understanding than her mother. 'Couldn't I try university first? I could still marry later.'

'Men with the pedigree of Charles Whitman don't grow on trees,' her father replied. 'Your mother's right.' With that he left the room, taking the easy path, as he so often did, of not crossing her mother, whose strained silence if she didn't get her own way was more uncomfortable than the loudest quarrelling.

Her mother followed him out, and Evelyn understood that no further arguments would be permitted. She was to marry

Charlie. Unless she took matters into her own hands. But, in the meantime, there was something else she had to do.

Evelyn waited in her room until she was sure everyone was asleep. Then she crept down the stairs and out the back door, took her bicycle and cycled to the hospital. As she entered the building, she worried for a moment that someone from her father's time as a doctor might be working and would recognise her, but then realised it would be unlikely – he'd given up his career soon after Evelyn was born, when he'd come into an expected inheritance from a childless uncle and thus become the gentleman her mother had always intended him to be.

The corridors inside the hospital were quiet. Evelyn tiptoed along like a girl on her way to a secret meeting with a lover.

'Can I help you?'

'Oh!' Evelyn clapped a hand to her mouth in shock, turning to see a figure standing in a doorway.

The speaker was a young nurse. 'Sorry,' she said. 'We don't normally find people walking the halls at night. Unless it's the mad patients trying to escape.'

'I'm definitely not one of those.'

'I can see that.'

Evelyn laughed and relaxed. 'Can you keep a secret?'

The nurse studied her. 'You don't look like the sort to have a very bad secret, so I'll say yes. Come and have a cup of tea. I'm Anne.'

'Evelyn.'

Anne took her to a large kitchen and made two cups of tea that were as strong and bracing as a winter storm. They sat down at the kitchen table.

'I'm looking for a baby.' Evelyn hesitated, not sure how to say it. 'A woman gave birth this morning. By the river.'

Anne sipped her tea. 'I heard about that. A tragedy. Poor little thing, to lose its mother before it knew her. Most likely the mother is better off, though. She could move as far away as the moon and the shame would still follow her.'

'I wonder if I could see the baby?'

'Well, you could except the baby's gone.'

'Gone?'

'It was strange.' Anne leaned closer and lowered her voice. 'We don't get many cases of that kind but ordinarily it takes a few days to organise and then the baby is sent to an orphanage in Boston. But this baby didn't go to Boston.'

'Where did it go?'

'To an orphanage in New York. Probably the Foundling. It went by private car with a hired nurse and a chauffeur. Imagine that. It's a funny thing to do when there's an orphanage only thirty miles away. Someone didn't want the baby close by, I expect.'

Evelyn wondered if the nurse had read too many novels while working the night shift. 'You think someone took the baby to New York so it would be far away from Concord?'

'Yes. Someone's done something they shouldn't have and they don't want anyone to find the evidence of their mischief.' Anne stood up and motioned for Evelyn to follow her.

'I found something of the baby's on the path outside. I was going to get it washed and give it to the church. But you can have it if you like.' Anne led the way in to a room stacked with linen. She opened a drawer and produced a white knitted bonnet. 'I expect it fell off the baby's head when it was taken out to the car. It's not one of ours — whoever took the baby must have given it to the little mite.'

Evelyn reached out her hand. The bonnet was soft and had one or two yellowing age spots. The ribbons were coming away from the wool and were frayed at the ends. Evelyn had the strangest feeling that she'd seen this bonnet before, but that was probably just the effect of Anne making a mystery out of everything. Most likely every baby in Concord had been given a similar bonnet when they were born, knitted for them by a doting mother or grandmother. Someone had wanted to give the baby a small piece of homespun love. But they'd also sent the baby to New York. Why?

Anne was insistent, so Evelyn took the bonnet. She collected her bike outside the hospital. As she rode through the quiet streets, the bonnet in her coat pocket, she thought over the day. Her first instinct on seeing Rose had been to help. Not to run away. Her second instinct had been for the baby. Surely that told her something about herself? Didn't Evelyn have an obligation to Rose and her child? An obligation to help desperate mothers before they died alone and in secret shame by silent rivers? But Evelyn knew of no woman doctors, let alone one who delivered babies. It was unheard of. Shocking. Not something Evelyn Lockhart would ever do.

'Damn!' Evelyn shouted into the night. If only she lived in a Fitzgerald novel, in a world where girls rode around in cars with boys, necking and drinking and breaking all the rules, and there wasn't a damn thing their parents could do to stop them.

The maid knocked on Evelyn's door the next morning and passed her a note. 'He said I shouldn't give this to you at the table. He said it was private.'

The envelope bore the Whitman seal. Evelyn took it with a feeling of dread. It most likely contained the proposal that hadn't been forthcoming from Charlie last night after her jazz impromptu.

The breakfast bell rang and Evelyn had never been so glad to hear the sound. It meant she had no time to read the note. She tucked it into her pocket and went downstairs. She listened as her mother and Viola discussed Alberta's delightful manners and lovely hairdo, feeling every crackle of the letter when she moved. For once she wanted breakfast to last forever so she didn't have to open the letter, but all too soon the dishes were cleared and Viola had left the table.

'Do you think Charles's proposal will come today, Evelyn?' her mother asked.

Evelyn touched her pocket. 'I don't know.'

'Sit beside me for a moment.' Mrs Lockhart tapped the chair next to her own. She looked at Evelyn knowingly. 'You're concerned because you think you don't love Charles.'

Evelyn hadn't expected her mother to be so perceptive. So she replied honestly, 'I'm not sure if I do.'

'You've always been a romantic. But love isn't a requirement for happiness.'

'Are you happy?' Evelyn asked. She had to know if anyone else shared the same apprehensions when thinking of marriage, or if it was just her.

'As happy as most people are. And if you're worried about having to . . . entertain your husband, don't be. After the first child . . .' Mrs Lockhart stopped.

'What? Tell me. If marriage isn't so wonderful, why does everybody do it?'

'Because it's the way of the world. As a woman, it's how you get a house. Money. Children. You're my daughter. I want you to be looked after. There is no other way.'

As her mother spoke, Evelyn could see her hopes written in the plainest of languages on her face. Her mother had little to look forward to, beyond a shred of gossip or a new dessert recipe for the cook to try, and it seemed to Evelyn that Mrs Lockhart believed her life, in the sense of having dreams and desires, was over and she had to grasp at these infrequent joys through the lives of her daughters.

Evelyn felt her eyes fill with tears. When she had the ability to bring her mother some contentment by marrying Charlie, how could she be so cruel as to withhold it? But she plunged on, as she always did, asking one question more than she should. 'What if there'd been a female doctor who could have helped you, in a hospital, with your babies?' she said. 'All you had was a midwife and a bowl of hot water, and me, holding your hand. What if things were different in the world?'

Her mother stiffened. 'What on earth are you talking about? A female doctor? Such a thing doesn't even exist.'

Evelyn averted her eyes. It would serve no purpose to correct her mother, to say that yes, there were a very few female doctors in the world and that Evelyn was wondering what it would be like to be one of them. Thankfully, Mrs Lockhart let her go.

⁓

Evelyn took the letter that would surely decide her fate down to the private walk between the yew hedges. The day was sunny, birds were out sky-dancing, flowers were budding and the clouds had eloped with the rain. Over the wall, she could see the Whitmans' apple tree.

This could be her last moment as Miss Evelyn Lockhart, she thought dramatically as she sat down on the bench. The last moment before she moved to New York – if Charlie ever finished at Harvard – and took her place in society as a banker's wife. She tried to picture Charlie's face but instead, inexplicably, she saw Thomas, the way he'd looked at her when they talked in the tree last night. And then she thought of Rose and her baby, and her own fledgling dream of helping women. Of doing something, being more than Mrs Charles Whitman. More than a mother to the little Charles Whitmans.

She opened the envelope and unfolded the letter slowly.

She didn't recognise the handwriting. Her eyes skipped to the bottom of the note. There, written in a bold flourish, was the name *Thomas Whitman.*

> *Dear Miss Lockhart,*
> *I hope this note is not presumptuous but I felt I had*
> *to write it after our conversation last night. I know a*
> *respectable man in New York, a former tutor of Charles's,*
> *who has also tutored some women to ensure their education*
> *meets the standard that universities such as Columbia*
> *require. His name is William Childers. Perhaps you could*
> *work with him to find out if your interest in science and*
> *your idea of helping women might become something more*
> *than an idea. I will send him a letter to advise that you*
> *may call on him in the future.*
>
> *You may also be interested to know that my mother*
> *is returning to New York next week and would be*
> *delighted to have you stay with her. She will send a*
> *letter to your mother inviting you to accompany her.*
>
> *Please disregard if this information is not of interest*
> *to you.*
>
> *Sincerely,*
> *Thomas Whitman*

Evelyn reread the letter. She folded it up and let out a breath she hadn't realised she was holding. The relief that it wasn't a proposal from Charlie! She put the note back in the envelope. Then she took it out and read it again because perhaps she now had a plan that excited her more than the prospect of marriage to Charlie ever had.

'Thank you!' she shouted excitedly at the Whitman house, even though she knew Thomas would never hear her. She couldn't help but blow an impulsive kiss his way.

What if she went to New York to see what might be involved in pursuing this unlikely idea of becoming a doctor? She could test her interest and her strength. She'd say that she was going to New York to shop. No one had to know what her true plans were. Not until she knew which life she wanted to lead, and which life she was prepared to leave behind.

Chapter Four

'What are you up to, my dear?' Mabel Whitman asked as Evie settled beside her in the rear of the car, exactly a week after she'd received Thomas's letter.

Evie blushed. 'I hoped nobody thought I was up to anything.' She looked out the window as the chauffeur picked up speed and Concord passed by in a rush of pastel, the colours of candy and cake and childhood. 'My plans are probably very foolish.'

'Even the best plans can seem foolish to begin with,' Mrs Whitman said.

'What did Thomas tell you?'

'He mentioned something about university. And he said not to tell your mother.'

Evie laughed. 'That about sums it up. Remember I told you I wanted to continue at college but my parents disagreed?'

Mrs Whitman nodded.

'I didn't know then what I wanted to study. But now I want to see what might be involved in studying medicine.' As soon as Evie said it, she wanted to take it back. It sounded shocking when said aloud in her girlish voice.

But Mrs Whitman didn't flinch or look disgusted. 'It's a fine idea.'

'After seeing Rose – the woman at the river – with the baby ... I thought perhaps I could become ...' Evie's voice faltered on the final, ridiculous phrase. She looked down at her gloves, at the white fabric covering her hands as if they were something appalling to behold without the gloss of silk. 'I thought about becoming a doctor who helps women give birth.'

'An obstetrician.'

It sounded simple when Mrs Whitman said it. Still, Evie felt she had to mock her own absurd ambition. 'It's like saying I want to be a lady of the night. Unthinkable. More than unthinkable. Most people, my mother included, would never speak to me again.' She paused before continuing, encouraged by Mrs Whitman's expression. 'But I thought if I found out what I'd have to do, I could go to Papa and show him that some universities allow women to study medicine and then he might reconsider. I mightn't mention the obstetrician part for now, though.'

Mrs Whitman laughed. 'That's probably a good idea. One hurdle at a time. You should try the College of Physicians and Surgeons. It's now a part of Columbia University. They have the best reputation.'

Evie recalled Thomas's letter. He'd also referred to Columbia. 'I will. And I'm glad you don't think I'm being outrageous.'

'It's outrageous that only male doctors or midwives help women with birthing, especially now that so many women are going to hospitals to have their babies. Now there'll be fewer midwives and more men involved in giving birth, which makes no sense to me. If young women like you try to become obstetricians and scientists or even the mayor of a city, then more people will start to believe women can do such things.'

'You make it sound as if it's possible.'

'I hope it is.' Mrs Whitman smiled at Evie. 'Have you said anything to Charles?'

Evie sighed. What if Mrs Whitman was only helping her because of Charlie's attachment to her? Should she mention to Mrs Whitman her doubts about marrying Charlie? It was hardly honest of her to be silent. But she also needed Mrs Whitman's help more than she'd ever needed anything. So she prevaricated. 'I haven't,' she said. 'It's hard enough saying it to myself.'

Mrs Whitman nodded and surprised Evie by saying, 'Some advice: it's much easier to be dissuaded from something when you don't yet have it all worked out in your head. Don't tell Charles about your idea until you're ready.'

Through the window of Evie's bedroom at the Whitmans' the next morning, Central Park sparkled with dew like a Tiffany diamond. Evie's feet itched to go outside. Both New York and the Whitmans' Upper East Side mansion were like a dive into cold water; a visceral and brilliant shock that made her whole body and mind feel alive and exhilarated. She wolfed down some waffles for breakfast and left for an adventure. It was only when she began to walk down Fifth Avenue that she realised she was unsuitably attired for adventure. The young women on the street wore vivid shades of teal, red and emerald. The waistlines of their dresses had been relocated to their hips and their sleeves draped like wings from the shoulder to the wrist. Evie wore a pale grey suit that made her feel invisible and not up to the task she'd set herself for the day. She needed armour, something to both protect her from and give her strength to handle the meeting she'd organised with the tutor Thomas had recommended. If she dressed like Evie Lockhart, medical school explorer, then perhaps she'd feel less like Evelyn Lockhart, the girl from Concord who'd never had a real adventure in her life. She quickly found Saks & Co., where a stunning array of shoes greeted her — silk, satin, brocade, velvet, lace. The perfect pair caught her eye in the same way as the dew of Central Park had, beckoning with a similar air of promise.

'I'd like to try these on, please.' Evie pointed to the shoes in a way that she hoped suggested she frequented Saks regularly. In fact, she had only ever been shopping before in the company of Viola and her mother, on their twice-yearly expeditions to Boston for reclothing.

As soon as she slipped the shoes onto her feet she knew they were going to be lifelong friends. She paid for them with money given to her by her father and stuffed her old shoes in a rubbish bin. It was reckless, she knew, but she couldn't bear to keep anything that made her feel as young and unworldly as she probably was. In the clothing department she found a dress to match, plus another for evening, and then stared at the rouge and lipstick in the toiletries department for at least ten minutes before she worked up the courage to buy some. Afterwards, she quickly hid the packages in her purse, even though she'd already noticed that many women in Manhattan wore cosmetics. Here, going outside without rouge seemed almost as unthinkable as going outside without a hat, whereas in Concord to be seen wearing makeup was to declare yourself a harlot.

Evie sailed outside and heard 'The New York Glide' swirl onto the sidewalk from one of the nearby restaurants. She hummed along to the words — *Just grab your partner, 'round the waist, hook her lightly in her place.* Her shoes were dancing shoes, covered in tiny silver beads and clear glass crystals, with a rhinestone button on the sides to secure the strap. They were out of place on a city street at noon but she didn't care. They made her feel brave. She could imagine them sparkling in a jazz club after the sun went down — a side of the city Evie desperately wanted to see. She'd have to show her smile to Charlie tonight when he arrived from Harvard for the weekend, in the hopes that he'd take her out. He was her only chance to see the city at night; she knew nobody else in Manhattan.

Just lay back and do the shimaree; Buzz up to your baby like a bumblebee, the song continued. Perhaps in New York, things would be different. Charlie would judge women with scientific aspirations less harshly. His behaviour by the river would prove to be an aberration. She reminded herself that they'd been great friends forever. And who knew what might happen between them, locked in a foxtrot on a dance floor somewhere?

Evie grinned and checked her wristwatch. She had to hurry. She was due at Mr Childers' rooms in Greenwich Village in half an hour. Enough time to stroll along Bleecker Street, where her body loosened, shifted into the shape required to wear the dress she'd purchased. Her legs seemed to lengthen, her gait unbuttoned itself and she strolled like the other young women on the street: freely, unconstrained by a corset of mothers.

She was so busy looking around that she kept bumping into people and apologising. Unlike Concord, with its street after street of wooden houses in shades of lemon, salmon and cream, standing far away from one another as if to get too close would be presumptuous, here everyone lived on top of each other, in row houses with windows lined up precisely, the only sign of discipline Evie could see. Otherwise it was a jumble of coffee houses, tearooms, fish shops and grocers draped in sagging awnings declaring the name – usually Italian – of the proprietor and what goods one might find through the doors, everything from *Pizza!* to headache powders. And in the midst of it all were wonderful buildings like the Jefferson Market Courthouse, a Victorian Gothic confection whose spired tower rose above the Village like a fairytale palace that had taken a wrong turn but was having too much fun in bohemia to return to its royal duties.

Evie could have kept walking forever, but she didn't want to be late so she backtracked to Carmine Street, found the right building and knocked on the door.

'Miss Lockhart?' The man who opened the door was younger than Evie had expected, only a little older than Thomas. 'I'm William Childers,' he said. 'Pleased to meet you.' He indicated that she should sit down in the front room. Evie carefully picked her way past teetering stacks of books and towers of paper that fluttered in the wake of her new dress.

She sat and took a deep breath. 'Thomas Whitman was concerned there might be gaps in my schooling that would prevent me from being offered a place at university. I'm considering studying medicine at Columbia.'

She paused, waiting for him to snigger at the thought. But either Thomas had already explained the situation to him or he had excellent composure because he only said, 'You've been to Radcliffe or Vassar?'

'I took literature at Radcliffe. I was top of my class. But discussing the merits of a Petrarchan sonnet is fine for dinner conversation and not much else.'

'Thomas is probably right. Most women are disqualified because they were taught to bake a pie rather than understand it's also a number.'

'I know what pi is,' Evie snapped.

'And did you know that a collegiate course of four years is considered the most desirable preparation for studies in medicine at Columbia?'

'Four years! But I've only studied at Radcliffe for two.' Evie's flash of anger vanished like champagne in the hands of a flapper.

They regarded one another for a moment. Mr Childers wore a look of resignation on his face, as if he had better things to do than bother with a silly girl who had too much time on her hands and not enough knowledge to understand she hadn't the schooling required to study medicine. Her dress no longer felt like armour. Instead the modishness of it and the deep violet fabric seemed to underscore his clear belief that she ought to be serving pie to her husband rather than sitting in his office.

Evie hesitated. She ran a hand over her dress. She tried to claw back some of her earlier exultation.

'Did Thomas speak to you about me? she asked.

'He did,' Mr Childers replied.

'Then if you know Thomas, you know he's not inclined to hyperbole. If he thinks I'm worth tutoring, perhaps I am.' Evie kept her eyes fixed on Mr Childers as she spoke, needing him to listen to her, to believe that she spoke the truth, even if she hardly believed it herself.

Mr Childers sighed. 'I said four years was the *most* desirable. However, the college also states their minimum requirement, which is two academic years – a minimum of seven months per year – at an acceptable college of arts and sciences. Radcliffe is deemed acceptable.'

So Evie had one thing in her favour. 'But is literature?'

'Ordinarily, no. You need to have taken one year of physics.'

'I've taken none.' This was worse than Evie had anticipated. Of course you would need physics. Anyone with a modicum of intelligence would know that. Her plan was being shown up as worse than foolish.

'If you read the college catalogue, you'll see that one year of physics is the equivalent of eight semester hours,' Mr Childers went on resignedly. 'It's the same with inorganic chemistry. You need to have completed one year, but that's an aggregate of six to ten semester hours.'

Evie needed to be certain of what she was hearing. 'One year of physics is only eight hours per semester?'

'That's correct. And your literature degree means you meet the requirements for English, and for French.'

'So literature has helped me with something other than analysing the finer points of Mr Fitzgerald's fictional kisses? But I don't think the chemical reactions in those novels are quite what the College of Physicians and Surgeons has in mind.'

Mr Childers surprised her by laughing. 'You're not what I expected. When I opened the door and saw you –'

'You thought I was a bored society lady wanting to fool around with science in between organising tea parties? It's my own fault, I suppose,' Evie continued. 'I bought the dress for courage without considering that bright purple might somehow magnify my intellectual failings.'

Mr Childers laughed again, a warm laugh, with an edge of friendliness to it. 'Perhaps the college could do with someone like you.'

Evie used the moment of apparent conviviality to find out a little more about him. 'Thomas said that you used to tutor Charles?'

'Yes. Through the winter break. Charles was close to failing. So Thomas dragged him down here every morning and sat with him while he worked. He thought that if he left his brother to his own devices, Charles would most likely find something else more entertaining to do.'

'And did it work?'

'He's still at Harvard.'

Evie relaxed. Despite the pi comment, she liked Mr Childers. He'd helped Charlie stay at Harvard, which was no small feat, he was forthright and he knew what she needed to do to make her idea a reality. Another thought struck her. 'Even if one year's worth of chemistry and physics is only thirty-odd hours, I'm not enrolled in a university to take those classes.'

'The college has a summer school from early July to mid-August. Registration is this week. You'll be able to take all the classes you need to meet the minimum requirements for entry into medical school in September. But you'll need someone to tutor you as well. The catalogue also states that meeting the admission requirements does not guarantee admission, and that . . .' Mr Childers opened a handbook and read aloud, '"The entire premedical record of each student is carefully examined by the Committee of Admissions in order that those who are adjudged most capable of meeting the exacting demands of the course and of the profession of medicine may be selected." Your grades have to be the highest possible. You want to be sure the admissions board can't overlook you because . . .'

'I'm a woman,' Evie cut in.

'Yes.'

'Will you tutor me?'

'I have a test you need to take before I decide whether to take you on.'

'I can pay you.'

'I'm sure you can, Miss Lockhart. But you may not be worth teaching.'

Evie was speechless. It was the first time in her life anyone had ever given her the true measure of herself. At the Academy, and at Radcliffe, her piano performances, her poetry, her French accent and her deportment were always praised. She did better than her peers at most things. Based on that praise, Evie had thought she was clever. But Mr Childers was implying that her cleverness might stretch only so far as the womanly arts. What if he was right? Life had been so easy until now. She had never really had to try at anything. Except sewing. And because she found it boring and difficult, she'd given it up. Perhaps it was finally time to work hard at something, to see what she was truly capable of. She didn't imagine Thomas had made it through Harvard Law School and up to his position as vice-president of the bank without having to work at it.

'Can I sit the test now?' she asked, either bravely or foolishly, she wasn't sure which.

'Certainly.' Mr Childers passed her some papers and stood up. 'I'll be in the other room. You have one hour.'

The equations in the paper seemed to go on forever, like rows of sheep on a sleepless night. Evie remembered the gentleness of her literature examinations, predictable essays on the use of punctuation in Emily Dickinson's poetry, and she almost despaired. But as she started to work, she began to see that mathematical and chemical equations had some similarities with the essay form: she was given the beginning paragraph and it was up to her to structure a coherent middle section and a logical conclusion. In one hour she didn't finish all the questions. There were many she didn't know the answer to. She understood now that schooling at a ladies' academy, followed by two years of literature at a ladies' college, was very different to schooling for a man.

Crestfallen, she handed the test papers back to Mr Childers. 'I expect I'm a great deal more ignorant than I thought.'

He shook her hand enthusiastically. 'But at least you're aware of your limitations. For most, that's half the battle. I'll telephone in two days to advise if I'll tutor you.'

In two days it might all be over, Evie thought as she walked back along Bleecker Street. A week ago it wouldn't have mattered. Now, because of Rose and her baby, it mattered more than anything.

When she returned to the Whitmans', nobody was about. Evie went into the drawing room and put on a recording she'd purchased in the Village. The title of the song suited her mood: 'Tain't Nobody's Biz-ness if I Do'. Daringly, she poured herself a glass of brandy from the decanter on the chiffonier, unable to stop the doubts. What if she failed Mr Childers' test, was unable to enter university and had to return to Concord? Then she'd have no choice but to marry Charlie.

She sat down in an armchair sideways, with her legs tucked over the arm in a way she would never have done at home and in a way she probably shouldn't do amid the grandeur of the Whitmans' home. But somehow, despite the brilliant green cloisonné vases that writhed with colourful dragons, the magnificent Picasso harlequins painted in shades of rose, and the elegance of the frescoed ceiling, Evie felt as if she was in a room meant to be lived in, rather than one that was purely decorative. She could see herself reflected in the mirror over the fireplace. Hazel eyes flecked with gold; blue eyes would have looked better with her blonde hair, her mother always said. Slender figure – too slender, her mother's opinion again; she needed to stop running around and learn to sit still. Pale skin and long hair that felt too heavy against her neck. It was the same skin, the same body, the same hair she'd had for twenty years. But none of it seemed familiar to her, because now it was filled with longings she might not be able to satisfy. She sipped her brandy and listened to the song, crooning to her that no matter what she did, she'd be criticised for it. The singer clearly knew Mrs Lockhart well.

She felt her eyes tear up and wiped them angrily. The old Evie Lockhart would cry and sulk. The New York Evie Lockhart wouldn't give up. She had to square her shoulders and hope for the best. Even if she was only pretending and underneath it all she felt as scared as hell.

～

'What adventures have you been having, my dear?' Mabel Whitman asked when she bustled into the drawing room. 'New York seems to agree with you; you look like a different woman.'

Evie laughed, gratified. 'I've been shopping.' She pirouetted to display both the shoes and the dress and then sat down again. 'I bought a dancing dress too,' she said. 'I'd love to wear it out one night. If I'm able to stay in New York.' She proceeded to tell Mrs Whitman about her meeting with Mr Childers and the disastrous test.

'Don't give up on Mr Childers yet,' said Mrs Whitman. 'He might be the kind of person who looks for possibility over performance.'

She'd just finished speaking when Thomas walked into the room. He kissed his mother on the cheek and greeted Evie formally.

Mrs Whitman smiled at her son. 'I was saying to Evelyn what a shame it is that Charles won't be here until tomorrow. I'd wanted Evelyn to go out and meet some young people.'

Evie looked at Mrs Whitman in surprise; she'd been saying no such thing. It was the first time Evie had heard about Charlie not arriving today. So much for her fancy of treating herself to a night of dancing.

'I thought you could take Evelyn with you tonight and show her the city,' Mabel Whitman continued.

'Oh really, I'm fine,' Evie said. 'You don't need to —'

Her protestations were cut short by Thomas. 'Of course. We'll leave after dinner.'

As he left the room, Mrs Whitman said, 'Now your shoes and your dress will have the outing they deserve.'

Chapter Five

Evie stood in her bedroom, staring at her new rouge, powder and lipstick. Did she dare? *Ladies' Home Journal* was no help. Its advice on makeup use was 'don't'.

She sat down at the dressing table and opened the powder first. It looked the easiest to apply. She dabbed a little on her nose. Too little; she couldn't tell the difference. She patted on some more. Better. Then the rouge. She brushed what she thought was a small amount on one of her cheeks, then examined herself and almost jumped back in horror. She looked like she'd spent too long in the sun. She wiped at it with her hand, but the wiping only made her cheek redder. Perhaps she should just take it all off. She ran the water and was about to wash her face when she stopped. What had she decided that afternoon? To not give up. And here she was, ready to consign cosmetics to the same fate as the sewing basket. She looked in the mirror again. Her cheek had settled to a gentle flush. It looked almost the way she'd hoped it would. Before she had any more time to think, she rouged the other cheek and applied a little lipstick. When she'd finished, she was taken aback. She looked different.

Not quite older, but as if she knew more than she really did. If only that were true.

Then she slipped on her new dress, which was daringly black. A sheer overskirt, decorated with amethyst-coloured embroidered flowers, fell to a few inches above ankles, enough to show off her new shoes. A sash draped around her hips, tied in a rosette at the side and then fluttered down her leg. The cap-sleeved bodice was also embroidered and Evie knew that was all she needed for decoration.

But as she walked down the stairs, Evie worried that she might have taken things a step too far with the cosmetics and the shorter skirt. What if the Whitmans thought she was fast? She had no idea what the rules were for well-brought-up young ladies in New York and she had no one to ask. It would be good to meet some people her age, as Mrs Whitman had suggested. It would be nice to have one friend in New York whom Evie could ask about the subtleties of lipstick.

When she stepped into the hall, Thomas was waiting. To her relief, he didn't recoil as if afraid to be sullied by her brazenness, nor did he laugh at her as if she looked like a clown. She hoped that meant she'd got the rouge right and that he wasn't just too polite to show his appalled reaction. He looked good, and Evie was glad to see he was wearing a tuxedo, rather than a tail-coat, which perhaps meant they were going somewhere fun. She felt a flutter of excitement at being escorted out into a New York night by such a handsome young man.

He ushered her to a waiting cab. 'We're going to Chumley's.'

'Chumley's?' Evie couldn't decide from the name if it was the kind of place she was hoping for.

'In the Village.'

Evie knew her question would sound gauche but her curiosity got the better of her. 'A speakeasy?'

Thomas nodded.

'Even after sharing a flask of whiskey with you in a tree, I can't quite imagine the Vice-President of the Whitman Bank at a speakeasy.'

'But Chumley's is the cat's pyjamas.'

Evie saw that Thomas was smiling at her and she laughed. 'You're teasing me. "Cat's pyjamas" is not something Mr Thomas Whitman would say.'

'No, but Tommy Whitman might.'

They rode the rest of the way in a companionable silence. When they stepped out of the cab, Evie felt sure that Thomas was teasing her again. They were in the middle of a residential street lined with townhouses. There was no sign of dancing or illicit drinking.

'That's Edna St Vincent Millay's house,' said Thomas. He indicated a three-storey red-brick townhouse that was so narrow it looked as if it was made for dolls, rather than people.

Evie had obviously misunderstood Thomas's intentions. Instead of going dancing, she was being taken on a tour of Greenwich Village, and although she felt a little silly, she couldn't help being struck by the thought of St Vincent Millay being able to write so beautifully while living in a space so small. For all its vastness, New York seemed to compress its people, geniuses or otherwise, into very tight spaces. Unless of course you were a Whitman and could afford a mansion.

Suddenly Evie heard the call of a saxophone coming from somewhere. Thomas led her to a nondescript two-storey townhouse on the opposite side of the street and, without knocking, opened the door and motioned for Evie to step inside. She hesitated at first, not used to walking into strangers' homes without an invitation, but if Thomas thought it was all right then she supposed it must be.

They went up one set of stairs and down another. At the bottom, they were most certainly not in a private residence. It was a square room with a bar in the centre and a crowd of people dancing and drinking. The walls were papered with the jackets of books; Evie could see F. Scott Fitzgerald's name on one cover, beside William Carlos Williams, Willa Cather and, of course, St Vincent Millay. Fireplaces created from old forges sent out a heat that probably wasn't needed given the number of people crammed into the room, but which had the effect of making all of the women remove their capes, revealing a backless dress here and a raised hemline there. The noise was exhilarating: jazz music, laughter and uninhibited conversation rose to the ceiling, along with a haze of cigarette smoke. Evie put a hand on the wall to steady herself. To have lived for so long in a world where nothing happened that was different from the previous day, week, even year, and to now be in a place where every single thing was new and unexpected was making her feel dizzy.

'Are you all right?' Thomas asked as he waited for her to move off the bottom step.

Stupidly she blurted out, 'When the biggest excitement of one's week has been the delivery of a new *Ladies' Home Journal*, a first outing to a speakeasy is a bit overwhelming.'

Thomas didn't laugh at her. 'We can leave if you prefer. But I thought you might like to meet some New Yorkers.'

Evie smiled. Thomas was proving to be very perceptive. And here she was in a speakeasy. Her whole body wanted to join in the gaiety; she could always hold onto the wall to balance herself if she needed to.

'Tommy!' someone called.

Thomas ushered Evie over to a booth where a man and a woman were sitting. 'Lil, Leo, may I present Miss Evelyn Lockhart,' he said and Evie found herself being welcomed by a chinking of crystal tumblers that certainly weren't supporting the Volstead Act.

She was pulled into a chair by the woman, Lil, who had the eyes of a cat and the cropped black hair of a movie star. 'Welcome to Chumley's, Evelyn.'

'I'm Evie. Not Evelyn.'

Lil laughed and swallowed her drink, and Evie found that Thomas or Tommy or whoever he was in a speakeasy on a New York night had put a drink in front of her.

She raised it in his direction. 'Thank you.' She sipped. It was gin. A deliciously warm and prohibited gin.

'So you decided to come out instead of working late tonight,' the man – Leo – said to Tommy. 'That must make Miss Evelyn Lockhart a very persuasive woman.'

'Oh, I didn't persuade him at all. He's only brought me here on his mother's orders,' Evie replied.

'If only my mother would order me to take beautiful women out dancing, life would be grand,' Leo said.

Evie laughed. 'Thanks for the compliment. I'll try not to be a nuisance.'

'Here's to beautiful nuisances.' Leo, who was as blond as Evie and handsome to boot, tilted his glass at her.

Rather than looking away and blushing as she might have done in Concord, Evie said, 'And here's to me meeting more of the scoundrels that my mother warned me were lurking on every street corner in Manhattan.'

Leo fell back against the booth as if she'd shot an arrow through his heart. 'I'm no scoundrel.'

'I think she's called it right, Leo,' said Thomas.

Lil sighed. 'Unfortunately, scoundrels are my favourite men of all.'

Evie had to sip her drink to stop herself from gasping aloud at what Lil had said. Her mother would need the smelling salts.

The band began to play again, loud and hot and full of excitement. Evie's shoes shifted under the table like showgirls ready to dance. But no one at their table moved, yet.

The men began to talk together so Evie turned to Lil and tried to think of something they might have in common. 'You must know Alberta then?'

'Can't say I do. Should I?'

'Thomas's, I mean Tommy's, fiancée.'

Lil tapped Tommy's arm. 'Tommy, Evie says the reason we haven't seen you for a while is because you've been busy proposing to a girl named Alberta.'

'I didn't say that!' Evie was horrified at the thought of sounding like such a gossip. 'I thought Lil would know Alberta because . . .' Her voice vanished under the *boom-di-boom-bang* of the drum; it was just as well, as she couldn't remember whether Thomas had actually proposed to Alberta at the dinner party or not.

'Alberta is back in Boston,' Tommy said unconcerned. 'I didn't propose to her. Lil hasn't met her because I've never brought her here.'

'Does your mother know?' Evie pushed her glass away. She had to stop drinking. It was making her impertinent.

But Tommy smiled. 'Yes. I think Mother was pleased.'

'Alberta. She sounds like a snob anyway,' said Leo, and Evie felt as if the world had somehow tipped when Tommy replied, 'She was actually.'

'Besides, I don't think Tommy's in any danger of dying a lonely old bachelor. Break open the ribs of any Upper East Side girl and you'll find a heart beating Tom-Tom, Tom-Tom,' said Lil. 'Of course, Tommy's oblivious to it, or he pretends to be, which is all part of his charm.'

Tommy laughed at the shock written plainly across Evie's face. 'You look as if Lil had just said I was a Yiddish butcher.'

'Everyone seems very different in New York.'

'Stay any longer and you'll be different too,' Lil said, and it sounded like a promise.

Leo stood up to dance with a woman who actually asked him to join her. Evie was astounded. Then she looked at Lil. 'You don't mind?' she asked.

Lil grinned. 'Leo and I aren't an item. We're just friends. Both too committed to fun and variety.'

'Oh,' Evie said, wondering what it would be like not to think about marriage at all. 'Your parents must be a great deal less conservative than mine.'

Lil laughed. 'That's why I live by myself in a boarding house around the corner. Because they're probably just as conservative as yours.'

A boarding house? What freedom, Evie thought. It was almost impossible to imagine.

'Let's go dance,' Lil said.

Evie shook her head, preferring to watch for a while. She didn't want to look like the unsophisticated Concordian she must seem. As Lil stood up, Evie saw that she was even taller than Evie and that she didn't try to hide it as Mrs Lockhart always suggested Evie should, because apparently tall girls were unfeminine and intimidating to men. Not here. Evie saw several men turn their heads to follow Lil's sashay into the centre of the room, and one of them immediately asked her to dance. It was like watching a carousel spin, the way the men danced with Lil. One would survive a few short turns only to be replaced by another, and then a new man would come cutting in. Lil laughed with them all and didn't seem to be in a hurry to settle on any one partner.

After a short time, Leo held out his hand to Evie. 'It's the only way I'll forgive you for calling me a scoundrel.'

The crowd was moving to the music with a contagious combination of heel kicks, arm crosses and knee knocks. Evie joined in as best she could, and was glad to see that while dancing classes at the Ladies' Academy had most certainly not taught her this particular style, they had at least given her a sense of rhythm. She had a couple of false starts, which to her relief Leo did not laugh at; instead he showed her what to do, and she was soon matching him kick for kick. The song got louder – 'Toot, Toot, Tootsie' – and Evie started laughing as Leo twirled her around.

Leo pretended to be hurt. 'Is my dancing really so funny?'

'No,' said Evie. 'But I can't decide if my mother would be more horrified about me dancing to a song in which the man is asking for a kiss, or about the possibility of him ending up in jail.'

'Keep dancing like that and we'll all be asking you for a kiss,' said Leo, and Evie couldn't believe this was happening in real life, to her, rather than in the pages of a novel hidden between the covers of a magazine.

The song finished, another girl Leo knew cut in and a tango began, forward and back across the floor. Evie decided to watch from the safety of her seat. As she sat down she spotted Tommy and Lil amid the dancers and was unable to move her eyes away from them, straight-backed and with arms held aloft, engaged in a sultry battle. The impeccable posture that Evie and Charlie had once mocked served Tommy well in such a dance, and he moved with grace. For a moment, Evie saw a flash of what all the lovesick girls on the Upper East Side must see when they looked at Tommy.

He caught Evie watching him and he smiled at her over the top of Lil's head. His smile lit up her insides in a way that surprised her and made her wonder how she could ever live somewhere like Concord again.

~

All too soon, Chumley's was closing its doors.

'But I don't feel like going home,' said Evie.

Lil raised one eyebrow at Tommy. 'Did you get an invitation to the party tonight?'

'I did,' he said.

'Then we'll show Evie one of the sights of Manhattan.'

The four of them squeezed into the back seat of a taxi together, in a blaze of liquor and laughter. The driver had to ask them three times where they would like to be taken as he couldn't hear anything sensible among the noise. At the corner of Fifth Avenue and Fifty-Second Street he let them out, complaining of his aching head.

'Let's get a wiggle on!' Lil called as she set off along Fifth Avenue.

The sidewalks were quiet now, the stores closed until morning. But the street was busy with taxis taking young people up and down town as if night was not a reason to sleep but was just another serve of time to be consumed leisurely and at length like a good glass of brandy. After a few blocks, Lil stopped outside a palace that was obviously the scene of a party, judging by the cars parked on the sidewalks like vagrants, obstructing the way, and the music and laughter pealing through the windows.

'In you go,' said Lil, nudging Evie towards the front door of the enormous house.

'In there?' said Evie. 'But I haven't been invited.'

'Let's go together,' Tommy said, and held out his arm.

She slipped her arm through his and felt the warmth of his body beside hers. She was surprised at the clutch she felt in her stomach when she touched him; no one, not even Charlie, had ever made her feel like that. She glanced up at him but he didn't seem to notice anything as he walked up the steps.

Several people nodded at him as they went in through the front door. Evie barely noticed, because the scene around them was as astonishing as seeing the Brooklyn Bridge for the first time and understanding that man could make something so grand. In this case, the grandeur was there for one private household to enjoy, rather than for the benefit of many, and Evie wasn't sure if she was impressed or horrified at the extravagance. She was staring at a three-storey art gallery hung with Rembrandts and Titians, the space larger than a public art museum and more gilded than Versailles.

Evie assumed the house was the sight Lil and Tommy had wanted her to see until he pointed to her left. 'There,' he said.

Evie turned to see a woman, someone she recognised from the newspaper and the *Ladies' Home Journal*. A Vanderbilt? Yes. Evie was in the Vanderbilts' infamous mansion.

The woman was wearing a dress covered with thousands of tiny electric light bulbs, stitched to the fabric by hand as if they were sequins or beads. All the bulbs on the dress were illuminated. It was as if falling particles of luminescence from a firecracker had dropped onto her dress and still shone there. Evie had never seen anything so striking: a woman aglow, the brightest point in the room.

The woman saw Tommy and smiled. He held up his hand as if to say, *I'll be there in a minute*, but someone claimed the lady's attention and Tommy quickly guided Evie back to the front door.

'If we say hello, we'll be stuck here for hours,' he explained as they rejoined Lil and Leo, who had taken possession of a bottle of champagne and were sitting on the sidewalk sipping from the bottle as if they were at a college party rather than the home of one of the richest families in New York.

'Wasn't that the elephant's eyebrows?' Lil asked with a grin.

'More like the butterfly's boots,' Evie responded.

Lil laughed. 'See, you talk like a city girl already.'

Lil and Leo got up and began to wind their way through the cars and away from the house as if what Evie had seen was nothing all that remarkable and could be dispensed with in one throwaway remark.

'But how does she move around in that dress? Wherever did she get it? And wasn't she Mrs Vanderbilt?' Evie asked, unable to be as nonchalant as her three companions.

'Could have been,' said Tommy, smiling.

'But that means you know the Vanderbilts,' Evie said. That was bordering on the impossible, the Vanderbilts being heretofore the kind of people who were so fantastically wealthy they existed only in stories in newspapers and photographs in magazines.

'Perhaps he's just an accomplished gatecrasher,' said Lil.

Clearly being a New Yorker meant that one became used to extraordinary surprises being sprinkled through the city as ubiquitously as litter. Evie shook her head.

Then Lil kissed her and Tommy on the cheek, linked arms with Leo and began to walk downtown. 'See you again, Evie Lockhart!' she called over her shoulder.

'You will!' Evie called back, clutching her purse which held a scrap of paper on which Lil had scribbled her address.

Lil and Leo's laughter faded with their footsteps. Tommy and Evie continued walking up Fifth Avenue, on the opposite side of the street from Central Park. In the darkness, the park had lost its Tiffany-esque appearance and now resembled the night sky: an expanse of blackness, dotted here and there with constellations of lamps. The summer air was warm and the park sent them a slight breeze that settled on Evie's skin like a blown kiss. If she'd been more sure of Tommy, Evie would have held onto his hand and run down the street with him, calling into the darkness, *I've had the time of my life tonight*. As it was, she found the silence uncomfortable and rummaged around in her head for something to say. Eventually, she settled on: 'You're very close to your mother, aren't you?'

Tommy smiled. 'I am.'

'It must be nice to know that she's always on your side.'

'Perhaps your mother will be too, once she gets used to the idea of your studying.'

Evie stopped and looked up at him so that he couldn't lie to her under cover of darkness. 'Do you really think she might?'

'I don't know. I hope so.'

Then the most surprising thing of all the night's many unexpected events happened: as they started walking again, Tommy slipped his hand into hers. Her stomach cartwheeled. How good it felt to walk along Fifth Avenue hand in hand with a man who was decidedly handsome, not to mention kind and charming and fun. Evie was very aware of his body, just an inch away from hers.

Thankfully, Tommy spoke, interrupting her wildly running thoughts. 'William Childers telephoned this evening while you were getting ready,' he said.

'Oh?' Evie said nervously.

'He wants to see you at nine o'clock tomorrow morning.'

Evie stopped again. 'Does that mean he's going to help me?'

'He is.'

She'd done it! She had taken her first step towards something that, until this moment, had seemed unattainable.

'Hurrah!' Evie's jubilation was short-lived. 'Oh no!' she cried as a new thought struck her.

Tommy tilted his head. 'I thought it was what you wanted.'

'It is. But I'm certainly tipsy or blotto or whatever Lil calls it and might still be in the morning. At the very least, I'll have a headache. Why didn't you tell me earlier?'

Tommy pushed open the door to the Whitmans' house. 'Because I wanted to see what you looked like when you were enjoying yourself.'

~

Evie lay in bed that night, her whole body aglow with the memory of holding Tommy's hand, the thrill of Tommy's words, and the look on his face when he'd said them. *Because I wanted to see what you looked like when you were enjoying yourself.* She was sure her face still shone more brightly than Mrs Vanderbilt's dress, and her smile was so enormous that she rolled over to hide it in the pillow.

Then she groaned when she recalled how she'd responded. She'd blushed for the hundredth time that evening, murmured something about needing to get to bed so she'd be ready for Mr Childers, and dashed up the stairs. She'd virtually run away from Tommy. And now she couldn't get to sleep for thinking about him.

Chapter Six

The next morning, Mr Childers gave Evie her corrected examination paper. There were some ticks. There were a lot of crosses.

Evie's head throbbed as if it was being trampled by the entire charlestoning throng from Chumley's.

'I'd thought it might be worse,' Mr Childers said.

'I'd hoped it might be better.'

'Optimism will be useful.'

'I'd prefer intelligence.'

Mr Childers laughed. 'You *are* intelligent. I can see that in your workings. You just haven't been taught what you need to know.'

'You must like challenges if you've agreed to work with me.'

'I do.'

Evie rubbed her forehead with her hand.

'Thomas telephoned earlier and said you might be in need of coffee. I have some brewing,' Mr Childers said.

The same smile Evie had hidden in her pillow the night

before bloomed on her face. Thomas had been thinking about her too. 'Coffee would be just the ticket,' she said.

While Mr Childers made coffee, Evie glanced through the selection of books he'd placed on the desk. One was a book about the human body, with chapters entitled: Osteology, Angiology, Neurology. And then: Embryology. The Ovum. The Spermatozoon. Fertilisation of the Ovum. Segmentation of the Fertilised Ovum. On it went through language she hadn't known existed.

Mr Childers placed a mug in front of Evie. She took a sip of her coffee – Irish, she noted with a grin. It gave her courage. 'What kind of doctors do women become?'

'There are so few it's hard to say. Columbia's first female doctors will graduate this year – that's only about five women. Cornell has graduated a handful. I know there are some female paediatricians at the Babies Hospital on Lexington.'

'Only five from Columbia?'

'Something like that. And, while I've tutored several women who wanted to be admitted to science degrees, I've only tutored one who wanted to be admitted into medicine.'

'Did she get in?'

'No.'

Evie digested this fact along with her coffee. 'Are any of these women obstetricians?'

'I don't know of any university-trained female obstetricians in New York City. Is that what you want to do?'

Evie hesitated. No female obstetricians in Manhattan. Then how on earth could someone like Evie ever become one? She took another sip for fortitude. 'Back in Concord, I saw a woman giving birth. I could have helped her, if only I'd known what to do. She died.'

'It won't be easy.'

Evie felt a sudden flash of anger. If she'd been Charles or Thomas Whitman, a man with money, nobody would question her. But little Evie Lockhart wasn't supposed to do whatever she wanted. 'It won't be easy staying in Concord and watching my whole life disappear as I sew hankies, all the while knowing that women are dying with no one to help them. I don't want to be a nurse – that would be exactly like taking orders from my father. I want to be a doctor. And if you won't help me, I'll find someone who can!'

As soon as the words were said, Evie realised she was being idiotic. No one else would tutor her. She'd fired off her pistols and ended up shooting herself.

But rather than throwing her out the door, Mr Childers said, 'You'll need to keep that level of passion if you want to succeed. And you'll need to study harder than any man, because the only way you'll get what you want is to be twice as good.'

Evie reholstered her guns, let out her breath and held up her coffee mug. 'Here's to you helping me be twice as good.'

Mr Childers clinked his mug against hers and sat down beside her. 'And you'll need to find your own reason for wanting to study obstetrics. Not a reason that's about other women, but one that's about you. That's how you'll stay the course.'

'What better reason is there than wanting to help others? I delivered Rose's baby. It was as if I knew what to do even without being taught.'

'It might not be enough to get you through what you're bound to encounter.'

'You make it sound as if I'm facing an execution.'

'I'm very sure you'll lose a part of yourself if you pursue this.'

Evie stared at Mr Childers. His expression was serious. She hoped he was wrong. Which parts of her life could she give up? Charlie? Her family? Thomas? She squeezed her eyes shut, wanting to block out what he'd said. 'Where do we start?'

'With summer school, you'll meet the minimum requirements to put in an application for medical school. But you'll be competing with candidates who have four-year pre-med courses behind them. The last step is a personal interview with the dean of the college. It'll come down to whether you can persuade him of your ambitions. Remember, the college catalogue said that they receive many more applications than they have places and that they choose the applicants they consider to be most capable. They don't define what capable means, of course.'

'Well, let's start making me capable,' she said, with more confidence than she felt.

With that, the books were opened. They worked until late afternoon, when Evie began to confuse calculus with an oriental language, and a second Irish coffee proved to be more of a hindrance than a help. Mr Childers suggested they call it a day, which Evie supposed was his way of saying he'd had enough of her for the time being. As a parting blow, he said that her knowledge of physics was at the level of a fifteen-year-old boy's, which only made her realise how lucky fifteen-year-old boys were. Large chunks of knowledge had simply never been passed on to her in her schooling.

As she walked away from Mr Childers' rooms, she ran through in her mind all the things she had to do: wrestle calculus into submission, write to her parents asking permission to stay on in New York for six more weeks, convince the dean that he should admit her. There'd be no shopping, no nights out, no drinking and dancing for now. No more enjoying herself with

Thomas. And then, if she was admitted – even saying it in her mind made her smile at the possibility – she would have to persuade her parents to let her attend college and to pay for it. More obstacles than a steeplechase up Fifth Avenue. But meeting Lil last night, so fearless and daring, had given Evie a sense that a life freely chosen here in New York City was worth fighting for.

Two girls of about Evie's age exited an Italian restaurant that drenched the street with the smell of garlic and melanzane. Beside the restaurant was a bakery called Zito's, whose delicious-smelling loaves made Evie's mouth water. Further along was the delightfully named PingPank Barber Shop, with red velvet chairs, rows of shaving mugs lining the window, and a calendar of scantily clad ladies from late last century sitting proudly at the front of the shop. Then Mandaro's, its balls of cheese hanging like Christmas baubles in the front window. Evie resolved to come back once she was settled in New York – because she *would* settle here – and have a celebratory meal of Swiss cheese on freshly baked bread, washed down with a bottle of the most exotic wine she could afford.

Further down the street, she was cheered along by a fast, foot-tapping mix of saxophone and brass, which she would later discover was called the 'Bugle Call Rag'. At the moment all she knew was that the song blasted away her worries and blew her hopes up as high as the notes trumpeting from the window above.

She checked her watch. It was half past five. Would Lil be in? She continued on to Minetta Street, located the right boarding house and knocked on the door. A middle-aged woman whose gimlet stare could quench the desire of even the most ardent gentleman caller answered.

'I'm here to visit Lil,' Evie said.

'You mean Miss Delancey? Second floor, room three.'

Two girls dressed in robes with their hair wrapped in turban-towels were laughing as they crossed the second floor landing. A third girl poked her head through a doorway and called, 'Nancy, I need to borrow your irons.' Another door opened and a girl with the reddest lips Evie had ever seen appeared with a curling iron in hand. They were all so relaxed, so free, unburdened by parents with outdated rules. Evie knew she was staring but she couldn't help it. The boarding house itself was like a cheap department store. The flooring was scratched, the walls undecorated, but the scent of the residents' perfume, the colour of their clothes and the constant stream of chatter transformed it into a place where Evie would be happy to spend her time.

Lil answered Evie's knock with a grin, pulled her inside and produced a bottle of gin and two glasses. She patted the bed, which took up most of the small room. The only other furniture was a chair piled with clothes and the chest of drawers, which also served as the liquor cabinet and a place for the gramophone to sit.

'Let's get comfy,' Lil said. She kicked off her shoes and wriggled to the top of the bed, then leaned back against the wall with her legs extended out in front.

Evie did the same even though she'd never in her life sat on anyone else's bed – not even Viola's. 'How long have you lived here?' she asked.

'Since last year.'

'Are you from New York? You must be if you know Thomas.'

'I am. One of the few. As for the rest, it's a city of immigrants and looking-for-a-better-life dreamers.'

'You're not an immigrant, so that must make you a dreamer. Like me.' Evie grimaced into her glass. 'Does that mean I'm a cliché?'

'You and me and a few thousand other women.'

They sipped their drinks and Evie felt her head relax back against the wall as the gin and the conversation warmed her throat and loosened her tongue.

'Are your grand plans coming to fruition?' asked Lil.

'I have to go to summer school. And I still might fail to be admitted to medical school if the other applicants are deemed more qualified than me. If that happens, I don't know what I'll do.'

'Get a job and try again next year.'

Evie laughed. 'You're assuming I'd be allowed to stay in New York. And what kind of job would I get? I've never been around women who work on anything other than their manners. Do you have a job?'

'No one pays for this low-rent room besides me. I work at J. Walter Thompson. Advertising agency. I write copy.'

'Do you like it?'

'I'm going to get out and have my own by-line in a newspaper or magazine one day, Evie. Until then, I'm going to learn to be the best writer I can be. And if that means working on what the fellas are too embarrassed to write about, like how Kotex are Jake because you can ask for them by name instead of having to blush your way through requesting sanitary pads from the drugstore, then that's what I'll do.'

Evie shook her head. 'Jake?'

'Jake – you know, great.'

'See, I don't even understand the language.' Evie paused. 'What if it doesn't work out for you?' she asked, because she wanted to find out if anyone else in New York had doubts like she did.

'Then perhaps I'll marry Tommy.'

Evie's head snapped to the side. She hadn't even thought about whether Lil might have her heart set on Thomas.

But Lil was grinning at her. 'I thought you might be sweet on him.'

'I hardly know him.' As she said it, she knew it wasn't true. Even though they'd only had a couple of conversations, she felt as if she knew Thomas better than she had ever known Charlie. And Thomas certainly knew more about New York Evie than Charlie did. 'How do you know Thomas?'

'My family and Tommy's family have been pals for years. When you're born in that circle you know everyone in it. Luckily Tommy was never a high hat. So we stayed friends after I was thrown out.'

'Thrown out?'

'When I finished school, I started going out at night and coming back the next morning. My folks told me to stop. But I didn't want to. So I left. Found a job. Found a room in Mrs Lomsky's boarding house. Here I am.'

'You sound like a character in that novel.' Evie nodded at the copy of *The Beautiful and Damned* lying on the chest of drawers.

'It's not just words on a page. It's life. Who wants to marry and ask permission to go out or to buy a new dress when I can dance with whomever I choose, wearing whatever I please.'

It was as if Lil had put into words all the doubts Evie had felt when contemplating marriage to Charlie and had also shown Evie that there really was another choice. She swung her legs over the side of the bed. 'Can you show me around? I've never been in a boarding house before.'

It didn't take long. There were four floors of rooms, each room inhabited by one or two girls; downstairs was a dining room where they all took breakfast together, so long as they made it down by half past seven. On the very top floor, Lil nodded towards a single door. 'That's the best room. A whole floor. Because the roof slopes she couldn't divide it up, but even with the low ceilings there's still plenty of space. Charlotte and Irina are moving out next month. If I had someone to room in with me, I'd take it.'

'And you'd be a long way from Mrs Lomsky on the first floor.'

'See, one turn around the house and you're already an expert.'

When Evie returned to the Whitmans', she asked the maid to bring her some milky tea in the small sitting room off the library. She needed to be alone to think. She felt nauseous and wasn't sure if it was the result of too much champagne the night before, the gin at Lil's, or the thought of all the obstacles that still stood in her way.

But she hadn't yet sat down or collected her thoughts when the door opened and Thomas walked in. He stopped when he saw her. 'Evelyn. I didn't realise anyone was here.'

Evie sighed. How quickly one changed from being one thing to another. From Evie to Evelyn. From Tommy to Thomas. From wonderful possibilities to rigid formalities. Last night must have been a dream. The workings of a splendid city on her foolish and impressionable mind. Perhaps everything she wanted was foolish and she should stop now before she lost too much.

The door opened again and in swept Charlie. 'Evie!' He crossed the room in a second and kissed her on the cheek.

Evie's hand moved to the place where his lips had touched her. She felt nothing. Not a stir, not a flutter, not a quiver of excitement. It was so different to how she'd felt last night when Thomas took her arm and walked with her up the steps of the Vanderbilt mansion, and when he'd held her hand as they strolled along Fifth Avenue. She realised that Thomas was looking at her and that he might think she was touching her cheek because Charlie's kiss had affected her. She pulled her hand away, but Thomas had already turned to the window.

'You can help us celebrate tonight,' Charlie said. 'Mother's putting on a dinner party. It's a bit last minute so we'll probably only get fifty guests.'

'What are you celebrating?' Evie asked.

'Getting rid of Tommy.' Charlie laughed and patted his brother on the back in a show of fraternal affection. 'Father decided today. Tommy's off to London next week to set up our European operations. Time to expand, and Tommy's the man to do it. He won't be back for a couple of years, so we thought we'd farewell him in style.'

Two years in London? 'Two years is a long time.' What a silly thing to say. Evie sat down on the sofa and sipped her tea, which was now cold. 'What a wonderful opportunity for you.' But she mightn't have said anything, because Thomas still wasn't looking at her.

'Thank you. I'll leave you two to talk,' he said. He left the room without a smile. Obviously the only person feeling jolts when they touched was her.

Charlie took a seat opposite her and stared at the teapot as if he had no idea that tipping it up would cause the tea to land in his cup. 'How have you been amusing yourself?' he asked.

Evie hadn't the strength to resist his expectations, so she picked up the pot and poured for him, unconcerned when some of it landed in his saucer. 'I've been shopping.'

'The perfect New York occupation. You'll have to wear your new clothes tonight.' He smiled at her indulgently.

His smile made Evie say something she knew she shouldn't. But she had to see how somebody from her old life would react when she told them what she was doing. 'I've been looking at medical schools.'

Charlie laughed. 'And I've been down to the docks looking for work.' He reached over and took Evie's hand. 'I know my beautiful Evie isn't going to give her life away to books. Just as I'm not giving mine away to manual labour.'

'I want to help people, Charlie. Why is that such a bad thing?'

He put his cup back down in the saucer. 'Do you remember that woman by the river?' he asked coldly. It was a tone Evie had never heard him use before and his contempt made her wonder what else she didn't know about him.

'Of course I do.'

'She was one of the Radcliffe students who came across to Harvard for the medical school courses. Waste of time really, since neither Harvard nor Radcliffe award medical degrees to women.'

'I know that,' Evie snapped, forgetting, in her anger, to ask how he knew so much about Rose.

'There was talk that she had an affair with a fellow at Harvard. He turned her away, of course; how could he believe the child she was carrying was his?'

'There's a very tenuous moral to that story: if you go to medical school, you're likely to end up dead by the river. I'm sure there are other women who've been to university and had more success.'

'What about the Butterfield's daughter? She has a degree in mathematics but the only thing she has to add up now is the number of men lining up to marry her younger sister. No man wants to marry a woman who can calculate the down payment on an Oldsmobile quicker than he can.'

'You're being ridiculous.' Her head started to pound with the realisation that Charlie was behaving exactly the way she'd feared, the same way her parents would; they'd absolutely refuse to let her stay in New York to attend summer school. Right now Evie was too tired from her late night and her day with Mr Childers to argue any more. It was easier to revert back to being the Evie that Charlie expected her to be, for now.

'The university plan is a far-fetched one,' she admitted. 'Coming to New York has shown me that.'

Charlie nodded. 'Your father thought that coming here would put you off the whole idea.'

Evie resisted the temptation to get up and walk out of the parlour and back to the Village to bunk in with Lil, where everything was said to one's face and deals weren't done behind one's back with all the finesse of a bootlegging thug. At least now she knew what Charlie really thought. It hurt a little, but not as much as it ought to have. She sank both rows of her teeth into the flesh on the inside of her mouth, biting off all the words she wanted to shout at him. Because she had a favour to ask, and now that Thomas was leaving she couldn't think of anyone else who might be able to help. 'Let's not quarrel. Please? I want to ask you something.'

'Anything.'

If only that were true. 'Could you make some enquiries about the baby? Apparently it was taken to New York. I want to find out if it's all right. It's been bothering me.'

Charlie patted Evie's arm as if she was five years old. 'Of course.'

This time, Evie couldn't swallow the words. She stood up. 'You're not going to, are you?'

'I just want to look after you, Evie. More than anything.'

Charlie stood too and leaned towards her. She was struck by how different he looked to the picture of him that she carried in her mind. His face was paler and the skin on his cheeks looser than she remembered. She suddenly understood that it was the tanned, blond, lean and always outdoors Charlie of a few years before that she held so dear.

With impeccable timing, the clock on the mantelpiece struck seven in a flurry of circling porcelain figures. 'I need to dress for dinner,' she said. She stepped away before his face could get any closer to hers.

~

Back in her room, Evie sat down at the dressing table and wrote a letter to the Foundling, the orphanage the nurse had mentioned. She enquired whether a baby born in Concord on June seventeenth was in their care and if any assistance, financial or otherwise, was needed. Every night she dreamed of the baby, its eyes on her, watching her leave. She had to locate it. 'Please,' she whispered as she sealed the envelope. Then she put on her new dress and shoes and went downstairs.

She was in no hurry to see Charlie again and so she drifted along the halls, taking the circuitous route past the outer rooms of the house, rather than through the middle to the drawing room. There were so many lovely things to see, beautiful Flemish tapestries from the eighteenth century, their blues and reds still bright, warmed by the last rays of the day that fell gently through the skylight above. The buttery Siena marble lining the floors and the walls was lustrous, and the fountain near the entrance was ornamented with lotus flowers, water hyacinths and floating candles. She was walking past Mr Whitman's study when she heard Thomas's voice. 'Don't be too hard on Charles while I'm away.'

She stopped. If she stood by the fountain with her back to the study, she could pretend to be looking at the flowers, rather than eavesdropping.

'He'll amount to little more than a prankster if he doesn't start to do some work.' Mr Whitman's concern carried out to Evie in the hall. 'I've let him go, thinking he'd sow his oats and then settle down to study, but . . .' The sound of a sigh and Evie imagined Charlie's father sitting in a chair, hand rubbing his chin as he worried over his younger son. 'I'm starting to think he's lazy.'

'Me being in London might be good for him. He'll have the chance to step up.'

'I hope he takes it. Spends his time trying to be more like you rather than being resentful.'

'He might surprise us all.'

Mr Whitman harrumphed. Evie studied the lotus flowers for a moment, part of her mind marvelling at how many petals each flower was able to accommodate, while another part considered envy. Envy grew piece by piece, petal by petal, until it was so large it was all you could see. Evie knew this, because she had once envied her sister's ability to please their mother.

'Evie?'

She whirled around. Thomas stood outside the study door.

'I remember that dress dancing up a storm last night,' he said. 'Would you rather be at a boring dinner party or back at Chumley's?'

I'd rather be here, because that's where you are, thought Evie. But she said, 'Your parents' parties are always fun.'

'Let's find out.' Thomas held out his arm to Evie, who took it gladly, feeling the thrill of the night before rush back over her, and they made their way towards the drawing room together. Then they saw Charlie approaching.

'I'll take Evie in,' Charlie said. He was holding out his arm for her and Evie could feel the tension between the two brothers. It would be yet another petal to add to Charlie's jealousy if she didn't take his arm. So she did. And Thomas let her because, as Evie now knew from her eavesdropping, he looked out for his younger brother, even if Charlie had rarely been heard to utter a kind word about him.

After that, Charlie was insistently by her side. He brought her a glass of champagne, a napkin, a morsel of food, and another champagne because he thought she'd finished the first. She could feel his fingernails biting through the fabric of her dress but she had to stand politely beside him as he showed her off to everyone in the room. The men looked her over and tilted their glasses at Charlie, hardly bothering to speak to her.

Eventually they found themselves back beside Thomas. Evie gripped her champagne glass a little tighter; she wanted to reach out and loosen his tie, take his hand and run away to a place where the saxophones blared, where they could lose themselves on a dance floor. Thomas smiled at her and the room fell away; it was as if the music stopped, voices hushed and movement halted.

'Who'll look after business here while you're in London?' Evie asked, desperate to have one more conversation with him before he left.

'Tommy's just a vice to Father's president,' answered Charlie, as if the question had been directed at him. 'So it'll be business as usual, with the old man in charge. But when I graduate next year, maybe it'll be me running the bank. The only thing I'll need then is a wife by my side.' As he spoke, Charlie pulled Evie towards him.

It was an announcement. The plan for Evie and Charlie spoken aloud. By saying it in front of so many witnesses, Charlie had made it impossible for Evie to tell him how she felt. She wished he'd take his hand off her. Most of all, she wished Thomas hadn't heard.

Thomas tipped his glass at her. 'Good luck,' he said. Then he walked away.

Evie had to leave the room. There were too many thoughts swirling around in her head and the champagne wasn't helping. 'Excuse me,' she said, drawing away from Charlie. She was walking down the hall in the direction of the bathroom when she felt a hand on her arm. She turned, half furious, expecting that Charlie had followed her, and half hopeful, wondering if Thomas might have.

It was Mrs Whitman. 'Come with me,' she said.

Evie let herself be led upstairs to Mrs Whitman's private sitting room. It was decorated in the softest shade of duck-egg blue, and as Evie walked across the thick carpet she felt as if she was floating on a pond in springtime. It was so different from the sensation that always overcame her in her mother's room, which was like a gilded cage, full of oversized mirrors with gold frames, little tables scattered like birdseed around the room, candlestick holders that were no longer used but were preserved as some kind of romantic keepsake of pre-electric times, and the Lalique and Baccarat perfume bottles her mother collected.

Evie was overwhelmed by a feeling like homesickness, but it wasn't home she yearned for. It was a motherly embrace she craved. If only she could crawl into her mother's lap and tell her everything: about medical school, about Charlie, about New York, and maybe even about going to a speakeasy with Thomas. Instead she sat down and felt her eyes fill, because she knew that would never happen. She couldn't tell anyone how she felt; Viola would faint, her mother would be speechless, her father would lock her up, Charlie would scold, and she didn't know Lil well enough to laden her with so many burdens.

'You look as if you're trying very hard to enjoy yourself but aren't really,' Mrs Whitman said, passing Evie a handkerchief.

'I'm sorry. The party is lovely.' Evie wiped her eyes, blew her nose and tried to hide her sadness, to show Mrs Whitman that she really did appreciate everything she had done for her.

Mrs Whitman took hold of Evie's hands. 'I'm very happy to listen.'

At this invitation to finally speak, everything rushed out. 'To get into medical school, I need to go to summer school for six weeks. But I'm certain if I tell my parents, they'll say no. It's not their fault they think the way they do. They're not mean or unkind; they just don't understand that the world is changing. So I'd rather do the work and see if I'm accepted into medical school before I say anything to them. Then they might be persuaded. But I'm supposed to be going home next week, and I don't know what to do about any of it.' *And Charlie has turned out to be less than I expected. Whereas Thomas has turned out to be more.* Two things she couldn't say aloud to their mother.

'What if I telephone your parents and ask that you stay on with me for the six weeks? I'll tell them I've so enjoyed your company that I'd like you to stay for the rest of summer. Which is true.'

'Oh no, you can't do that. You wouldn't want to if you knew . . .' Evie hesitated, wishing for a moment that she had no morals and could selfishly take what she needed. But she couldn't lie to someone who'd already done so much to help her. She forced herself to go on. 'Charlie hasn't asked me but he said something downstairs that makes me think he might. I can't marry him. I'm so sorry. And I know I should have told you earlier, but I've only just realised it myself.'

Mrs Whitman squeezed Evie's hands. 'Don't apologise, my dear. It's the right thing. You wouldn't have made each other happy, no matter what Charles thinks. You want a different life to the one he wants.'

'I understand if you'd prefer not to help me now, though.'

'Nonsense. I'd be more likely to refuse to help if you had said yes to him. I want him to marry someone who loves him. And I want the same for you.'

What a strange and wonderful place the world was. Evie kissed Mrs Whitman's cheek. 'Thank you.'

'Be gentle with Charles when you tell him. He isn't good with having his feelings hurt. Especially if Thomas is the one who –'

The door opened and Evie jumped up, thinking it might be Charlie and wondering what Mrs Whitman had been about to say. Evie's mood lifted a little when she saw Thomas's face. He stopped when he saw his mother and Evie. 'Sorry, I was trying to escape the fuss.'

Mrs Whitman smiled at her son and beckoned him in. 'Your father is having the celebration for you that he wished he could have had when he established the bank thirty years ago.'

Thomas kissed his mother's cheek and Evie saw again how well they understood one another, that the son's ambitions for business success were supported by his mother. She realised again how precarious her own position was without support, with her secret tucked away like a hanky in her pocket.

'How was your meeting with Mr Childers?' Thomas asked Evie.

'Astonishingly good for making me realise how many holes there are in my education. The Swiss Cheese Academy of Concord, it should be called, not the Ladies' Academy.' Evie sighed. 'And next week, I'm supposed to be back in Concord.'

'You're going back?' Thomas frowned.

Evie could see that he thought she'd given up. She could also see that her giving up bothered him. The differences between Thomas and Charlie, differences she used to laugh over, now seemed anything but laughable.

Mrs Whitman interjected. 'I'm trying to convince Evie to stay with me so we can get her through summer school.'

'I can't let you get involved. My mother would . . .' Evie stopped, because she honestly couldn't imagine what her mother would do if she found out that Mrs Whitman and Evie were colluding on a project that could make Evie unmarriageable. 'Stab you with her sewing needle, perhaps.' For the first time that night, Evie laughed, as did Mrs Whitman and Thomas.

'I'd like to help,' Mrs Whitman said. 'Please allow me.' She spoke as if Evie would be doing her a favour by agreeing.

'But if I'm staying in the house and Charlie is too . . .' Evie paused, glancing at Thomas, who probably still thought she wanted to marry Charlie. 'Won't that be awkward?'

Mrs Whitman also looked at her elder son, who seemed puzzled by the direction of the conversation. 'It won't be awkward,' she said. 'Charles has finished his examinations, so his father is sending him on a tour of the bank's east coast branches. You won't need to see him after you've refused him.'

Evie blushed furiously at Mrs Whitman's unequivocal words. Now Thomas knew. Would he care? 'Thank you,' she said to Mrs Whitman.

'I'm going back downstairs.' Mrs Whitman stood up. 'Why don't you write to your parents tonight? And I'll telephone them in the morning.'

After his mother had gone, Thomas sat down beside Evie. 'I wanted to be the one to tell you about London. It was only decided today, otherwise I would have told you last night. I doubt that I'll see much of you between now and when I go because I'll be spending all my time at the office getting things organised.'

'I feel as if I'm losing one of the only people who believes in what I'm doing,' Evie said tentatively, hoping that what she was saying would make him understand that she . . . what? That she was attracted to him? What was this thing she felt for him? She didn't even know how to explain it to herself, so how could she expect Thomas to comprehend?

'Mother believes in you. So does Lil. I asked her to keep an eye on you.'

Evie knew her smile was ridiculously huge but she didn't care. He'd asked someone to keep an eye on her. That meant he must care a little.

And then he asked, 'Can I write to you?' and Evie almost got up and danced around the room.

She pushed her feet firmly into the floor so they wouldn't take off for a twirl all by themselves. 'I'd love it if you wrote to me. And I promise to write back.'

Now Thomas's smile matched Evie's and all she could think was, how did I ever overlook a man as sublime as Thomas? 'I should return to the party,' Thomas said. 'Guests of honour probably aren't supposed to disappear like this. Although I'd rather stay here with you.'

Evie knew she would hold onto those words for the next two years. 'Good luck,' she said. 'And good-bye.'

'For now.'

The way he said it seemed to suggest that they were unfinished, like a love song truncated, the coda still to come in another time and place. Evie hoped that was true. And Thomas seemed to confirm it because, after he'd reluctantly stood up and walked to the door, he turned to look back at her and she knew she wasn't the only one who couldn't bear to drag her eyes away.

'I'll miss you,' he said.

Evie felt pinwheels of joy spin in her stomach as she replied, 'I'll miss you too.'

Chapter Seven

After her conversation with Thomas, Evie returned to her room and did something despicable. She almost couldn't make herself do it. But she knew she had to. An invitation from Mrs Whitman might not be enough to convince Evie's parents to let her stay. But an implication that an engagement to Charlie was imminent might.

So Evie wrote her mother a letter, telling her that Charlie had announced to the party last night that he would soon need a wife, and that he'd embraced Evie as he'd said it. That part was true. But then she wrote that a few more weeks in New York would guarantee an engagement between her and Charlie. She remembered her mother's face when they'd spoken two weeks ago, the hopes she had for Evie. Evie knew she had it within her power to bring her mother some much-needed joy by saying yes to Charlie, and that in this letter she was toying with her mother's wishes. She told herself it wasn't such a terrible lie, that she had no choice.

But she loathed herself all the same.

The following week, after her mother agreed to Mrs Whitman's request to keep Evie in New York for the summer, Evie left the house before anyone else was awake and caught the subway to Columbus Circle, which was a riot of colourful billboards advertising cars and gaspers, Rubber and Fisk tyres, and whiskey; anyone would think Manhattanites did nothing but smoke and drink and drive. All she needed was a car to pull up and offer her a ride to nowhere, along with a throat-warming beverage, and she might have left her first day of summer school behind. Anything other than test her grand plan and have the holes in it revealed as unstitchable.

But she smoothed down the skirt of one of her conservative Concord dresses, which she hoped would allow her to blend in, and walked on past the statue of Christopher Columbus. It stood tall, proud and so high it seemed to suggest that only in reaching for the sky could you be certain never to knock your head against the ceiling. Evie smiled her agreement and took heart. The city was on her side.

She continued onto Fifty-Ninth and was soon outside the College of Physicians and Surgeons, the oldest medical college in New York City. And here was Evie, hoping to be let in the doors. She found that she hadn't the courage to look at the imposing exterior of the building. Instead, she hurried inside, where a corridor ran east and west. She had no idea which way to go. She turned right and almost ran into a cabinet full of bones. Skulls, ribs, leg bones – they looked smooth and tactile and she imagined they might feel like pearl buttons if she ran her fingers over them.

At last she found the main lecture hall, a vast room with dozens of chairs. Evie's shoes clacked loudly on the wooden floor, announcing her arrival more emphatically than she wished. Heads turned, and Evie realised that every one of them was male. Never before had she been in a room with so many men, and nor had so many men ever looked at her at once. She blushed and took the seat nearest the door.

'Hello,' she said awkwardly to the man beside her. She struggled to think of something else to say and stupidly asked, 'Are there any other women taking summer school, do you know?'

The man opened his notebook and studied the blank page. 'I don't think women should be assigned to the same lecture rooms. Too much chatter.'

'I see.' So that was the medical understanding of women and their habits: they were gossips who would disrupt the serious business of men's learning.

Evie's optimism shrivelled like a dowager's skin in the sun. But the lecture soon started and within a few moments she forgot everything else. For the language of medicine, she discovered, was even more beautiful than that of literature. The professor spoke about oscillation, how vocal folds move in a wavelike dance to allow us to speak. Even the strange hieroglyphs of calculus on the blackboard seemed to have their own beauty. Never had a day passed so quickly.

It was early evening when Evie raced through the Whitmans' front door, eager to tell Mrs Whitman about her day. There was a letter waiting for her on the hall table; seeing the return address stamped on the envelope, she stopped to open it.

It was from a Sister Mary of the New York Foundling, advising that they had a baby whose birth details matched those Evie had supplied. Evie was welcome to visit the child whenever she liked.

'Thank you!' she shouted up at the beautiful cherubs frolicking in white clouds on the ceiling fresco. At last things were starting to work out for her! Even though it was only her first day, she knew that summer school was going to be the best thing she'd ever done. And she'd found Rose's baby!

'Mrs Whitman!' she called, wanting to share her excitement with somebody. She burst through the drawing room door and then stopped dead, unable to suppress her dismay and couldn't stop herself saying, 'Oh no!'

Viola, sitting stiffly on the sofa in a positively Edwardian style dress, looked up from her embroidery. 'Surprised to see me?'

'Why are you here?'

'Mother wondered what was taking so long. Are congratulations in order yet?'

'I wrote Mother a letter last week. You didn't need to come.' Evie sat down in the nearest chair, her elation gone. How would she go to summer school every day with Viola here? 'How long are you here for?'

'You don't sound pleased to see me.'

'Having you here will be hotsy-totsy, Vi,' Evie said sarcastically.

'You're not a character in a novel, Evie. Mother sent me here to find out what was happening.'

'To spy on me, you mean?'

The sisters stared at one another and, exasperated as she was, Evie couldn't help but feel a wave of fondness at the familiarity of Viola's motherly and unsmiling face. Amid so much that was new, it was nice to see something connected to home.

'You've seen that Viola's here.' Mrs Whitman had come in unnoticed while they were bickering. She appeared unruffled, as if she was perfectly happy to accommodate another guest.

'Yes,' said Evie. 'Surely it's too much to have both of us stay?'

'Your mother telephoned this morning while you were out to let me know she was concerned about you and that Viola was on her way here.'

How like her mother to call after she'd dispatched Viola, when nothing could be done about it. 'But we're so busy with ... with ...' Evie stuttered, trying to think of an excuse for all her absences from the house over the coming weeks.

'Well, I thought you could take on organising the gala by yourself so that I have time to show Viola around the city,' Mrs Whitman said, raising one of her eyebrows ever so slightly at Evie.

'Certainly! I'd be happy to! I'll start tomorrow. There's so much to do I'll be all over the city like a blizzard!' Evie laughed as if she was delighted to be given the responsibility for organising a fictitious gala, when in fact she was so grateful to Mrs Whitman for her quick thinking.

'Excellent. That's settled. Viola, we'll leave at ten o'clock tomorrow to pay some calls, and Evie, you do what you need to do. It's important that the gala is successful.'

'I'll do my best.'

'I'll show you to your room, Viola.' Mrs Whitman let Viola pass, then whispered to Evie, 'Charles is looking for you.'

'Thanks for the warning.'

Evie turned on the phonograph and selected 'Somebody Stole My Gal', wishing somebody would steal her away from this uncomfortable moment. She had barely a minute to think about what she would say before Charlie burst into the drawing room with his usual dramatic exclamation of 'Evie!', as if she was the most wonderful thing in the world. He kissed her cheek, holding her closer than was necessary. Evie pulled back a little.

'Life is about to get a whole lot better for you,' he said.

'Oh?' she said, wanting nothing more than to leave the room.

'I've been shopping at Tiffany.'

Now was the moment. She had to tell him she didn't love him before she humiliated him by refusing his proposal. But her courage had deserted her. The memory of Mrs Whitman's words — *be gentle with Charlie when you tell him* — made her quail inwardly. Was it her fault? Had she been wrong to let Charlie love her? She had once felt something for him. But she'd changed so much of late and it seemed that he hadn't changed at all.

'Do you want to know what I bought?' Charlie asked, smiling at her.

Oh God! He was excited, thrilled with the thought of giving her whatever he'd bought. He was expecting her to respond with equal joy. She had to say something before his hopes climbed any higher. She had to open her mouth. How was it possible to say what she had to say kindly? She took a deep breath and tried to look penitent and kind.

But Charlie spoke before she had a chance. 'You know what I'm going to say. I've been trying to ask you for the last couple of weeks. But things keep getting in the way.'

'Things like medical school?' Evie said lightly, hoping to remind him how unsuited they were, trying to get him to see that he shouldn't ask her to marry him.

'You're bored,' he said dismissively. 'You need a house to run. A husband to manage. Parties to organise.'

'Charlie, I can't think of marriage right now.'

Charlie stepped closer to her. 'I can wait for you, Evie. Enjoy New York for a couple of months. We don't have to be married straight away.'

Evie kept her voice soft. 'We've always been such good friends. We had so much fun together every summer. But I think that's all we're meant to be. Friends.'

'But we're practically engaged already. Everybody expects it. You can't say no to something that everybody thinks is a fait accompli.' Charlie's expression was that of a hurt child and it made Evie feel so desperately sad.

'Charlie,' she touched his arm gently, 'I don't love you. Not the way a woman should love the man she marries. I love you as a very old and dear friend. And I want us to stay friends. Please?' Her voice wobbled as she said it, as if she was unsure, but she was really terrified, because there was no softening the blow of these words. And she could see their effect on Charlie.

His hand was frozen on his jacket pocket, covering the Tiffany box that was no doubt hidden inside. The Tiffany box that any other girl in the world would give her right arm for. For a single moment, Evie wished she was normal. That all she wanted was to be married and have babies. Then she could say yes and Charlie would smile, rather than looking at her as if she'd stabbed him.

He'd had no idea she would say anything other than yes.

Neither spoke. Into the silence sang the words from the phonograph, and as Evie heard them, really heard them, she recoiled. Why had she chosen such an unfeeling song to play at this moment? *Gee, but I'm lonesome, lonesome and blue. I've found out something I never knew. I know now what it means to be sad, For I've lost the best gal I ever had.*

Charlie picked up a brandy glass and studied it. 'I haven't asked you to marry me.'

She knew he was trying to claw back his pride. So she let him, because it was the least she could do. 'You haven't,' she agreed. 'I know you're saving your proposal for a woman who loves you as much as you deserve to be loved. Besides, this morning I did something you wouldn't like. If you needed more proof that we aren't suited, this is it. I attended summer school at the Columbia College of Physicians and Surgeons.'

'Why?'

'Because I want to be a doctor.'

'Women aren't doctors. You won't be accepted into medical school.'

Of all the things he could have said, that was the one that hurt the most. He was voicing the secret fear that gnawed away at her every day, that she tried to ignore, that she hoped wasn't true. Because if she wasn't accepted into medical school, then she had nothing. And if she was honest with herself, her chances were so slim as to be almost impossible. She removed her hand from his arm. She should leave the room before either of them wounded the other more deeply.

But Charlie spoke again, casually. 'I hear you went out with Thomas the other night. You didn't tell me.'

'I met some of his friends. That was all.'

'Are you trading up?' His voice was no longer casual. It was accusatory.

Evie felt her heart stop. And with the worst possible timing, the song on the gramophone moved to the chorus: *Somebody stole my gal. Somebody came and took her away* . . . 'What do you mean?' she said.

'Are you moving on to the vice-president? The brother who's not a dumbbell?'

'You're not a dumbbell, Charlie.'

'Thomas thinks I am.'

'He doesn't. And nor do I. He's trying to look out for you.'

'By taking you out? How do you know what Thomas thinks?'

Because he's a good man, Evie wanted to say, but she knew that would be the end of everything. If she left the room now, they could both recover some dignity. 'I'm going out for a walk.'

'I wouldn't have married you anyway, Evelyn. You're not that sort of girl.'

Bite your tongue, her better self screamed at her as she hurried out of the room and out of the house.

Dusk was beginning to settle on the city like a fine cloud of soot, the street lamps were alight and people marched past, returning home from work. Evie walked as they did, with purpose, because to do otherwise was to risk being pushed aside or trampled and she had had enough of both. She went over and over in her mind the conversation with Charlie, searching for a point where she could have handled it better, where she could have been kinder, where she could have hurt him less. She'd somehow done exactly what Mrs Whitman had warned her not to do. She'd made him angry. She'd let him hurt her too. And now he was suspicious of her feelings for Thomas, and given his jealousy and resentment of his brother, that would only make things worse.

When she reached Lexington Avenue, she turned and walked south. She checked the number written on the envelope in her pocket. She was in the right place. But the building looked so ordinary, red brick with white stone trims and rows of arched windows. Beside it were regular houses, windows lit up, full of people going about the business of living. Nothing about the building or its location suggested pathos and tragedy; comfort sat in the lap of despair as it did everywhere across the city.

A nun answered the door; she was a little older than Evie but her mouth was pinched as though she'd swallowed too many bitter pills. Evie couldn't imagine this woman caring for an abandoned child.

'Are you Sister Mary?' Evie asked.

The woman nodded, and looked suspiciously at Evie.

'I think you're caring for the baby I'm looking for.' Evie showed her the letter.

Sister Mary stepped aside and motioned for Evie to come in, then led her down a hall and into a dormitory that looked like the infamous old woman's shoe. There were so many children. Babies, both newborn and older, as well as girls and boys who were old enough to understand that fate had not been kind to them.

'This is the baby from Concord.' Sister Mary gestured to a whimpering baby lying in a crib. It was wearing a white suit with a pink ribbon pinned to the front. Its face was clenched and wrinkled like a fist that had caught hold of sadness and couldn't let go. Evie couldn't help herself. She bent down and picked up the baby. 'It's a little girl,' she said in wonder.

The baby's face relaxed. Her eyes opened and she looked at Evie, who had no idea if this was the baby she'd seen by the river in Concord. The blood had been washed away and its sad little mouth grizzled quietly, as if it knew that crying any louder would simply waste energy but grant it no extra attention.

'Sister Margaret!' Sister Mary called. 'Please look after our visitor.'

Another nun appeared, this one younger, but she already had a strip of white in her hair, just visible at the front of her wimple, as if what she had seen of life had given her the greatest fright.

'Thank you for writing to me,' Evie called to Sister Mary's departing back.

She returned her attention to the baby. It was so small. Defenceless, unable to do anything for itself. How could anyone have thought of leaving such a tiny and helpless thing to die by a river? Evie swayed from side to side and the grizzling began to quieten.

'She seems to like you,' Sister Margaret said.

'I'm glad she's stopped crying. She sounded so sad. Is she healthy?'

'Yes, she's healthy enough. But she cries most of the time. She stops if I hold her. But I can't carry her around all the time. Sister Mary –' Sister Margaret pressed her hand over her mouth and stared at the floor.

Evie looked around the room. Most of the other children were unnaturally quiet; there was no rough and tumble bois-terousness or show of high spirits as one might expect. Sister Mary was nowhere in sight, nor were any other nuns. Still, she lowered her voice. 'Has anyone claimed the baby?'

'No. She will attend nursery school here and then be sent on the orphan train to Maryland when she's six or seven.'

'The orphan train?'

'We place babies with Catholic families out of state. Sister Mary says it's for the best.'

'Can I keep visiting the baby while she's here?'

'I should think so. We can do with the help. If one of the children is looked after for even an hour, it's a blessing.' Sister Margaret's voice dropped to a whisper. 'And it's so nice to have a visitor when you live somewhere like this.'

Evie heard the wistfulness in Sister Margaret's voice, but before she could respond, footsteps approached behind them.

'It's late.' Sister Mary was back. 'Time for the children to get ready for bed.' She took the baby and placed her in the crib.

'I'll be back again next week,' Evie said.

Sister Mary nodded frostily, then indicated that Sister Margaret should walk Evie to the door.

They walked back through the big room full of so many lost and unloved children. Evie wanted to take them all with her. But she could barely help one, let alone so many. She glanced at Sister Margaret. It would be good to have somebody looking out for the baby. 'Thank you for talking to me,' Evie said. 'I wish there was more I could do for her.'

'I could check on her each day. Then when you visit I can tell you how she's been,' Sister Margaret said eagerly, so desperate to help, desperate for friendship. Desperate for a visitor too.

'Were you an orphan here?' Evie asked with sudden intuition.

Sister Margaret blushed and nodded.

Evie felt her eyes fill with tears. 'I'll bring some chocolate with me next time. To say thank you.'

Sister Margaret looked down, too overcome to speak.

'I'll see you next week,' Evie whispered, stepping outside.

As she walked back to the Whitmans', her head was full of the baby's cry, a sound that seemed as if it could go on forever, and would go on forever in Evie's head until she could visit her again. What a day it had been. And now the prospect of sitting at dinner with Charlie and pretending nothing had happened. She couldn't do it.

She crept into the house and told the butler she wouldn't be coming down for dinner. Then she telephoned Lil. She changed into a dress she'd bought in her first week in Manhattan and not yet worn because she hadn't been sure if she was ready to become the bold and reckless woman it would best suit. But perhaps now, after refusing Charlie, after severing that strong link to her past, she was.

As the cab sped downtown, Evie wondered if the world had been turned upside down, that the city was in fact the night sky. The illuminated windows of the skyscrapers were as bright as any star, and Manhattan was hung with a necklace of lamps, shining from each of the bridges that surrounded the city – the Brooklyn, the Madison Avenue, the Manhattan, the Washington, the Williamsburg. Watching the lights, Evie began to understand she had to concentrate on the points of radiance in her life, rather than the shadows. She jumped out of the cab, pretending that with each step she was skipping from constellation to constellation, an astrologer learning to read the signs of her city.

'Let's get half-seas over and have a gay old time!' a familiar voice shouted. It was Lil, striking in a breathtaking silver dress.

Leo pushed himself away from the wall and threw his cigarette onto the ground. Lil and Evie linked arms with him and waltzed through the door of Chumley's.

Before they sat down at their table, Evie let the gold and black brocade shawl she'd worn in order to avoid scandalising the cab driver fall onto a chair. The dress beneath was sapphire blue. It had a tulle skirt that fell to just below the knee. The bodice was sequined and the neckline dived gracefully to end at her sternal notch. An inset of semi-sheer flesh-coloured fabric was artfully placed over the middle of her chest, but even knowing that, Evie had blushed when she looked in the mirror. Her hand had moved to her breasts and she'd turned to the side to see how the fabric both revealed and concealed the line of her cleavage. Now she didn't blush. She stood tall and proud, because she knew she had nothing to be ashamed of.

Leo smiled at her. 'Evie, you look magnificent.'

'Hear, hear,' said Lil.

Leo bought their drinks but Evie barely had time to sip hers before he took her hand. 'It's "Hot Lips",' he said, and Evie recognised it as the song she'd tried to play on the piano at the Whitmans' in Concord, the song that had so angered her mother and Charlie. The song that had made Thomas say she had a beautiful voice. Tonight it was fast and loose and full of brass that made her limbs shimmy along with the dipping and rising of the trumpets.

'So will you be sticking around?' Leo asked as they danced.

'I don't know. For six weeks anyhow.' She twirled under his arm and hoped her dress wouldn't shift around too much, but it seemed the dressmaker knew exactly what a girl might get up to when wearing it and everything stayed where it should.

Soon she was smiling in a way she couldn't remember doing since she was a child. It was as if she had risen to the top of the Woolworth Building and the whole city lay at her feet. The song finished and the next one began. Another man – Frederick – asked her to dance, and then another – Caleb – and another, until she left the floor, breathless and laughing.

She rejoined Lil and Leo for another drink until a man by the bar caught Lil's roving attention. 'I might go see if he takes cash or cheque or just a bit of chin music.'

'I think I'm meant to say good luck,' said Evie, 'if I've interpreted right.'

'You have,' said Lil with a wave of her hand as she walked away.

Evie watched Lil approach the man without a hint of shyness. She turned to Leo. 'Let's dance some more.'

'I'll never say no to that,' he replied.

The music segued into a slower song, meant for lovers and not-yet-lovers.

'Why don't you have a girl?' Evie asked.

'I like too many girls.'

'Really?' There was something about the way he said it that made Evie not quite believe him.

'Well, there's really just one, but she doesn't know I'm alive. Not in that way.'

'Then she's a fool.'

As they danced, Evie found that their bodies had moved closer together and that it was not at all unpleasant. And because he'd told her he was in love with someone else, and because she still wanted to know what it was like to be kissed and she figured it was better to find out with someone who had lots of experience, someone who was in no danger of falling for her, Evie rested her cheek against his. Then she looked up and saw that his eyes were intent on her face. She smiled.

'Have you ever been kissed, Evie?' Leo asked.

'Is it so obvious that I haven't?' she said.

'No, but you're looking at me like someone who's curious to know what happens next.'

'Is this a service you offer to all girls newly arrived in the city – first kisses in exchange for a dance?'

'Only the beautiful ones.'

Evie laughed. Her lips touched his and her hand moved up to the back of his neck. After a minute, she pressed her mouth to Leo's a little more firmly until it opened against hers and she lost herself in the wonder and joy of casually kissing.

Chapter Eight

The next day, Evie's head was still spinning when she woke to the blessed news that Charlie had embarked on his tour of the bank's east coast assets. Viola seemed uncharacteristically glum at the news but Evie was thankful she wouldn't have to see him for some time.

While Mrs Whitman kept Viola busy paying calls, Evie threw herself into summer school with a will but was met with sneers. No one wanted to speak to her. She became so used to men looking at her with derision and contempt that she had to remind herself that this was not what men were really like. She told herself they would become accustomed to her if she kept quiet and studied hard, but so many small incidents threatened this optimistic viewpoint.

There was the time the anatomy lecturer asked her to leave the room because they were going to discuss the male genitalia. Evie hadn't replied; she'd simply sat in her seat and stared at her desk and refused to move. She knew that her cheeks were the brightest of reds, but it wasn't because of the male genitalia that were apparently too shocking for her; it was because she could hear the sniggers, could sense the disapproval from the lecturer and the other men in the room. In the end, the lecture went ahead with her present, but she was too afraid to look up lest she catch anyone's eye. At the conclusion of the lecture, one of the other students sidled up to her and asked if she'd like to study some of the finer points of anatomy with him, which sent him and his pals off into boisterous fits of laughter. Again, Evie didn't respond. She slunk off, feeling as if she'd been the one who'd done something vulgar, feeling the men's mockery sit like filth on her skin.

But her mind soon became used to the rigours of study and she concentrated hard on what she needed to learn, rather than the jeers directed at her. She spent every day at the college, or with Mr Childers working on physics, chemistry and mathematics. She returned to the Whitmans' house late at night and had dinner on a tray in her room, talking to Mrs Whitman about the things she'd learned that day: that an eye behaved in the same way a camera did, and that it contained parts with such wonderful names as vitreous humour. She talked about the weather with her sister when they passed in the hall; for some reason, Viola had decided to leave Evie alone, and Evie was so grateful for this that she never once thought about what Viola might be up to.

After the first couple of tests, in which she struggled, Evie's grades slowly improved, until by the last two weeks she was consistently achieving marks in the highest range. When she received her first perfect score, she almost wept. To think that just a few weeks ago she knew so little about physiology and now she was able to answer everything correctly. She began to feel more confident of success. Surely the medical school would have to admit somebody who was one of the strongest students?

Six weeks passed with the speed of a jazz pianist's fingers, during which Evie tried many times to write to her mother to tell her that she'd refused Charlie. Finally, with one week to go – it would take at least that long for the letter to arrive in Concord – she sent a short note admitting she'd turned Charlie down and apologising for not being able to do what her mother wanted. She tried not to think about what would happen when her mother read it.

Then it was the day of her last tutoring session with Mr Childers. The following day would be her admissions interview with the dean of the medical college.

That morning, Evie caught the El down to Bleecker Street as she always did. To her, the El symbolised all the contradictions of New York City: inside, the trains had mahogany walls, leather seats and carpeted floors, but the engines dropped soot and oil on the heads of everyone who passed beneath the elevated tracks with more precision than a Central Park pigeon. The El was grimy and grand all at the same time.

Once off the train, she smiled at the Italians selling fresh ears of corn and lush broccoli stems from the stalls along the sidewalk, and at the newspaper boy calling out, 'Extra! Extra!' as if in Manhattan there was always something new worth hearing. She sang as she walked, because she was so close to victory, and when a passerby stared, she gave him the full force of her smile and said, 'Manhattan can make one a little mad.' He nodded as if that was a perfectly reasonable explanation.

'Your admissions interview is tomorrow,' was Mr Childers' greeting.

Evie sat down in her usual seat; by now she was used to the way he gave the climax before the warm-up. 'How do you think I should approach it?'

'The same way you approach everything in life, Miss Lockhart. Boldly.'

'I wondered if I should try to be less like myself.'

Mr Childers laughed. 'Why?'

'I want them to admit me. If the way my parents react to me is any indication, I have a habit of irritating conservative people.'

'If any woman can convince the college to accept her, you can. You're more determined than when I first met you. And more adept.'

It was the best compliment she'd ever received. She *was* becoming adept. Physiology especially was her strong point. 'Thank you,' she said. And then because they'd shared a lot of Irish coffees over the last six weeks and because he'd been patient with her, she told him what she'd told nobody else. 'I've staked everything on the interview tomorrow. I can't return to a life I've outgrown. I belong to New York now.' Mr Childers nodded as if he agreed. They settled down into a final session of calculus, at the end of which Evie stood up and shook Mr Childers' hand. 'May I let you know how I get on?'

'I'd very much like to know.'

~

When Evie returned home, earlier than usual, nobody was around. But there was a letter for her. And this time it was from Tommy!

Evie curled up on the sofa in the sitting room and read about what he had been doing in London, in between employing men to work in the bank and meeting the people he hoped would become their clients. It all sounded so grown-up and independent, and no one thought twice about him being adventurous because he was a man. A man, as it turned out, with a rather nice turn of phrase; after reading his description, Evie almost felt as if she was walking through St James's Park with him. Her smile widened when she came to the end of the letter: *How is summer school?* Tommy had written. *I hope I'll find you well on your way to becoming a doctor by the time I return. Even though I've only been away a few weeks, I'm already looking forward to seeing you again.*

She stood up and spun around, feeling impossibly happy. Despite being so busy, Tommy was thinking about her. And for the first time in her life, Evie herself was on the brink of doing something that mattered. One interview to get through tomorrow and then she'd hopefully be accepted into medical school! She danced a few steps, pretending Tommy was with her, reaching out to take her hand.

Ouch! She'd knocked her knee against a table. Rubbing it, she laughed at herself, dancing alone in the cosy room. It was a room that lacked fuss, a room Evie loved spending time in; the walls were covered in cream silk, the Aubusson carpet on the floor was gently patterned with lutes and swans, and there were touches of the outside everywhere. Ferns and palms stood in vases by the door, and roses sat in loose bunches on the occasional table that had injured Evie. Above the fireplace was a recent portrait of Mrs Whitman and her two sons, gathered together in an embrace of love. Evie studied the portrait and decided that the artist had not done justice to the rich blackness of Tommy's eyes.

She sat down, picked up a pen and paper and began to write back to Tommy. She told him about her perfect score and how good Mr Childers had been to her. At the end of her letter she wrote: *I talk to your mother every evening about my days. But I often wish you were here, so I could talk to you too.*

'You look happy.'

At the sound of her sister's voice, Evie dropped the pen on the floor and hastily folded over the letter.

'I'm happy too,' Viola continued, stepping further into the room. 'I'm especially happy with *my* correspondence.'

'Correspondence?' Evie realised that her sister was dressed up more than was usual for a family dinner, in a shapeless plum-coloured velvet shift that overemphasised her solid frame.

'With Charles.'

'You've been writing to Charlie?'

'You need to come to dinner tonight,' Viola said, not elaborating any further. 'Mother and Father are here.'

'What?' Evie spluttered as her mind raced. What elaborate ruse could she conjure up in order to escape to her interview tomorrow? Then another thought struck her. 'Why are they here?'

'To see us, of course. They arrived while you were out. I took them for afternoon tea. You'd better get changed.' Viola nodded at Evie's dress, which was creased from the day spent squashed behind a desk. 'Charles is here too.'

Evie stopped herself groaning aloud. Viola sounded more assured than usual, almost as if she were challenging Evie. Was she going to tell their parents that Evie was up to something? Surely Viola hadn't a clue what Evie was doing.

Evie decided to play nicely. 'Thank you for not telling Mother that I've been . . . busy during the days.'

But Viola clearly wasn't susceptible to charm. 'Just make sure you're at dinner in half an hour.'

Damn. Evie left the room wondering why this had to happen today, of all days. She had so few fences left to hurdle, and ideally she'd spend the night preparing for her interview. Now she was going to be stuck at dinner with her family and Charlie. How awkward.

At the top of the stairs, she saw Mrs Whitman. 'Now you have even more of my family to accommodate,' Evie said. 'I'm sorry.'

'I don't mind. It's my husband and Charles I'm most worried about. I have to get them through the evening without killing each other.'

'That doesn't sound good. Anything I can do to help?'

Mrs Whitman patted her arm gratefully. 'You can try to keep George occupied in conversation and his attention directed away from Charles. You always manage to lighten George's mood.'

'I thought Charlie was away for a couple more weeks?'

'He's supposed to be. But he's come home early. He told his father he'd learned everything he needed to know after visiting the first two branches of the bank. Heaven only knows what he's been doing for the rest of the time he's been away.' Mrs Whitman sighed and Evie saw that beneath the always warm exterior lay a woman who spent her life managing the intricacies of being married to a successful man who had one successful son and one son who always felt second best. 'And his father told Charles he was an idiot and that Thomas would never have offended the branch managers by telling them he had nothing to learn from them. Of course he's just frustrated with Charles, but . . .'

'But he would have hurt Charlie badly all the same.'

'Yes.'

'And in the middle of it all, you have to put up with a gaggle of Lockharts around your dinner table.'

Before Mrs Whitman could answer, her eyes moved past Evie, and her worried frown was replaced with a polite smile.

'Evelyn darling!'

Evie would know her mother's voice anywhere. She turned and received her mother's kiss, wishing she wouldn't always put one hand on Evie's shoulder to keep her at a slight distance. Hang decorum! They hadn't seen one another for nearly two months. Evie tried to put her arm around her mother but before she could, Mrs Lockhart whispered in her ear, 'You have some explaining to do.'

Evie flinched. Her parents must have received the letter.

Then her mother smiled and said something surprising. 'Luckily we've had some good news to make up for your foolishness. So we'll celebrate tonight and deal with you tomorrow.' She raised her voice. 'Evelyn, you're not dressed. Hurry up.'

'I'll just be a minute.' Evie raced to her room. *Good news.* What good news? Had her parents found out what she had been doing in New York? And instead of coming here to tell her to stop, were they here to congratulate her? It was a faint, and probably fanciful hope. Because her mother had also said, *I'll deal with you tomorrow.* Was she referring to Charlie? Or medical school? Evie changed her dress slowly, making sure to choose one that would please her mother. As long as she stayed in her room, she didn't have to find out which scenario was the right one. But then she remembered that she'd left Thomas's letter and her reply in the sitting room. Damn. She didn't want anyone to find them. She buckled her shoes and slipped downstairs, past the dining room where she could hear that everyone was already gathered, to the far end of the hall.

When she pushed open the door, she couldn't believe what she saw. Charlie. Reading her letter. Reading Thomas's letter. Both of which would confirm, in his mind, the accusation he'd hurled at her during that last, angry exchange.

'Can I have those?' she asked coldly.

Charlie turned to Evie, his face hard with anger. 'I thought you said there was nothing to tell about you and Thomas. But you both seem to have such a lot to say to each other.' He held out the letters, indicating that she should come and take them.

She walked across to him warily, half expecting him to snatch them away and hide them behind his back, but instead he put his hand on her arm.

'Charlie, please don't.' She pulled back but he didn't let go.

'I was right,' he said. 'You traded up.'

'I haven't traded anyone for anyone. The reason I don't want to marry you has nothing to do with Thomas. And Thomas and I are just writing letters to each other, nothing more.'

'"I often wish you were here, so I could talk to you too".' Charlie mimicked Evie's words. 'Is that what you say to every man you meet?'

'Of course not.'

'Just the special ones.'

Evie took a deep breath. She reminded herself that he'd just had a confrontation with his father that would have cut him to the quick. And now on top of that had come these two letters. She softened her voice. 'You're hurting me, Charlie. Please let go.'

Rather than releasing her, he caught hold of her other arm and made her face him, holding her so firmly she couldn't move. His breath hit her full in the face and it smelled like too much wine and too much whiskey. He propelled her towards the door and pushed his back against it to make sure no one could enter. Evie shivered, suddenly feeling cold despite the summer night.

'I thought I was one of the special ones,' Charlie said. 'Once upon a time. But you never said anything like that to me.'

Fear made Evie's breath quicken. She couldn't get enough air. Why was he holding her so tightly? Why was he standing against the door? She tried to pull her arms away but it was just like that time at the river when she realised how much stronger he was than her.

Then he lowered his face to hers. Oh God. He was going to kiss her, and given the way his fingers were digging into her flesh, she knew there would be nothing of love in what he did.

Charles's foul, wet mouth pressed against hers and his tongue tunnelled between her lips. She gagged and tried to twist her head away. But he took both her wrists in one of his hands behind her back and pulled her arms up higher until she thought they might snap. With his free hand he groped at her breasts, pinching her. Then his hand slipped down and lifted her dress until he found her thigh. Evie squirmed, frantic now. She couldn't call out, let alone scream and howl like she desperately wanted to. Why didn't someone come to find them?

She shifted her leg away a little but he grabbed hold of her thigh and squeezed so hard that tears stung her eyes. His mouth was still squashed against hers, making sure she couldn't utter a sound. She felt as if she was standing outside her body, watching herself on the verge of ruin, being kissed in a way she never wanted to be kissed, being touched with such violence and hatred that she wanted to shout, *I'm sorry, I didn't mean it, I will marry you, I'll do anything if you just stop!* She managed a single 'Please!', but he swallowed it with his mouth and it was clear to Evie that there was not a thing she could do to get away.

She was trapped. Trapped by his awful lust, which she could feel jabbing against her hip. She was the woman by the river. She was the one at the mercy of a man. She was the one about to get into trouble she hadn't asked for, trouble she didn't deserve.

The hand under her skirt moved inside her knickers. That was when Evie stopped moving. Her body froze. She stopped crying. She stopped thinking.

'I'll see if he's in here.' It was Viola's voice, coming from behind the closed door.

Viola! Help me! Evie wanted to cry out. But Charles reacted first. He pushed Evie away and jumped forward. She fell to the floor, knocking the brandy glasses off the table. The sound of shattering glass rang out.

The door opened and Viola came in.

Charles's face was flushed. He was panting. Spittle shone on his lip. One of his hands was clenched, as if he still had Evie's thigh in his grip. Evie was shaking, crouched on the floor, her face turned from Viola in an attempt to hide the shock and the pain and the tears.

'Evie?' Viola said. 'What's going on?' Her tone was accusatory, as if it was Evie who had been doing something wrong.

And Charles always had the right words for any occasion. 'Your sister was asking me why I hadn't yet proposed marriage to her. She became upset when I told her it wasn't ever my intention to ask for her hand.' His voice was controlled.

Viola walked over to Charles's side and smiled up at him with devoted eyes. And Evie knew then that Viola would never believe her, let alone help her. Nobody would believe that Charles Whitman had tried to force himself on Evie while his guests drank champagne further down the hall. Her face was awash with tears. She looked like the guilty one, the one who was out of control. Whereas Charles looked proud, as if he knew that even though he hadn't been able to finish what he'd started, he'd won. Evie had been thoroughly beaten.

Before Evie could escape, Charles put his head through the door and summoned the butler. 'Call everybody in here.'

Evie's whole body shook uncontrollably. She had to leave. At the very least, she had to see if she could stand. With her hands braced on the table, she pulled herself to her feet just as her parents and the Whitmans came into the room.

Mrs Whitman noticed Evie's face and gave her a concerned look. Mrs Lockhart was beaming, and Evie wondered how it was possible that her mother could be so oblivious to her daughter's anguish.

A fork rang against crystal. It was Charles, getting everyone's attention. What was he going to say? Evie cringed against the table.

'I have an announcement to make, now that we're all here,' he said, glancing at Evie. 'This is one of the happiest days of my life.'

Evie took a step back.

'I must be the luckiest man alive to have a woman so incomparable agree to spend the rest of her life with me,' Charles continued.

What? Evie struggled to make sense of what was happening.

Charles looked directly at Evie as he spoke. 'I'm proud to announce my engagement to Miss Viola Lockhart.'

Viola smiled as if she'd caught herself a king.

'No!' said Evie. Everyone looked at her.

'But . . . but . . .' Evie stopped. What could she say? That Charles had tried to do unspeakable things to her and she didn't want him doing anything like that to her sister? The pent-up tears began to pour down her cheeks and she knew she looked exactly like a spurned and jealous lover.

'Evelyn,' her mother snapped. 'What is wrong with you?'

'Evie's been feeling unwell all day.' Mrs Whitman stepped in, and Evie had never been so grateful to be rescued in all her life. 'She made such an effort to come down to dinner but I think she should really be in bed.'

'It's not every day that one's sister gets engaged.' Mr Lockhart's lips were pressed tight with disapproval.

'Please?' Evie whispered.

'I think it's for the best.' Mrs Whitman swept Evie through the door before her mother could protest.

'Oh, my dear,' Mrs Whitman said when they were in the hall. 'Are you upset about Charles and Viola?'

Evie shook her head. She wouldn't allow herself to speak because she could never tell Mrs Whitman that her son was the worst kind of man.

'You've had an extraordinary few weeks. My prescription is bed rest for tonight so you're at your best for the interview tomorrow. I'll handle your mother. And I'll do my best to pretend I'm happy for my son and your sister.'

'Why is he marrying Viola?'

'That's a very good question. He seems intent on proving himself, but in all the wrong ways.' Mrs Whitman hugged Evie. 'Now go upstairs to bed. Try not to think too much about the interview.'

Evie nodded. She slipped upstairs and closed the door of her room. Her legs collapsed and she slid down the wall, onto the floor. Another sob escaped loudly, too loudly, so she swallowed it and all the rest that wanted to come pouring out.

Rose's face flashed before Evie's eyes. Rose's desperate, lonely face. And it made Evie so angry to remember what had happened to Rose while the father of her child had suffered not at all. It turned Evie's wretchedness to fury. 'Damn you, Charles

Whitman,' Evie whispered. 'Damn you if you think that's the way to get rid of me.'

This was *her* reason to stay, the reason that Mr Childers said she had to find. Charles's attack meant she had no choice but to become an obstetrician. Because Evie would know, every time she saw a shamed and pregnant woman walk into the hospital, that it could so easily have been her.

Chapter Nine

Evie hardly slept that night. The next morning, her eyes were circled with shadows and her face was red and puffy. Powder helped very little. She tried to concentrate on her interview with the dean, on her one and only chance to be admitted to the Columbia College of Physicians and Surgeons. But other problems were demanding her attention. She couldn't stay in the Whitmans' house any longer. Not with Charles here. Where would she go? And should she warn Viola what her future husband was really like? She decided to walk to the college rather than take a taxi. The fresh air would calm her down. She stood up to leave but the door to her room opened.

'Evelyn!' said her mother, billowing into the room, followed by Mr Lockhart. 'What fun we can have now that we're all in New York. We'll be able to find a dress for Viola and a dress for you for the wedding. I might even see if the stores of Fifth Avenue have something for me. We'll plan a date for late autumn, I think. November would be ideal.'

Mr Lockhart placed his hand on his wife's arm to quiet her and turned to Evie. 'Last night you didn't behave like the lady I know you to be. It was your sister's engagement announcement and you were in bed. It made you look petulant, which I know you are not.'

Mr Lockhart lifted Evie's chin so she had to tear her eyes from the floor and look at him. He smiled at her, benevolently, and Evie's lip trembled. 'What we need is to find one of Charles's friends for you. Then you can forget about Charles and be happy for your sister. Charles didn't behave like a gentleman should, so I can see why you might be upset. When he asked me for Viola's hand, he told me that you understood his preference for your sister. But I can see now that he was wrong, and I'm sorry for it.'

Evie sniffed back tears. How could she even begin to tell her father how mistaken he was? Besides, he was being kind to her, and what she needed right now was a little kindness. 'Thank you,' she said, deciding it would be simplest to go along with his assumptions. She kissed him on the cheek, wondering how she could get her parents to leave the room. It was only half an hour until her interview. But then the door opened again and in came Viola.

Mrs Lockhart beckoned Viola over. 'You haven't shown Evelyn the ring.'

Viola held out her hand. Her finger was bejewelled with a diamond that could light up Broadway.

'It's impossible to miss,' said Evie.

'It's from Tiffany,' said Viola.

Evie's heart sank. Charles wouldn't have given Viola the same ring he'd bought for Evie, would he? But it wasn't Viola's fault if he had, so Evie tried to be nice. 'I hope you'll be happy. But I have somewhere to be in half an hour, so if you let me finish getting ready, we can talk later. We'll have afternoon tea.'

'But we're going shopping!' Mrs Lockhart exclaimed.

'What if you and Viola go this morning and I'll come next time?' Evie said, wishing everyone would leave her alone, because her fragile facade could crumble at any moment and she needed to leave now or she would be late.

'Charlie told me that Evie's been going to summer school.'

There was utter silence in the room. Evie was filled with cold and bitter hatred for her sister. Who was probably filled with cold and bitter hatred for Evie, if she believed what Charles had said last night, that Evie had been begging Charles to marry her when Viola walked in on them.

'I don't understand,' said Mrs Lockhart, with disbelief.

It was time to come clean. 'I have been going to summer school. Because I want to be admitted to medical school. Are you happy now, Vi?' Evie asked her sister. 'You got the prize and I'm the black sheep. Let's leave it at that.' She turned back to her parents. 'My interview with the college is in twenty-five minutes. I have to go. You can shout at me about it later. Please?' Evie took her father's hands in hers. She tried to look chastened and apologetic. He'd been feeling so sorry for her only a moment before. But the look on his face was anything but sympathetic now.

'How dare you lie to me all this time,' he said coldly, with-drawing his hands. 'How dare you spend the money I gave you to enjoy New York on summer school. You've been dishonest – worse than dishonest, because you haven't just lied, you tried to convince us that things were going well with Charles when they were not.'

He was right. She had been deceitful. She had lied and cheated and dissembled. And not just once, but over and over again. She turned away, unable to face her father's gaze.

Through the window, on the pavement below, Evie could see two women, one older and one younger, walking along Fifth Avenue. It was like watching herself and her mother, out strolling for the purpose of being seen. The two ladies noticed nothing beyond themselves: not the finger-bone tree branches ringed with late and faded blossoms or the girl hurrying past in a Bergdorf's uniform with a frown on her face because perhaps she was late for work and perhaps she cared about that. The older woman was smoothing her cuff, ironing out a wrinkle as fine as the smile lines that would adorn her face if she forgot herself and had a momentary lapse into humour. Evie knew that a wrinkle in a sleeve could be the biggest trouble in one's day, because she'd witnessed such fussing over trifles at home. No one would speak of a woman dying by the river, but much ado could be made out of a misplaced button. Why did she care about losing the approval of a family whose lives were filled with such trivial concerns? Because they were *her* family. They were supposed to love her no matter what. If they couldn't love her in spite of what she chose to do, then who would?

She turned back to the room. 'I'm sorry,' she said. 'I knew you'd be surprised. But can't you be proud as well? I can show you my summer school grades. They're among the highest of all the students'. Of all the *male* students'. I'm good at this.'

'How can we be proud of something that will make you a pariah?' Her mother shuddered.

'The world is changing, Mother. There are women all over New York who work and take care of themselves.'

'Those women are typists and laundresses and teachers. They are not doctors.'

'And if you're truly sorry, you will not go to the interview,' her father added.

Evie picked up her purse and tried to keep her voice steady. 'I am going. I'm sorry I had to lie. But I'm not sorry I did it.'

'I think you should leave me to talk to Evelyn,' Mr Lockhart said to his wife and Viola, who left the room, Mrs Lockhart clutching Viola's hand in shock and Viola looking as if life was now just about perfect.

Mr Lockhart didn't begin to talk straight away. He let the silence fill the room, fill Evie's mind with fear and worry. This was the moment when she would discover whether her father's love for her stretched only so far as social convention, or whether it was big enough to fill the wide open space that existed beyond propriety.

Finally he spoke. 'Let's imagine for a moment that you do go to medical school, as preposterous as that is. What do you intend to do after that? Become an intern?' He laughed. 'It's not even possible.'

'Yes it is,' said Evie, feeling a little more courageous as she said it. 'New York Presbyterian has just appointed its first female surgical intern, Virginia Kneeland Frantz. She graduated second in her class this year from the Columbia College of Physicians and Surgeons.'

Then her father began to shout and Evie flinched. He reminded her of Charles, wanting to bend her to his will. 'So there is one other deranged woman in the whole of Manhattan. One! Do you have any idea what it will be like to be the freakish oddity everyone laughs at and nobody speaks to? You threw away your chance with Charles Whitman. I can't see any other fellows lining up to ask you to marry them. You've been wasting your time on a foolish idea that will make you unmarriageable to any decent man. You'll look back on all this ridiculousness in a few years' time and be glad we stopped you.'

That her own father would call her a freakish oddity galvanised Evie to fight. 'You were a doctor,' she shouted back. 'Surely you're pleased that I want to do something useful?'

'You have no idea what being a doctor is like.'

'Yes I do,' said Evie firmly, although she knew it was a lie. 'You may have found it too difficult to stick at. I won't.'

Mr Lockhart stared at her and Evie wished he would shout at her again. Anything other than look at her as if she was someone he'd encountered for the first time and didn't particularly like. She shouldn't have said what she had. It was mean-spirited. 'I'm sorry.'

'You don't know what you're talking about. You cannot be a gentleman and a doctor. And you certainly can't be a lady and a doctor.'

There was something about the way he spoke, a wistfulness that Evie would never have expected from her father, that made her say, 'Did you want to be a gentleman rather than a doctor? Or is that what Mother wanted?'

'Your mother wanted what was best.'

'But for whom?'

Her question hung in the air, unanswered. What had her father given up for her, for her mother, for Viola? A busy life, a useful one. A life where he mattered. He'd exchanged it all for a bigger house, a position in the foothills of good society and a life of extreme boredom. No wonder he'd spent so little time with her and Viola when they were children. What did he see when he looked at them? A life forsaken? No wonder he spent so much time sequestered in his study reading, or going to Harvard to meet with his old cronies from his university days. It was to rediscover for a short time the person he might have been.

Evie stepped over to her father and touched his shoulder. He looked at her, and although she tried to hide the pity in her eyes, he must have caught its barest flicker because his voice when he spoke was cold and the moment for truth was lost. 'You have some romantic idea of helping people,' he said. 'You can help your mother organise the Concord Hospital fete. That's what *ladies* do.'

'I don't want to spend the rest of my life idling by a fireplace, drinking cups of tea and commanding a housekeeper. Surely you understand that?' she pleaded, willing him to admit that he didn't want her to suffer the same life of tedium that had so wearied him.

'Many people would be extremely pleased to live a life of such ease.'

'Then let them have it.'

Her father landed the final blow. 'If you are accepted, which I doubt, we will not pay the college fees. If you won't rescue yourself from a future of shame and ridicule, then I will have to save you.'

To save her. Just as Evie had once tried to save her half-dead pet mouse from the jaws of a cat, a mouse who thereafter walked with a limp and sported a chain of toothmarks around its neck. She marched out of the room, ran down the stairs and hailed a cab.

Climbing in, she gave the driver the address and asked him to hurry. She needed to be at the college in fifteen minutes and she had to compose herself. She had to pretend that the sudden insight into her father and his refusal to allow her the freedom he himself coveted didn't upset her. She had to imagine that the dean would be unlike most other people and would not think her deranged and a freakish oddity for wanting to study medicine.

Most of all, she needed to remember Rose dying. To remember, as much as she wished to forget it, Charles and what he had almost done to her last night. That was *her* reason for wanting to be an obstetrician. The difficulties involved would just have to be surmounted.

She looked at her watch. A horse and cart laden with blocks of ice was clip-clopping along in front of them as if this was Central Park and not a busy street. 'Can you go around him?' she asked the driver.

'Not unless you want to get yourself killed,' the driver replied.

Finally they reached Tenth Avenue, and Evie paid the driver and jumped out of the cab. She ran to the college, losing her hat, and arrived bright red in the face. Perhaps the interviews might be running late and she'd have time to compose herself. But of course she was ushered straight in, hatless and panting, and asked to sit down.

'Miss Lockhart,' the dean said. 'You're applying to medical school with a literature degree.' Every word was suffused with sarcasm.

'No,' puffed Evie. She took a deep breath and tried to settle herself. 'I've just completed summer school, here at the college. I meet all the requirements for pre-med.' She ran out of air and had to stop.

'Literature is very different to medicine,' the dean replied.

As if she didn't realise that. The dean was so in control, serene even; he barely moved his lips when he spoke, only his tone belied his rudeness. Evie felt even more flustered and breathless. 'I understand that.'

'Medicine is highly competitive. Our applicants are men with the highest grades from the most reputable colleges.'

'And my grades are also of the highest standard and are from a reputable college. First Radcliffe, whose alumni include such notable women as Gertrude Stein.' Gertrude Stein? Why of all the names would she pick that one? The dean hardly looked the type to favour experimental writing. Evie blundered on. 'And your own college —'

'Where you've attended summer school only.'

'When I began at Radcliffe, medical colleges weren't open to women,' she said. 'Most of them still aren't. So there was little point in taking a pre-medical degree. I've tried to rectify the gaps in my education with summer school, and you can see how well I've done.'

'It's difficult to see how a literature degree makes you a good candidate for admission into medical college.'

Suddenly exasperated, Evie said, 'A literature degree doesn't make me a good candidate for medical college. But a desire to learn does. I wish more than anything to become an obstetrician. And when I want something, I work my hardest to get it. The men in your course have probably never had to consider the impossibility of getting something they want. But I have. And it makes me even more resolute. I'm a good candidate for admission because you need female doctors in this city and I'm set on becoming one.'

The dean closed the file in front of him. He hadn't bothered to write anything in it. 'Thank you for your time, Miss Lockhart. Your aspirations may be higher than your abilities.' He stood, indicating the end of the interview.

It was over. Evie was shocked, finally, into silence.

The dean's parting words about her aspirations and her abilities shadowed her as she walked away. She returned to Columbus Circle in a daze, unable to believe what had happened. She'd failed utterly. The statue of Columbus no longer inspired her as it had on her first morning at the college. Evie wanted nothing more than to give Christopher a push off his perch so he could see what it was like down there on the more democratic space of the ground.

She didn't want to go back to the Whitmans', where she'd have to tell her parents that the interview had gone badly. She'd buy some chocolates and go to the Foundling, she decided. A place where she could focus instead on the baby, who had far more troubles than Evie did.

Mary, the baby had been called at last, now that it seemed it would survive. 'Mary,' Evie murmured when she picked up the baby, wondering how many other children had had to suffer from Sister Mary's lack of imagination. She walked around the big room until Mary fell peacefully asleep in her arms. As she rocked the baby, she noticed Sister Margaret watching and she smiled to encourage her to approach.

'I have some chocolates for you,' Evie whispered. 'In my purse on the chair over there. Make sure Sister Mary doesn't see them or she might eat them all herself!'

Sister Margaret giggled, her face transformed from a map of woe to a picture of delight. 'Thank you.'

'How has Mary been?' Evie asked as Sister Margaret found the chocolates and slipped them into the pocket of her habit.

'Much the same. Crying a lot. But a gentleman came to see Sister Mary about her yesterday.'

Evie stopped rocking the baby as she took this in. 'Do you know why?'

'He left some money to help care for her.'

Mary stirred and Evie jiggled her arms, puzzling over the mysterious gentleman. Why provide money for the child but leave her in an orphanage? Unless the nurse in Concord had been right: someone had done something they shouldn't and they wanted the evidence out of the way.

'Can you tell me if he comes again?' Evie asked. 'And perhaps try to get his name.'

Sister Margaret nodded eagerly, clearly pleased to have been asked to help, and Evie's heart ached for her. That chocolate and a request for assistance could make such a difference to someone's life.

She kissed Mary and placed her back in the cot, then thanked Sister Margaret for her help. Setting her shoulders, she returned to the Whitmans', where she knew her family would be sitting in a row in the drawing room like a line of hungry gannets waiting to peck her to pieces. She slipped in the door, hoping to get to her room before anyone noticed her, wanting to lie down on her bed to think. But the butler saw her and gave her a telephone message. Evie recognised the number straight away. She was sure Mr Whitman was at the bank, so she let herself into his study and dialled the Columbia College of Physicians and Surgeons.

The dean was quick to advise that her application had been unsuccessful. He hadn't even waited to write her a letter, she realised; they wanted to be rid of her as soon as they could.

Evie didn't respond; she simply hung up the telephone. What was there to say? She was devastated, so stricken it was impossible to think. She had nothing. No dignity; Charles had stolen that last night. No family, because how could she continue to see Viola once she was married to Charles? No husband, because she'd stupidly thought she could have a better life than that. No man she really cared for, because the one she admired had moved to London. And no home, because how could she ever go back to a life of Concord tea parties now that she'd lived in New York?

But the college had refused to admit her. She'd lost everything. No matter how hard she'd worked, it wasn't enough. What she wanted was beyond the bounds of possibility. The absoluteness of this made her gasp aloud, too loud; somebody would surely hear and discover her when she most wanted to be alone.

And somebody did. 'Evie, what is it?' Mrs Whitman's voice came from the doorway.

'My ambitions overreach my abilities. I haven't been accepted into medical school.'

'Well, that's wrong, plain and simple.'

Evie stood up and walked over to the fireplace. She reached out a hand to touch the big heads of white hydrangea that sat like fallen clouds in two matching porcelain vases on the mantel. She clenched her fists and rubbed them against her eyes, which were dry but tired and blurred, as if they were not seeing the world as it really was.

'I might be able to help,' Mrs Whitman said.

Help, thought Evie. She was always needing help. She seemed unable to do anything on her own. She was the very opposite of independent. A fungus, requiring a host to survive.

'Mr Whitman and I are benefactors of the college,' Mrs Whitman continued. 'Our donations allow the college to provide services for the poor. I'm sure that if I was to express an interest in you, they could revise their decision.'

'I wanted to be accepted based on what I know.'

'My dear, once you have a start, you can show them what you're made of. But you won't be able to do anything without a start. The men who've applied have all used their connections to get ahead. Men are so much better at that than women, who are always too afraid to ask. It's not the time to be polite. It's time to put up a fight.'

Mrs Whitman reached out and took Evie's hand in her own; it was such a motherly gesture that Evie couldn't help but feel a cut to her heart. She knew her mother would never say such a thing. And Mrs Whitman seemed to know Evie better than her mother did; she couldn't have used better words to rouse her. A fight was exactly what Evie felt like.

'Thank you,' said Evie. 'For everything. It's more than I deserve.'

'It's exactly what you deserve.'

Evie left the study and simply told her parents that she hadn't succeeded. That they wouldn't have to worry anymore. She didn't wait to listen to their satisfaction at the news. She went to bed, but she didn't sleep. She listened until she was certain everyone had retired for the night, then she crept downstairs, uncertain who would answer the telephone at this time of night but hoping someone would still be awake.

'Yes?' came a voice from the other end of the line.

'Could I speak to Lil, please?' Evie asked.

Evie waited forever, then heard Lil's wide-awake voice say, 'Hello?'

'Lil! It's Evie. Is the attic room still vacant?'

'Sure is.'

'Would you share it with me? I can't stay with the Whitmans any more. And even if I don't get into medical school, I can't go back to Concord.'

'I'll talk to Mrs Lomsky in the morning. When are you coming?'

'Tonight.'

Chapter Ten

*E*vie packed one suitcase with the new dresses and shoes she'd bought, plus a couple of old frocks that would be fine for life as an impoverished student, if she was lucky enough to be one; half a dozen books; her new rouge, powder and lipstick; and a clean hanky, because some habits were hard to lose. She'd delivered a knockout punch to her conscience by stealing into her parents' room while they were at dinner and opening the bottom drawer of the desk where it was her father's practice to keep a little emergency money. Thankfully he'd kept up the custom here at the Whitmans' and so Evie made a small donation to her own forthcoming emergency – just enough, she hoped, to get her through two weeks in Manhattan without a job.

She wrote a letter to Mrs Whitman, thanking her and telling her where she was going. She also wrote a letter to her parents, but didn't include her forwarding address.

Then she picked up her suitcase and tiptoed out onto Fifth Avenue, ready to walk almost seventy blocks downtown with her suitcase in hand in the middle of the night. At first her progress was slow, but further down Fifth Avenue, the buildings changed from stiff and formal Beaux Arts carved limestone to stores selling fur coats and furnishings, ornate bronze traffic towers, the triangulated glory of the Flatiron Building, and Ladies Mile, where six caryatids the same size as Evie looked down on her from above the awning of a store, as if they were giving her their blessing. She smiled at them and began to walk faster, counting off the blocks, her excitement rising with every step she took closer to Minetta Street.

Lil was watching from the window and came downstairs to let her in. 'Shhh,' she whispered. 'Mrs Lomsky'll make us scrub the floors if she finds I've had a guest in my room. Luckily she sleeps through everything, from fires to gentleman visitors, so we should be safe.'

They hustled up the stairs and into Lil's room, where Evie leaned on the back of the door and began to giggle. 'That's the craziest thing I've ever done in my life! I've just walked from one end of Manhattan to the other in the dark of night carrying everything I own.'

Lil laughed too. 'It'll be the first of many crazy things you do if you live with me.'

'Promise?'

'Promise.'

Evie spent the next day hiding in Lil's room while Lil was at work. Hiding meant that she wasn't allowed out, but a steady stream of girls came in to introduce themselves. They offered to lend her everything from hair rollers to 'rubber goods', a euphemism Evie had some trouble deciphering until a packet of the articles was produced and Antonia from the ground floor, who was the most theatrical person Evie had ever met and whose hands spoke as eloquently as her mouth, used a curling iron to conduct a demonstration of the correct way for a man to put one on. Having only recently experienced her first kiss, Evie couldn't imagine ever being in a situation where rubber goods would be required, and she knew her mouth and eyes were wide open during the entire procedure; in the end, though, she was laughing so hard at the ludicrous sight of a curling iron covered in sagging rubber that she had to be shushed lest she bring Mrs Lomsky to the door.

At about six o'clock Lil appeared. 'I see you've been inducted into the life of a single girl in the city,' she said, nodding at the curling iron, still dressed in its rubber raincoat. 'I've just rented us the attic room.'

A cheer erupted from Evie and the two other girls in the room, Antonia and Betty, who were kindly sharing their cigarettes and gin. The gin was making them all so loud that the dreaded Mrs Lomsky soon appeared.

'I rent my rooms to quiet girls,' she said, staring at Evie, who had moved quickly and desperately to stand in front of the curling iron.

'I'm ordinarily very quiet,' Evie said. 'I just got a little excited about moving into this wonderful boarding house.'

'Yes, well,' Mrs Lomsky gave Evie a nod of approval, 'I like a girl who appreciates what she has. Just make sure you keep it down.'

All of the girls were silent until the door closed and the sound of Mrs Lomsky's footsteps had faded, and then the laughter began, muffled by hands over mouths, but no less infectious for being stifled.

'"I just got a little excited about moving into this wonderful boarding house",' Lil mimicked, and they all began to laugh again. 'You sure got Mrs Lomsky on side. Which will come in handy, mark my words. Shall we get all this upstairs?'

The girls swung into action, carrying up Lil's dresses, gramophone and the all-important liquor stash. Lil didn't own a lot and Evie had just one suitcase, so it didn't take long until they were all moved in.

'Evie!' Evie heard her name relayed up the stairs, from the first floor to the second, onto the third and finally up to the attic room. There was someone downstairs to see her.

It was Mrs Whitman, with a letter in hand. 'This came for you by special courier. I thought you'd want to see it right away.'

Evie was both pleased and apprehensive at the sight of Mrs Whitman and the envelope, on which were embossed the words *Columbia College of Physicians and Surgeons*. The paper was creamy and thick; it even smelled important. She pushed her finger under the seal. 'Do you know what it says?' she asked in a shaky voice.

Mrs Whitman shook her head.

Evie took out the letter, her good mood vanished. What if the college still refused to admit her? She began to read.

```
Dear Miss Lockhart,
Please be advised that your application for
admission to the Columbia College of Physicians
and Surgeons has been accepted, conditionally.
    The conditions of your acceptance are such:
that you will not, for the time of your asso-
ciation with the college, behave in such a way
that would bring the college into disrepute.
```

```
Should such behaviour occur, your place at the
college will be withdrawn immediately.
    Please send notice of your acceptance of
these conditions within seven days.
```

'They said yes! Oh God, they said yes!' Evie's relief was so acute she thought it might bowl her over. 'I did it! Or, rather, you did it. I'm going to be a doctor.'

'You were the only one who ever doubted it, my dear.' Mrs Whitman smiled at her.

'Thank you for everything, and for bringing the letter. I didn't expect you to come all the way downtown.'

'But then I would have missed seeing how happy you are. It's a more than satisfactory reward for the very little effort required to have the driver bring me here.'

Then Evie remembered why she was standing on the steps of a boarding house in Greenwich Village and not in the Whitmans' parlour. 'Did my parents say anything when they found my note?'

'Very little to me,' Mrs Whitman replied diplomatically. 'I can take a letter back with me if you want to write one now.'

Evie shook her head. 'No, I don't think I will. I might just enjoy this moment and celebrate.'

'I'll forward Thomas's letters here until you write to him with your new address.'

Evie blushed. 'Thank you.'

Mrs Whitman sighed. 'All the subterfuge of the last few weeks has kept me feeling much younger and more entertained than I've felt in years. I'll miss having you in the house, but coming down here is the best thing for you. I'm very much looking forward to seeing the woman you'll become. Now, kiss me before we both end up blubbering on the steps.'

Evie threw her arms around Mrs Whitman and hugged her as hard as she could. She waved until the car was out of sight and then she walked up to Bleecker Street, to Mandaro's, and purchased a supper of cheeses, just as she'd promised herself she would.

When she arrived back to the grandeur of their attic room, Lil had found a bottle of wine from who knew where and they sat on the bed together eating cheese and drinking wine. When she couldn't eat any more, Evie took a deep breath. 'I need a job. College is five hundred dollars a year. That's a lot of money.'

'You know the average wage is twenty-five dollars a week.'

'Twenty-five dollars?' Evie was dismayed. 'But I need to put aside at least fifteen dollars a week to cover college costs, then there's food and board and getting around. And I can't work during the day – I have lectures to go to. What kind of job will pay better than the average wage for skills I probably don't possess?'

But Lil had an answer for every problem. 'You could get a job that pays you for skills you hadn't considered.'

'What skills?' Evie asked warily.

'Aside from the women who make work out of pleasure, there's only one way I know to earn a whole lot of cash after hours. Can you sing?'

'What do you mean?'

Lil rolled her eyes. 'Open your mouth and tweet like a canary.'

Evie laughed and thanked God for Lil, who always made her feel better. 'Actually, I sing quite well.'

'Ever heard of the Ziegfeld Follies? Land yourself a gig as a Ziegfeld Girl and you'll get some decent mazuma. Fifty dollars a week.'

'Fifty dollars!'

'So I've heard.'

'Just to sing and dance? I don't believe you.'

It was Lil's turn to laugh. 'Yes, Evie. Fifty dollars a week just to sing and dance. Hell, if that's all it took, I'd be doing it too.'

Evie took a large swallow of wine while Lil continued. 'Ziegfeld's auditioning to find one hundred girls for this year's Follies. Trouble is, two thousand blonde hopefuls from Kansas'll turn up with a set of gams longer than any country girl's life in show business. The fellas like a lady with Ziegfeld's approval branded on her butt — she's a glorious American girl. So long as you're a perfect 36-28-38 — which you look like you are — and you don't mind wearing fewer clothes than a visitor to Coney Island, you've got a chance.'

'How few clothes are we talking about?'

'Most of the girls get to keep their bubs and duds covered, but some of them like to give their perfect thirty-sixers an audience. But that's only in the Midnight Frolic. We're aiming for the Follies. The least you'll wear is a corset.'

'Is that supposed to make me feel better? No one, besides the maid, has ever seen me in just a corset.'

'Evie, you're gorgeous. Make a quick buck out of it while you can. Think of the money you need and it'll be worth a few men ogling your chassis.'

There were so many objections in Evie's mind that she didn't know which to voice first. 'But I'm not a performer.'

'You don't have to be a performer to be in the chorus. The stars sing and dance. The chorus girls strut. The only skill you need is deportment. And fine ladies like us have that in spades. Ziegfeld chooses girls for their face and their figure. He trains them to do the rest. You're a prop on the stage. Window dressing – or undressing as the case may be.' Lil laughed.

'I wish there was some other way . . .'

'Besides selling yourself, I can't think of another way to get the dollars you need from only working nights.'

Lil was bold and brave and Evie wanted to be like that too. She wanted to stop feeling like a naughty child who'd soon be dragged home and scolded by her mother. She wanted to believe that she was the kind of woman who could go to medical college and pay for it herself. Besides, the wine had gone to her head, as had the bugles calling from the gramophone. 'When are the auditions?'

'Friday.'

'So me and two thousand others are heading to Broadway on Friday. There are a lot of ifs and maybes in this plan, Lil.'

'Just like in life.'

Over the next two days, Evie did her homework. She found out everything she could about the Ziegfeld Follies and the infamous girls who worked there. For the auditions, she borrowed from Lil a demure ensemble of a white silk-chiffon blouse with cap sleeves, a strand of pearls, and a white cloche hat with navy trim. She'd discovered that while a Ziegfeld Girl might put herself on show in the theatre, outside the doors Ziegfeld expected her to be a paragon of late-nineteenth-century respectability. Evie found the hypocrisy momentarily difficult to digest, but for fifty dollars a week she thought she could probably manage the dissimulation.

On Friday morning, Lil kissed her cheeks and told her to break a leg.

'At the very least, I'll damage my pride,' Evie replied with a nervous smile. 'I still can't believe I'm doing this. From not knowing what rubber goods were at the start of the week, to auditioning to be a showgirl at the end of it, I think we can safely say I'm now a New York girl.'

Off she went to the New Amsterdam Theatre on Forty-Second Street, between Seventh and Eighth. The building wore a curved facade and it stood like a regimental soldier above its far shorter and less elegant neighbours. Inside, it looked like an expensive hotel. The ceiling was an Art Nouveau fairyland onto which scenes from *A Midsummer Night's Dream* had been transposed in iridescent silver, pink and gold, elegant colours that made the red velvet chairs of other theatres seem tawdry by comparison. Across the proscenium, a line of peacocks preened in a relief that continued around to the cantilevered balconies, which hung seemingly without support, suspended only by applause and ovations. Each box was adorned with flower reliefs – buttercups, goldenrod, violets – garlands of glamour, outshone only by the furs and jewels of the audience ordinarily seated within. At the centre of it all was a sweeping staircase begging for a grand entrance.

But today there were too many beauties. Blondes, brunettes, redheads with hair the colour of toffee apples, all with legs as long as skyscrapers and figures as curvaceous as the Shimmy Queen's. Girl after girl took to the stage, most of whom quickly found out that even a gilded staircase couldn't make exits with dashed hopes any less distressing. And there was still a long line ahead of Evie and a long line behind.

Then, at four o'clock, before Evie had even had the chance to meet him, Ziegfeld stepped on stage and announced that it was over. He'd seen enough. He had his girls.

If Evie had thought the room couldn't handle any more drama, she was wrong. Hundreds of girls who, like Evie, hadn't yet auditioned broke out in histrionics. So much wailing and desperation. So much melodrama. Their shoulders slumped and they began to leave the theatre, giving up all too easily.

Not Evie. She needed this job. Without the Follies, she couldn't afford to go to medical school and she'd have to suffer the mortification of returning to Concord, which she wasn't prepared to do. She remembered the stories she'd read about Ziegfeld. Apocryphal or not, there were enough of them to make her hope they were true. According to legend, if Ziegfeld saw a girl he liked in an elevator, he chased after her. If he saw a girl he wanted crossing the street, he got her. He could always have more girls. And Evie hadn't grown up in a Kansas cornfield. She'd been in the drawing rooms of wealthy men, the kind of men who patronised Ziegfeld's. She could offer him something different to what he already had.

So she shouldered her way through the sobbing girls, stepping on a few toes. She climbed the stairs to the stage, stood beside Ziegfeld and began to sing – 'A Good Man Is Hard To Find' – as if she had had any experience of having her heart broken by a man fooling around with another gal. But she pretended she did. She thought of Charles and how he'd once been her pal and how she now knew he wasn't a good man. She was counting on the fact that, even though Lil said the chorus didn't need to be top-class singers and dancers, Ziegfeld would recognise a good voice when he heard one. He could still take her. If he wanted her enough.

Ziegfeld let her sing right to the end. Then he just stared at her, as did all the other girls.

Although she was dying of embarrassment inside, Evie let him look. She kept her chin up and pretended she was at a party at the Whitmans', surrounded by men who were made of money.

At last Ziegfeld spoke. 'Join the rehearsals. Keep hold of that upper-class, I'm-better-than-you thing you've got going on and you'll have men feeding you gems like they're chocolates.'

Evie kept her excitement to herself until she left the theatre; then, unable to contain herself, she spun around on the street. She'd done it. In two weeks she'd start medical school. And to top it all off, she was now a Ziegfeld Girl.

PART
TWO

Chapter Eleven

*G*iven that I possess one, I think I have a more intimate knowledge of the vagina than any man could ever lay claim to. That should make me well qualified to be an obstetrician,' Evie said.

It was lucky she'd been trained in resuscitation, because Dr Kingsley looked as if he was about to have a fit right before her eyes. His face was redder than a whore's knickers and his cheeks puffed in and out, making him look like one of his birthing mothers would if only he didn't knock them out as soon as they began to make a bit of noise. But Evie had had enough. Two and a half years of swallowing her words meant there was no room inside for any more. And now that she'd opened her mouth, even Evie couldn't believe what came pouring out.

'If you continue to speak in that manner, Miss Lockhart, you'll no longer have a place at this college,' Dr Kingsley huffed.

'All the other students have assisted with a delivery. I'm the only one who isn't allowed to do anything more than watch from the side of the room. You're supposed to be teaching me.'

'I'm teaching the students who show the most skill.'

'At what? It can't be at being a doctor, because my grades are better than theirs.'

'They're better at being a doctor in a hospital setting,' he said flatly.

'Oh, you mean being a man. The only obvious difference between the other students and me, apart from their inferior grades, is what they're carrying between their legs.' Evie snapped her mouth shut. The years of study, hard work, daily abuse and no sleep would end right there if she said another word.

The clash had begun as a whispered exchange across the main desk of the Sloane Hospital for Women, where Dr Kingsley had been seated, alternating between sucking on a cigarette and slurping the second of his five-a-day Coca-Cola habit. He'd been smiling, pleased at the joke he'd made to the students about a patient who was so modest it was a miracle she'd opened her legs long enough to let a baby inside in the first place. Where would they be without scopolamine? he'd laughed. Still prising the lady's legs open with a vice. And then Dr Kingsley had had the gall to blame the woman's modesty for the fact that he'd overlooked the size of her pelvis. The baby's head had been too large and the patient's pelvis had snapped in two. Evie had told Dr Kingsley that it certainly wasn't the woman's fault. He'd replied that Evie wasn't qualified to have an opinion. And so it went on, louder and louder, until Dr Kingsley stood and shouted at her, 'Start doing rounds immediately!'

Now the other students, the interns and the residents were all watching, parties to a tactic that Evie had thought would end after her first year of studies. When it didn't, she'd accepted that it might continue into her second year. But for everyone to still be trying so hard to keep her away from the obstetrics patients in her final year of studies was disgraceful. And she felt her damned mouth open again before she could stop it.

'Besides,' Evie said, 'most men have never even seen a vagina. Their only experience of one is via their penis, which, according to *Gray's Anatomy*, doesn't have eyes. They go about the business of lovemaking with their eyes closed so they can thrust away and pretend their wife is the blonde who sold them a bottle of perfume at Saks.'

One of the interns snorted back a laugh, and that did it. Dr Kingsley slammed his fist on the desk, making his cola bottle tip and land on the floor, spilling brown syrup all over his shoe. He kicked the bottle against the wall. The echo of smashing glass rang on and on, the only sound in the now-silent ward.

Evie knew nobody would defend her. The nurses didn't speak to her unless they had to; they thought she should have been one of them. She had no friends at college; of the two other women in her year group, one had quit because of the constant browbeating, and the other thought Evie should take her medical degree to the peace and quiet of the decorous-in-comparison-to-obstetrics pathology lab.

Dr Kingsley leaned right in to Evie, using that typical trick of a man at his wits' end — threatening her with his physical size and strength. 'I'm reporting you to Dr Brewer,' and off he waddled, his overindulged bulk bouncing furiously.

Evie walked away to the wards, hoping to God she wasn't about to be shipped off to Bellevue Hospital to assist with the bruises and lacerations of the alcoholic homeless. She'd learned a lot in the past couple of years, including how to tame her mouth, so why the hell had she let it run off like a virgin at a petting party? Her behaviour for the rest of the morning would be faultless, she vowed. She'd keep her eyes down, her mouth shut, stay out of Kingsley's way and hope Dr Brewer, the hospital director, was in a benevolent mood.

The first room she came to was private. It was occupied by the woman whose legs hadn't opened to Dr Kingsley's satisfaction until she'd been sedated. Evie had been sitting with the woman and encouraging her to relax and to breathe through her labour until Dr Kingsley appeared and reassigned Evie to a space along the wall to view yet another birth, while a student on his first obstetrics rotation was asked to step up and assist.

'How are you, Mrs Cunningham?' Evie asked.

'Sore,' was the reply.

Even though it wasn't permitted, Evie sat down on the bed and held Mrs Cunningham's hand. Her face was pale and she looked confused, her eyes darting anxiously around the room, searching for something. 'Your baby is beautiful,' Evie said.

'You've seen him?'

'Yes. And I've asked the nurse to bring him down so you can see him too.'

'Thank you.' Mrs Cunningham's eyes teared up. 'I can't remember anything. I remember coming to the hospital and talking to you. But nothing else. The nurses tell me I had a baby. But they also tell me . . .' her voice dropped to a whisper, 'that I'm broken.'

'The baby was stuck in your pelvis. I'm so sorry.' Evie wished she could offer more than an apology – an apology she knew wouldn't be forthcoming from Dr Kingsley. It was how she always felt when she spoke to the women after their births: as if she should have done something – even though she wasn't allowed to; as if she was still walking away from women who needed her.

'But why can't I remember?'

'It's the effect of the scopolamine,' Evie explained. 'It makes you forget what's happened.'

'Will I remember soon?'

'The drug works by taking away the memory of the experience. So no, you won't remember.'

'How do I know the baby is mine?'

Luckily Evie recalled her vow to behave impeccably. It was the only thing that stopped her from cursing Dr Kingsley, Dr Brewer and all the men in charge who thought it best to render a woman completely insensible at one of the most vulnerable times in her life. She recalled her first observation of a birth, the strange experience of seeing a woman senseless but thrashing – a side effect of the drugs she'd been given – absolutely unaware of what was being done to her, unable to give permission for anything, her body under the total control of the doctor and his whims.

'Dr Kingsley is very professional,' Evie said, forcing the words from her lips. 'The baby is certainly yours. And even though you won't be able to get up and move around for several weeks, I'll make sure the baby is brought down to you as often as you like. I can also ask Dr Kingsley to speak to you. He was in the delivery room and might be able to reassure you.'

'Oh no, I couldn't talk to Dr Kingsley about it. Will you be here if I need to . . .' Mrs Cunningham's voice trailed off.

'Yes. I'll be here until half past five. Have the nurse find me any time.'

'Thank you.'

Evie left the room and walked straight into Francis Sumner, the intern given the job of supervising her.

'Do you ordinarily loiter outside patients' rooms?' Evie asked after she'd removed her face from his chest and stepped back.

'I need you to check on Mrs O'Rourke.'

'A whole case just for me? What have I done to deserve that?' Evie realised she was leaning forward like a boxer about to throw the first punch. Always ready to attack, because attacks were what she'd become used to. She corrected her posture.

'You wanted to do more, so I saved Mrs O'Rourke especially for you.'

Evie should have known it was too good to be true. But she was so pleased to be given a chance that she didn't stop to think. Instead, she took the stairs down to the ward reserved for the patients with no money.

'How are you, Mrs O'Rourke?' she asked the woman in the first bed by the door, whose scrawny body and haggard face indicated to Evie that she suffered from a relentless cycle of birthing and being pregnant and giving most of her food to her children because there wasn't enough to go around.

'Damn sight better if that doctor hadn't cut me from here to Sunday. It's a wonder I've got anything left to stitch down there — that's the third time they've taken to me with a pair of scissors.'

Evie checked the patient's chart. 'I need to take a look at your wound. One of the nurses thought there might be signs of infection.'

'Go on then, have a look. Everything needs to be in good working order before I leave here or my husband'll throw me and the kids out. Sometimes I reckon the only thing he comes home for is the barney-mugging.'

Evie smiled; one thing hospital work was good for was extending her vocabulary. She put on her gloves and asked Mrs O'Rourke to roll onto her side and slide down her knickers. Then she inspected the episiotomy and bit down hard on the insides of her cheeks — God, they were raw. The smell from Mrs O'Rourke's wound was worse than the back alleys of the Bowery on a fetid summer's day, and Evie cursed Dr Kingsley for thinking that his job ended once the baby appeared. For thinking that the only thing to do in every birth was to cut the woman up like a Sunday roast so the forceps would fit inside. The wall of the vagina was so badly damaged that faecal matter was leaking in. Evie remembered a nurse telling her, many months ago, that two-thirds of the patients in the gynaecology clinic were there because of obstetric trauma. Evie had been astounded. Thousands of women were so damaged from having a baby, but nobody thought anything needed to be done about it.

'You need an antiseptic wash,' Evie said. 'I'll have one of the nurses organise it immediately.'

'Ain't no one washing my jelly-box 'cept me,' replied Mrs O'Rourke.

Evie pulled up the sheet. 'Mrs O'Rourke, if you don't let one of the nurses help, then there'll be no barney-mugging ever again.'

'Miss Lockhart.'

Evie recognised Dr Brewer's voice. Kingsley had wasted no time in telling tales. 'I suppose you want a word with me,' she said.

'When you're finished.' He strode away.

Evie spoke to Mrs O'Rourke. 'I'll send the nurse in now?'

'Reckon you'd better.'

Evie pulled off her rubber gloves, gave them to a nurse for sterilising, released her jaw, briefed another nurse and readied herself for presentation to Dr Brewer. On the way to his office, she passed Francis Sumner. 'I can see why you saved Mrs O'Rourke for me.'

He smirked. 'You said you had an intimate knowledge of the vagina. It's clearly a case that needs a certain level of expertise.'

Instead of ranting, Evie laughed. She'd probably got what she deserved. And if you could overlook his toadying to Dr Kingsley, Francis was actually quite handsome. Besides, it felt good to laugh, to share a moment of possible friendship.

Francis smiled. 'I knew there was a sense of humour lurking beneath the frown.'

Evie was still laughing as she walked away.

~

'Miss Lockhart. Take a seat,' said Dr Brewer when she knocked at his door.

Evie did as she was told, eyes facing the back wall of the office, which was covered with rows of framed certificates celebrating Dr Brewer's qualifications and expertise. Beneath them was a bookcase filled with leather-bound editions of medical textbooks. And on the desk, a cigar case, opened, but not offered to her. She sat without speaking, determined to be as meek as a bride on her wedding night. Anything so she could keep her obstetrics clerkship and not be transferred elsewhere.

'Rather than shouting profanities across the ward for everyone to hear, why don't you show Dr Kingsley that you're the good doctor you think you are,' Dr Brewer said, standing behind his desk and looking down at her from on high.

Evie looked down at her lap. 'It's difficult to do that when he lets the other students assist but not me.'

'You help on the wards. I saw you talking to one of the patients just then. Take what Dr Kingsley gives you and do it well. And smile a little more, like the nurses do. You're prettier than most of them, after all.'

Evie cringed. He wanted her around for decoration, nothing more. But if it saved her clerkship . . . Evie forced herself to smile. She was expert by now at doing what she needed to. 'I'd love to be able to assist with a birth.' She couldn't stop herself from adding, 'Like the male students do.'

'Day-to-day patient management is up to Dr Kingsley, not the hospital director.' Dr Brewer picked up a cut-crystal paperweight heart from his desk and began to transfer it from hand to hand, like a juggler warming up. 'I told you from the outset that I didn't know if this would work. But I allowed you to do the clerkship. Please don't make the mistake of proving me wrong.'

'I'll do everything I can to make it work.'

'Dr Kingsley isn't the only person in New York who can't comprehend the idea of a female obstetrician. I sometimes wonder if you're the only person who can.' Dr Brewer put the heart down on a pile of papers unruffled by their conversation and flipped the lid of the cigar case closed.

It would be so easy to rage, to scream, to cry, but that was what everybody expected her to do. Exhibit the uncontrolled emotions of the weaker sex. 'Fine. I'll be the best medical student at bathing pus-ridden episiotomies, at holding the hand of the woman dying of puerperal fever, and at learning everything I can from watching rather than doing. That should satisfy everyone, for the time being.'

'It should.' Dr Brewer smiled at Evie like one of the patrons from the Follies, reminding her he'd done her a favour and she'd be expected to pay for it sooner or later. Evie made a note never to walk down the stairway late at night with only Dr Brewer for company.

'I won't tolerate any more complaints about you from Dr Kingsley,' he added, dismissing her.

Evie stood up. The paperweight caught the light, winking at her. She imagined taking it in her hand and pitching it at the certificates lining the walls, shards of glass from the frames tinkling to the floor, the thick crystal heart falling like a stone, unbroken, before rolling away to hide in a dusty corner. She touched her hand to her chest and felt her own heart tuck itself away in sympathy, concealing the little that was left of her feelings.

~

After she left Dr Brewer's office, Evie stopped at the bathroom. By the time she got there her breath was a series of gasps, like a woman in the final stages of birth, panic and hysteria a few breaths away. The events of the morning – the argument with Dr Kingsley, the butchered genitals she'd seen, and Dr Brewer's warning – were catching up with her. She washed her hands three times, then took a cigarette out of her pocket, stuffed it into her mouth and inhaled deeply. As the smoke rushed into her lungs she felt her breathing level out. Inhale, exhale. Inhale, exhale.

In Evie's first year at college, Dr Kingsley had stood before the group of eager students and said, 'You're privileged to be assisting in a fundamental change in society: you'll preside over the first generation of women to be brought to bed in a hospital and serviced by a specialist obstetrician.' It should have been exciting, and it was, until Evie came to realise exactly what being brought to bed in a hospital meant.

All of the births, even the successful ones, had one thing in common: not excitement but fear. The doctors loved to make their patients fearful; they stoked the fear, because it accentuated their mighty power to extract life. And they extracted life in the way prescribed by Dr Joseph DeLee, author of the rules of obstetric practice that Evie was made to memorise like a child in Sunday school. Dr DeLee had decreed that birth was a pathological process that damaged women. Thus doctors should always intervene, with sedation, forceps and episiotomies, which apparently saved women from the evils of labour. But it seemed to Evie that those tools left women desecrated.

'If labour is so evil,' Evie had asked in her first lecture, 'then why have women been made to give birth in that way?'

Dr Kingsley's answer was, 'God made men into doctors. He foresaw what assistance would be required.'

One didn't have to be a literature graduate to hear the subtext in that.

Dr Kingsley had then quoted Dr DeLee's opinions, which he obviously shared, on the deleterious effects of labour. '"So frequent are these bad effects, that I have often wondered whether Nature did not deliberately intend women to be used up in the process of reproduction, in a manner analogous to that of the salmon, which dies after spawning."'

At that moment, Evie realised what she was up against in her quest to become an obstetrician. It wasn't just a question of her breaking into an occupation that few other women had dared to enter, it was a matter of changing the way everyone working in that occupation thought: that a birthing woman was like a salmon who should go ahead and die once the business was over. As Rose had. It strengthened Evie's determination to rein herself in, to never say what she thought. All she had to do was get through college. Then she could help women bring their babies into the world with joy rather than fear.

It had been the same when Evie began her first obstetrics clerkship in the operating room at the Sloane Hospital for Women, which had rows of seats at one end so the students could sit back and watch the show. A pretty nurse who couldn't resist one of the flirting medical students let on that the woman on the table was not only poor, but also fifteen, pregnant and unmarried. Oh, what a joke that had been to the men gathered in the room. How funny that this stupid girl had allowed a man to have his way with her. Evie clamped her lips shut and watched the girl's drugged and convulsing body, ignoring the jests about how the girl should have closed the bank before the cheque was cashed. She realised again how lucky she'd been. When Charles had held her arms and refused to let her go, when he'd forced his tongue inside her mouth and left the precise imprint of his hand in a bruise on her thigh, she'd been in a sitting room with people nearby and he'd had to stop before . . . whatever it was he'd intended. This girl was from the wrong end of town, but that didn't mean she was stupid. Maybe a man had pinned her down and refused to let her go too. But nobody had stopped him.

Chance and circumstance were the only things that separated Evie and the girl on the bed. Which was why Evie had to say nothing. Because if she shouted at them all to shut the hell up, she'd be asked to leave the room and she'd never become a doctor who could help and defend these girls whose position she might have been in, but for the grace of God.

So she concentrated on watching Dr Kingsley, storing every detail of each procedure in her mind. It was how she learned everything. Memorise each step. Write down the steps later, with diagrams. Revise the drawings, revise her notes, imagine herself carrying out the procedure. In her mind she was always perfect. She had no idea whether she would be in reality.

That was why Evie was at the college or the hospital from seven in the morning until six at night, why she danced at Ziegfeld's from eight in the evening until almost midnight. It was why she never went out, why she did nothing but watch and learn and study and make just enough money to keep watching and learning and studying. It was for all those women whose faces filled Evie's dreams, women who'd had the misfortune to bolster the statistics: becoming a mother was the second highest killer of women, after tuberculosis. In her dreams, Evie was finally allowed to give each mother more than her heart; she gave them the skill of her hands.

Evie flicked the butt of her Lucky Strike into the toilet bowl and pulled a much-refolded piece of paper out of her pocket. She reread the words, even though she knew them by heart.

> *Evie, I'm returning to New York soon. I don't know exactly when, but I hope to be able to let you know in my next letter. I'm looking forward to seeing you — I haven't met another woman since I've been in London who has the courage you have, nor the same agility at climbing apple trees.*
>
> *Love,*
> *Thomas*

Evie smiled when she reached the last line, and then smiled a little more at the penultimate word: *Love*. She put the letter back in her pocket, resolving to write back to Thomas that very night. She'd been putting it off, because, now that he was returning, there was the matter of her evening employment as a showgirl to confess to. And the unorthodox way she spent her days, which he knew about of course; but knowing about it and seeing the effect it had upon people, especially the kind of people who were clients of the Whitman bank, was another thing altogether.

Evie had told his mother about her other life as a Ziegfeld Girl. Mrs Whitman had asked her what she was doing for money, and she never lied to Mrs Whitman. In response, Mrs Whitman had said, 'I trust you to do whatever you need to do.' Evie had tried to believe that that was absolution, but of course it wasn't. There was no excuse for never once mentioning it in her letters to Thomas.

Checking herself in the mirror, she patted down the blonde curl on the right-hand side of her head that always tried to cancan its way from her ear to her eye. Cutting her hair had been her way of celebrating her first paycheque from the Follies. Losing the heavy lengths had caused waves to form, curls even in some places, so she always looked a little bit jaunty, as if she was too busy to bother with the tedious ritual of combing. She put her hand in her pocket, pulled out a bobby pin and fastened back the sweep of hair falling across her brow.

She touched her fingers to the skin below her eyes and stretched it a little, smoothing away the finest of lines, a consequence of the hours she worked. If she held her hands there and puffed out her hollowed cheeks, she almost looked like the old Evelyn Lockhart, the one who'd marched down Fifth Avenue with a suitcase in hand and a feeling that she'd look Manhattan in the eye and it would be the one to blink first.

'Catch!' Evie rolled the ball across the grass of Central Park to the little girl opposite. Mary squatted, scooped the ball into her hands and threw it as high as she could, but forgot to catch it, so it came down with a gentle bounce on top of her golden hair. A normal child would have laughed spontaneously, but this child looked first across at Evie, who nodded. Then Mary began to laugh, unfettered, the sound rushing out like trapped air from a popped balloon.

Evie laughed too, casting Dr Kingsley out of her mind and into the yet-to-be-endured tomorrow. 'Shall we do it again?'

'Yes!'

Evie rolled the ball again and Mary picked it up, threw it, and let it fall on her head. The same laugh followed – twice in an afternoon. Evie beamed.

All too soon, dusk fell and it was time to leave. As they walked away from the park, Mary pointed to the puffs of steam rising from the tops of the buildings, like the ghosts of those who'd tried New York and failed. She pointed to a bird flying, a leaf plucked off a tree by the wind and tossed up, up, up and away. Departing things always caught Mary's attention.

'I'll come again in a few days,' Evie said as they got closer to the Foundling.

Mary's mouth opened, but closed again before she made a sound.

Evie bobbed down so they were at eye level. 'What is it?'

Silence followed, then at last a tiny sound: 'Park?'

'Of course we can go to the park again.' Evie stayed crouching before Mary and pulled something from her bag. 'I wanted to show you this. You can't keep it because the sisters won't let you, but I'll keep it safe until . . .' She stopped. That sentence had no easy ending. 'It's a bonnet. I think your father gave it to you when you were born.'

Mary put the bonnet on her head. It was too small, but she pulled on the ribbons and it slid down a little, leaving a bunch of golden curls to gather like buttercups next to her cheeks. As she tugged again, one of the ribbons broke away, and Evie gasped. A look of fear replaced the smile on Mary's face.

'You're not in trouble,' Evie said quickly. 'I can sew the ribbon back on. I made that sound because you look . . .' She paused. 'So pretty,' she said, instead of what she really thought, which was: I've seen a picture of you somewhere before, in a white bonnet surrounded by curls.

She reached out and hugged Mary, even though she'd been told not to by the Foundling sisters, and the child wilted against her chest. Passers-by were forced to step around them, and one woman said, 'What a pretty tableau you and your daughter make.'

Evie shook her head at the very thought of having a daughter.

Mary took the bonnet off her head and handed it back. 'Sorry.'

'You have nothing to be sorry for. Let's wipe your eyes.'

Mary reached into her pocket and took out a hanky. Before she touched it to her face, she showed it to Evie.

'You've still got the hanky!' Evie exclaimed, noting the crooked M in the corner that she had embroidered for Mary's second birthday.

Mary nodded.

'I'm glad.' Evie took Mary's hand and they walked as briskly as they could across to Lexington Avenue and the Foundling, where a line of sisters greeted them at the door.

'We've been waiting for you,' Sister Mary said.

'So I can see,' replied Evie.

'Sister Margaret, take the child inside.'

'Goodbye, Mary,' said Evie.

'Goodbye,' Mary said, staring up at her with the eyes Evie could never forget.

Evie turned to leave but Sister Mary stopped her. 'You can't see Mary again.'

'You said you wouldn't send her away until she was six.'

'She's not being sent away.'

'Then why can't I see her?' Evie demanded.

'It isn't good for Mary.'

'Being taken outside to play isn't good for a child?'

'Not in this case.'

'I won't take her to the park again. We'll stay inside.'

'It won't make any difference. It's been decided that Mary can't continue her visits with you,' Sister Mary said firmly.

The frustrations of the day seethed inside Evie. How she wanted to yell at Sister Mary the way she'd yelled at Dr Kingsley. But she knew it would be as fruitless as it had been at the hospital, and would likely cause her just as much trouble. She tried to put forward a reasoned argument. 'I'm the only person who visits her. Surely every child deserves a little fun and companionship from time to time? It's not as if I'm here all day every day getting in the way.'

'Mary has the companionship of the sisters and the other children.'

Evie cast around in her mind for a possible explanation. Surely the sisters didn't know about her job at the Follies? No, if that were the case Sister Mary would have simply shut the door in her face. She remembered Sister Mary's words: *it's been decided that* . . . 'Who decided I couldn't see Mary? You've let me see her until now. Why would you change your mind?'

Sister Mary pressed her lips together and Evie knew she was getting closer to the truth. But who else in the city knew that Evie visited Mary, much less cared? 'Who decided?' she asked again.

'It recently came to the attention of someone who has an interest in Mary that you'd been visiting her. We've been asked not to allow any more visits.'

'Who has an interest in Mary besides me? Nobody visits her. How can someone make a decision like that if they never see her?'

Sister Mary didn't reply.

'Now's a fine time to invoke the vow of silence!' Evie said in exasperation. The conversation had done at least two laps of the track and she didn't intend for it to take another. Sometimes it was easier to retreat and wait for the next race. She'd come back with a stronger argument once she'd had time to think about it. 'Mary will miss me,' she said as her parting shot. 'And you'll have to deal with that.'

And I'll miss her, Evie thought as she walked along Sixty-Eighth to Fifth. This little girl she had watched grow from a baby into a tiny person who trusted Evie, who would not understand why Evie had abandoned her yet again, just as she had that day at the river. She *would* see Mary again, and soon. And she'd find out who'd said she couldn't visit.

She strode on past the cream stone facades of the homes of industrialists and bankers who liked the number and height of their windows to proclaim their wealth as well as any Times Square billboard ever could. Stables were scattered here and there, many with horses in them, because now that motorcars were de rigueur, the novelty and expense of maintaining a set of redundant horses was a more effective way to show how rich one was. All that money wasted on horses nobody rode when it could be spent caring for a child. Evie knew, because Sister Margaret had told her, that the mysterious person involved with Mary occasionally sent money, but the little girl needed more than that; she needed someone to look after her. She certainly didn't need someone who took away Evie, the only thing Mary had to look forward to.

Chapter Twelve

*A*bove the New Amsterdam Theatre, sparkling like Fourth of July crackers, were neon signs announcing to all that inside the doors were the Ziegfeld Follies, with *New Stars!* and *New Girls!* The Follies attracted the rich and wealthy: bankers took their clients there, bored husbands acquired mistresses there, and for a few hours a night inside the theatre, bare legs could be paraded, midriffs exposed and necklines lowered. In the morning, those same theatre patrons would put on their suits and look down their noses at the flappers, who they said were corrupting the morals of the city.

Evie put a finger to her lips as Bob, the stage manager, noted her tardiness with a pointed stare at his watch.

'I'll be ready on time,' she called, fixing on her showgirl smile. 'Don't tell Flo.'

The smile worked. Bob nodded. 'Do it again and I will though.' Evie knew that was her first and final warning. It must be the day for it.

Backstage, she passed by Louise Brooks's dressing room – Louise was happily lost in the pages of *Ulysses*, from which no one expected her to emerge alive – and made her way over to a pretty redhead who was sitting before a mirror and blackening her lashes. Evie bent down to kiss her cheek.

'Evie!' Bea said. 'I thought you weren't going to make it.'

'You and Bob both.' Evie slipped off her clothes, donned the pink silk kimono that had been a gift from Bea on her last birthday and sat down in front of a mirror. 'I was uptown.'

'At least you'll save time on rouge tonight with those ruby-red cheeks.'

Evie looked in the mirror and saw that her face was flushed from the exercise. She hoped Bea was right and that the powder wouldn't dilute the effect too much.

'What were you doing?' Bea asked.

'Visiting Mary,' Evie replied.

'Honestly, Evie, you've got the bleeding heart of Jesus sometimes. Looking after stray kids, birthing babies – I don't see how you ever get any sleep.'

'I get enough,' Evie said.

'Well, you're still young enough to burn the candle at both ends. Not like me. Everyone says twenty-five is when you start looking like a face stretcher.'

Evie laughed. 'You're a long way off needing to worry about looking anything other than gorgeous.' But the truth was that some of the girls backstage were as young as sixteen. Ziegfeld, and Manhattan, liked their girls barely ripe.

'For that, honey, I'll do your hair while you fix your face. Then you won't be late for curtain-up. Now, flour up.' Bea passed Evie the powder.

Evie smiled at her friend. They'd met on Evie's first day of rehearsals when she'd made her way through the backstage area for the first time, mouth hanging open at the sight of more spangles and cosmetics than she'd ever seen. A woman who was tall, thin and long-limbed caught Evie's eye. Her makeup was a thick layer of marzipan and she was wearing nothing but a brassiere and knickers. She strolled over to Evie. 'I thought Ziegfeld wanted you for your class, not like us Midwestern hoofers. Close your mouth before he reconsiders.'

Evie snapped it shut.

'So, you aiming for the moving pictures or do you want to marry a rich man who thinks it's a triumph to have a Ziegfeld Girl at his table and not just in his boudoir?'

Evie shook her head. 'Neither. I need to pay my college fees. I've got a place in medical school.'

The woman began to laugh. 'Goddamnit, Ziegfeld was right. You sure are different. But seeing as we won't be competing for the same prize, I'll show you around. I'm Bea, by the way.'

Bea took her to Ziegfeld's office and pointed to a painting above the desk. It showed a woman with her head tipped back, one hand holding a red rose close to her red lips. Her mouth was parted to show a glimpse of white teeth. The woman was wearing a black silk gown that had slid down her shoulders and opened across her chest so that both of her breasts and their vivid red nipples were fully exposed. The woman was holding one of her breasts in her other hand; her fingernails were painted red to match her lips, and the expression on her face suggested that sensual satisfaction was only an exhalation away.

'That's Olive Thomas,' Bea said, nodding at the painting. 'She's a real Ziegfeld Girl. If you get my meaning.'

Evie thought she did. 'We don't have to do that, do we?'

'No. But you have to make every man in the audience think you might,' Bea replied.

By following Bea's advice, Evie had survived at the Follies for almost as long as she needed to. And now, after two and a half years, the end was in sight. 'Do you think Flo will give me a week off in a couple of months' time?' she asked.

'I think I'll fly an airplane to China before that happens. Why?' Bea said.

'For my final examinations. I just need a bit more money and a bit more time and then I can be a doctor and nothing else.'

'You slay me, Evie. You're the only one who wants to be a doctor over all of this.' Bea waved her arm around to indicate the jostle and bustle of a hundred girls wearing more fur and feathers than could ever be found in a zoo. She stood behind Evie and combed her hair, wetting down the curls and adding starch and powder with the flair of seven years' practice at being a Ziegfeld Girl.

'Evie?' Dottie, another chorus girl, appeared at Evie's side. 'I need help.'

Evie knew instantly what Dottie meant. 'Come with me.'

'You don't have time,' said Bea. 'Dottie can wait. You need lipstick.'

'I'll be quick,' said Evie as she led Dottie behind a screen to a disused corner of the dressing room that had been nicknamed The Confessional because anything that happened there was a zipper-tight secret.

'I'm peeing broken glass,' said Dottie.

'Is that all?'

Dottie nodded, and Evie was relieved it was something so easy to fix. That wasn't always the case with the ills that the Ziegfeld Girls brought to her. 'I've got something in my bag that'll fix it,' she said. 'No sex for a few nights will help.'

'I can't take more than a night off.'

Evie squeezed Dottie's hand. She understood what Dottie was saying – that her patron and his cash would move on to some other girl if Dottie couldn't give him what he wanted. She gave Dottie the medicine. 'Let me know if this doesn't fix it.'

Then it was time to go on stage and sing and dance and flirt until interval, when there was no time to rest because costumes had to be changed, faces re-made and hair fixed. Evie was just darkening her lashes again when Mr Florenz Ziegfeld himself strode into the room. The silence was instantaneous.

'I need a blonde,' he announced.

'I'm blonde.' Evie leapt up not knowing what Flo wanted a blonde for but hoping it'd be worth her while. Anything to earn a few extra dollars.

Ziegfeld ran his eyes up and down her body in the manner of a housewife selecting the best cut of meat. He turned to Bob. 'She's skinnier than Kitty. Get Zalia to pin the costume.' He said to Evie, 'You're on the moon. You know the song?'

Evie hummed the intro and sang the first verse, clear and loud and not needing the piano to key her in as some of the girls still did.

'Get her fitted,' Ziegfeld said to Bob. Before he left, he pointed his finger at Evie. 'Raise the roof.'

'I always do,' Evie called.

Bob filled the girls in. 'Kitty's gone home. She's got the grippe.'

One of the girls sniggered. 'Grippe? Or recovering from a visit to Madame Bonny? Hope her crochet hook was clean.'

Most of the girls laughed. Not Evie. 'I told Kitty to come and see me at the hospital,' she whispered to Bea. 'Or go to the place off Canal.'

'He charges twice what Madame Bonny does,' said Bea. 'And Kitty knows there's only so much you can do at the hospital.'

'The fellow at Canal sterilises his instruments. Madame Bonny wouldn't be able to find the word in the dictionary.'

Bea shrugged. 'You can't save everyone. There's only so much you and your Confessional can fix.'

'I hope she survives it.' Evie looked over her shoulder to her makeshift treatment room; there she did more than she was ever allowed to at the hospital, but some problems, like unwanted babies, couldn't be solved in a back room of the theatre.

'Get a move on.' Bob prodded Evie in the direction of Zalia, their Russian wardrobe mistress, who had her usual mouthful of pins and a pencil tucked behind each ear like horns on a miniature bull.

Zalia selected a white leotard covered in red and blue stars and helped Evie into it. She swore in Russian. 'You need to eat more. I cannot sew this in five minutes.' She muttered as she stitched. Then she passed Evie the headdress, an elaborate wire construction of several circles, each studded with silver stars. The circles grew outward, ever larger, so that the final circle was wider than Evie's shoulders. The headdress was pinned into her hair, and the finishing touch, a single silver star affixed to a hidden headband, was arranged to drop from the centre part of her hairline to sit in the middle of her forehead. Evie smiled. Even she had to admit she looked like the Queen of the Night she was supposed to be.

Bea squealed. 'Pos-i-lute-ly perfect! But if you forget a line, Ziegfeld'll land your ass in the middle of Forty-Second Street with a one-way ticket to Minnesota.'

'Believe me, I know,' Evie said as she bent down to check her face in the mirror one last time.

'Then I'll dye my hair blonde and be Queen of the Night tomorrow,' said Bea, and Evie knew that, in spite of their friendship, she was only partly joking; Bea would love the chance to take a lead role too. But then Bea delved into her purse. 'Wear this for luck,' and she slipped her four-leaf clover ring onto Evie's finger.

'Thanks, Bea.' Evie embraced her friend.

She took her place in the wings. The music began and the chorus of girls hoofed it onto the stage wearing gold-sequined leotards that raised their busts higher than any of them were ever likely to reach. Five men were comets, their 'tails' lit up with phosphorus, which Bob was convinced was going to catch fire one night. Evie knew she had a couple of minutes before the papier-mâché moon would drift up and out, into the sky of the theatre, so she took her seat on it, leaned her head against the crescent and closed her eyes. She was particularly tired tonight. The rush of minutes always sweeping past too quickly paused while she rested.

But why was she moving? Was she on the El? Her ears registered music and singing. She was on the damned moon and she'd fallen asleep and now she was suspended above the stage. The girls below had formed their clusters and the piano had paused briefly; it was her cue. Evie could see through the tiny slit she'd made with one eye that Ziegfeld, sitting in one of the balconies, looked as mad as Dr Kingsley had earlier that day. What the hell was wrong with her? Everywhere she turned, she made the man in charge furious with her.

Evie thought quickly. She was the Queen of the Night. She could make it a part of the show, pretend to be waking from the day's slumber. What man wouldn't be titillated at the thought of watching a beautiful young woman wake from her sleep right in front of him? Now to get the right mix of innocent awakening and the suggestion that, whatever she'd been doing before she slept, it had left her rumpled and flushed.

She opened one eye further and peeked out theatrically. Then she opened the other eye and faked a big, round, startled 'Oh' with her mouth. She raised one arm, stretching, arching her back, allowing her chest to lift to full advantage. Then the other arm, up, up, up. There wasn't a sound in the theatre. The piano was still waiting, as were the girls on stage. And the crowd – well, they were staring mesmerised at Evie. It was time to sing.

Evie reached down into her diaphragm and pushed out the words harder and stronger than usual. Tonight her voice wasn't supposed to blend with those around her – it was on show. And boy, did it respond. In spite of her earlier tiredness, her voice caught hold of the song and sent it right out into the far corners of the theatre, to the tops of the boxes, to the foyer, and up to the roof garden. The piano couldn't hold the final note for as long as Evie could and so the song ended on the long and strong echo of one perfect C. The audience waited until it had absolutely faded away before they started to applaud, and then they stood and cheered.

The moon lowered to the stage. Evie hopped off and did the Ziegfeld strut – arms outstretched, head tilted forward to balance the crown of stars – to the centre of the stage, where she bent her knees and performed an upright curtsey. She winked at a man in the front row, who actually blushed and turned to the lady beside him with a shrug, as if to say, *That time, it wasn't my fault.* The lady frowned at him and Evie laughed, wondering why anyone would bother to marry someone who might leave them for a showgirl's wink.

It wasn't until Evie flicked off her cape to reveal the star-spangled leotard beneath that she saw Thomas Whitman in the New Amsterdam Theatre, watching Ziegfeld's Girls fluff their feathers like hens on heat. For the moneyed men and women of Manhattan, coming to Ziegfeld's for a night of entertainment was the bee's knees. Let the poor people have their moving pictures; those in the know got the live show in three dimensions, with a splash of titillation on the side.

But what the hell was Thomas Whitman doing inside her theatre when he was supposed to be on the other side of the world, in London? He'd said he'd tell her when he was coming back, but here he was, studying her face, his expression inscrutable.

The jolt she felt at the sight of him was even stronger than when he'd looked at her for the last time before he'd left for London. She wanted to run over to him, whisk him away for a dance and a drink, catch up on the long years that had passed, years when she'd dreamed of him almost every night. But then he stood up and strode towards the exit and she remembered where she was and what she was doing and that she hadn't told him. The shame of her situation struck her full force; he'd never speak to her again.

Evie took her curtain call quickly, stepping away from the front of the stage, anything to move the damn spotlight off her. The curtain came down, the show was over and Evie was pushed backstage by the combined hot air of a thousand questions and compliments: 'Who told you to change the show?' and 'You were darb!' and Louise Brooks, who didn't like any competition, saying, 'You'll be lucky if Flo lets you out of here alive.'

'Told you she was a star,' said Bea, drowning out Louise. To Evie, Bea whispered, 'Why waste that voice on a lifetime of dealing with the ladies and their ace of spades?'

'Because this isn't a lifetime,' Evie whispered back. 'You can only go to the moon a few times before it's just like going to the corner store.'

'Bob says there's a queue at the stage door the likes of which he's never seen and they all want to see you.'

But would it be enough? Evie worried. Louise was right: no one messed with Ziegfeld and got away with it.

She was about to find out. Florenz Ziegfeld was striding towards her. It was impossible to tell whether he was still as angry as he'd been when it looked as if she'd slept right through her cue.

'That was your moon tonight, Evie,' he said. 'And it'll be your moon for as long as this show runs.' He kissed her hand, ever the gentleman, except when he was making whoopee with his leading ladies. But as he straightened, he said in her ear so no one else could hear, 'Change anything in my show again and you'll be working at the Creep Joint off-Broadway.'

'Thanks, Flo. And you're going to pay me like I own the moon too, aren't you?' Evie said in a loud voice, knowing that Ziegfeld didn't like to be seen as anything other than the big man in town.

'I've got the extra right here for you.' Ziegfeld handed Evie a ring box with a folded five-dollar bill tucked into the velvet inside. It was all part of the show, and the girls in the dressing room oohed and aahed as he'd intended.

'There's one more thing.' Evie knew she had to take advantage of her star turn here and now — she might not get another chance.

'There always is with you.'

'I need a week off soon. I've got some examinations to prepare for.'

'Two nights. No more. The doctoring doesn't get in the way.'

'Except when I'm fixing up your girls so they don't ruin the show by taking a night off. You could always create a little doctor number up there on the stage for me, Flo, and then I could get both jobs done at the same time.'

Ziegfeld allowed himself a smile. 'For the run of this show, if you sing like you did tonight, you get two nights off for your examinations and your extra five dollars a week and I won't fire you for having another job.' It was both permission and a warning and Evie understood.

'That's all I want, Flo.'

'For this week,' he muttered as he moved away.

'You might be one of Flo's favourites now, my love,' Bea said. This was something to both long for and dread. While taking a starring role might bring in more cash, they both knew that what he really liked was the class bred into Evie's bones and up there on stage, dressed with only the bare essentials covered, and with the suggestion that it could maybe be bought for a drink and a dollar later. It was how he groomed all his mistresses.

But Evie had five whole dollars a week extra. She was practically rich! She kissed the clover ring. 'You'll be lucky if you get this back.'

'It's never brought me as much luck as it has you. You should keep it.'

'If I find a rabbit's foot, it's yours,' Evie promised.

'I'd rather a gentleman's foot. Or his body.'

They laughed and hugged, and Evie found herself doing one of the most ridiculous things she'd ever done. She was standing in a room full of girls dressed as stars, so she made a wish — that this was the point at which life would suddenly get a whole lot easier.

But then she remembered Thomas's unreadable face. His swift exit. There was also her promise to the college that she wouldn't do anything to bring it into disrepute. And while she didn't think Thomas would tell anyone what he'd seen tonight, she couldn't quite bring herself to believe that he'd want to have anything more to do with a girl who was paid to flirt every night with a theatreful of men. How stupid she'd been to think that he'd never find out she was a Ziegfeld Girl, that when he came back to New York they'd just pick up where they'd left off, dress up and dance to the jazz at Chumley's, arms wrapped around one another.

Evie didn't bother to scrub her face or change. She had to get out of there, avoid any contact with Thomas and maybe he'd forget he'd seen her. If only she could forget she'd seen him, could pretend that nothing had changed, that he would still sign a letter to her with the words 'love, Thomas'. She pulled off her headdress, threw on a coat over her leotard and charged out the door, desperate to make her way unnoticed through the crowds of men who waited by the stage door every night, holding flowers and gifts and hoping to escort a Ziegfeld Girl to whatever party was kicking up its heels. Tonight there were more men than usual, all salivating like thoroughbreds over a bucket of molasses. Luckily her coat and lowered head hid the fact that she was the woman who'd woken up on the moon, and she managed to escape with the imprint of only one hand on her ass.

Rolls-Royces, Duesenbergs and Buicks were parked in the gutter outside, ready to whisk girls like Bea off to their happy-ever-afters — an after that rarely extended beyond the bedroom.

Once past the cars, Evie boarded the El and sat with her feet propped on the opposite seat, resting them for the first time all day. At Eighth she hopped off and ran all the way to the boarding house on Minetta, praying that Lil would be home to help her solve the Thomas Problem.

Their street was one of the few curved roads in New York City, built over and following the course of a stream. Evie liked to imagine the water running beneath her feet, cleaning out all the bad things from the day and ushering in the new, fresh and full of optimism. It was hard to believe that the area had once been the heart of Little Africa, home to men with names like No-Toe Charley, black-and-tan saloons, and the easiest place to get yourself murdered just for minding your own business. Now it was inhabited by Italians and artistes, who filled the streets with garlic and jazz and the morals of Zelda Fitzgerald. Or the morals of Evie Lockhart, incompatibly a Ziegfeld Girl and a medical student, who'd been spotted strutting her stuff by a high-society Upper East Side banker who'd know she was breaking all the rules for standards of conduct.

Evie pushed open the door of the attic room and slammed it shut behind her.

'Is the big bad wolf after you?' Lil asked, looking up from the dressing table, where she was rubbing cold cream into her face.

'Maybe.' Evie took off her coat, threw it on the bed and stood with her hands on her hips and a frown on her face.

'Nice,' Lil said, nodding at the patriotic leotard. 'Think I could wear that to the Black Rabbit tomorrow?'

'Zalia will bump me off if I don't return it.'

Lil shrugged. 'Worth a try. Let's get back to the wolf.'

'Thomas Whitman was at Ziegfeld's tonight. He recognised me. Of all the nights I get a solo, he's there. Why isn't he still in London?'

'A solo? Do tell,' said Lil, conveniently ignoring the real issue.

'No, do tell me what to do about Thomas.'

'This came for you today.' Lil held out a letter. 'It's somehow taken three weeks to get here. You can finally replace the letter in your pocket that's about to fall apart. I expect it has the news of his arrival.'

Evie ripped open the letter to find that it was dated just three days after his previous one. Sure enough, in it he said that he thought the letter would arrive at much the same time as he did, and he would telephone her when he was in New York.

Evie refolded the letter. She didn't believe he would telephone her after what he'd seen tonight. Instead of telling Lil her fears, she said, 'I came down from the sky as Queen of the Night and sang a little tune about the moon. Ziegfeld's given me an extra fiver a week. This morning I got a scolding from Dr Brewer, and tonight I had praise lavished on me by Ziegfeld. I'm succeeding at what doesn't matter and failing at what does.'

'Don't you ever want to quit college and use all that money to get a nice place and have fun?'

Evie arched an eyebrow as she scanned their room, taking in the double bed pushed over to the side and left unmade all day, the dressing table for two with a handy crack down the centre so each of them never took up more room than was her right, the wardrobe whose doors were always splitting apart like a fat lady in a dress three sizes too small, the single armchair which meant that most of their conversations took place while sitting on the bed, and the table that Evie had found in the basement and claimed for those times when she had to bring her books home with her. That left a narrow gap for them to funnel their way through the room. 'You mean this isn't a nice place?' she said.

Lil laughed. 'The only good thing about this place is you and me, and we know it. But enough about that. What about Tommy?'

'He saw me on stage.'

'So Tommy's been back in town for a day and he's already hitting the Follies. That man doesn't mess around. It was bound to happen, you know. Especially if you're going to take a solo number. Someone would eventually look beneath that blonde cap of hair and see what Concord Evie is doing to pay the rent.'

'I thought I was safe. My parents never come to New York – or maybe they do now that Vi lives here, but they'd never go to Ziegfeld's. Nor would Vi. She'd have apoplexy at the thought. And Thomas was supposed to be in London. But now he's back and you don't seem surprised.'

'He telephoned earlier. He didn't know you worked nights. I was going to organise for us all to have a little celebration. He wanted to talk to you.'

Yesterday Evie's heart would have belted out a tune of its own at the thought that Thomas was back and wanted to see her. But now she sat down on the bed, lit a cigarette, handed one to Lil and then asked the question she was most sure of the answer to. 'Do you think he'll tell the college?'

Lil sank down on the bed beside her. 'Tommy won't tell a soul. But you already know that. Charles is the one you should watch.'

Evie shivered. 'I've been lucky so far.'

'Damn right.'

In some ways, Evie thought, the glacial shoulder her family had shown her had made things easier. There was so much less to have to explain. When she'd first moved in with Lil, she'd given them two months to abhor her, which she thought would be enough. Then she'd sent a letter home, enquiring after everyone's health, telling them she was happily studying at medical college, promising to pay back the money she'd taken and giving her address. No reply ever came. She'd tried every month but there was only silence from Concord. In the end, Evie read about Viola's wedding in the newspaper. Then Charles and Viola had gone abroad for a year and Evie had waited until they'd returned to New York before writing again. Viola didn't write back. So Evie had stopped trying. Lil, Leo, Bea and Mrs Whitman had become her family.

To distract herself, Evie picked up a magazine. 'You got *The New Yorker*. Did you read Lipstick yet?'

'Nope. I went to the Black Rabbit with Leo and some others.'

'How is Leo? I haven't seen him for a while.'

'That's because you're always at work. But he's the same. Still a scoundrel. I left two ladies vying for his affections on the dance floor.'

Evie laughed. 'I wonder if he's still got eyes only for that girl?'

'What girl?'

'I don't know. Just something he said a while ago.'

'There's no girl. Leo's like me. He likes variety.'

'Variety is for ice-cream, Lil.'

'You're such a romantic!' Lil teased, and Evie hit her with the magazine.

'Let's see what Lipstick has to say about life in the land of just-have-fun.' Evie found the page she was looking for, entitled 'Tables for Two' and signed off by 'Lipstick', a woman whose identity was Manhattan's best-kept secret. The latest column was about the opening of the Nineteenth Hole Club. Evie began to read aloud.

'"The great feature of this was the informality achieved by the tricky putting greens on either side of the dance floor. What with the girls' skirts being as short as they are nowadays, and the additional uplift contingent upon the position required for putting, the evening was not without humour. Really and truly, something ought to be done by Congress or somebody about the lingerie shortage in this country."'

Both girls laughed. 'I thought I'd heard everything,' Lil said. 'A nightclub with putting greens? I bet it's a real clip joint. Next there'll be one with circus elephants.'

'Ziegfeld's just bought an ostrich for our next show.'

'Do you have to ride on that?'

'I hope not!'

'Look at this.' Lil pointed to a poem – 'The New York Girl' – at the bottom of the page. It read:

She shines in high society,
And dances at receptions.
The picture of propriety –
A mistress of deceptions.

'Is she real, do you think, this New York Girl? Or is she a figment of advertising and journalistic imaginations?' Lil asked as she rolled onto her back and examined the one thing of beauty in their room, a genuine crystal chandelier that Mrs Lomsky couldn't be bothered dusting and so had consigned to the attic room.

'If you can afford to be her, she's real. Half of Ziegfeld's Girls charleston the night away at high-society parties in Great

Neck with married men. But they work hard for their money – and I don't mean at the theatre.'

'Maybe there should be another line to that poem – *and of hard-earned affections.*'

'Imagine living like Lipstick,' said Evie. 'With no cares for anyone but yourself.'

'I expect one day you'd wake up and realise the consequence was that no one cared for you.'

'That won't happen to me. I spend every day caring for people.'

'I don't mean the kind of care it takes to clean out a lady's basement. I mean the kind of care that comes with a man attached to it.'

'And when would I fit that in? Besides, I thought you didn't believe in romance?'

'For me, I don't. But for you –'

Evie didn't let Lil finish her sentence. 'Perhaps I should have settled for being a poet.'

'You'd be a terrible poet. You need to fall in love first.'

'I don't know anyone who wants to fall in love with me.'

'Don't you?'

Evie got up and walked over to the phonograph, seeing only Thomas's face. His very handsome face, which had once smiled at her in a way that made her blush and run up the stairs. What she wouldn't give to transform his blank face of earlier into a smile.

She selected 'Oh, Lady Be Good'. 'In honour of the fact that Thomas will most likely think I've been anything but.'

'Don't underestimate him.'

Evie shook her head and slouched back onto the pillows. 'Something strange happened today.'

'Stranger than watching a woman push a baby out of a pinhole?'

'Yes!'

'Now I'm listening.'

'The sisters at the Foundling told me I couldn't see Mary again. I got the impression they were following someone's instructions.'

'Someone like who?'

'I don't know. Maybe the same person who took her from Concord to the Foundling. Her father?'

'Are you going to add playing detective to your list of extracurricular activities?'

Evie laughed. 'No. But who cares if I see Mary? Which is exactly why I have to see her: no one else cares about her. And I've been trying to remember every conversation I ever had with Rose, Mary's mother, but I can't recall her ever speaking about one particular man.'

'Does anything ever go smoothly in your life?'

'Living here with you is as smooth as a flapper's bob.'

'Amen!' Lil hoisted an imaginary glass in the air and began to examine one of the pages of *The New Yorker*, as she was wont to do, studying ad copy the same way as Evie pored over anatomical illustrations. 'I could do better than that.' She pointed to an advertisement with the headline 'Often a Bridesmaid, Never a Bride'. The words were emblazoned across a picture of a desperately sad-looking young lady by the name of Edna. There was a bottle of Listerine in the corner of the advertisement, a supposed cure-all for Edna's dire unmarried straits.

'I bet all she needs is to learn how to kiss properly. Bad breath probably has nothing to do with it,' said Lil, as if she was an expert on the causes of spinsterhood.

'You know Listerine used to be sold as a cure for gonor-rhoea?' Evie said.

'No wonder it rips the lining off your tongue quicker than a stubbled chin.' Lil closed the magazine. 'I asked to do the copy for the Listerine ads. I wanted to do something other than terrify single girls into buying Listerine to cure them of being old maids. But they said no and told me to stick with the cold cream. Listerine is too scientific for a woman to write about, whereas cold cream is just fat in a jar.'

Evie sat up and hugged her friend. 'We're not exactly succeeding in changing the world, are we?'

'But we're trying. That's what matters.' Lil looked at the clock. It was after midnight. 'Game of mahjong?' she asked, gesturing to the black leather briefcase and wooden racks stacked on Evie's desk, next to her *Gray's Anatomy*. Mr Childers had bought the mahjong set as a gift for Evie when he found out she'd taken her place at college. 'Or lights out?'

'Let's play. Sleep is for those who aren't lucky enough to live in Manhattan.'

'And let's listen to something else or you might find me dangling from the chandelier,' said Lil as 'Oh, Lady Be Good' reached its dreary chorus and even Evie had to admit that the infantile ukulele was giving her a headache.

Evie chose the 'Charleston', hoping the romping piano might dance her worries away, and Lil tipped the mahjong tiles onto the bed. It was a traditional set, made from bone and bamboo, and probably the most expensive thing Evie owned. Mr Childers had ignored her protestations that it was too much, telling her it would teach her two things: firstly, that it could quickly become ordinary to hold a bone in your hand, and secondly, that if one knew the rules and applied the right tactics, victory was possible. After starting at the college, she could see why he'd thought it an appropriate gift.

As the girls sorted the tiles, Evie said, 'I made a wish tonight. That luck would turn its face my way. Maybe my parents will forgive me. The sisters will let me see Mary. Kingsley will let me practise something. Tommy will forgive my nocturnal activities. And I'll win at mahjong!'

'I hate to get in the way of luck,' said Lil, 'but you might have to settle for four out of five.'

Evie smiled as she drew a bouquet and a concealed pung of east winds from the wall and hoped Lil might be wrong, which seemed possible when Lil's first discard was, inexplicably, a south wind.

Evie picked it up to pung her pair. 'Are you trying to lose?'

'Special hand. I've got a good feeling.'

'Me too,' said Evie.

'Let's see who's right.'

After that there was silence until Lil clacked all her tiles onto the top of the rack. 'I did it!'

Lil had got herself a set of Heads and Tails, and Evie's grand attempt at Four Blessings Hovering Over the Door was two winds short of completion.

'I thought I'd win that,' Evie said, downcast.

'I could tell. You get quiet when you're excited.'

'No blessings hovering over my door tonight.'

'Come out with us tomorrow night and we'll find you a blessing to hang over your bed.'

'Lil!' Evie cried, and then yawned. 'Four hours till I have to get up.'

They threw on their pyjamas and jumped into bed. Evie remembered lying down and switching off her lamp but that was all until she awoke with a start, gasping, as if she'd forgotten to breathe while she was asleep. It took her a minute to stop snatching at air, to understand that she'd only been dreaming of blood and births. Lil was still asleep, her side of the blanket smooth as if she hadn't moved all night. Evie, on the other hand, had lost her blanket; she was white-sheeted, tangled in the linen as if she'd spent the night with a hundred lovers, or perhaps just one lover, suitably wild.

She rolled over and squeezed her eyes shut. The phosphenes beneath her lids glowed yellow, blue, red, a mass of galactic shapes that eventually settled into the image of her parents. Evie wondered how her mother was, her father, and Viola. Whether they missed her at all. Whether they ever thought about her at four o'clock in the morning.

Chapter Thirteen

After a day of lectures at the college, it was time for Evie to roll up to the great circus of Forty-Second Street, where Ziegfeld reigned supreme as the ringmaster of tickle and tease, cracking his whip at his glorious girls so they performed their tricks with just the right blend of conceal and reveal. The first half of the show went off without a hitch. Evie was having her headdress fitted for the second half when Bea approached, looking over her shoulder as if pursued by something that she'd be happy to have catch her.

'Gentleman caller!' she hollered, whereupon a row of girls turned their heads towards Evie in a perfectly choreographed manoeuvre. 'Been a long time since you had any gentleman callers,' Bea went on. 'Different to when you started.'

'That was beginner's curiosity,' replied Evie. 'I now know everything I need to know about men.'

A *la-di-da-boom-bing-bang* of squeals and titters followed, Bea's the loudest.

Evie walked over to the door, where there was indeed a gentleman in a dinner suit. His head was turned away to protect the modesty that none of the girls in the room possessed, but Evie still knew immediately that it was Thomas.

'You've come to warn me off, I suppose,' she said.

Thomas turned to her and smiled, and Evie couldn't help but smile back, even though for all she knew he could actually be laughing at how ludicrous she must look – the girl next door transformed into the Queen of the Night.

'I have,' he said.

Evie's smile disappeared. She didn't know why she'd expected anything different, but she was so disappointed in Thomas Whitman for being less than she'd thought he was. For being a stuffy Upper East Side banker who thought it was his duty to chastise Evie over the folly of what she was doing.

She gestured at the corridor. 'We're in the way. You'll have to come in,' she said, wanting to see if he would. He did.

Evie saw the room through his eyes – the racks of frocks cut up to here and down to there, revealing enough of the girl inside to make sure the seats of the theatre were filled every night of the run; vases of flowers, mostly chrysanthemums, from the men who cherished the frisson of buying flowers for someone other than their wives; ribbons sprawled immodestly across the counter top; hatboxes leaning in towers, ready to spill their secrets onto the floor; headdresses vying for attention from fur and beads and jewels. The lights above the mirrors showed all too clearly what wasn't visible from the stage – that the girls were wearing too much makeup, that what looked like flesh was actually body stocking, and that you could light a fire with the stuff they put in their hair to make it do what Ziegfeld wanted.

Evie sat down in a chair and left Thomas standing, wondering what he'd fix his eyes on: Bea in her knickers doing her best to show a hint of buttock as she bent over to buckle her shoe, a couple of pert breasts awaiting a costume, or Evie in her constellation headdress that made her temples ache. He chose the latter.

'Forget you saw me,' she said.

'I wish I could,' he replied.

'I need the money,' she said, and she might as well have been naked the way she was giving Thomas Whitman the truth.

'I didn't come to tell you to stop performing,' he said. 'I came to warn you that Charles is here. He was here last night too. Didn't you see him?'

'I only saw you,' Evie said honestly. They were both silent a moment, watching each other, then she added, 'Perhaps Charles didn't notice me.'

'How could he not?'

As he spoke, Evie thought she saw admiration in Thomas's eyes. Admiration for her as a woman. Not the girl next door any more.

'The ship arrived yesterday,' he said. 'Charles had organised an evening out as a welcome home, and I thought, since he'd made the effort, that I should spend time with him. I didn't know you worked here, otherwise I would have turned him around at the entrance and made him go somewhere else. He's brought a group of clients back here tonight. I've come to try to limit the damage.'

'Damn.' Evie lit a cigarette and then studied the red ring she'd made around the butt; she'd have to redo her lipstick before she went on stage. 'I'll skip the solo, tell Ziegfeld I'm sick and hope he doesn't fire me.'

'Charles has already seen you. Pretending to be sick won't change that. He'll do whatever it is he's come here to do whether you go back on stage or not.'

'You know I'm supposed to have an unblemished reputation and not bring the college into disrepute?'

'I thought that might be the case.'

'Does Charles know?' she asked, worried.

'If he didn't, he's probably made it his business to find out.'

She appreciated his honesty. But it made her so mad at Charles. 'Why does he care what I do? Nobody knows I'm his wife's sister, and if he keeps his mouth shut, nobody need ever find out.'

'He's angry. I went to London partly because my father wanted to test Charles's mettle. He's been making a string of poor decisions and has lately become so reckless that the bank could have suffered huge losses if we hadn't found out what he'd done in time. And father wants to retire so I was made president of the bank today. Charles fights with Viola. He told the world he was going to marry you. But you refused him and he's still resentful. And he thinks you didn't marry him because of –' Thomas stopped.

'Because of you?' Evie looked straight at him when she said it. She had to know how he felt. Whether he was as scandalised as he should be by her leotard and her spangles and her naked legs.

But he only nodded, and a rush of relief made her say, 'I'm sorry I didn't tell you I worked here.'

'I understand why you didn't.'

Right then, when it seemed as if Charles might be planning to threaten the life she'd made for herself over the past two years, Evie realised how much she loved it all. Even with the fatigue of studying at college and clerking at the hospital, backed up by long nights at the Follies, she wouldn't change it for the world. She could never be Concord Evie again, whose parents gave her money to buy dresses, who had to request permission to walk to the main street, who didn't know how much it cost to rent a room in New York City. She was doing what she wanted to do, living the life she chose to live, not the life someone else had chosen for her. And Thomas was back. That made her happiest of all.

She put out her cigarette, leaned into the mirror and reapplied colour until her lips were as red as cherries, hoping that Thomas was watching. And he was.

'I need to go wait in the wings. Will I see you after the show?' she asked.

'You will.'

Evie couldn't hide her grin.

~

Now that she knew he was there, Charles was impossible to ignore. He watched Evie from the front row for the entire second half, eyes crawling down her legs, over her chest and up to her throat.

Might as well go out with a bang, Evie thought as the moon was lowered over the stage and she began to sing, digging deep into her lungs so it wasn't just another number but a showstopper. The applause at the end told her that the audience had loved every minute of her in a way that Charles, unclapping but giving her one slow wink, had not.

When she went backstage there was a note for her in Charles's handwriting: *Charles Whitman requests the pleasure of your company on the rooftop after the show.*

Evie screwed it up. She scanned the costume racks, got dressed, added another layer of red to her lips, sprayed herself with perfume, then walked upstairs. She used the showgirl's entrance, rather than the patrons', which meant she had to traverse the glass runway Ziegfeld had installed to allow theatregoers the best view up the skirts of his girls. When she stepped out onto the roof, most heads swivelled her way.

The costume she'd chosen had a polka-dotted silk bodice. But the fabulousness really began with the skirt, a waterfall of white feathers long at the back and short in the front so that trails of feathers covered only the tops of her thighs, leaving the rest of her legs on display. In her hand she carried a fan with feathers as long as her arms. It was a fan to be carried aloft, with her elbow bent and her hand raised as if she was soon to plant her flag in territory she intended to claim.

The crowds had to part to let her through, because the skirt was as wide as the backsides of the Italian ladies serving up pasta on Bleecker Street. Charles was waiting for her, flanked by Thomas and a man she didn't recognise.

'Evie!' called Charles. His voice was loud and she knew he wanted all the men on the roof to hear him, Charles Whitman, not just on first-name terms with a Ziegfeld Girl, but on shortened first-name terms, a sure sign of intimacy.

'Charles,' Evie said in a voice that had nothing of gladness about it.

'This is Stanley Shields. A client of ours,' he said.

Thomas nodded at Evie as if they were barely acquainted, and she kept up the charade with a nod of her own. She could feel Charles watching them and she was glad Thomas had forewarned her.

'Spectacular show,' Charles continued.

Evie fluttered her fan in reply and turned the full beam of her smile onto Stanley, who giggled like a little girl.

'Stanley liked the look of the dark-haired one over there,' said Charles, gesturing towards Louise Brooks, who, though only eighteen, worked harder than most to get her rent paid because her preferred domicile was the Algonquin Hotel. 'Thomas, you should arrange an introduction for Stanley.'

Thomas clearly couldn't refuse, because Stanley was a client. And Evie also knew that Thomas couldn't stop Charles from doing whatever he had planned just by his presence.

'Say whatever you have to say, Charlie,' she said, after Thomas and Stanley had moved away. He looked more thickset than when she'd last seen him, the skin on his face was pouchy and, were it not for the unmistakable quality of his suit and the diamond-studded signet ring that proclaimed his wealth, she'd bet that few women looked at him the way they used to, just a few years ago.

'Always in such a hurry, aren't you? I thought we were friends,' he said.

'Friends who haven't seen each other for almost three years.'

'You make it impossible for someone in my position to be your friend.'

'I'm your wife's sister. It's not that hard.'

'But your lifestyle isn't what anyone would call desirable.'

'It's desirable enough for you when you're sitting in the audience watching a line of thighs go by, but not when you're sitting in a drawing room on the Upper East Side?'

'Watching the Ziegfeld Girls is an Upper East Side requirement. Being one isn't. You wouldn't have had to do this if you'd married me.'

No. I'd have had to do a lot of other things that would have left me with less dignity than I have right now, Evie wanted to say, but she knew she couldn't afford to make Charles angry. She said nothing.

Then Charles surprised her. 'I miss you, Evie,' he said.

For a second, beneath the bluster, she could see the boy she'd once had so much fun with, the humiliated man who didn't get the bride he'd wanted, the disappointed man whose brother arrived back from London one day and was made president of the bank the next. But then she saw his eyes travel over her cleavage and down her legs and remembered the evening when he'd tried to take what he wanted from her. 'Goodnight, Charles.'

But Charles hadn't finished. 'I could be your patron,' he said, his desire for her showing plainly on his face.

'You're married to my sister.'

'Which is why I need a mistress.'

Evie's mouth said what it wanted to before she could stop it. 'I came up here to see Thomas. Not you.' She pulled a hanky out from between her breasts and passed it to him. 'You're salivating.'

She'd underestimated him though because he leaned over and slipped the hanky back into her bodice, making sure his finger grazed the tip of her nipple. Evie backed away.

'Rediscovered your morals?' Charles asked. 'Too late for the college though. Didn't they ask you to uphold a good moral character?'

'Why does it matter to you what I do?' Evie demanded, suddenly angry, even though she knew that would just make things worse.

'Quit the Follies. I'll pay your college fees.'

'I'll never be beholden to you for anything, Charlie.'

Charles smiled at her. 'You don't have to decide now. Come to dinner tomorrow night. Viola's expecting and we're having a celebration. You can let me know what you've decided then.'

Viola was having a baby and nobody had told her? Evie hoped that Charles couldn't see how much the news hurt her. To cover it, she lashed out. 'What's taken you so long? I'd have thought a man as virile as you would have had Viola pregnant long before now. I'll come to dinner. But to see Viola, not you.' She turned and walked away, wanting a bath, wanting to scrub herself clean. She began to walk downstairs when a voice called her name.

Thomas was leaning over the balustrade. 'I want to see you. Somewhere without Charles. And,' he smiled at her outfit, 'without feathers.'

'I have to have dinner with Charles and Viola tomorrow night. I might need moral support.'

'I'll make sure I'm there,' he said before Stanley Shields tapped him on the shoulder and drew him back into the crowd of tuxedoed men.

So now she had something to look forward to and something to dread, all on the same evening. And less than twenty-four hours to work out how to prevent Charles from killing her dream of ever becoming a doctor.

Chapter Fourteen

The next morning, Evie made the rare decision to skip the first lecture of the day. She had an errand to run. Ever since the nuns had told her she could no longer visit Mary, she'd been worrying over how to show the little girl that she still cared for her.

She caught the El to Gimbels department store. As it rattled up Sixth Avenue to Herald Square, she remembered the first time Mary had recognised her on one of her visits to the orphanage, how she'd smiled at her. She remembered the first time she'd been allowed to take Mary outside; Evie had been so afraid something would happen that she'd taken Mary back after just ten minutes. She remembered the first time Mary had said her name, and when Sister Margaret had told her that the child had been saying nothing but Evie for the past three days. At that moment, Evie finally knew that Mary was fond of her and looked forward to her visits.

At Gimbels, she went straight to the toy department, where she found a doll that looked just like Mary, with blonde curls and light brown eyes. Evie knew the little girl would love it, and it could be her companion for all the long days until Evie was able to convince Sister Mary to let her visit once again.

Then she rode the train to Columbus Circle, where she walked westwards to a set of buildings stretching the width of a city block. At Tenth Avenue stood the building where Evie wanted to spend all her time: the Sloane Hospital for Women. In the Ninth Avenue corner was the college itself, looking as regimented and orderly as the instructional practices conducted inside. The arched entryway was the only non-linear part of the building; all else was rectangular, with windows precisely aligned and an east wing and west wing of equal proportions. A covered walkway led from the college buildings to the Vanderbilt Clinic, which treated the ailments of hundreds of thousands of the city's poor. On her first day of training at the clinic, Evie had been assigned catheter duties for a long line of male patients. She knew that she'd been given the job because her supervisors expected her to refuse. But she'd told herself that a penis was just another appendage, really no different to an arm, albeit hopefully less rigid, and she went ahead and inserted catheter after catheter without complaint. The patients didn't complain either. It was the first of many humiliations, large and small, the doctors had inflicted on Evie in the unspoken hope that she'd give up. But she never had.

She caught the end of the lecture and then walked across to the hosptial, where the morning passed uneventfully. Evie had just sat down to eat her lunch when Francis Sumner came to find her in the staff dining room.

'You can take the toxaemia case on Ward One,' he said. 'She's neurotic. I saw her last week and told her not to overeat and to attend to her hygiene and she'd feel better.'

Francis's way of speaking about the patient didn't surprise Evie. She'd become used to the doctors' perceptions of pregnant women: as neurotic and highly excitable, purveyors of their own complications, most of which were nervous conditions that could be overcome by greater mental fortitude. What did surprise her was that it was the fourth day in a row he'd come to find her at lunchtime. He turned away to load up his plate with food.

'Now?' Evie called after him.

'Yes.'

'If you saw her last week, it doesn't sound very urgent.'

'I'd like you to see her now.'

Evie put one forkful of food in her mouth and stood up. Lunch was served at precisely noon and finished by half past. She knew that if she went up to the ward now, she'd miss her only chance to eat a square meal. Just as she had the past three days. At the tables around her, the other students and doctors were all happily eating. It was only Evie who had to go without food. Francis had found a use for her: she could deal with all the cases he didn't want, especially the ones that came in at lunchtime. But if she complained, she'd be found unsuitable for the obstetrics rotation. So she went upstairs to Ward One and found the patient vomiting uncontrollably.

Evie checked the chart. 'I'll get you cleaned up, Mrs Latimer,' she said. 'Then I can examine you.'

What was a bit of vomit to have to navigate, Evie told herself. Compared to Mrs O'Rourke's infection, it was almost pleasant. She lifted Mrs Latimer's arm, which was as weak as a paper doll's, and took her blood pressure. She could see that the woman's ankles were hugely swollen, more so than they should be even considering the patient's weight.

Evie scanned Francis's notes from the week before. *Patient is significantly overweight and in a nervous state. I suggested breathing exercises to relieve pelvic congestion, and discussed the importance of overcoming food cravings and overeating, all of which are certainly contributing to the patient's vomiting. I asked the nurses to wash out the patient's stomach and colon with soap and sodium bicarbonate to improve her hygiene. Should the neurosis become extreme, induction or abortion is recommended as the only possible cure.*

'Congestion!' Evie repeated, tired of the ridiculous, lazy label that was given to toxaemic women by obstetricians. This woman's vomit was black. That was not due to 'congestion'.

She went to the dining room to find Francis. 'Dr Sumner! What was Mrs Latimer's blood pressure last week?'

'How should I know?' Francis replied. 'Check the chart. I'm eating lunch.'

'It's not on the chart.'

'Check again.'

'It's not there.'

'He said to check again,' Dr Kingsley interrupted, and Evie realised that every single doctor, resident, intern and student was staring at her with irritation. She was interrupting their meal.

She turned away to do as she was told, even though she knew the blood pressure wasn't recorded in the chart. But then she stopped and turned back around. 'It's eclampsia. Not toxaemia. Her blood pressure is the highest I've seen. She has oedema of the face and ankles.'

'She's fat, Evie,' said Francis.

'*Congested*, you mean?'

'Yes.'

'Miss Lockhart, you've wasted enough of Dr Sumner's lunch break,' Dr Kingsley said. 'Do as you've been asked.'

Evie walked out. She reached the ward in time to see the patient begin convulsing. 'Nurse!' she shouted. 'We need castor oil. And a Voorhees bag. She has to have the baby now.'

When the nurse saw the patient's state, she dropped the equipment on the bed. 'I'll get Dr Sumner,' she said, as if Evie couldn't help at all.

The nurse had more luck with rousing Francis from his lunch, but he still strolled into the ward as if it was Sunday afternoon in Central Park. He quickened his pace when he saw Mrs Latimer. 'Do your rounds,' he ordered Evie. Then he shut the curtain so she could no longer see.

Instead of doing her rounds, Evie went to the bathroom and smacked her palm on the basin. What kind of a fool was she, putting up with being belittled and ignored when she could be spending her Ziegfeld's cash on a life that didn't involve the uncertain workings of another woman's pineapple? The harder she worked, the further she seemed to get from what she wanted. How foolish and idealistic she'd been when she first had the idea of becoming an obstetrician. Perhaps everybody had been right to warn her off. This was the hardest thing she'd ever done in her life. She prayed for the thousandth time that it would all be worth it in the end, that everything would turn out right.

She discovered later that Francis had got away with his mistake. The baby and the mother survived the emergency caesarean. When Evie checked the chart, she saw that he'd written into his earlier notes, *Dx: eclampsia*. She'd been right. Francis had almost fatally misdiagnosed. But nobody had acknowledged she'd been right, or reprimanded Francis for his mistakes. And God she was starving. She should be used to it by now, but being on her feet all day and missing lunch four days in a row was wearing. Thankfully it was time to go home.

'Miss Lockhart!' Dr Brewer called her name as she was leaving. 'I need to see you.'

What was she in trouble for now? Or perhaps he'd heard about today's events and was going to commend her for her quick thinking. Evie followed him to his office, eager to be sitting pretty for the first time since she'd started medical school.

'Charles Whitman called earlier,' Dr Brewer said. 'He enquired about your progress. I didn't realise he was your benefactor. Of course, given the money he's investing in you, I gave him a full report.'

Oh, Charles was good. Turning the screws before their meeting tonight. Making Evie understand that he could pick up the phone to Dr Brewer any time he liked. And she was such a dumb Dora for thinking things would work out. 'I hope the report was satisfactory,' she said.

'It was. Satisfactory.'

God damn you to hell, Evie thought, sitting up straighter in her seat. 'My grades are the highest in my year group. Surely it was more than *satisfactory*.'

'I know that after our last conversation, you're working on your manner of address to the doctors.'

'Soon I'll be just like Kingsley,' she said sarcastically but Dr Brewer chose to ignore her meaning.

As she left the office, she bumped into Francis. 'Eavesdropping?' she asked coldly.

'No. I was wondering what you're doing tonight.'

'Working,' she lied. 'I work every night.' As Evie said the words she wondered how she'd ever, even fleetingly, thought Francis was handsome. Compared to Thomas Whitman, he was a bug-eyed Bobby who didn't have the balls to admit he'd made a mistake. That was what loneliness did to a girl.

Ruined her judgement. She could feel her heart creep further back into her chest, hiding as deeply inside as it possibly could. Because she had another battle to fight now. With Charles. Who was going to be an even more ruthless opponent than Dr Kingsley.

⁓

What did one wear to dinner on the Upper East Side when the intention of the dinner was blackmail? 'And on my one night off from the Follies too,' Evie complained, hair done, face made up, but body clad only in underclothes. 'I should be revising otolaryngology.'

'You'd rather look at tonsils than have dinner with Charlie?' Lil asked.

'So long as he stays away from my tonsils . . .'

Lil laughed. Then she jumped up, crying, 'I know!' She delved into the bottom of the wardrobe, reached right into the back and pulled out a rolled-up black garment. It unfurled, and there before the girls was a silk chiffon dress with an asymmetrical hemline, cut higher in the front than the back. The neck was scooped low, but not too low, and a piece of chiffon floated from the back of the dress, almost like a pair of wings. 'It's a Chanel.'

'And you've got a gorgeous Chanel dress bundled up in the back of the wardrobe because . . . ?' Evie reached out a hand to feel the fabric drift like hundred-dollar bills between her fingers.

'It was the one expensive thing I took with me when I left home, but I haven't needed to wear a dress so undemocratic yet. You do.' Lil thrust the dress at her.

Evie dropped it over her head. It fell across her body with a sigh, as though coming home.

'Divine,' said Lil. 'No jewellery, no watch, nothing. Just you and Chanel. And catch a cab. They'll be expecting you to walk from the train. Don't do what they expect.'

'Thanks, Lil.' Evie kissed her friend on the cheek.

She walked up to Bleecker and hailed a cab. The driver nodded at her as if the Chanel combined with her destination made her someone important. Through the window, Evie watched the grand buildings of midtown Manhattan fly by – the Flatiron, the Met Life Tower, Grand Central, the Plaza Hotel – until she arrived uptown.

'Can you drive on to Lexington?' Evie called. She directed the driver to the Foundling and asked him to wait while she knocked on the door. There was no answer.

'It's Evie Lockhart,' she called. 'I just want to see Mary.' But the door remained resolutely barred against her. 'I miss you, Mary,' she whispered and hoped that somehow, huddled under her rough grey blanket, Mary would hear and would know that Evie hadn't turned her back on her again.

'You going to stand there all night?' the taxi driver called.

Evie shook her head. They continued on uptown until the driver pulled up outside a five-storey bow-fronted house on East Seventy-Ninth. Its facade was limestone, with more pillars than a Roman temple and enough stone carving to compete with the cathedral. Viola's taste, Evie was certain.

She rang the bell and the butler answered. His bow was merely a nod of the head, as if he'd been instructed by Charles that this was all she deserved. She said, 'Don't worry, I don't bite,' and the butler blushed all over his bald head. God, she was in a mood. A mood to attack everybody before they attacked her. She'd better calm down and think what to do or else she'd walk away from tonight with a debt to Charles that she'd die rather than repay.

The hall was lined with oak panelling and dominated by an enormous walnut grandfather clock. The wall tapestries were probably expensive but so conservatively brown it was like walking out of the light and down into the earth, into a place devoid of colour and sunshine. Evie shivered, wondering if Viola had greyed also, in keeping with her surroundings.

The butler led her into the drawing room. Evie almost laughed aloud at the song warbling its slow and sad tune into the room: 'A Good Man is Hard to Find'. The song she'd sung at Ziegfeld's nearly three years before. An appropriate song choice for someone married to Charles Whitman.

As she paused in the doorway, Evie saw Charles look at her in her beautiful black Chanel, worn with just the right amount of rouge and red lipstick. She'd put on a new pair of silk stockings to make her legs look long and lean right down to the tips of the first pair of shoes she'd bought at Saks when she didn't care about how much things cost. Then Charles looked at his wife beside him and the comparison was silently made. Viola, round with pregnancy, stared aghast at Evie.

She heard a gasp and registered that there were two other people in the room. Her parents.

'Hello, Father,' she said. 'And Mother.'

The Lockharts stared at Evie, making no move to go to her, to hug her, to say that they'd missed her. She might as well have been a stranger. Evie felt tears sitting in the corners of her eyes, and blinked to hide the ache she felt at realising she was truly forsaken, lost to them forever. She tried to act as if she didn't care. 'You weren't expecting me? Nor you, Vi? Seems Charles has been saving me up as a special treat.'

'We were not expecting you,' said her father, looking at Charles as if he were a wild duck ripe for shooting.

'I thought it was time to build a bridge. Mend relations now that the family is getting larger,' Charles said. He nodded at Vi, who blushed and placed a hand on her belly.

'Attagirl, Vi. You must be pleased,' said Evie.

'I am pleased,' Vi said, then put a hand over her mouth as if she'd forgotten that she wasn't supposed to speak to her runaway, thieving sister.

'Don't worry, you and the baby won't be any the worse off for having seen me. Besides, dinner will be a touch uncomfortable if Charles is the only one talking to me.'

Viola glanced at Evie as if to say, *Don't flirt with my husband*, and it was all Evie could do not to shout, *I wouldn't flirt with him if we were the only people alive in the Garden of Ede*n.

'I could do with a drink,' she said instead. 'Gin and tonic. You can't invite the black sheep to dinner and have her die of thirst.'

'Don't start, Evie,' said Viola.

Evie decided to be the magnanimous one. The view was surely better from the moral high ground. 'You're right. We're here to celebrate. Here's my drink.' She took it from Charles eagerly. 'Good to see you don't support the Volstead up here either. Let's toast to the baby.'

'We don't need to talk about it quite so loudly,' replied Vi, with a sideways glance at the butler.

Evie couldn't resist. The low ground was much more fun, after all. 'I spend my days watching women give birth. Talking about it is a lot tidier.'

Charles, who must have felt his dinner party disintegrating around him, stepped in. 'Perhaps we'd better move to the table.'

They filed through to the dining room in silence, Evie knocking back her drink. Where was Thomas? The alcohol and her fear hit her stomach at the same time. What if he'd changed his mind? What if he'd decided, rightly, that he could do so much better than a female medical student who earned her living as a showgirl? And all day Evie had come up with nothing to counter Charles. He would tell the college. Unless she accepted his offer.

The decor of the dining room didn't improve her mood. The walls were covered with portraits by the Dutch masters, black and brown the favoured shades. The sitters in the paintings were stiff with their own importance, and the general impression was of being observed by an assembly of stern schoolmasters who wouldn't hesitate to rap the knuckles of those who couldn't extract the flesh of a boiled lobster from its shell without said lobster landing in their lap. Evie was seated beside Viola and her father, and was grateful that Charles was some distance away on the opposite side of the table.

'Why don't you tell us about life in Greenwich Village?' Charles said, cracking the claw of his lobster with the practised hand of an executioner.

'Never visited?' Evie asked.

'Wall Street and the Upper East Side keep us happy,' Charles replied smoothly.

'Where do you live?' Viola asked, curiosity getting the better of decorum.

'In a boarding house. I share with a friend. Life is cheaper that way.'

'The cheap life has its charms for some people,' said Charles. 'Cheers. Here's to the family reunion.'

Evie noticed her parents hesitate before picking up their glasses, but it would be rude to ignore the toast so they raised the goblets to their lips and drank thirstily, appreciating the liquid part of the action rather than the sentiment.

Mrs Lockhart began talking pointedly to Charles, and Viola used the cover of their conversation to ask Evie, 'Do you actually help at a hospital? Or do you just go to lectures?'

Evie thought she heard something in her sister's voice, a new pensiveness that made her question sound genuine rather than mocking. 'I help at the hospital a little. Today I saved a woman's life.' As Evie said it, she realised it was true. If she hadn't badgered Francis about Mrs Latimer's blood pressure, the woman would probably be dead right now. Despite the battles she had to fight every day at the hospital, and her regular defeats, she was making a difference. She smiled. 'It's hard work but I love it.'

Mr Lockhart cleared his throat and Evie realised he'd been listening to her. 'What happened?' There was a gleam of interest in his eyes although his face was still stern.

'I don't think it's suitable conversation for a dinner party.' Charles's words seemed to lift the trance that had settled on Viola and her father, to bring them back to themselves.

'You're right,' nodded Viola, looking over at her husband.

In spite of her sister's smile, Evie thought she didn't look happy. But Evie didn't ask. What was the point in speaking? Charles would block her at every turn.

The rest of dinner continued with stilted conversation that studiously avoided her. Thomas still didn't appear. And Charles was making Evie wait through the whole of dinner for the denouement.

After dinner the ladies withdrew, in the old fashion, to the drawing room. Rather than sit down with her mother and sister, Evie excused herself to go to the bathroom. Viola gave directions, adding, just like her old self, as if the person asking questions at the dinner table had been an apparition, 'Your nose doesn't need any more powder.'

'But your face, on the other hand, could do with a touch of rouge. Pregnancy is making you look decidedly peaky,' Evie replied.

Mrs Lockhart pressed her lips together and patted Viola's hand. It was just as it had always been, Evie in trouble, Viola and her mother in agreement. Evie understood that she had not been forgiven, not by any of her family. But perhaps she deserved it. She could only imagine the gossip and whispering that must follow them everywhere — that Evie had thrown her life away to become, of all things, a medical student. Nobody in Concord, nobody in Viola's circle, would ever have contemplated that such a thing was possible, let alone in any way desirable.

She trailed down the hall, her attention caught briefly by the library, but after seeing an entire shelf full of the gloom of Thomas Hardy, she moved on. Then she heard her name, spoken by her father. She stopped near a door that was not quite closed, and listened.

But there was silence for a dozen ticks of the clock. A chinking of ice in a glass. The ting of the decanter lid being replaced. The gulp of swallowed brandy.

Then Charles's voice. 'I'll do what I can to help you with this business.' Another swallow. 'People should always be in your debt, don't you think?'

Which was an ominous sign for Evie, given Charles's interest in paying her college fees.

The door opened. Evie had just enough time to continue walking, as if she'd only just come down the hall. Her father didn't see her as he huffed out of the room, but Charles did.

'Evie! Just the person I want to talk to. Brandy?'

'Thank you.' Evie entered Charles's study, which had been decorated in red velvet and yet more dark wood. The head of an animal hung in the centre of each of the four walls: a moose, a bear, a stag and a bison.

'Shot them yourself, did you?' Evie asked, nodding at the heads.

Charles laughed and remained sitting behind his desk. 'I don't dirty my own hands with sport.'

'Except with me.'

'Is that what they teach doctors, to jump straight to the business at hand?'

'Only with those who waste our time.'

'So you'll accept my offer? The College of Physicians and Surgeons won't want a Follies whore as part of its student body. And Viola and I don't want the embarrassment of somebody we know recognising you.'

'I think I'm unrecognisable from the girl I used to be, Charlie.'

'That's true. But I can't run the risk. And you don't have to repay me in cash, if that's what's worrying you.' He stood and began to walk towards Evie.

A sickening vision of the kind of interest Charles would expect on his loan passed through Evie's mind. She swallowed her brandy to shut out the memory of his finger reaching for her nipple last night at the Follies. How the hell was she going to get out of this one? She'd come with no plan and now she was euchred.

Being combative hadn't worked, so she tried honesty. 'I have no other way to pay my fees. I have to work at the Follies.'

'I've offered you another way.'

'I can't accept it.' Evie hesitated. She hated herself for what she was about to say, hated having to appeal to vicious, cruel Charles, but she'd run out of ideas and he was standing right in front of her now. 'We used to be such good friends. For the sake of that, please forget you saw me at the Follies.'

Charles laughed joylessly. 'Friends? Back when you promised to marry me and then threw me off, not just for my brother, but to be a laughing-stock? Nobody quite knew which was the best part of the joke, but everybody knew the joke was on me.'

A movement near the door caught Evie's eye. A man stepped into the room, and Evie found that, in spite of the conversation she was having with Charles, she couldn't help but smile. Thomas had come after all. He smiled at her too, and as soon as he did, Evie knew it was a mistake. That Charles would notice.

'You two seem pleased to see each other.' Charles poured another brandy and offered it to his brother, who declined with a shake of his head, leaving Charles standing in the middle of the room with his arm outstretched.

'It's good to see you, Evie,' said Thomas.

'You too.'

'I hope I haven't interrupted anything,' said Thomas, looking at Charles.

'You have,' said Charles. 'We'll be in the drawing room shortly.'

Instead of leaving, Thomas sat down in the chair behind Charles's desk. He picked up a pen, examined it, and then put it down as if he found it lacking. 'You wouldn't believe who I just saw,' he said.

Charles looked annoyed at having his grip on the conversation loosened. 'Should I care?'

'It was Ada Griffin,' said Thomas. 'She was walking along Fifth Avenue. I told her I was on my way here and she was so interested in seeing you that I almost invited her to come along. Perhaps I'll bring her next time. Viola would love to meet her, seeing as she's such a pal of yours. Wouldn't you ordinarily be seeing her at this time of night?'

As if the room wasn't already decidedly chilly, the air suddenly hit freezing point. Evie shivered. She had no idea who Ada Griffin was, but at the sound of her name Charles had turned his back on his brother.

'You can forget about the business we were discussing.'

At first Evie thought Charles was talking to Thomas. But then she realised he was talking to her. He was letting her go. Somehow, she'd won that round.

'Thank you,' she mouthed at Thomas before she slipped out and left the brothers to whatever it was they were discussing. She didn't bother to stop in at the drawing room. Instead, she let herself out of the house and extended her arms into the warmer air outside.

Thomas had managed to hand her a victory this time. It would give her an excuse to see him again, to thank him. But Evie was also sure it was a mere delay, that there'd be another round to fight with Charles soon.

A voice she loved hearing called her name. Thomas hurried to catch up to her. 'I'll take you home.'

'I thought I'd walk.'

'Then I'll walk with you.' He fell in step beside her. 'Are you all right?'

'Yes.' Evie paused. 'Is Ada Griffin Charles's mistress?'

'Yes.'

'Does Viola know?'

'I don't think so. Nor do my parents. Otherwise they'd probably cut off some of his funds.'

'So now he hates both of us.'

'Probably.'

'I wish I wasn't the reason for it.'

'Evie, even though he's my brother, you're worth a thousand of Charles.'

Evie had to look down at the pavement to hide her smile. But she said, 'I'm a showgirl with the Ziegfeld Follies, Thomas. That hardly makes me someone to admire. And I want to be an obstetrician, which most people think is even more scandalous than dancing on a stage in my corset. I'm sure your clients at the bank would think so.'

'But I don't.'

'Why?'

'Because I know you and I respect why you're doing it. More than that, I hope you succeed.'

'So in spite of the fact that you shouldn't, you still want to walk me home?'

'Yes.'

Evie couldn't help laughing. 'Of all the people to sit with in an apple tree and plan a disreputable future, I don't think I could have chosen better.'

'It was your apple core that chose me, not you. It was a very good shot.'

Evie laughed again but stopped when she realised that Thomas had taken her hand, that she was walking along Fifth Avenue on an evening spotlit by a round full moon, hand in hand with a man she'd been unable to stop thinking about for nearly three years. It made her shy, and perhaps Thomas too, because they walked together in silence for several blocks, a silence that was loud with questions. Should she let him walk her home? Should she tell him to find someone more suitable than her? Or should she just enjoy the moment, her hand in his?

Before her doubts could make her thank Thomas politely and hail a taxi, she said, 'Tell me about London.'

'London was . . . a city you'd like. I worked in an office building that looked out onto Westminster, so I was surrounded by the palaces and churches where all the kings have walked. Then I'd go out into the streets at lunchtime and see a row of policemen standing guard in front of the Bank of England and I almost wished they were wearing courtiers' clothes so they looked more a part of the city. And I'd sit in St James's Park and write letters to you.'

'Whereas I'd write my letters to you at the dressing table at the New Amsterdam Theatre during intermission. Now you know why they were always spattered with rouge. Your story is much more —' Evie cut herself off. She'd been about to say 'romantic', but worried that that would sound presumptuous.

Thomas stopped walking. 'I might have to go back to London in a month or so.'

At his words, Evie tightened her grip on his hand, as if that would prevent him from leaving. 'Why?' she blurted.

'To finish up some business. It would only be for a few weeks this time I hope. I had to come back now because of . . .' Thomas hesitated and then said diplomatically, 'the situation with my father and Charles. But I was in the middle of a deal with some English lords and I'll have to go back to see it through.'

'English lords?' Evie teased to cover up what she really wanted to say, which was *Please don't go away again!* 'It's times like this when I realise there's another world spinning in parallel with mine, where people keep their hands a lot cleaner and babies are definitely not the outcome.'

Thomas laughed. 'I want to see you again, but tell me if the back and forth to London is more than you can put up with.'

'You put up with what I do. It'd hardly be fair if I couldn't return the favour.' Evie smiled and realised they were facing each other, within kissing distance. Even though she was no longer the inexperienced girl she'd been the last time they were together, she felt skittish because Thomas mattered to her so much more than any other man ever had. Instead of stepping closer she said, 'Look.'

She pointed to a woman carrying a wicker basket filled with steaming, just-baked pretzels. 'I'm ravenous. I couldn't stomach much of dinner.' She led Thomas over to the pretzel woman and pulled some coins from her purse.

'I'll get it,' Thomas said.

'Allow me,' Evie said with mock grandeur. 'They're a penny each. Which I bet you didn't know.'

'I didn't.' Thomas took his pretzel and bit into it.

'I bet you also didn't know that the *Times* once said it wasn't fitting for a bank president to be seen munching a pretzel.'

Thomas laughed. 'You're making that up.'

'I'm not! Pretzels are saloon food meant for those of us who live downtown.'

'Well, bank presidents don't know what they're missing. What else are you going to show me on our impromptu tour of the city?'

'That's it for tonight. You'll have to see me again to find out more,' Evie said boldly.

'I will.'

Thomas looked at her, his eyes dark with desire and the effort of restraint. Evie bit her lip. God, she wanted to kiss him. Hang restraint. She reached out to him, her face turned up towards his.

'Evie! I thought it was you!'

Evie whirled away from Thomas to see Lil and Leo running towards them.

'We missed you!' Lil's greeting for Thomas was effusive and she kissed him on both cheeks. Evie wished she'd been as daring. Thomas and Leo shook hands, clearly pleased to see each other.

They all walked back to Minetta Street together, and as much as Evie rued the kiss she didn't have, she was still ridiculously pleased that Thomas had not once let go of her hand. Thomas told them more about London, and about visiting Paris. About attending the wondrous exhibition of modern and decorative arts that had been so full to bursting with unusual ideas it was impossible to do it justice with words. Evie was glad to listen, to find out more about this man who was the only person who'd ever made her feel like Times Square on New Year's Eve – alive with the possibility of what the future might hold.

In the flurry of goodbyes when they reached the boarding house, Evie found herself cheek to cheek with Thomas. He held her there for a moment and she was sure she heard the intake of his breath when she put her hand on his chest to balance herself.

'I'll see you soon,' he whispered, before he and Leo walked back across to Fifth Avenue.

Evie could have stood there all night, watching him and dreaming of what might happen the next time they were together.

Chapter Fifteen

*C*harles was banging on the door, he was coming after her, coming to finish what he'd started in the sitting room two and a half years ago.

Evie's eyes flew open. She'd been dreaming. Charles's presence was imaginary, but the banging on the door was real.

'What's happening?' Evie asked Lil, both of them fumbling awake, grappling with sheets that seemed to be pinning their bodies to the bed, fingers tussling with the inside-out sleeves of robes that caught on their arms like persistent admirers.

Evie gave up on her robe and turned on the lamp before opening the door wearing just her pyjamas.

'Can you help us?' begged a girl in a bedraggled coat. Evie recognised her as someone she'd seen in the neighbourhood.

'What is it?' Evie asked as Lil came up behind, having beaten her robe into submission.

'Mum's having another baby. But it's bum first, she reckons, 'cause it won't come out, and the ambulance must be coming from California, it's taking so long. I heard you're learning how to be a doctor who gets babies out.'

'I'm only a student.'

'But Mum's been going at it since yesterday. She's in bad shape.'

Evie could hear the panic in the girl's voice. She checked the clock. Four in the morning. New York was determined to make her an insomniac. She found her stethoscope. Then she and Lil followed the girl down the stairs and into the apartments next door; a woman's screams could be heard from the entry. The landing was abuzz with people who'd come out to see Evie, as if she was the feature at the picture theatre.

'She's the doctor I told you about,' she heard whispered as she ascended the stairs.

'The dark one?'

'The blonde.'

'Oh.' This was said as if Evie had been found wanting. It did nothing for her confidence, and she realised that, much as she hated Dr Kingsley, she wished he was here right now. Anything rather than be alone with a mother whose baby was possibly presenting as breech. Hopefully the ambulance would come and Evie wouldn't have to show everyone how little she knew.

The apartments were yet to be redeveloped into à la mode Greenwich Village living, and the sight of the grim, poky room made Evie wish that more women would give up the practice of birthing at home in spite of the doctors' cavalier treatment of them. The sheets on the bed were dirty with grime that had long preceded the bodily fluids of birth. It was grime that spoke of the difficulty of washing bedsheets in a two-room tenement housing seven people and with no laundry facilities. The room was barely lit by a single uncovered bulb that dropped a puddle of light on the floor. Evie could just see the woman on the bed, who was flushed, sweaty and breathing rapidly. She needed help.

Evie felt her anxiety, for the woman and the situation she was in, increase.

'I'm Evie,' she said. 'I'll help until the ambulance arrives.'

'It's the doctor lady I told you about, Mum,' said the girl who had banged on the door in the middle of Evie's dreams.

'Damn ambulance . . . Arrrrgh!' Another scream burst from the woman's mouth. When the contractions stopped, she lay still as if she had no more strength left.

'What's your mother's name?' Evie asked the girl.

'Gladys. But everyone calls her Glad.'

'And yours?'

'Patty.'

'Lil,' Evie said, 'can you sit behind Glad so she can lean against you? She needs to be more upright.'

Lil nodded, climbed onto the bed and wriggled herself in behind Glad.

'Find the cleanest towel or blanket to wrap the baby in when it comes. And get everyone else out of here,' Evie said to Patty, gesturing to the onlookers at the door. She was anxious to rid the room of extra people in case everything went to hell.

Evie took out her stethoscope and listened to Glad's stomach. This part was easy. She knew how to find a heartbeat. She had the mother in a better position. She made herself smile as she listened, because she needed Glad to have faith in her, even if Evie had no confidence in herself. 'Excellent. Beautiful strong heartbeat. Baby's not tired yet, but let's get it out as soon as we can. I'll examine you now.'

Again, this part was simple; Evie had conducted lots of examinations. She found what Glad had suspected, that the baby was breech. She could see that Glad was more tired than it was possible to imagine, her body already having climbed a mountain, only to find another mountain to climb on the other side. What Glad needed was someone who could soothe her and keep her pushing until the baby came out.

Evie forced herself to speak calmly. 'Your baby is bottom first. That's why it's taking so long. But a baby's bottom is the same size as its head, so it still fits perfectly in the birth canal.'

'You'd better be right,' said Glad before she let out another howl.

I know, thought Evie. She'd seen only one breech birth, and that from her usual position against the wall in the delivery suite, peering between Dr Kingsley's arm and his torso, so that her entire visual experience of the birth had been cylindrical, as if she'd watched everything through a rolled-up newspaper. But she remembered her lecture notes as clearly as if she'd just written them: she had to birth the hips by lateral flexion, and then the shoulders and the head would follow. She prayed to whoever it was that heard wishes flung into a New York night that the head wouldn't get stuck and the baby wouldn't asphyxiate. Or that the ambulance would come.

This was the chance Evie had wanted. To be allowed to help a woman give birth. And now she wished to be anywhere else. Because what if she did something wrong? She'd seen mothers die and babies die, and mothers forever ruined by birth, and she'd thought she'd be able to do better than those other doctors. But what if she couldn't?

She looked at Lil. And Patty. They were staring at her as if they trusted her. Evie remembered Rose, and she knew that, this time, she wouldn't walk away.

'Glad, you need to give a big push when I tell you to,' she said. 'Then as soon as the baby's bottom is out, I'm going to need you to push again, as hard as you can, because we need to get the baby's shoulders and head out straight after. Does that make sense?'

A nod from Glad.

'Here comes another contraction,' said Evie. 'Push, Glad. And Lil, keep holding her up as much as you can. We need gravity to help us.'

Please let this work, Evie prayed again. *It's not this woman's fault that I'm all she has.*

In spite of her exhaustion, Glad pushed hard, grunting with the strain. Evie began to guide the baby's bottom out. Glad was doing her job. Evie needed to do hers.

'Two more big pushes,' Evie said.

The buttocks turned slightly. Evie said a silent thank you. 'I need that towel, Patty!' she shouted, and the towel appeared, with only one brownish stain, which she ignored.

Evie wrapped the baby's hips to keep it warm and to give her something less slippery to hold than vernix-covered skin. She gently manoeuvred the baby towards Glad's sacrum and the anterior shoulder came free. Then she lifted the baby's buttocks up into the air to help the posterior shoulder move out. Just the head to go. The most difficult part.

If Evie didn't control the birth of the head, there could be a disastrous change in the pressure on the infant's brain, resulting in a haemorrhage. Or . . . Evie stopped herself. Listing the potential complications wasn't going to help. Her teeth were drawing blood from the insides of her cheeks. She grasped the baby by the ankles with one hand and began to pull with some force, but not so much that the neck would bend backwards and break, or so she hoped. She raised the baby's feet straight up into the air and placed one hand against Glad's perineum so that the head didn't come out too quickly. Finally she saw what she wanted to see. A mouth and a nose. And then the slow and steady appearance of the baby's head. Suddenly there it was. There *she* was.

A baby girl. Intact and perfect and howling like the wind down Bleecker on a winter's day, a sound Evie was so glad to hear.

'It's a girl,' she announced. She realised she had tears in her eyes and that she felt as proud as if she'd been the baby's mother.

Lil propped Glad against a pillow, slithered off the bed to take a look, and began to squeal and applaud. Glad reached out her hands and held her daughter.

'She's beautiful,' sniffed Evie.

'You're amazing,' said Lil, giving her friend a hug.

Evie laughed as she watched Glad kissing her daughter's forehead. Glad was pale and tired but awake and elated. It was a birth that had needed only skill and a shared understanding between the mother and the doctor. Mother and baby were alive, well and in love.

Then she leaned back suddenly against the wall. Her legs were shaking. For the first time, she realised how afraid she'd been. Not just tonight, but all through her studies. Afraid that being ignored, being made to watch rather than assist, never having a chance to practise, would make her a doctor with excellent grades but no skill. Sure, she could fix up most of the gynae cases that the Ziegfeld Girls presented her with. But she'd had no proof that she could deliver a baby. Until now.

Evie remembered Thomas's smile from earlier that night. As she thought of him, and about what she'd just done, she knew that this was why she'd come to New York. To feel as if she mattered. As if she was, finally, full of life.

When Evie left the boarding house later that morning, still soaring from the glorious adventure of the night before, she wasn't expecting to hear a voice as familiar as her own.

'Evelyn?'

The only people who called her that were her mother and father. And Evie was astonished to see that her mother had ventured across the frontier of Broadway and was now standing on the sidewalk outside Evie's boarding house.

'I want to talk to you,' Mrs Lockhart said. She clutched her purse in front of her, looking quaint and out of place among the melting pot of Greenwich Village's inhabitants.

'Well, I wanted to talk to you two years ago, but you didn't write back,' Evie retorted. She began to stride off to catch the El but then relented and turned back. After all, it was her mother. 'What do you want?'

'Seeing you last night was a surprise.'

'You can blame Charles for that. Let's get coffee,' Evie said, leading the way to Bleecker Street. She pushed open the door of the cheapest coffee house on the block, where yesterday's crumbs and a lifetime of sticky marks came for free with your order, and sat down at a small corner table.

Mrs Lockhart hovered by the table, as if unsure what to do.

'Two coffees,' Evie called to the waitress. 'Take a seat. I'll get it,' she said to her mother. 'I seem to remember I owe Father some money. I only have five minutes or I'll be late for college.'

Her mother sat down gingerly. 'How have you been passing the time here?'

Evie burst out laughing. 'You want me to fill in nearly three years in five minutes? I've been studying and working. That's about it. And you?'

'We visit Viola and Charles occasionally.'

'Now you know where I live, you can visit me too.' Evie looked her mother in the eye, this person with whom she'd lived for twenty years of her life, but who'd been happy to disclaim her. How could a parent do that? Did their estrangement hurt her mother at all, the way it hurt Evie? Or did her mother truly believe that she had only one daughter now?

The coffees arrived. Evie took hers gladly, tiredness crashing over her at last.

Mrs Lockhart waited for the waitress to leave. 'And what else do you do?'

'I don't have a lot of time for anything else.'

'But you must do something besides study.'

'Not really.'

'Does anyone visit you?'

'What do you mean?'

Her mother sipped her coffee and then stared at the cup as she spoke. 'Your father. Does he come to visit you?'

'Last night was the first time I'd seen him since I left the Whitmans'.'

'Oh.' Her mother seemed disappointed by Evie's answer.

'Had you asked him to visit me?' Evie said, trying to grasp her mother's meaning, her heart leaping a little at this first inkling of maternal concern.

'No.' Her mother shook her head and Evie's heart dropped back to the ground. Of course her mother hadn't sent her father along to New York to enquire after her.

She stood up. 'I'm going to be late.' She left some money on the table to pay for the coffees.

But before Evie could leave, her mother put her hand on her arm. 'He's been to New York once or twice to stay with Charles and Viola. He didn't take me with him.'

Evie was silent. The thought of her father voluntarily spending time in the Gomorrah of New York City was incongruous. And then there was the fact that he hadn't bothered, on any of those visits, to see Evie.

Mrs Lockhart looked down at her coffee cup. 'It's so quiet when I'm at the house by myself.'

Evie shut her eyes. She didn't want to hear this, didn't want to imagine her mother alone in the house in Concord, perfecting her already flawless embroidery, surrounded by the silence she'd always wished for. She remembered the conversation she'd had with her father when he'd refused to pay her college fees and she'd suddenly understood that he might also find his Concord life dull and confining. Did he come to New York to escape the gentlemanly responsibilities he'd taken up like a manacle, chaining him to the proprieties of the upper-middle class? But how could she say that to her mother? Evie opened her eyes. In spite of her own sadness, she tried to comfort her mother. 'Perhaps he came for some sort of business and didn't want you to be bored.'

'Of course you're right.' Her mother affixed a familiar smile to her face, a smile Evie used to think of as cold; now she wondered if it was the mask her mother wore to hide her own hurts.

'I could start writing to you again?' Evie said.

Mrs Lockhart nodded but Evie wasn't sure she'd heard. She left the coffee shop more confused than when she'd entered, wondering why her mother had sought her out after all this time. Was this just a momentary peek at her mother's heart, one that Mrs Lockhart would never wish to put down on a sheet of notepaper in a letter to her daughter? And even after this encounter, if Evie wrote to her, would her mother be venturesome enough to write back?

~

'Better get your glad rags on, your sugar daddy's here,' Bea said to Evie that night, giving her a not-so-subtle elbow in the ribs.

Given the giggles of the girls, Evie knew a man must be coming through the dressing room, walking between the rows of performers who were changing out of their costumes, taking off their faces and dressing down from sequins to silk dresses.

'He sure must be somebody if Bob lets him come back here rather than making him wait at the stage door with all the wannabes,' added Bea.

'Swell,' Evie muttered, expecting it was Charles, come to wield his power like a dog with its leg cocked, but realising – just in time to remove the snarl from her lip – that it was Thomas.

'We'll have to stop meeting like this,' she said, indicating her leotard and headdress in the mirror. She was stupidly gratified when he blushed. Most of the men she'd met at Ziegfeld's were too suave to blush at anything. She turned to face him. 'You know, outside the Follies I'm a regular girl,' she said, hoping to put him at his ease.

'You'll never be a regular girl, Evie,' said Thomas.

Now it was her turn to blush. She looked at Thomas in his beautifully cut dinner suit and the smile on his lips that was all for her and she thought what a fine-looking man he was. So fine that the sight of him commanded all her attention and she didn't even notice Bea raising her eyebrows suggestively.

'Would you like to get a drink?' he asked. 'I know it's late but we could go somewhere nearby.'

'I delivered an unforeseen baby last night and I'm so tired that if I have even one drink I'll be scrooched.' She saw the corners of Thomas's mouth dip with disappointment and added hastily, 'But we could do something else?'

He thought. 'The pictures?'

'Love to. Let me get changed and I'll meet you at the stage door. Don't let the crowds put you off.'

'Crowds?'

'You'll see.' There weren't words enough to explain the chaos surrounding one of the most famous stage doors on Broadway.

When he'd gone, Evie quickly pulled her clothes out of her bag. 'Damn. I've been wearing these at the clinic all day. They look . . .'

'Like a line of hoofers has trampled them.' Bea stood up on her chair, stuck her fingers in her mouth and whistled for quiet. 'Girls! Evie's got herself a date with a fella who's gen-u-inely the gnat's whistle and she ain't got nothing fit to wear. Whaddya got?'

The effect of Queen Bea's whistle and holler was as powerful as if Flo himself had said, *Thou shalt find Evie something to wear.* The girls mobilised. The idea that there was at least one man in the world who was the gnat's whistle, and that this man wanted to date, rather than merely deflower, a Ziegfeld Girl was enough. Because if it happened to one girl, it might happen to any of them. Maybe there was a way out of shimmy-shaking for cash.

Bags were searched and outfits laid out in various combin-ations, some of which said gun moll, while others screamed, *Hang the cheque, it's cash all the way.* Evie eventually decided on a divine sailor-style dress in navy linen with white contrast trims. It had a prim little bow at the collar, fell to just below Evie's knees and made her look as if she'd stepped off a yacht on the French Riviera.

There was a sense of occasion to Evie's plans now. Her tiredness was abandoned, to be taken up later, whenever there was time. A new pair of silk stockings was discovered in someone's bag, a pair of cream heels – fortunately in Evie's size – with cunning pearl buttons was declared a perfect match, and red lipstick was absolutely insisted upon by all the girls as the ideal finishing touch. Her hair was brushed till it shone and her dress smoothed down. She gave a final twirl, was pronounced ready, and set off for the stage door accompanied by a wistful chorus of *good luck*s.

Good luck? Evie wondered as she pushed open the door. What exactly was she hoping might happen? Truthfully, she'd settle for another of Thomas's smiles. A girl could re-live a thousand dreams with one of those tucked safe in her memory.

Evie ignored the queue of men at the door and went straight to Thomas. He was standing a long way back, looking uncertain, and Evie realised how long it had taken her to dress. 'Sorry,' she said. 'My clothes had the distinct smell of the hospital about them and I had to scrounge around for something less pungent to wear.'

'Should I call you Captain?' Thomas said teasingly, nodding at her sailor dress.

'Only if you don't want to walk the plank.'

And then and there, Evie got what she wanted. Another smile from Thomas. She stopped him as he put out his arm to hail a cab. 'Let's take the El,' she said. 'Evie's tour of Manhattan continues.'

'Lead the way.'

Once on board the train, Evie showed Thomas the things she saw every day and every night as her train snaked through Manhattan, things she was sure Thomas had never seen before. The train curved a few feet away from office buildings and apartments, giving the passengers a view inside the places people lived and worked that was like no other. 'This is my favourite part,' she said as the train rattled past the second-floor windows of Macy's at Thirty-Fourth Street.

'For window shopping?' Thomas asked, and Evie laughed.

'No. Because no matter how late it is, there's always someone in there. See.' Evie pointed, but Thomas shook his head as the train sped by too quickly for him to see. 'It's the same guy every night,' she said. 'I suppose he's working, checking the stock, making things ready for the morning. But sometimes he looks like he's dreaming, staring at the clothes or shoes or haberdashery and thinking of all the things he could do and be in that pair of two-tone brogues, and wearing those maroon pinstriped trousers, and with cerulean bedsheets instead of plain old white.' She grinned. 'Of course, he's probably sleepwalking or something else much less romantic.'

'I like your story better.'

'Me too.' The train drew into the station. 'We'd better hurry or we'll miss the last session,' Evie said as they stepped off.

Thomas began to run, surprising her with the suddenness of his movement. 'Keep up, Captain,' he called.

'I will!' she shouted back, and they ran on together, arriving at the cavernous Sheridan Theatre on Twelfth Street just in time. Every seat in the house was filled at every session, such was the appetite of New Yorkers for sheikhs, swashbucklers, phantoms and other dashing unrealities. The lights were about to dim, the piano had struck up its accompaniment, and Evie and Thomas were both flushed, out of breath and laughing as they were ushered to seats near the back. They earned themselves at least one reproving stare, from a man who evidently preferred his movies silent and unstirred.

The newsreel flickered on and Evie sighed aloud as she sank into the seat, feet glad to have the load taken off.

'Okay?' Thomas asked.

'Yes,' Evie replied, thinking how comfortable his shoulder looked.

The next thing she knew someone was stepping past her and people were standing. 'What happened?' she said as she sat up, realising that she had indeed fallen asleep on Thomas's shoulder. Not only that, she'd slept through everything – the newsreel, the shorts, the serial and the feature.

'I'm sorry,' she said.

'Why?'

'I'm terrible company. I've ruined your evening.'

'No, you haven't,' Thomas said, gently helping her to her feet.

Outside, he slid his arm around her waist, and as they walked back to her boarding house together, Evie realised that she'd set her goals for the evening far too low. A smile from Thomas was wonderful, but this, his side warm against hers and the touch of his hand at the top of her hipbone, was better than anything. She could feel that his body was strong and muscular, and she imagined touching the skin beneath his shirt, or his hand moving lower, to turn her towards him. Heat rushed through her, from top to toe.

But they'd reached Minetta Street. 'This is it,' Evie said reluctantly.

Thomas stepped back and tipped his hat to her. 'Goodnight, Evie. I'll look out for the man at Macy's on the way home.'

'You're taking the El?' she asked in surprise. 'Well, report back and tell me what he's up to.'

'I will. And make sure you check your mail tomorrow.'

'Why?' Evie called, but he just smiled as he walked away. She leaned against the lamppost and watched him, reluctant to let him go but also secretly delighted that he was probably the only man in New York who'd take a Ziegfeld Girl out for the night and leave without stealing so much as a kiss.

Chapter Sixteen

MR AND MRS GEORGE WHITMAN
REQUEST THE PLEASURE OF THE COMPANY OF
EVELYN LOCKHART AND LILLIAN DELANCEY
AT THEIR EGYPTIAN BALL
TO BE HELD ON MAY 10TH AT 8 PM
AT THEIR HOME.

*O*n the back of the printed invitation was a handwritten note. *Evie and Lil, I know how much Evie likes the El but what if I send a car to pick you both up? You can avoid the soot for one night. Thomas.*

A ball, and with Thomas! Evie hugged the invitation to her chest.

'A man after my own heart,' Lil said when she'd read the note. 'I'm sure Cleopatra always used private transportation. We'll need new dresses. Let's go shopping on Saturday.'

'I should spend Saturday revising my vaginal infections.'

'Say that any louder and no one will sit next to you on the train.'

Evie laughed. 'Well, maybe I could find something to wear that'll spin Tommy's head faster than a pinwheel on the Fourth of July.'

'Attagirl!' said Lil.

The thought of dancing with Thomas at a ball gave Evie something to dream about for the rest of the day spent at the Vanderbilt Clinic treating a room full of johns and quiffs for VD. The girls she felt sorry for, and she tried to help them, although most didn't want anything more than a quick fix. The men angered her but she kept her lips pressed shut and ministered to them the way she was supposed to. She was glad when her shift was finished. Seeing that it was only half past five, she took her gift for Mary out of her locker and stepped outside into the wet heat of an unseasonably warm spring day; it was like walking into the bathroom after Lil had been broiling herself in the tub like a Maine lobster. But that was New York, a city of extremes, and Evie knew better than anyone that accepting the humidity and living amid a forest of skyscrapers rather than trees was worth it to experience the living firework of Manhattan at night, when everything from Times Square to the Brooklyn Bridge to a young woman's hopes and dreams were spotlit, as if the city was a stage set for the world's greatest show.

She walked to the Foundling determined to at least deliver her gift, even if she couldn't see Mary. This time when she knocked and called out, she heard a faint sound within. 'Evie!' Mary's voice, Evie was sure. Calling for her, forlorn.

Evie banged once more, but she knew the front door wasn't going to be the way in. She hurried around the side of the building; there must be a service entrance somewhere. She peered in the windows until she saw a face. Sister Margaret! The young nun's hands were pointing, indicating that Evie should continue on ahead. Evie did so, until she came to a laneway behind the building. A door opened.

Sister Margaret's head popped out. She looked around in an overdramatic, Chaplinesque manner, as if she'd wanted all her life to be a stooge in a moving picture. Evie held back a laugh. Then Sister Margaret produced something from behind her skirt. Or rather someone.

'Mary!' Evie cried, sweeping the little girl into a hug.

'You didn't come,' Mary said.

Evie kissed her on the top of her blonde head. 'Sister Mary asked me not to. I missed you.'

'I missed you. No park.'

'I can't take you to the park today. But we can sit here on the step.'

'Just two minutes,' said Sister Margaret, wringing her hands.

'Thank you,' said Evie.

'She was fretting for you. It isn't right,' said Sister Margaret before she retreated to keep guard inside the doorway.

Evie passed Mary the doll. 'This is for you. She can be your friend when I can't be here. I'll ask Sister Margaret to look after her for you.'

Mary touched the doll's hair carefully, then withdrew her fingers as though frightened of dirtying it. She looked up at Evie, who nodded. 'It's all right. She's yours. You can stroke her hair.'

'She's beautiful,' Mary whispered.

'You need to come in now, child.' Sister Margaret was back, pulling Mary to her feet.

'How has she been?' Evie asked as she kissed Mary's cheek.

'She's been upset.' Then Sister Margaret's face crumpled. 'It's my fault! I told him about you. The man who gives Sister Mary the money. I said to him how much Mary liked your visits. He shouted at Sister Mary and said you weren't to be allowed to come any more. That you should never have been allowed to come.'

'He knows me?' Evie was taken aback. 'Did you find out his name?'

Sister Margaret shook her head. 'No. I was going to ask him but I made him angry by mentioning you and then it was too late.'

The unmistakable sound of voices rang through the hall inside the building.

Sister Margaret began to push the door closed. 'You have to go.'

Evie had time for one last hug and one last glance at Mary's too-sad face before the door was locked. Was it her personally, or did this man object to the thought of anyone visiting Mary, she wondered as she walked away from the Foundling. Did that mean Mary's father was someone Evie had met? She tried to remember if she'd ever seen Rose with a man and was certain she hadn't. And the only men from Harvard she knew were Charles's friends. Evie's heart stopped. And Charles. No, that wasn't possible. He'd seen Rose by the river and shown no concern for her or the baby. He wouldn't have been so heartless towards his own child. Would he?

⁓

By the time Saturday arrived, Evie had convinced herself that she was being foolish. That Sister Margaret had misunderstood. Whoever this mysterious man was, he hadn't specifically forbidden Evie from visiting; he simply hadn't wanted Mary to have any visitors. Although it didn't make the problem of getting in to see her any easier to solve. But perhaps with time, Evie would find a way.

The shopping expedition for the ball was a welcome distraction. Evie and Lil went to Saks, accompanied by Leo, who was going with them to the ball and had promised to offer honest opinions on whether their dress choices made them look more like mutton or lamb.

Lil held up a dress with a silver fringe that tinkled down from the hemline like the crystals on a chandelier to a spot at least two inches above her knees.

'Egyptian ball means a long dress, doesn't it?' Evie asked.

'I bet Cleopatra would have loved it, though,' Lil sighed as she hung it back on the rack.

Leo proved to be more useful than Evie had expected. He held out his arms and let the girls load him with dresses, barely raising a sweat under the weight of so many beads and crystals. 'Didn't Cleopatra wear gold?' he asked when his arms were full. 'Find the right necklace and you'll be as Egyptian as Tutankhamen.'

'But hopefully more lively,' Evie said as she lifted half the dresses off his arms and carried them away to the fitting rooms.

'Well, scram then,' said Lil to Leo. 'Shoot down to accessories and find us a scarab beetle while we work our way through this lot.'

In the end, the girls went against expectations. Evie bought a dress that she couldn't remember selecting from the rack; something about Lil's satisfied smile when Evie emerged in it told her that Lil had chosen it for her. It was short, bold and gold and there was no hiding from it, like the midday sun in July. In his fossicking, Leo had found a piece of jewellery that could only be described as a collar, thick gold and azure blue, which draped perfectly over Evie's clavicle. Lil declared that she looked like the bust of Nefertiti come to life.

Lil chose a long dress, a sheath of white silk which looked stunning against her dark hair. It was ruched and gathered to a point on her hip and she adorned it with an iridescent scarab beetle that Leo had so obligingly located in accessories, along with the name and address of the sales clerk. As Lil did one last twirl, Evie noticed that Leo had screwed up the paper with the salesgirl's name on it and was looking at Lil as if she was being served for dessert. His expression reminded Evie of the night they'd spoken about the girl he thought he couldn't have and Evie suddenly realised who it might be.

Lil went back into the fitting rooms to change, so Evie seized the chance to see if her intuition was right. 'You could ask the girl from accessories to come with you to the ball,' she said to Leo.

'Not her,' Leo replied.

'But you always have a lady on your arm.'

'I'll have two ladies on my arms tomorrow night.'

'Lil and I don't really count.'

'You'll be the belles of the ball.'

'Lil will be in that dress.'

'She will.' Leo's eyes hadn't shifted from the place where Lil had stood, showing off her dress and making a man fall more in love with her.

Evie smiled and touched his arm. 'Remember what you said to me at Chumley's the night you kissed me?'

Leo laughed. 'I kissed you? I thought it was the other way around.'

'You're changing the subject.' Evie elbowed him in the ribs. 'Why don't you say something to her?'

'What?' Leo looked like a man caught by the bulls with a boxful of bootleg.

'Say something to Lil. Otherwise you'll never know.'

'But she's . . .' Leo stopped, lost for a way to describe the quintessence of Lil.

'Perfect for you,' finished Evie. 'Leave it to me. I'll give you a helping hand.'

'Helping hand with what?' Lil asked, reappearing in her everyday clothes.

'With finding Leo something to wear,' Evie answered, observing Leo's faint blush.

He recovered quickly. 'With the two of you on my arms, all I need is a tuxedo. No one will be looking at me.'

As they left the store, Evie wondered how she could possibly wait until tomorrow night for the car to come and collect them for the ball. Not only would the delicious anticipation of seeing Thomas keep her in such a high state of excitement that it would be impossible to study, but she might also be able to do Lil a favour. Perhaps Lil felt the same way as Leo but was so convinced of his preference for variety that she'd overlooked an affection that was more than friendship – an affection that could burgeon into something beautiful if Evie nudged her friends a little closer together.

For the rest of the afternoon, Evie and Lil did nothing but sit on their bed, bubbling with the exhilaration that can only come from an invitation to a ball held in the beating heart of New York's moneyed and magnificent society.

Every girl at the boarding house played a part in the production that was Evie and Lil Going to the Egyptian Ball. They'd all read about balls in the society pages but no one thought that a girl from Mrs Lomsky's would ever be invited to more than a carouse around the local dance hall. They crammed themselves into the attic room and each took a job – fingernails, hair, makeup – so Evie and Lil only needed to sit and be togged to the bricks.

'This is a New York moment,' proclaimed Antonia with her typical flamboyance. 'Just like when Douglas Fairbanks and Mary Pickford waved to me from the steps of the Algonquin.'

'I think you're selling Fairbanks and Pickford a little short there,' said Lil. 'And don't burn my hair with those irons.'

Antonia came back to the reality of life on Minetta Street in time to save Lil's hair from a scorching. 'Well,' she said, 'if you don't both find yourselves a beau at the ball, you'll have wasted the chance of a lifetime.'

Someone turned on the gramophone and selected the 'Charleston'. As the accelerating piano chords of the opening bars jangled into the room, Lil began to tap her hands on Evie's desk like a jazz drummer. A couple of the girls began to dance, all of them started to smoke, and what with the music and the squeals over Evie's golden collar, it wasn't long before Mrs Lomsky appeared at the door.

'You know parties aren't allowed,' she snapped.

'This is serious business,' declared Antonia. 'Evie and Lil'll be the only women from south of Washington Square at the ball tonight, and we don't want anyone to hold that against them.'

Playing on the grand narrative of girl from skid row makes good appealed to Mrs Lomsky's sense of pride. She took a cigarette from the pack beside Lil and stuck it behind her ear. 'You warn 'em I can tell jet from a gem with one crack of my teeth.'

This silenced the girls until Mrs Lomsky had left, whereupon they all began to laugh, especially when Antonia stood up and did her best impersonation of Mrs Lomsky checking a length of beads with her teeth and finding it wanting.

Soon the call came that their car had arrived. Leo was waiting outside looking like the snake's hips in his swanky tuxedo. At the sight of him, Lil whispered to Evie, 'Look at him. So beautiful. Shame he's such a flirt.'

'I bet he'd stop for the right woman,' Evie replied, and was delighted to see Lil eyeing him appraisingly.

The night was as sultry as midsummer, the three of them were half-shot with excitement and Evie had high hopes that Lil might be as stuck on Leo as he was on her. She made sure they were seated next to each other in the car.

Leo produced a bottle of champagne and three glasses.

'Oh, good,' said Lil. 'We need to be spifflicated on entry so we can tolerate meeting my mother.'

'Will she be there?' Evie asked, intrigued.

'She'd consider it highly damaging to her reputation if she didn't attend. Which is all she cares about.'

'She must care about you.'

'Only in small doses. Like absinthe.'

New York seemed to gather the unmothered, Evie reflected as they drove away. Lil. Evie. Mary.

Soon they were at the Whitmans', where the butler had been dressed for the occasion as an explorer of Ancient Egyptian tombs à la Howard Carter. He handed them each a linen pouch, which contained a gold amulet with one bejewelled eye, red for the ladies and blue for the men.

'Spoils from King Tut's burial chamber, no doubt,' said Leo with a grin as he pinned the amulet to his lapel.

'You've obviously never heard of the mummy's curse,' said Lil as she put hers back in the pouch.

Evie laughed and pinned hers on. 'It's just a party favour. Oh.'

They had just entered the ballroom, the sight of which had elicited Evie's *Oh*. It was like stepping inside a pyramid. One wall of the room had been transformed to look like the stone facade of a grand temple, complete with hieroglyphs and illustrations from *The Book of the Dead*. An obelisk stood tall and proud in the centre. Placed throughout the room were gilded statues of Horus, Isis and Osiris, gold-foiled sarcophagi, statuesque black cats with gold collars, and long-handled fans in peacock blue and emerald green adorned the walls. There was even a chain of three live camels resting on the ground, apparently worn out by the rigours of being admired and exclaimed over. A band was playing all the latest songs at one end of the room and waiters circulated with trays laden with prohibited champagne, which everyone was drinking. Leo summoned a waiter over, took three glasses and handed them around.

'It's like being inside a Macy's Christmas window,' Evie said.

'Here's to a night we'll never forget,' Lil toasted.

They finished their drinks quickly and Evie decided to act. 'You two should dance,' she said, elbowing Leo a little closer to Lil. As she spoke, she continued to look around the room; something was missing but she wasn't sure what until she felt the lightest touch of a hand at her back. It was funny, she thought, that without sight or sound, you could know when a certain person was near. It was like phosphorescence, an unconscious drawing in of another's energy, which then sparked back out into the room through the static charge on her skin. When she turned and saw that it was indeed Thomas Whitman behind her, the smile that lit her face was as spontaneous and uncontrollable as the appearance of the moon in the night sky.

Lil offered her cheek to be kissed, which made Evie feel as if she could do the same. When Thomas leaned towards her, she breathed in a scent that had been lurking in her dreams since the night at the movie theatre when she'd fallen asleep on his shoulder and inhaled him with every breath.

'What a show!' Lil said.

'I feel as if I've been living in Cairo for the past week,' Thomas said.

'That might be fun,' Evie said.

'Only if you enjoy being hit on the head by fake pillars that fall down every time you walk past.'

Evie laughed. 'Tutankhamun's curse? Perhaps it mistook you for an animal ready for sacrifice.'

'Surely you're not calling my Tommy a fatted calf?' An English voice Evie didn't recognise interrupted the conversation. A blonde in a backless black number that bore more resemblance to a Ziegfeld costume than an Egyptian ensemble threaded her arm through Thomas's and spread her smile around. Even though she knew she was being unkind, Evie was pleased to see that the girl had crooked teeth.

'I'm Winnie. Nice to meet you.' Winnie's diamond earrings were more than a match for the chandeliers in the ballroom, and as if the blinding effect of those danglers wasn't enough, she'd strung a few spares around her neck. Evie couldn't take her eyes off Winnie's arm resting on Thomas's. She was glad that Thomas hadn't summoned up much of a smile for Winnie, but still. An unpleasant feeling sat heavily in her stomach and she knew it was jealousy.

'Winnie,' Lil repeated. She drew herself up, enunciated her vowels more clearly and became the epitome of what she used to be, the rich girl from the Upper East Side who had no time for interlopers. 'And how do you know the Whitmans?'

'I arrived in New York a few days ago. London wasn't the same without Tommy. Now,' Winnie actually pouted at Thomas, 'I don't know anyone here, so you need to make some introductions.' With that, she and Thomas set off, arm in arm. Evie wanted to think Winnie was the one steering him away and that Thomas was too polite to make a scene, but she couldn't be sure. In any case, Thomas didn't look back as they walked away.

'What a billboard,' Lil said. 'It takes talent to make all those jewels look cheap.'

Evie laughed but even to her ears it sounded false. A wealthy English lady was exactly the kind of woman Thomas would be expected to invite to a ball, not a showgirl in a frivolously short skirt who danced and sang so rich men could pay her bills. How did Thomas feel about Winnie? Was there some kind of understanding between them? Winnie had come all the way from London after all.

'Let's dance,' she said, to get away from the place where Winnie had stood, to get away from the warm spot she still felt on her cheek where Thomas had kissed her. 'Take Lil's hand and move in close,' she whispered to Leo as they joined the whirl of dancers. 'I'll scram.'

'You think so?' Leo whispered back.

'I know so.'

As soon as she could, Evie let herself be whisked away by a handsome man whose charleston could put the Tiller Girls to shame. Catching glimpses of her friends through the crowd, she eventually saw Leo place his hand on Lil's face and run his thumb along her cheekbone. Lil's unusually shy smile made Evie's feet skip a little higher. Then Leo rested his cheek against

Lil's and they looked so happy that Evie knew it would take a firecracker to separate them. At least two people would leave the ball happier than when they arrived.

The song ended and Evie let her heels try a few kicks with a blond-haired stranger. He turned out to be a dead hoofer, and Evie extricated herself after suffering one too many blows to her shins. She wondered if she should go straight to the bar and admit defeat. Then she felt a familiar hand at her back.

'I asked the band to play the next song for you,' Thomas said.

'What is it?'

'Wait and see.'

Evie followed him to a spot in the middle of the dance floor where they were hidden by all the other people spinning around them. The first bars of the song began to play. The band had taken out a bandoneon to add to the violin, the double bass and the piano. It took Evie a moment to place the tune, but then she remembered that night, years ago, when she was a different person and Tommy had taken her to a speakeasy he thought was the cat's pyjamas. There in Chumley's, Tommy and Lil had danced a majestic tango. The same music now filled the room.

'I've wanted to dance a tango with you ever since Chumley's,' Thomas said.

Evie had to know. 'What about Winnie?'

'Winnie came to New York for no one but herself. I'm not interested in Winnie. I want to dance with you.' His voice sounded warm and sincere, and Evie let herself relax into his arms.

If petting and necking and climbing into the back seat of a struggle-buggy were the aphrodisiacs of the men and women of the 1920s, Evie felt sorry for them. Dancing the tango was the most exquisite way to express desire, with hands clasped together, bodies nearer than ever a waltz would allow, knees fitted between knees, Evie's shoulder tucked under Thomas's right arm, her hip bone pressed against the top of his thigh. They were holding each other so close that Evie could feel that Thomas was as attracted to her as she was to him. His eyes were fixed on her face, and the intentness of his gaze was almost unbearable; it made her stomach clench and she yearned to be alone in a room with him. Each dip of her back brought his face nearer to hers, until the distance between their lips was no more than a breath. She would only have to incline her head just a little for their lips to touch. The longing that swept through her was so acute that she knew the kiss they were about to share would be anything but chaste. She closed her eyes. His lips touched hers.

'Evie!'

The music and the lights and the people crashed back into Evie's senses, like an emergency at the hospital. She was no longer leaning back, supported by Thomas's arms, about to dive into a kiss she'd been dreaming of for years. She was standing and so was Thomas and they were both looking, none too pleased, at Charles.

'You didn't come to say hello so I . . .' Charles began.

'Hunted me down,' Evie supplied tersely.

'Charlie,' Thomas said, warningly.

But Charles's boorish voice carried right across his brother's. 'That's right, jump in and save her again.'

'I need a drink,' said Evie, aware that people were beginning to stare. Mrs Whitman didn't deserve to have her party spoiled by her younger son's petty jealousies.

'A drink? Allow me.' Charles stepped towards Evie, tripped, and his glass of bordeaux went all over her, so that she no longer looked like a shimmering Nefertiti but a decidedly wet, annoyed and bloody victim of the Hudson Dusters.

A look crossed Charles's face, more like mirth than horror.

Thomas was quick to react, pulling a folded handkerchief out of his pocket and passing it to Evie. She took it gratefully, then stood staring at it in shock.

There in the corner of the handkerchief was an embroidered M, a crooked and imperfect M, one Evie had stitched there herself, on a gift for Mary.

Her fist tightened around the handkerchief and she pretended to smile at Thomas. 'I'll be right back. I'll clean this up in the bathroom.'

She hurried out of the ballroom but instead of going to the bathroom, she left the house. She almost fell down the front steps. Her mind was disordered, images and words flashing through it, presenting an argument that she wanted to deny. Surely there was another explanation. She walked faster, then began to run; a past she couldn't get away from was snapping at her heels, demanding she wake up to the reality that had been staring her in the face from the time she'd first encountered the baby by the river.

There was only one way Thomas could have got Mary's hanky. He had to have visited her. Which meant he was the mysterious man who'd wanted Evie to stay away from the Foundling. While he'd been taking her to the movies and holding her hand at midnight on Fifth Avenue, he'd been hiding the fact that he was Mary's father. Not Charles. God, it had been easy to believe it was Charles. It was almost beyond belief to think it was Thomas.

She stopped running because she had to bend over and hold on to the wall. The force of the discovery felt like a physical blow, winding her. It was agony, to still be able to feel the touch of Thomas's lips on hers, even as she realised that he'd lied to her all along.

Someone walked past and knocked her sideways. She stumbled, hit the wall with her knee and her shoulder and grazed the skin. She touched the scrape and saw blood on her hand but she didn't feel anything. The blood was the same colour as the wine on the handkerchief. How could he have done this to her? She felt a sob escape, the sound like a streak of white against the night sky. She clapped her hand over her mouth.

A couple strolled past, arm in arm, the woman's head tucked into the man's shoulder. 'What a night,' the man said.

And it was. It was warm and starlit, a night made for lovers to walk clasped together over the Brooklyn Bridge, stopping to kiss, backlit by a perfect circle of moon in the sky. It wasn't a night for heartbreak.

Goddamnit! Evie wanted to howl, because howling was better than thinking. If she could howl then maybe she could get it all out of her, just as a scalpel let the blood flow until the vein was empty.

She walked on, not going anywhere other than away from Thomas. City block after city block passed by until she reached Fifty-Ninth, opposite the elegant white facade of the Plaza Hotel. She saw a string of merry people make their way down the steps of the hotel and into a cab. How could they be so happy? How could they laugh and joke? How could they even breathe?

Evie wasn't breathing, not properly, and the world around her began to spin. She was stuck on a carousel that blurred the merrymakers in the cab with Thomas's smiling face at the ball and the hanky stained with red until she could no longer see. Until she felt as if she had stepped outside her body. Because New York wasn't real. Unless you were born at the right address and could buy your way out of trouble the way Thomas had, it existed only in a head-in-the-clouds, pie-in-the-sky kind of way, a city of skyscrapers built from fairytales. Fairytales that lured people like her to the lights and the jazz and the promise that, once there, you'd have the freedom to be nobody's daughter, nobody's intended, nobody's mistake. But that was the great and grand myth of New York City. And Evie was the biggest sucker of them all to have believed it.

'Do you need help?' somebody asked her, taking hold of her elbow, steadying her. Evie took a deep breath, as if she'd just remembered how, and felt the dizziness recede.

She nodded and walked forward, closer to the hotel, carried along by the people on the sidewalk. She reached the bottom of the steps and the doorman opened the door. It looked dazzling inside, too lustrous for heartache and defeat, and Evie thought, why not? She was still in her glad rags and had no place to go. When you earned fifty-five dollars a week and spent eight dollars on board, even after the College of Physicians and Surgeons had been paid you still had some money put aside for a rainy day, and here it was now, drizzling down.

Evie walked up the red-carpeted steps as if all her life she'd been staying at hotels like the Plaza. The doorman bowed to her as if he believed it too, and she averted her red eyes and damp cheeks in case he figured her out.

She strode to the front desk. 'I need a room for tonight,' she said in a voice that was loud and firm.

The desk clerk handed her a key and she was accompanied to the elevator by the bellboy, who enquired after her luggage.

'I travel light,' she said, and he nodded as if he'd expected her to say that.

At the tenth floor, the lift stopped. She followed the bellboy to a door, which he held open for her to walk through – into another world. She pressed a quarter into the boy's hand and he left her alone to stand at the window. From up here all she could see was the beauty. And the tears at last began to fall.

I'm so damn stupid, she thought. Because she knew like the way she knew her own skin that she'd been in love with Thomas. How could she not have been? What was love but a sudden jolt out of real life and into the unmapped, the possible, the strange and splendid. A place where another person became as familiar as the breath in your lungs. She'd relented on the promise she'd made at the hospital to keep her heart tucked away where it could never be hurt, and now it was shattered into pieces that could never be put back together.

Because everything had been a lie. Their conversation in the apple tree. The letters he'd written to her from London. The encouragement he'd given her to pursue her dreams and become a doctor. His arm around her waist. Dancing a tango. The way she'd thought he felt when he held her in his arms. An album of memories that Evie wanted to wrench out of her head and drown in the fast moving waters of the Hudson River.

Forgetting Thomas Whitman would be a lifetime's work, and Evie doubted it could ever be done.

She slid down the wall beside the window and onto the floor. How was it possible to cry so many tears and still find more waiting, ready to be shed? For the whole night she sat weeping in her room at the Plaza Hotel, with its marble bath and soft featherbed and views of a life she couldn't afford, as if those things could comfort her for losing the love of her life before it had even begun.

Chapter Seventeen

The next morning, Evie's first thought was relief. Relief that she was awake and the awful dream that had soaked her pillow in tears after she'd crawled into bed in the early hours of the morning was over. But immediately after followed the sickening realisation that it hadn't been a dream. It had really happened. Thomas was Mary's father and Evie had fallen in love with a liar, a deceiver of the worst kind because he'd not only told her a series of untruths, he'd made her believe that he loved her.

She squeezed her eyes shut. How could she get out of bed? How could she walk around the city, the college and the hospital when every breath brought with it a physical pain that made her want to coil herself into the smallest possible shape in an attempt to bring some solace? She opened her eyes again and stared at the windows, at the dawn brightening over Manhattan, and knew she could never see Thomas again.

She had to get up. Some part of her brain was telling her that she was on rotation at the Vanderbilt Clinic. She was supposed to spend her day lancing boils and peering into infected throats. All she needed to do was stand up, get dressed, go to the clinic, and then she would be so busy that she wouldn't have time to think or feel or remember. Her legs felt so heavy when she lowered them over the side of the bed that she thought they might not hold her weight, but she steadied herself and shook her stupefied head. Coffee. That would help. She would start there, with the most basic of things.

She put on her wine-stained dress from the night before, not even caring how it would look in the Palm Court of the Plaza Hotel at half past seven in the morning. She caught the elevator downstairs and sat with her coffee, watching people come and go through the doors of the hotel. Her thoughts began to centre around one thing: the necessity of avoiding Thomas. He knew she spent her days at the college and at the hospital or clinic, he knew she spent her nights at the theatre, and he knew where she went to lay down her head. He could find her easily, *if* he wanted to. Would he come looking? She shuddered. She couldn't imagine looking at his face, hearing his voice, seeing his hand that had once held hers.

She sipped her coffee, which was better than anything Mrs Lomsky had ever served for breakfast. In fact, compared to the cramped boarding house on Minetta, the Plaza Hotel was as luxurious as a palace. She didn't want to leave. And Thomas would never look for her here. Right now, Evie felt that she could lie in the feather bed and sit in the chair by the windows and soak in the tub in her room forever. But forever would have to be paid for. And she couldn't afford more than a night of this kind of fantasy.

Just then there was a crash and an exclamation beside her, and a half-empty pot of cold tea landed in her lap. The waiter had tripped over a suitcase left in the thoroughfare and doused her for the second time in twelve hours. He began to apologise profusely.

The manager came hurrying over, as did the other staff in the vicinity. Taking in the scene, the manager turned on the bellboy – the same boy who'd shown Evie to her room the evening before, the one who hadn't raised an eyebrow at her lack of luggage, who hadn't commented on her grazed shoulder and knee, her tear-stained face.

'Mr Dunning!' the manager barked at the bellboy. 'It is your job to place suitcases in storage.' The manager turned to Evie and his voice softened. 'Madam, I am terribly sorry.'

Young Mr Dunning was stammering apologies at Evie too, and he really did look so contrite that it made her feel like crying all over again. She didn't know why she said what she did next; it was a kind of reflex action to be kind to another person in pain, a person on the verge of losing something he held dear – his job – all because of a little spilled tea.

'It's my fault,' she said. 'Not Mr Dunning's. I insisted on putting the case there. Mr Dunning tried very hard to dissuade me.'

'Well,' the manager said, looking taken aback. 'Well. It is still not right.'

'Mr Dunning has been very helpful,' Evie insisted. 'I'd be so upset if he found himself in trouble over this. I'll never wear this dress again anyway.'

'I shall organise a new dress for Miss Lockhart immediately,' the bellboy said.

'Very well,' said the manager. And then, to Evie, 'If you're sure.'

'I am,' she said and was almost grateful for the spilled

tea because it meant she hadn't thought of Thomas for five whole minutes.

She returned to her room, bathed and, shortly after, the bellboy, who was so endearingly young and baby-faced, appeared with a dress. 'I telephoned Bergdorf's, explained your requirements and told them this would be your size,' he said – and it was.

Evie stepped behind a screen, shrugged off the Plaza's black silk robe and slipped on the dress. It was pure white silk and made her feel, for an instant, like the girl in her early twenties she actually was, not the cynical woman for whom the world had become unsurprising in its constant repetition of the same old stories.

When she reappeared, the bellboy produced a box. 'Perhaps these would suit?'

Inside the box was a pair of shoes in the lightest shade of tan; when she put them on she felt as if she was walking in bare feet across silk carpet. 'You should be helping the ladies at Bergdorf's instead of opening doors for them here,' Evie said as she fastened the buckle.

'But this position has greater advantages,' the bellboy replied.

Evie wondered for a moment what those advantages were – the tips, she supposed, handed over in fistfuls for service above and beyond, service of the kind she was receiving now. Alas, she was not yet so much of a cynic that she could lead a man with such impeccable taste along in a lie. 'You know I can't give you any of those advantages,' she said. 'I trade in smiles, rather than dollar bills. And I've clean run out of those too.'

'You look just like my sister. But when you came through the doors last night, I thought you were the saddest woman I'd ever seen.' As he spoke, his expression showed a compassion beyond his years and Evie was touched, her heart lightening a little. 'If my sister ever looked like that, I'd want someone to be kind to her. And you saved my job this morning. So I informed the manager about the problem with the elevator last night, and advised him that, considering you'd been trapped in there for some time, you'd been remarkably forgiving of the Plaza Hotel. In gratitude, the manager wishes you to know that last night's accommodation is courtesy of the hotel, as are your next two nights,' he finished, straight-faced.

Evie looked at him blankly. 'Problem with the elevator?'

'Yes, those elevators are always getting stuck with guests caught inside.' A small grin escaped.

Evie couldn't help but smile too. Where else but New York could a catastrophe also turn into something so fine? Three nights at the Plaza for free, all because of a bellboy's quick thinking. It was just what she needed. 'I'm Evie. And your sister is very lucky to have a brother like you.'

'And I'm William Dunning. Please call down if you need anything else.'

'I will.'

After he left, Evie knew she had to call Lil, who would be worried about her. She owed it to her friend, who'd always been there for Evie, to see if she'd found the happiness she deserved. Evie would just have to pretend that talking about love didn't grind to dust what was left of her heart.

Lil must have been hovering by the phone on the landing because she answered after only a few rings. 'Ordinarily, I'd be congratulating you for finding another bed to lie in for the night. But Tommy said you'd left last night without a word.

So you weren't with him, and you wouldn't have been with any other man. Where are you?'

'At the Plaza.'

Lil snorted with laughter. 'And I'm Lillian Gish.'

'You can telephone me here if you want to check.'

Lil was quiet. 'So you're at the Plaza. It's more serious than I thought. What happened?'

'He broke my heart.'

'That doesn't sound like Tommy.'

'We both had an inflated idea of Tommy.'

'But he doesn't know what he's supposed to have done wrong.'

'Which makes it worse.'

Lil sighed. 'He'll come here looking for you. He's that kind of guy.'

'Tell him I don't want to see him.'

'Evie —'

'Enough about me. How about you and Leo?'

'We don't have to talk about that.'

'Yes we do.'

Lil's giggle said it all. 'It was simpatico. Better than anything. Who knew that the goods had been sitting right under my nose the whole time?'

Evie whacked a smile on her face. 'I want to hear all about it. But I've got to get to the hospital. I'll telephone later.'

Dressed, shod, and armed with two more nights on the house at the Plaza, Evie set off along Central Park South, past the horse-drawn cabs that still took those in search of romance for a ride through Manhattan's verdant heart. Her luck was holding: Thomas wasn't waiting at the college when she arrived. She had a lecture to attend, then she was due at the Vanderbilt

Clinic. Her day and her head would be fully occupied. No time for any more thoughts of Thomas.

Evie went to her lecture, dutifully took notes, then realised she had half an hour to spare before she needed to make her way to the clinic. More empty time. To fill it, she decided to check on Mrs O'Rourke at the hospital, the one place on earth where – even if nobody else thought so – Evie knew she belonged.

She was walking into the ward when she heard Francis call her name.

'Do you have another infection you're too queasy to manage?' she asked. 'Oh no, that can't be it, it's not lunchtime. You only need me when I'm eating.'

'I need some help,' Francis said.

'From me?' Evie couldn't quite believe it but he sounded nervous.

'Kingsley's out at a Medical Association lunch.'

'I'm supposed to be at the clinic soon. Who's rostered on today?'

'Stevenson.'

'Well, ask him. You can only boss me around when I'm actually working under you.'

'Stevenson couldn't help deliver a baby if it crawled out by itself. Things aren't going well.'

Four words. Four words that none of the doctors had ever said to her before; they'd never diminish themselves by letting a woman know something was wrong. Evie took a proper look at Francis and saw that his face was dotted with sweat and his cheeks were red, like those of a child caught stealing.

'I need to change,' she said. She replaced the beautiful dress and shoes with something old and crumpled from her locker and was scrubbing her hands when Francis came to find her.

'Hurry up,' he said.

'I haven't scrubbed enough.'

'You need to come now.'

Still expecting a mildly inflamed situation, perhaps a tired mother and a second stage that was taking too long, or a breech presentation, Evie walked over to see what all the fuss was about.

One look was sufficient for her to say, 'There's too much blood.'

'I know.'

'What happened?'

'It's a brow presentation. I attempted podalic version.'

Evie moved her stethoscope higher, lower, further around to the right, and heard a beat that was too slow. 'You've carried out podalic version before?'

'No.'

'You've seen Kingsley do it?'

'No.'

'You've seen Manners do it?'

'No.' Francis looked helplessly at Evie. Even the nurses were looking at Evie, obviously having witnessed Francis's bumbling and unwilling to trust him further.

Evie took a breath. She said as calmly as possible given that there was a stupefied woman lying on the delivery table and a situation that, based on what Evie could hear in the stethoscope and see in all its red glory on the bed, didn't look good, 'Tell me you know something more about brow presentations and podalic version than what you were taught in lectures.'

'I don't. But you've seen it,' the nurse said.

'*Once!* That doesn't make me an expert. I was standing by the wall with Kingsley's head in the way, which is a bit like standing on top of this building and watching from behind a pillar while an ant carries a crumb down an anthole!'

'It didn't work. It's still a brow presentation and it's taking too long,' he said pleadingly.

'I can see that! You've given the mother too much scopolamine. She won't be capable of doing any pushing.'

'She was screaming.'

'All women scream in labour. You'd scream if you had a football coming out of your anus. And knocking yourself out wouldn't make it any easier to extract.' Evie began to examine the patient. 'It's a face presentation, not brow. It must have rotated. But why is there so much blood?'

All the risks of podalic version, where a doctor reached up past the cervix and grasped the baby's foot to turn it into a more favourable position, were scribing themselves across Evie's mind in white chalk, the key risk being uterine rupture and haemorrhage, which she hoped she wasn't seeing now. The mother was too pale, or perhaps that was just in contrast to the blood, red as Bea's oriental silk robe and just as shocking. Unaccountably, Francis seemed to be relaxing, as if the situation was more under control than the quantity of blood and the slow rate of the foetal heart would suggest.

'I thought at first it was breech,' he said.

'That's a mouth I'm feeling, not an anus. An ass like you ought to be able to tell the difference. This baby had better be posterior,' Evie muttered as she palpated. 'Damn!' She turned to one of the nurses. 'Send someone to wherever Kingsley's having lunch and tell him to come back now. And get Matron. Check the mother's vitals.'

'Matron's sick,' the nurse replied. 'Sister Veronica's in charge today, but she's been called over to the Vanderbilt Clinic. There's a woman in labour over there.'

'Of course there is,' snapped Evie. 'Everyone's in labour at the wrong place and the wrong time today.'

'Is it posterior?' Francis asked hopefully.

'No. And you should have known that before now.'

'The baby descended more quickly than I expected.'

'Yes, but what is it, her fifth baby? They fall out with one contraction. And you probably brought it down when you were attempting version. How is it possible for you to be an intern and not know this?' Evie placed her hands on the bed and shook her head.

Her mind desperately flicked through the scribbled pages of her lecture notes. There was a chance they'd be lucky, that the baby would rotate and present anteriorly, which Evie might be able to manage. But how long should she wait? If the rotation had occurred as much as it was going to spontaneously and the baby was stuck facing the wrong way, the only option was a caesarean, which she couldn't do, and nor could Francis without Kingsley present. But Kingsley wasn't here and Francis was clearly incompetent. There was nobody else.

'Wake the mother up. You got her into this, you can at least help get her out of it,' Evie said.

'What are you going to do?' asked Francis. He was looking at Evie as if she was Jesus Christ and would perform the previously unheard-of miracle of final-year medical student delivering a baby presenting as left mentum posterior.

'Check the baby again. Unless you'd prefer to?'

'No. You seem to know what you're doing.' He began to try to rouse the mother.

Or at least I'm pretending to, thought Evie, as she felt once more into the birth canal and breathed a sigh of relief. The chin was securely in an anterior position. 'We're in business. I'm going to apply pressure to the brow while you deliver.'

'Right,' said Francis as he shifted back to the bottom of the bed.

'You need to be quick. There's barely a heartbeat.'

Francis cut the episiotomy, took up the forceps and placed them around the baby's head. 'The neck isn't flexed enough. I can't deliver the chin.'

'You need to control the head. Hurry up!'

'I'm trying!' Francis's head twitched to the right, a motion Evie could see was involuntary, as it happened again a few seconds later. His face was awash with sweat and, as far as Evie could tell, he wasn't doing anything other than placing his hands on the forceps and hoping for the best.

Evie took out her stethoscope and listened again. 'I can't hear anything. We have to get it out.'

'What do you think I'm trying to do?' Francis retorted.

'Pull harder! And on a different angle. You don't want to hyperextend the neck. Raise the handles of the forceps higher!'

No reply from Francis. Evie watched the clock tick past the seconds: fifteen, thirty, then sixty seconds, and Evie could see no improvement in the position of the baby. Francis was pulling with more force now but the angle of the forceps looked wrong to her; all she could see was the baby's neck extended to a degree that was dangerous. Then his head began to twitch in time with the second hand on the clock.

Evie lifted up the mother's eyelids. Her pupils were dilated. Dead eyes, Evie thought. Why am I always haunted by eyes?

'Move over.' Unable to watch any longer, Evie butted Francis out of the way with her hip. She withdrew the forceps and placed her hands on the baby's head firmly, guiding and controlling until she could get the chin out. That was all she had to do, because then the mouth, nose, eyes, brow, anterior fontanelle and finally the occiput would all follow. Downward traction first, she recalled, and thus she pulled.

Within two minutes she had the chin. 'The baby's coming! Help the mother!' she shouted to Francis, but she realised he wasn't looking at her. He was staring over her shoulder towards the door and Evie felt the sudden presence of Dr Kingsley in the room, but she couldn't turn because she was delivering a baby.

Then it was out. Evie could see that there was extensive oedema of the trachea. The baby would need help to breathe. Its head was monstrously distended. There was a gush of blood – too much blood – and Evie knew that her fears had been well founded; the mother was haemorrhaging. Francis's attempts at podalic version had hurt rather than helped.

'Step back!' Dr Kingsley shouted. Evie did as she was told, but only after she'd given the baby to the paediatrician, who'd arrived hot on the heels of Dr Kingsley, and urged him to check its airways.

There was a rush of hands to the mother. Now there were more doctors in the room than there had been for the past half hour – was it really only half an hour since Francis had called her name? Evie stood back against the wall in her accustomed position and watched as the mother bled all over the floor, and the baby stubbornly refused to allow a tube to be inserted into its bruised and swollen larynx.

Evie knew it would be her fault. She had been the one holding the baby when Dr Kingsley walked in.

And perhaps it was her fault. Who could say for certain that it was Francis who had caused the oedema, or that his ridiculous attempts at podalic version had caused the mother to haemorrhage? What if Evie had done something wrong? She'd been tired. Distracted. Upset. And she was only a medical student. She wasn't supposed to be delivering babies who presented as anything other than routine.

'The neck is broken,' the paediatrician said.

Oh God. Evie could see Francis's hands on the forceps, pulling on the wrong angle, attempting to shift the position of the head and instead breaking the baby's neck. And her hands on the baby's head. She had pulled too.

Instead of helping, Evie had been party to murder. At last Dr Kingsley had found something to blame Evie for.

~

The baby died. The mother died. Both things happened at the Sloane Hospital for Women from time to time, but mostly not together.

As soon as Evie heard, she ran. Down the stairs, outside, but then she didn't know where to go. The college building was like a second home, so she went in there. In the west corridor, she hurried past the students' reception room, and the study room where she spent large parts of her days when she wasn't clerking at the hospital or the clinic. The osteology cabinet that she'd regarded with awe nearly three years before when she'd started summer school was still there, a little lending library of bones and skeletons. How she wished she could exchange the last fine grains of her heart to recapture the wonderment and promise of that day, when she'd thought that becoming an obstetrician was a glorious and useful thing, when she'd believed that Thomas Whitman was a good man.

She kept running, up to the second floor, past the college museum and on to the third floor. At last she reached the dissecting room on the top floor and she had to stop. There was nowhere left to go. She'd once thought this room was marvellous, a hundred and five feet long, with skylights flooding sunshine onto the tables where the students worked. She remembered the first time she'd worked in the room; the body of a pauper woman was laid out in front of her and Evie had seen inside a womb, to that remarkable place where a child could grow. Now when she closed her eyes all she could see was the mother and baby she'd failed. They were sitting on the table before her, two angels, their white robes stained red with blood. They held out their hands to Evie and said, *Why didn't you help us?* Evie opened her eyes and the ghostly manifestation of her guilt disappeared, but she knew it would be back again that night, in her dreams.

Her mind circled around the thought: was it Francis who'd pulled the baby's head at the wrong angle or was it Evie? Regardless, nobody had survived. She deserved to be punished. She could run from Thomas and desperately push away the crushing sadness she felt whenever she thought of him, but she couldn't run away from a mother and a child who'd been harmed in her hands. She set her shoulders, retraced her steps back down through the college, walked back to the hospital and knocked on Dr Brewer's door.

'Come in.'

Dr Kingsley was there, grim, unsmiling. Francis was there too. He didn't meet Evie's eye.

'I'll speak to Miss Lockhart alone, gentlemen,' Dr Brewer said, his tone revealing nothing.

Dr Kingsley and Francis left without acknowledging her existence. She was worse than ignored. She was invisible.

'Sit down,' said Dr Brewer. 'I've checked your roster. You were supposed to be at the Vanderbilt Clinic.'

'I came to see Mrs O'Rourke.'

'You were in the delivery room.'

'Dr Sumner asked me to assist him. I thought it would be wrong to leave him on his own to deal with a difficult situation.'

'He seems happy to leave you to deal with this difficult situation on your own.' Dr Brewer reached for the crystal heart paperweight. 'I bought this the first time I delivered a stillborn child,' he said, matter-of-factly.

It was not what Evie had expected him to say.

'I wanted it to remind me of something,' Dr Brewer continued. 'That in obstetrics, one wrong move . . .' He stopped and opened his hand and the paperweight began to drop, at speed, towards the desk. Evie found her arm moving reflexively, without thought, to grab the heart, to break its fall. '. . . can be catastrophic,' Dr Brewer finished. 'Two lives are at stake.'

Evie stared at the glass heart in her hand.

'According to Dr Kingsley, you have an instinct for obstetrics. But you speak and act without thought.' Dr Brewer held out his hand for the paperweight.

Evie held onto the crystal a moment longer. She remembered being in the delivery room and how she'd thought through the steps she'd been taught in the lectures. She'd visualised the correct angle at which to deliver the baby. She hadn't been thinking of Thomas. She'd been thinking only of the woman on the bed, and of the baby. And she was tired, but not that tired. She would never have helped if she was so tired she couldn't function. She hadn't acted without thought. Dr Brewer and Dr Kingsley were wrong.

But she also saw that she should have done more to find a doctor who knew how to deliver a face presentation. She should have done anything other than follow Francis into the delivery room as if she knew what she was doing. She'd been trying to prove herself, and two people had died. Now, by telling her that Dr Kingsley thought she had an instinct for obstetrics, praise she'd always craved, Dr Brewer was delivering her final damnation. Giving her the encouragement she'd always craved right before he took everything away.

She tipped the heart into Dr Brewer's hand.

'Dr Kingsley has recommended that you and Francis Sumner go out on the ambulance service at Bellevue for the remainder of semester,' he said. 'If something goes wrong out there, you won't be sitting your final examinations with the rest of your group next month.'

The ambulance service. The one place where things were most likely to go wrong. She'd have as much chance of surviving that as a drunk locked in a gin mill. Dr Kingsley's chosen punishment would be a quick and effective way of ending her career before it had begun.

'The student who achieves the highest marks in their final examinations will be able to choose from the internships on offer,' Dr Brewer continued. 'That student will be guaranteed their first choice of position.'

Evie understood what he was saying. Nobody would offer her an internship at the Sloane next year unless she was the student who achieved the highest grades. But she'd be working the ambulance service while she was supposed to be studying. She'd have no time to prepare for her examinations. She had to make sure that no one, in all the emergencies she'd have to deal with, died in her hands. And she had to work with Francis, who'd hate her for his demotion, who'd gladly turn her in to save his own skin. Getting the highest grades and winning the internship she coveted was about as likely, in those circumstances, as becoming a nun.

'You should return home for the rest of the day. Report to the ambulance service tomorrow.' Dr Brewer dismissed her.

Evie left the room. Never had the walk down the hall taken so long. Everyone watched in silence as she passed. She didn't know what to do, other than return to the Plaza, sing and dance at Ziegfeld's, and stay awake for as long as she could so she wouldn't have any ghostly dreams.

'You need to write your report on today's incident before you leave,' Dr Kingsley called, loud enough for everyone to hear, as she passed his desk.

Evie nodded. She sat down and wrote slowly, each word a record of disaster.

What happened next cut Evie to the quick. Mrs O'Rourke, whose infection Evie had tried to heal, was taking a turn about the wards. When she saw Evie, she stepped back and pressed herself against the wall. She pointed. 'I heard what happened. I don't want that one anywhere near me.'

What have I got to show for coming to New York? Evie wondered as she walked away. A dead mother. A dead baby. An attachment to a man who'd lied to her, over and over again, while pretending to always be on her side. An attachment to a foundling child she was forbidden to see, a foundling child who was the result of the man Evie loved abandoning a woman who'd done nothing but trust him.

And now Evie had a reputation as a butcher.

Chapter Eighteen

When Evie put her white dress back on and returned to the Plaza that afternoon, having been banished from her clerkship, she had an unusual two hours to herself. Ordinarily she would have studied. What was the point of that now? She could try to visit Mary. But the thought of examining Mary's face for traces of Thomas turned her stomach. Thomas. Now that she'd thought of him once, she'd spend the whole afternoon thinking of him. Or if not him, of the mother and the baby who'd died. She closed her eyes. She needed something to do and she needed it now. She called down to William Dunning. 'Any chance you'll have a break soon? And is there a mahjong set around?'

'Certainly,' he replied.

'How would you like to spend your break on sandwiches, tea and mahjong in my room?'

'I'll be there shortly.'

The bellboy soon appeared with a plate of sandwiches — cucumber and potted crab — and a glass of whiskey.

'What happened to the tea?' Evie enquired.

'This seemed more suitable.'

'You're right.' Evie sipped the drink. 'Now, tell me about your sister.'

'She's eighteen and she's just started working in a typing pool. She's so proud to have money of her own.'

William's obvious love for his sister made Evie smile a little. 'Does she have a fella?'

'I don't think so.'

'Well, fellas are overrated. And then you'd only worry about her.'

'I do anyway.'

Evie sighed. 'Let her make her own mistakes. But with a brother like you, I'm sure she won't make many. Everybody needs a guardian angel.'

'Who's yours?'

'Usually, it's my friend Lil. But for now, it's you. So let's play.'

The bellboy played mahjong like Duke Ellington on piano – fast and with rhythm as the tiles clicked from his rack to the table in unexpected variations. The tempo of the game was quick and without pause. Evie lost three hands in a row but she was pretty sure Lil would never beat her again after all she'd just learned.

Then in the last round, William did something she'd heard of but never seen executed. 'I caught the moon from the bottom of the sea,' he said as he shifted his tiles to the top of his rack, exposing them; on the final tile he'd drawn from the wall was one perfect round spot. The moon. Caught as the last tile, and thus from the bottom of the sea. A moment of preciousness. Such things still existed.

Evie clapped her hands in admiration, happy to have been fairly beaten in honest combat, and happy not to have thought of Thomas or the hospital or the ambulance service for an hour.

She checked her watch. 'Have you ever been to the Ziegfeld Follies?'

'I haven't.'

'Swing by the stage door after your shift. I'll make sure they let you in.'

'You're a Ziegfeld Girl?' William asked, admiringly.

'Sure am. Sometimes I think I'm better at that than anything else. Maybe I ought to just enjoy a life of singing and dancing and the pleasures it brings and not worry about anything else.'

'If those pleasures make you happy.'

'They make everyone else happy. Why should I be any different?' Evie held out her hand. 'Thanks for a good match, William Dunning. Enjoy the show. Be sure to bring your sweetheart.'

'Thank you, Miss Lockhart. And you see, life is all carousels and Wonder Wheels. Nobody has given me tickets to the Follies before.'

'I hope you're right. I could do with my Wonder Wheel making its way up the other side.'

With one happy bellboy dispatched, Evie walked down to the New Amsterdam Theatre along the Great White Way, so called for its lights and billboards, the whiteness not a symbol of innocence but of the way it made everything shine like ambition. On one side of the street was showing *A Good Bad Woman* and *Ladies of the Evening*, a few doors down were *Bachelors' Brides* and *Flesh*, next was *The Devil Within* and *The Firebrand*. That was all before Forty-Second Street. Perhaps life was easier as a Broadway show, Evie thought. Everyone at the hospital thought she was a firebrand. She should take up her part in it properly, be the showgirl of whom nobody expected anything other than a wink and a giggle.

She left William Dunning's name at the stage door and made her way to the dressing rooms, which were unnaturally empty. Bob explained, 'Flo's bought ice-cream. Everyone's on the balcony.'

Ice-cream. On any other day, Evie would have been struck by the unexpected treat. Maybe it was a sign. That she was in the place she belonged.

She walked up the stairs and out onto the balcony and sat down next to Bea, who handed her a tub of strawberry ice-cream. Evie gave the spoon a long lick and then let her legs slip down over the edge, like the other girls. They were a row of half-made-up beauties in silk robes, like spring birds arranged in the branch of a tree, stockinged feet kicking the breeze.

'You look like you've had better days,' Bea said.

'I have.' Evie had to blink hard when Bea put an arm around her and brought Evie's head down to rest on her shoulder. A tear trickled down Evie's cheek. Bea used the tip of her finger to wipe it away and Evie was so glad that she didn't ask any more.

All the girls were quiet, watching the sky transform from late afternoon to dusk, which it seemed to do in an instant, as if Florenz Ziegfeld himself had dictated that the scene be changed and on with the show. The lights of the city and of the cars on the street turned on, frightening the shadows away, promising that not only would it be all right on the night, it would be all right forever and always. Evie wished she could believe it.

A few pedestrians looked up and exclaimed at the sight of the showgirls in a rare moment off-show. They looked girlish and vulnerable without their lipstick and feathers, some as young as sixteen, their dreams plain for all to see as they sat above the city they wished to make their mark on.

Below their feet was New York's spine, the width of Broadway leading through the theatre district and on to Madison Square, down to the triangular Flatiron Building and then Union Square, through Canal and finally out of grime and poverty and onto the yellow brick road of Wall Street, before terminating at the docks, where so many of New York's immigrant population had their first physical contact with the city. One street could tell the whole story of New York, Evie thought, and she noticed how many of the girls had their eyes turned uptown, towards riches and glory.

Then Bob arrived with a telegram from Ziegfeld, sent, as was his way, from the office at the back of the theatre to the girls on the roof. *Back to work*, it said. It continued on for another nine hundred words, as was also his way, with a pre-show chin-up spiel about how adored they all were, telling them that Ziegfeld wanted nothing more than to glorify the American girl.

Oh, they were glorified all right, thought Evie, looking around at the fresh, hopeful faces. Right up until they died young from too much opium and too little love, or they jumped out of a hotel window, or their livers failed from the drinking, or they simply got too old and spent their money too quick and died on a street corner from destitution. All the girls on the roof thought they'd be different from the ones who came before. But Evie suspected they wouldn't be any different at all. Perhaps neither would she.

One by one the girls stood up. They were chatting and laughing now, back to being sassy chorus girls, discarding their childish selves along with their ice-cream buckets and regaining their ambition to be the one driving away after the show in a Bentley to a party in Great Neck with a Wall Street businessman.

'Attagirl,' Bea said as Evie pulled herself up and they headed back down to the dressing room. 'Get your headdress on, the curtain up, the lights picking you out and you'll be the phoenix's feather.'

Evie was saved from replying by another girl hollering her name. 'Evie! Your fella's here again!'

Evie wanted nothing more than to hide. She hustled in to the dressing room, needing to get away from the stage door, away from Thomas.

Bea stopped her and raised her eyebrows. 'At this rate, I'll be expecting handcuffs.'

Evie shook her head, unable to interpret this one of Bea's many colourful expressions.

'You know, a ring on your left hand.'

'Can you tell him to leave?'

'You sure? His shoes looked like they were lined with hundred-dollar bills.'

'Please?'

'Is that what the tears were about up there?' Viv gestured to the roof.

Evie nodded.

'You won't mind if I flip up my skirt and show him my gams?'

'Show him whatever you like.' The words hurt to say but Evie tried her hardest to look as though she meant them.

With that, Bea was off to try her luck, but she came back looking disappointed. 'It was all about you. Could've taken off my robe and he wouldn't have noticed. He's going to wait at the stage door until after the show.'

'Then I'd better leave by the front door.'

Evie went through the motions that night, singing and moving about the stage as she was required to, but without any extra flair. She cast her eye over the audience and couldn't see Thomas. She saw William Dunning holding hands with his girl and she flicked him a smile. She saw Charles too. Whispering intimately into the ear of the woman beside him, who was definitely not Viola. He grinned at Evie and put his hand on the woman's leg, resting his fingers at the top of her thigh.

So many men wasting so much energy on keeping Evie in her place. Wouldn't it be easier if they let her do what she wanted? What did they honestly think would happen if they relinquished their control of her? As Charles continued to paw the woman beside him, eyes fixed on Evie, she understood that while it might be easy being a Ziegfeld Girl, it wasn't the forever she wanted. Because then every waking and sleeping minute of her life would be owned by somebody else.

As soon as the show was finished, she slipped back into her white dress and left with a crowd of people through the front doors. She sighed with relief when she made it to Fifth without anyone tapping her on the shoulder.

Once safely inside her room at the Plaza, she poured herself a whiskey from the flask William had left with her, finished it in one swallow and then lay on the floor, sinking into the plushness, cushioned like *putti* on a fresco cloud. She turned onto her side and looked through the window at the thousands of stars in the sky until she fell soundly and dreamlessly into an exhausted sleep.

~

The ringing of the telephone woke her and she had to lie still for a few moments, moving only her eyes, to work out where she was. Still on the floor where she had lain last night to feel the comfort of the silk rug against her skin, so tired and possibly drunk that she hadn't roused at all. Now it was morning and her neck felt as if it had been craning all night for a view of Rudolph Valentino on a film set.

Evie reached up her arm to the telephone. 'Hello?' she managed.

'A Miss Lillian Delancey for you,' said the desk clerk.

'Thank you.'

Lil's voice came down the line. 'So you really are at the Plaza. I'll have to come by for a drink.'

'You'd love the view. And the mahjong.'

Lil burst out laughing. 'You're the only girl I know who goes to the Plaza for the mahjong.'

'One of its many charms.' Evie didn't bother to sit up as she talked. The effort required was too great.

'Tommy was here last night and again this morning. You slipped through his fingers at the theatre.'

'Intentionally so.'

'I've never seen him like this, Evie. He's had girls chasing him all over New York and London since forever and he's always thought it was a bit of fun. He's never looked this sad before.'

Evie swallowed. Her mouth was dry from the whiskey, her eyes were damp from what Lil had said, and she wished it was the other way around.

'Tell him what's wrong,' said Lil. 'Don't see him again if you don't want to, but at least let him know why.'

'How's Leo?'

'Swell. But you're changing the subject.'

'Swell as in you've seen him every minute since the ball?'

'Yes, that kind of swell.'

Evie could hear the joy in Lil's voice, joy she was trying but failing to hide. 'Let's celebrate,' Evie said. 'I'll see you in the lobby at half past five. I'll be the one with whiskey and you'll be the one with champagne.'

~

It was hopeless. Evie watched as Francis performed a balletic tiptoe around the puddles of slop on the pavement outside the tenement in the East Village where the ambulance had been called. They'd be lucky to last an entire day without killing anyone. And where would that leave her?

Once inside, Francis stood in a corner of the room, careful not to touch anything, lest the dog excrement, or the buckets of diapers, or the scabs from the children's numerous scrapes and sores somehow leapt from their moorings and infected him with the trappings of poverty and filth. Evie did everything while he yelled instructions at her, some of which she followed and some of which she ignored, because he couldn't see what she was doing and he didn't appear to care. She spent the whole morning at each and every call-out inside her head, sorting through the lecture notes she'd committed to memory and the diagrams from *Gray's Anatomy* she'd revised, as well as recalling everything she could of the dissections she'd practised. She felt as if she'd learned more in one morning than she had in the last year of physiology. And she hadn't made a mistake, yet.

'If you'd been a man we'd have been sent to gynaecology rather than here,' said Francis grumpily as they left one block of apartments early in the morning.

'Of course you'd rather be injecting silver protein into gonorrhoeal patients than helping these people.' Evie gestured to the row of people sleeping on the fire escape to get away from the stuffiness of their tiny room. A rat was nosing its way between bodies.

As she replied to Francis, Evie felt a small piece of herself return. Perhaps her time on the ambulance service would prove to be a blessing. She had no time to think of anything other than the patient in trouble, no time for her mind to wander off to Thomas. And she was treating a range of medical conditions, most of which she would have to revise for her examinations. She was getting the best study preparation she possibly could.

So she climbed into the ambulance when it was called out, she worked on each patient, she delivered the patient to the hospital if necessary, reported her treatment and diagnosis, and set off again. In the afternoon, she'd return to the Plaza and spend fifteen minutes with Lil, long enough to find out about Leo but too short to discuss Thomas. That would leave her with half an hour to wash and walk to the theatre, where she'd perform until late at night. Then she'd collapse – hopefully, she thought as she tipped her head from side to side, onto the bed this time rather than the floor.

And she wouldn't think about Thomas Whitman ever again.

~

She wouldn't be the one with the whiskey, Evie decided as she walked up the steps of the Plaza. She'd be the one with the strong hot black coffee to give her the energy to expend on a song and a dance and a smile at the Follies before falling into bed.

William Dunning was waiting for her at the top of the steps.

'How'd you like the show?' she asked.

'It was excellent, Miss Lockhart. You're worth at least a week's stay at the Plaza.'

'I can see why you keep your job,' she teased.

'You might reconsider that if I tell you I've allowed a gentleman by the name of Mr Thomas Whitman to wait for you by the elevators all afternoon. I had no choice; he threatened to make a scene and I knew that would reflect badly on . . .' He trailed off apologetically.

Evie understood. 'On a woman who's been allowed to stay free of charge for a few nights after a hocus elevator entrapment.'

'Well, it mightn't be good to draw too much attention to yourself.'

'It's okay, William. He's a consequence I have to face sooner or later. Might as well handle it now.' And then it will be done, Evie added to herself.

'Please indicate if you need any assistance.'

'I'd better take this one on my own.'

Chapter Nineteen

Evie walked across the foyer to the elevator, wishing she'd worn the wonderful white silk dress of the day before, rather than the sturdy tan skirt and navy blouse she'd chosen from her locker as least likely to show the stains of her work. She looked rumpled and in need of a good press, as if she'd fallen to pieces and been unable to care for her own laundry.

God, it hurt when she saw Thomas.

He was standing between the elevators, cheeks stubbled and with his hair falling across his forehead, divine in his beauty. Evie wanted nothing more than to walk right over to him, run a hand down his cheek and kiss his lips. She forced herself to stand still, several feet away, and get no closer.

He watched her walk towards him and she could see that what Lil had said was true. He looked as if his heart was broken too. But she also knew what a master actor he was; after all, he'd had her convinced of his goodness for nearly three years.

'Evie,' he said, and he stepped towards her.

She backed away. 'Lil told you where I was.'

'Don't be mad at her. She was sick of me camping out on the doorstep.'

'Let's not do this here. Let's sit down.'

Thomas followed her to the overstuffed floral armchairs that were emptying of the afternoon tea crowd.

'I have ten minutes,' she said. 'Which should be enough.'

He reached out a hand towards her.

'Don't,' she said as she sat down. She waved away the overzealous waiter who was approaching with menus, as if they were about to have a cosy cup of tea and a scone, like a lady and gentleman in an English novel. The song tooting its brass through the room was 'I'll See You in My Dreams', which was all too true.

She decided to start with the question to which she most wanted the answer. 'Why did you tell me so many lies?'

He frowned. 'I've never lied to you, Evie.'

'You're lying now. I know you're Mary's father.' She looked directly at him as she said it, wanting to see how he'd sweet-talk the truth away.

Instead he shook his head, looking bewildered, as if of all the things he'd thought she might say, that was not even under consideration. 'Who's Mary?' he asked.

Evie laughed, a sharp and bitter sound. 'Mary, as you well know, is the baby who was born in Concord by the river. I've been visiting her. And you've been busily trying to stop me from visiting her, because you're her *father*.'

Thomas stared at her in consternation, his eyes wide. 'I thought you were mad about Winnie. I thought she must have told you that we kissed when I was in London. I was wondering how to make you believe the truth, which was that she kissed me one night when we were dancing and all I could think of, besides getting away from her, was you.'

Evie breathed in sharply. 'What about Mary?'

'I don't know why you think I'm her father. I'd never abandon a mother and child.'

Oh, he was good. She almost believed him. 'The hanky,' she said. 'The hanky you handed me to mop up the wine Charles spilled on me. I gave it to Mary. Why else would you have her hanky if you aren't her father?'

'Charles gave me that handkerchief,' Thomas said slowly, as if he was trying to understand what had happened. 'When I put on my jacket for the ball, the handkerchief I'd put in the pocket earlier wasn't there. Charles said he had a spare and not to trouble Barnes with getting another.'

'Charles gave it to you,' Evie repeated. Charles. Her mind struggled to piece together what Thomas had said. She wanted so much to believe him, to see the situation as it might have unfolded. Charles taking the handkerchief from Mary, knowing he'd be able to use it for something diabolical if only he waited long enough. Then, on the night of the ball, Charles stealing Thomas's handkerchief from his jacket, shadowing Thomas until he realised it was missing and then offering him Mary's. Charles had spilled the wine on Evie deliberately, knowing that Thomas would leap to her rescue and pass her something to mop it up. He'd hoped that Evie would believe what the evidence suggested: that Thomas was Mary's father.

'If Charles had Mary's handkerchief, then . . .' Evie faltered on the words. She tried again. 'Then he must be her father. He must have been the one visiting the Foundling, the one telling the sisters not to let me visit Mary.'

'Charles is the father of the baby born in Concord?' Thomas's jaw tightened, and his bewilderment of a few moments before was replaced by cold hard anger.

'He has to be.' Evie shook her head. Although she'd seen first-hand what Charles was capable of, she was still horrified that he could be so cold-hearted as to watch the mother of his child die alone by a river.

Neither Thomas nor Evie spoke for several moments as they tried to grasp not only what Charles had done to Rose and Mary, but what he'd done to them. Evie felt her shame at mistrusting Thomas grow and she could see that Thomas's eyes were as black as flint. Was it from rage at Charles, or rage at her?

'Evie, why didn't you tell me you'd been visiting the child?' Thomas asked at last.

'Because . . .' *Because there are so many things I longed to tell you,* Evie wanted to say, *but we've had so little time together.* How do you fit a lifetime of conversation into barely a dozen encounters? Encounters that Charles had tried to put an end to with a ruthlessness Evie could hardly believe he possessed. She felt as if she couldn't breathe. 'Charles tried to make me believe you were the father. That's how much he hates me. I'm so sorry.'

Thomas rubbed his jaw with his hand tiredly. 'No, he hates me. I'm president of the bank. Not Charles. I graduated top of my class at Harvard. Charles never graduated at all. Last week he came to a meeting with one of our biggest clients drunk and they nearly walked out. I had to ask him to take some time off. The way Charles feels stretches back to childhood, to everything he thinks I did first – or better – just to spite him. Except you. You were always his domain.'

'Until I was yours.' Evie said it without thinking and then it was too late to unsay it. An admission of the sure and certain knowledge that while she could survive without Thomas Whitman, she was only truly alive with him.

There were no words after that, just the two of them regarding each other across an elegant chinoiserie coffee table. All they wanted to say was caught in their eyes, a language that the other understood as instinctively as thought. It was a single perfect moment, full of what could happen, what was yet to happen, what they both hoped might happen.

Then Evie caught sight of William Dunning, her guardian angel, in her peripheral vision, pointing at his watch, and she shot out of the chair. 'Damn!'

Tommy laughed. 'That was unexpected.'

'I'm late. Hopefully I can bat my lashes at Bob and be forgiven. But I have to go. I've still gotta pay the rent.'

Tommy stood up too. Hang it, thought Evie. It was time to do something she'd been wanting to do for nearly three years.

She stepped over to Tommy, slipped her arms around him and ran her hands up the length of his back. He cupped her face in his hands, sliding his thumbs over her cheekbones, and her whole body yearned for him to touch her, everywhere. She pressed her lips against his.

Their mouths opened and they kissed, long and hard and without regard for anyone in the lounge, unaware that all eyes were turned their way, watching a man and a woman so clearly in love kiss for the very first time.

When at last they drew apart, Evie saw William Dunning smiling at her. Everyone else in the lounge was watching and smiling too, as if the whole of New York was cheering them on, enlivened by the thought that perhaps, against all odds, Thomas Whitman and Evelyn Lockhart might belong together.

It was impossible to do anything but smile. Bob didn't stand a chance as an effusive Evie rushed in the stage door, kissed him twice on each cheek, then took his hand and sent him into a spin. That night on the moon she glowed, as if a star itself had come down from the heavens and was now twinkling for all the world to see on a Broadway stage. Because tomorrow night she'd be meeting Lil and Leo and Tommy at Chumley's for a whole night of dancing and kissing, dancing and kissing. And when Chumley's closed its doors in the early hours of the morning, who knew what she and Thomas Whitman might do then?

When Evie jumped into the ambulance with Francis the next day, she was still full of the joy of the night before. She'd slept better than she had in a very long time. She felt rested, alert, ready for anything. Even hearing that they had to attend a woman giving birth couldn't get her down. It was the first birth she'd seen since the disaster at the hospital, but Evie wasn't nervous. Every successful doctor had at least one tragedy behind them. Maybe she'd had hers and she'd certainly learned from it.

A woman with a worried look on her face let them into the apartment. 'She's through there.' She pointed through an open doorway, and Francis pushed past Evie to go inside.

'Are you a neighbour?' Evie asked.

'Yes. Her husband works on the ships. She's been here by herself. I found one of the kids out on the landing with two days full in his nappy.'

'How long has she been in labour?'

The woman shrugged. 'Judging by the look of the kids, it's been a while.'

'Evie!' Francis called. 'Hurry up!'

'Coming!' Evie replied. She stopped when she saw the woman on the bed. She was unconscious limp and bloodless. Two children sat on the floor, huddled together, silent. Evie hurried them out of the room and closed the door. If she and Francis didn't act quickly, it looked as though the mother wouldn't survive.

'It's a face presentation,' Francis said grimly.

The look that passed between them spoke all too clearly of the last time they'd been in a room with a baby presenting face first. 'I'll look after the mother,' Francis was quick to add. 'You take care of the baby.'

'But you're the intern,' Evie protested. 'That's your job.'

'You're always asking for experience. Here's your chance.' Francis took the mother's head and began to check her pulse. Which left Evie at the bottom of the bed with the baby.

The examination proved that the baby was mentum posterior. Evie was certain, given the state of the mother, that the baby was impacted, and had been for some time. 'She needs a caesarean,' said Evie. 'We have to get her to the hospital.'

'She's too weak to move,' said Francis. 'What about a foetal heartbeat?'

'I can't hear one.'

'If the baby's dead, it's not worth risking the mother's life to move her to a hospital and have her undergo an operation she's unlikely to survive. You'll have to do a craniotomy to get the baby out.'

'A what?' Evie couldn't possibly have heard him properly.

'A craniotomy.'

She stared at him in horror. 'I can't.'

'If you don't, the mother will be dead in ten minutes. It'll be another death on your hands.' Francis spoke accusingly, as if the situation they were in was somehow all her fault.

You do it, Evie wanted to say, but she knew that Francis was a coward and that he wouldn't.

She also knew he was right. The mother wouldn't survive being moved down the stairs, into the ambulance and across town to the hospital. Which meant a craniotomy was the only option. But how could she extrude a baby's brain when her whole purpose in becoming a doctor was to help mothers and their babies to live?

'Do it now,' Francis ordered.

He was her superior. She was supposed to do what she was told. Even so, she checked for a heartbeat one last time. She placed her stethoscope all over the woman's abdomen but could hear nothing. The baby was almost certainly dead, and a craniotomy would therefore do nothing other than remove the obstruction and hopefully save the mother's life. 'Shouldn't you check too?' Evie asked Francis, needing to be sure.

'No. You should know how to check for a heartbeat.'

And you don't want blood on your hands. Evie understood all too well.

She opened her instrument bag and took out a perforator and a basiotribe, two instruments she'd never used before and had hoped never to have to use. She remembered listening in horror in the lectures as the craniotomy procedure was described, wondering how, in the modern world, such gruesome procedures were still performed.

As she stood there, about to do something barbaric, something that had to be done to save a woman's life, Evie realised she no longer felt any need to prove herself as a doctor. Because it wasn't about her. Nothing about Evie mattered right now. The point wasn't to be the one who helped people live; it was about being compassionate always, and regardless of the outcome. If you were the woman lying on the bed, would you want Francis, with his condescension and complete indifference, to be the one pulverising your baby's skull? Or would you rather someone like Evie did it, someone who had only ever wanted to help? Someone who would mourn for the baby because the mother was unable to.

When she'd finished, Evie sat on the floor of the tenement, heedless of the blood, and cradled the baby in her arms. She knew she was sobbing in huge, loud, gasping gulps. Swallowing snot and tears. But she didn't care what Francis or anyone else thought. She wasn't crying because she was scared. It was because she'd felt in her heart and in her body every cut she made. And she also knew she was, finally, a real doctor.

Chapter Twenty

'Come out with us anyway,' Lil said that night in their room at the boarding house. 'Come out and forget. You can't stay here by yourself and relive it.'

Evie let herself be talked into going out. She even put on the fabulous blue dress she'd worn the night she'd shared her first kiss with Leo. She let Lil make up her face so that she looked like a beautiful young woman without a care in the world. But every time she blinked, she saw herself piercing the baby's skull, and she wondered if it was possible to have too many cares, to be so weighed down by them that to even put one foot in front of the other was impossible.

Lil took her arm and walked her down the stairs from the attic room. 'You'll feel so much better when you see Tommy,' she said, and Evie thought this might be true: that to see his face would be such a relief, to know that there were still beautiful things left in the world.

But when they walked through the doors of Chumley's, all Evie could hear was the singer, sultry and sad, crooning to the beat of a slow but insistent tango, her voice like the cry of a motherless child calling out in its dreams for comfort it knows will never come.

How was it possible, Evie thought, looking at the singer, to sound so alone when the full glare of the spotlight was shining on you?

She saw Tommy's face, his smile turned to her with so much longing that she began to cry again, to cry as she had when the perforator first touched the baby's head, and now that she'd started she knew she could never stop so she turned and ran out of Chumley's, back to the boarding house, up the stairs, through the door and lay down on the bed, soaking the pillow with all that was left of her youth and her innocence.

Evie didn't know how long she'd lain there. She didn't know how Tommy had made it past Mrs Lomsky into the boarding house, or whether he'd knocked on Evie's door and she hadn't heard him. But suddenly he was standing beside the bed, and then he sat down and pulled her into his arms, whispering her name. 'Evie, my darling Evie.'

Which only made her cry all the more.

It took Evie another ten minutes to cry seemingly every tear she'd been saving since she'd moved to New York: tears over her parents acting as if she didn't exist; tears because she was tired from studying and working all day and dancing and singing all night; tears because she now knew that it was impossible for every baby to have a safe passage into and through this life; tears over Mary, who lay in her dormitory bed at night silent, awake, staring into the dark, unable even to imagine what she was missing – laughter and love and family – because you couldn't miss something you'd never known. Tears of gratitude over Tommy, that Tommy was here, that Tommy was the kind of man who would leave a gin joint and come after a woman and hold her while she ruined his jacket with weeping.

'I'm sorry,' she whispered eventually, pulling away from his embrace. 'Your jacket's the worse for wear now.'

'So's your dress.'

Evie looked down and saw that the flesh-coloured fabric that was supposed to partly conceal her cleavage was thoroughly soaked and not concealing anything. 'Oh,' she said, and blushed all the more when she saw that Tommy was looking at her with desire stamped deep in his dark black eyes.

His hand moved as if he was going to touch her, but then he stopped himself. Hang decorum, Evie thought. Unable to resist the pull between them, she leaned in and kissed his lips as hard as she could to let him know that all she wanted was his touch. She lifted her hands up to his chest and pushed back his jacket, her fingers fumbling with the buttons, damn buttons, on his shirt until finally she had them open and she could feel the flesh of Thomas Whitman under her palms. She heard his sharp intake of breath and felt the beat of his heart racing beneath her hands, his chest ridged with muscles that she traced with her fingertips.

Tommy returned Evie kiss for kiss but kept his hands decorously on her back until she felt his fists clench and he moved back. 'Evie, we need to stop.'

'But I want this more than anything.' She slipped off his shirt and reach around to unzip her dress. It puddled at her waist and she pressed her body against his. This time, Tommy forgot to be a gentleman.

Which was what Evie was hoping for.

Afterwards they both lay on their backs in the bed, staring up at the ceiling, unable to say anything, until Evie propped herself up on one elbow. 'Well, that was the most fun I've ever had,' she said.

Tommy laughed. He pulled her nearer so that her forearms were resting on his chest, and he idly traced his finger over her cheek and then through the curls of her hair. 'Whoever would have thought that Evelyn Lockhart, the loud girl from the house next door, would end up lying naked in a bed next to me, telling me she'd just had the most fun ever?'

It was Evie's turn to laugh. 'Nobody would have thought it, least of all me.'

Tommy hesitated before he said, 'I didn't realise you'd never been with a man before.'

Evie blushed. 'I was probably the only Ziegfeld virgin in existence. Flo would've charged extra if he'd known.' Then she spoke honestly, because she knew Tommy would understand. 'I've had enough meaningless kisses and groping hands to know there was no one else I wanted to be with like this. Until now.'

Tommy began to kiss her again, and Evie wondered how it was possible that even after everything they'd done, she still wasn't satisfied, still wanted more. There was a light tap at the door and she quickly sat up in time to see a piece of notepaper slipped underneath, then heard the sound of feet retreating down the staircase. Evie considered what the etiquette was when walking across the room in front of a man you'd just slept with, and then decided she didn't care. She climbed out of bed naked and walked over to the door to collect the note, smiling as she realised Tommy's eyes were on her the whole time.

'It's from Lil,' she said. 'She's going to spend the night elsewhere, so you can stay until I smuggle you out in the morning.'

'What will happen if Mrs Lomsky finds me?'

'I'm sure she has a dungeon somewhere that she'll lock you up in, and the rest of the girls in the house will eat you for breakfast.'

'I think I prefer the smuggling option.'

'Much safer, I'm sure. And that means we have at least another five or six hours together.'

'Perhaps you should come back here so we can make the most of it.'

Evie didn't need to be asked twice.

❧

Later: 'We have the worst timing,' Tommy said.

Evie rolled over to face him. 'I don't think I'm going to like this.'

'I've booked my passage to London. I'm leaving on Monday. I was going to tell you the night of the ball – I thought that would give us a week to spend together before I left, but . . .'

'But Charles got in the way,' Evie finished. 'For how long?'

Tommy sighed and sat up, leaning against the wall. 'I'd thought it might only be a few weeks. But now I think it'll be a few months. Maybe six.'

'That's a bit like hiding the cookie jar after giving someone their first taste.' Evie tried to hide her hurt beneath a snappy rejoinder, but Tommy saw it anyway.

'I'm sorry. The English lords I told you about are two of the wealthiest men in Britain. They want to do business in the States and they want to use Whitman's bank to do it. If I sign this deal with them, it'll make Whitman's one of the biggest banks in America. I have to do it.'

'I understand,' said Evie quietly.

'Business doesn't move quickly in London. That's why I think it'll take months, not weeks. Instead of just signing the deal, there'll be more dinners and weekends in the country than I –' Tommy broke off when he saw Evie's face. 'Now I'm making it sound as if I'm not going to be doing any work at all. The Bank of England also wants me to give some talks to a few of the gentlemen's clubs about doing business in America.'

'You really are very important, aren't you?' Evie teased.

'You mean you didn't know that already?'

Evie hit him with the pillow. 'Aren't English lords very stuffy? You'd have much more fun staying here with me.'

'English lords are very stuffy. I'll have to be on my best behaviour or they might take their business elsewhere. And there's nothing I'd rather do than stay here with you.' Tommy leaned over to kiss Evie, then noticed her sudden frown.

'I can put it off for a couple of weeks,' he said. 'Anything so you don't look so upset.'

Evie shook her head. 'No, don't put it off. I'm about to start my exams. I won't have much time to see you anyway. It's better if you go now and then, when you're back, I'll have finished my exams and I can spend every minute with you.' She smiled to push away the thought that had made her frown: *I'll have to be on my best behaviour,* Tommy had said. In nobody's mind would his best behaviour be defined as dating a showgirl who was also trying her hardest to become an obstetrician. But what were the chances of any English lords ever finding out about Evie Lockhart?

Tommy's next words distracted her entirely. 'Let's go to Newport tomorrow,' he said. 'Or today, if it's already morning. We'll use the family cottage. Spend the whole weekend together.'

'I have to work. Unlike you, I have a boss. Two, in fact.'

'Be sick. Have you ever been sick? Tell them you have a bacterial infection. You'll spread puerperal fever on the ward if you go in.'

'They'll know I'm not sick. I'm never sick. What about the Follies?'

'You have a rash. No man would touch a girl with a rash like the one you have.'

Evie began to laugh. 'You sure know how to flatter a girl.'

'I'm serious. Let's take this chance to have a weekend together. Fate or something kept us from noticing each other for the first twenty-odd years of our lives. Then when we finally did notice each other, I went to London. And now I'm going to London again. Let's beat fate to any other separations she may have planned for us.'

'So you *did* notice me before you left. I was never sure.' Evie couldn't help but smile at the thought of how they'd been back then, both too shy and uncertain to do anything other than write a few letters. Which thankfully wasn't the case now.

'Leo wrote to me to apologise; he told me he'd kissed you. If there'd been a boat at the dock leaving for New York that day, I would have jumped on it and come back and hit him and then kissed you.'

'Kiss me now.' Evie leaned down towards Tommy.

'You're beautiful, Evie. And strong and amazing and unlike anyone else I've ever known.' Tommy ran his hand up the back of her neck until it tangled in her hair, watching her eyes all the time. She moved her body on top of his as they kissed, her arms around his neck, his arms around her back, clinging to each other as if all they wanted was to be even closer than skin to skin.

He broke off for a moment to say, 'Does this mean you'll come to Newport?' and Evie whispered, 'Yes,' against his lips.

Chapter Twenty-One

*I*n the end, the smuggling was easy. Evie enlisted the help of all the girls at Mrs Lomsky's to create a diversion.

'Fire!' shouted Antonia.

It had the desired effect. Mrs Lomsky, usually so hard to rouse when anyone wanted anything from her, came crashing up the stairs like a Spanish bull. She was followed by a crowd of girls, who ensured that the landlady was hemmed into Antonia's room for as long as it took Tommy and Evie to run, laughing, down the stairs, hand in hand, and to kiss at the door until Evie had to push Tommy outside and close the door before their ruse was discovered.

Evie ran back up the stairs in time to hear Mrs Lomsky say, 'A girl should be able to tell a fire from a Lucky Strike.'

'I'm not as familiar with cigarettes as some are,' Antonia replied, which should have earned her a part on the silver screen, because everyone knew that Antonia couldn't stub out a gasper without lighting the next one off the end.

'Thanks!' Evie whispered as she passed.

'Has he got a brother?' Antonia asked hopefully.

Evie laughed. She closed the attic room door behind her and leaned against it, smiling so hard she thought she must surely look hopped up. Which she was, on love. It took her scarcely any time to throw some clothes into a bag, roll a scarf and tie it around her hair as a headband, letting the front curl fall over her forehead. She made her calls to the Follies and the hospital and was told to report to Dr Brewer when she returned on Monday. But even that didn't get her down and she stood waiting at the window, looking down into the street for Tommy's car, when Lil came crashing through the door.

'I'm in love,' Lil declared.

She took Evie by the hands and spun her around the room until they both fell onto their backs on the bed, laughing so loudly that Mrs Lomsky called up the stairs, 'Am I renting my rooms to ladies or monkeys?'

'Monkeys would know better than to live here,' Lil shouted back. 'There's more room in a cage at the zoo.'

'Shhh,' Evie whispered through her giggles.

When they had caught their breath, Evie asked, 'You're talking about Leo, I hope?'

'Yes! Even I don't move that fast onto another fella. Maybe I won't be moving at all.'

'Really?'

Lil looked shy for the first time in her life. 'Maybe.'

'I told him it was worth a try.'

'You told him?' Lil sat up, lit a cigarette and looked at Evie.

'That day we went to Saks together I saw Leo looking at you so goofily it had to be love. And I thought how perfect you'd be, like the Sheik and Diana. So I may have given him a push in your direction.'

'He never said a word. Thank you.'

'It was the least I could do.'

'It's the best thing anyone's ever done for me.' Lil kissed Evie on the forehead. 'Enough schmaltz. What about Tommy?'

'We're going to Newport for the weekend.'

'Whoopee! Even I've never been to the Whitmans' Newport digs. You won't want to come back here after a weekend of lollygagging there.'

'He said it was just a cottage.'

Lil snorted. 'And I'm just a coy girl from uptown.'

'Evelyn!' Mrs Lomsky's voice. 'Gentleman caller.'

Lil hugged Evie. 'Have a blast. And I want all the details when you get back.'

'I won't be sharing all of them!' Evie giggled as she grabbed her bag and left their room.

She would have slid down the bannister if Mrs Lomsky hadn't been eyeing Tommy suspiciously at the door. Given the landlady's presence, Evie and Tommy greeted each other with a chaste hello, which turned into a smooch of the best kind when the door was closed. Soon they were in the car and heading out of the city, laughing over all the night's misdeeds as the miles flew past.

They eventually fell into a comfortable silence, until Tommy said, 'I have to talk to Charles about Mary before I go.' He was no longer smiling.

'I'll do it.'

'I can't let you do that. He'll be furious and he'll take it out on you.'

'I know Mary. You don't know her,' Evie reasoned. 'And I know you'll do your best for her, but it's not the same. She's my responsibility because no one else cares. I have to be the one to talk to him.'

Tommy shook his head. 'I think it's a bad idea.'

'A bad idea is letting you do it. You two will just shout at each other and nothing will get resolved.' Evie put her hand on Tommy's leg. 'I know you want to do the right thing, but it'll be better this way.'

'I'll come with you.'

'No. If he saw the two of us together, it'd only make him worse. I'll talk to him next week, after you've gone. Which I still can't believe you're doing.'

'Neither can I.'

They were both quiet, trying to imagine several months apart. It seemed impossible.

'I'll put it off, go in two weeks' time,' Tommy said.

Evie shook her head. 'Let's get it over with now. It'll only get harder the longer we wait.'

He was silent for a moment, then sighed. 'I wish you weren't right.'

'Let's talk about something else.'

So Tommy said, 'What happened yesterday to make you cry like that?'

Yesterday. She looked out the window to the blue sea, the same colour as the dress she'd watermarked with tears. 'A baby was stuck. It was dead. The mother was dying. To save the mother I had to take out the brain of her half-born child.'

'Evie.' Tommy reached out his hand to take hers and he held it all the way to Newport. She was sure it was decidedly unsafe, but she was glad he did it anyway.

⌒

Around noon, the car turned into Bellevue Avenue in Newport and drove past glorious mansion after glorious mansion, each one bigger and grander and more European than the one before, their gardens full of huge blue heads of hydrangea. Tommy slowed at a set of open wrought-iron gates and proceeded up the driveway to a house built of white-grey stone, with pillars in front like mini skyscrapers. It resembled nothing less than a French chateau. Beyond the house, Evie could see an unspoiled vista of ocean, swirling and frothing like a blue silk skirt waltzing around a ballroom floor.

'You call this a cottage?' she said.

Tommy had the good grace to blush. 'Everyone calls their Newport home a cottage. It was habit.'

'I have nothing grand enough to wear in this cottage.'

'You can always wear nothing,' Tommy said.

The laugh bubbled out of Evie like champagne and she leaned across to kiss him.

A subtle throat-clearing interrupted them. 'Good day, sir.'

Evie pulled away reluctantly and stepped out of her opened door.

'Higgins,' said Thomas to the butler. 'This is Miss Lockhart.'

'*Miss* Lockhart. Welcome. Where shall I put the luggage?'

'In my room,' replied Thomas.

'All of it?'

'All of it.'

'Very well.' The butler picked up the suitcases, frowning.

'He doesn't approve,' whispered Evie.

'He doesn't need to.' Tommy took her hand. 'I'll show you the cottage. Then you can decide whether your clothes are inappropriate. I hope they will be.'

Evie laughed again and hit Tommy with her purse. 'The butler may not be so sure.'

As they walked inside, Evie tipped her head back and looked upwards. The entry was a marvellous void that soared up three storeys, ending at a skylight that let in the sun and warmth of the day. They walked past breakfast rooms and dining rooms and drawing rooms, all showing Mrs Whitman's impeccable taste; soft sea-green hues papered the walls, cool and buttery marble covered the floors. Opulence was reflected subtly in minutiae – a magnificent ormolu barometer clock, a set of lapis Sèvres mounted vases trimmed with gold, a chandelier falling like a veil of diamonds from the ceiling. The outer rooms were feminine in their colourings and furnishings, whereas the rooms in the centre, the heart of the house, were masculine. Sea-green gave way to burgundy, navy and a deeper woodland green in the library, the main sitting room and the private study.

'I'm not doing justice to your staircase,' Evie said as they walked upstairs. 'I should be wearing a gown with a train that ripples over the steps behind me.'

'We'd better come back here one day, with me in a suit and you in a gown, and we can dance on the lawn beneath the stars.'

Tommy made everything sound both easy, and possible. That there would be a *one day*. That they would come back. That they'd still be together. Evie squeezed his hand as if to seal in place the promise he'd made.

At last, after passing six bedrooms, they reached a seventh, into which Tommy showed Evie. 'This is the room I use. It's small, but all the gentlemen's rooms are. I can have one of the other rooms made up if you'd like more space.'

'You're forgetting I share an attic room in Greenwich Village. This is more than enough space for me.' Evie looked out the window to the sea, suddenly unsure what to do now that she was alone again in a room with Tommy.

'Let's go for a walk,' he said as if sensing her shyness. 'The path along the cliff is worth seeing.'

'Like everything here.'

'Especially you.'

How could she not kiss a man who said such things?

'Give me a minute to change.' Evie searched through her suitcase but her college and hospital clothes didn't look right, and she'd never imagined needing an outfit for strolling around Newport. She opened the wardrobe and found some clothes, Tommy's she presumed. She pulled on a pair of navy trousers that she tied at the waist with her scarf and rolled to mid-calf. She threw on a striped shirt and a boater hat that she found in the same wardrobe and, satisfied, made her way down the stairs.

Tommy smiled when he saw her. 'You'll have to keep the trousers and the hat. They look better on you.'

Evie slipped her arm through his and they walked along the top of a cliff that dropped steeply away to the waves below. The sun was warm but the breeze blew a little so it was neither too hot nor too cold, and the sea air carried away all the blood and death and anger that Evie had swallowed down over the past few months.

As they walked, Tommy pointed out the house where he'd drunk too much champagne as a sixteen-year-old and fallen asleep, unnoticed, in someone's carriage, waking to find himself being conveyed to Washington; and the particular rock that he and Charles had dared each other to jump from, into the roiling sea below, something he'd done only once, because his father had thrashed him when he found out about his ridiculous derring-do. They soon reached a point along the cliff where Evie could see the barest markings of a path down through the rocks to a strip of sandy beach below.

'That's the beach where we used to swim,' said Tommy. 'We'd scramble down the hill like a pair of mountain goats and splash around in the water for hours. We should go for a swim now.'

'I don't own a bathing costume. Visits to the seaside aren't a regular thing for me.'

'I dare you, Evelyn Lockhart, to go swimming with me in your underwear.'

Evie laughed, for what must have been the hundredth time since they'd arrived, and she realised how serious she'd become in the last few years, how seldom she laughed any more, except when she was with Lil. She used to laugh all the time, so much so that her parents would complain about the noise, claiming it gave them a headache, which only made Evie do it all the more. Tommy had brought happiness back into her life.

'I'll race you,' he said, and took off, scrabbling down the rocks, feet slipping here and there but somehow staying upright.

After a moment's hesitation, Evie followed, skidding to her bottom at one point but pulling herself up, determined to stay in sight of Tommy. He noticeably slowed before they reached the beach, allowing her to catch up to him, so they reached the sand together, flushed, out of breath and laughing some more. Once there, he wasted no time in shucking off his shirt. He hit the water first, diving in. Evie followed suit, remembering Concord summers spent at the pond until her skin was as red as a cherry. As she surfaced, both she and Tommy reached out at the same time, and drew each other as close as two separate bodies could ever be.

Tommy pushed the wet hair away from her cheeks so that he could see all of her face and she could see all of his. 'I love you, Evelyn Lockhart,' he said.

Evie reached up to kiss him, wrapping her legs around his waist and her arms around his neck. She could taste the salt of the man and the salt of the sea, the very essence of Thomas Whitman, and she knew that what she felt for him was something she'd be blessed with just once in a lifetime.

NATASHA LESTER

Their kiss deepened, mouths opening to one another, her breasts pressed against his chest with only the thin fabric of her brassiere coming between them. Evie felt the passion build as strong as the night before, and finally she breathed, 'Perhaps we'd better go back before I do something indecent.'

'Perhaps we should,' Thomas murmured against her lips.

They dressed quickly and hurried back to the cottage. She was shivering with cold when they reached the bedroom, so Thomas undressed her once more and wrapped her in an enormous soft towel. He lit the fire and sat her in front of it while he drew the bath. Then she lay in the warm water with her back against his chest, his arms around her waist. They talked of her studies and work – what she did and why – and of his, and when the water began to cool, he helped her out and dried all of her in front of the fire. He brushed her hair gently until the knots made by the sea were untangled, and when he was done, they went to bed.

~

Evie had been kissed and petted by men before Tommy. Being a Ziegfeld Girl guaranteed a steady supply of eager supplicants. At first she'd wanted to satisfy her curiosity but what she discovered was disappointing. None of those men seemed to realise that she might also seek pleasure in being touched until she felt like taking out her copy of *Gray's Anatomy* and showing them a diagram of the key points of interest.

Tommy knew. He understood that he could bring every inch of her skin to arousal, from her fingertips down to the soles of her feet.

And so his mouth moved down her neck and along her collarbone, his tongue swirled over her nipple before taking the whole of it inside his mouth. His hand moved at the same time, from her knee to her thigh, and grazed so lightly between her legs that, in the end, it was Evie saying, 'I can't wait any longer,' and Tommy grinning at her and saying, 'Neither can I.'

Evie sat astride Tommy, moving with him in perfect time. He reached up to take her breasts in his hands, fingers gently pulling on her nipples, then his thumb found the place between her legs that made her cry out and her whole body throb with want for him. They took a last breath together, cheek pressed to cheek, her arms stretched up over his head, hands clasped in his. Then an inhalation and a kiss, long and deep, which neither wished to break, because they knew that what they'd just shared was flawless.

On Sunday evening, after another day spent sleeping and kissing and making love, they decided to have an early dinner in the upstairs sitting room before heading back to the city, regardless of Higgins's insistence that they'd be more comfortable in the dining room. Tommy had said the sitting room was his mother's favourite, and Evie could see why. It had a wall of glass overlooking the sea, and the sky streaked with bronze. The cream and gold sofa made for two was turned towards the view, its back to the room, as if acknowledging that to be truly happy one needed only a lover and a house by the sea.

They were about to sit down to eat when there was a knock and Higgins appeared again. 'Sir.' He held something out for Tommy. 'Package from your mother.'

Tommy glanced at it, blushed slightly and tossed it onto the chiffonier. 'Thank you,' he said as Higgins nodded and stalked out.

'What is it?' Evie asked, curious to know what had made him look so bashful. She walked over to the chiffonier and saw that it was *The New Yorker* and that Tommy's face was on the cover. He looked handsome and serious, and Evie wanted to hug the magazine she was so proud. 'It's you!' she said and flipped open the pages.

'You don't need to look at it now,' he said, coming over and trying to take the magazine off her.

Evie batted his hands away. 'Of course I do! You should be showing everybody, not blushing and trying to hide it.'

She found the article and eagerly started reading. The opening paragraphs only made her prouder. They spoke of his business acumen, his tenacity, his place as one of America's rising stars in the world of business. That was Tommy they were talking about. Her Tommy!

But as she continued to read, her elation faded. Because she began to note other words: unblemished reputation, conservative, trustworthy, impeccable credentials. And then, in a paragraph near the end: *Rumours of a liaison with a Ziegfeld Girl have followed Mr Whitman, and also, ludicrously, rumours of an entanglement with a female medical student. But Mr Whitman has long been known as one of the city's most eligible bachelors, and now that he is set to double the family fortune overnight, it's likely that his return to Manhattan from London later in the year will see him looking to settle down, perhaps with some English blue blood.*

She tried to make light of it. 'English blue blood? Is that what you prefer?' She put on a smile as she said it, so he would know she was teasing.

'Newspapers love to make up stories where none exist.'

'I doubt that your English lords will be happy to read about your liaison with a Ziegfeld Girl and a ludicrous medical student.' Her tone was sober now.

Tommy stroked her face. 'I won't lie to you and say they'll be thrilled to see that. But it's one sentence. If I can't talk them around that, then I don't deserve their business.'

But one sentence buried at the end of the article could so easily become a newspaper headline, Evie thought. Like the salacious stories in the papers about Peaches and Edward 'Daddy' Browning, just because he was a wealthy real-estate developer and she was a sixteen-year-old who, amongst many other misdemeanours, wore a one-piece bathing suit that showed off her thighs on a day trip to Atlantic City. Or the interest in Evelyn Nesbit, the chorus girl involved with Manhattan's premier architect, Stanford White, whose life since his murder had been made into a story of illegitimate pregnancies and bawdy adventures on red velvet swings.

'What if you can't talk them round? And what about your father? What will he think when he reads this? He's given the bank to you and you're supposed to look after it, not –' Evie stopped, unsure how to finish. Not get entangled? Not have liaisons?

'I love you for being worried, but please don't be.' Tommy took her hand and led her to the sofa, pulling her down beside him. 'Maybe it's a good thing I'm going away. It'll give talk like this a chance to disappear and nobody will remember anything about it by the time I'm back. And you can concentrate on studying, rather than worrying.'

He smiled at her but she couldn't bring herself to smile back. 'Evie,' he said. 'Please? It's our last night together.'

'Shouldn't you be more concerned?'

'I love you. That's all I want to think about tonight.'

Tommy stood and drew her up. He touched her cheek with one hand and the other slid up her back. She moved closer so they were standing body to body and she felt a delicious tremor run through her.

He started to kiss her, deeply, and she couldn't help but respond. Soon she'd forgotten everything, because he was lifting her leg to wrap around him and her knickers were long gone, and she almost couldn't believe it but they were making love in the sitting room before a glass wall and with the butler in the house. But there was no question that she could stop herself, and nor could he.

'Hopefully nobody has a photograph of that for the newspaper,' she teased when they'd finished and collapsed together onto the rug.

Tommy laughed. 'Now that would be a scandal.' He kissed her again, both hands cupping her face. 'The boat leaves at five in the morning, so this is really our goodbye. I won't be able to kiss you like this when I drop you at the boarding house. How am I going to face each day knowing I can't see you?'

'I don't know how I will either.'

'I'll write you a letter every day.'

'Don't promise too much and disappoint me. Promise me once a week and then I'll be leaping for joy when there's more.'

'I won't disappoint you, Evie.'

'All the same, I prefer less extravagant vows.'

'So what should I expect from you?'

'I'll scribble you a line on the back of the calling cards that the men leave for me at the theatre,' she quipped, trying to push away the ache that was building inside. But when she looked at his face, she couldn't keep up the act. 'I'm quitting Ziegfeld's when I get back.'

'Why?'

'It's a week until study break. I have to do the best possible job in my exams. I'll only do that if I'm not working every night at the Follies. Luckily, Brewer's punishment of sending me out on the ambulance service has turned out to be the best thing I could have done. I've learned more there in a week than I would have in a year of studying my books. And I've saved enough money from Ziegfeld's to get me through until I can take up an internship next year. *If* I get one.'

She paused. She was so afraid he wouldn't come back, that he might realise, once in London, that someone like Winnie would be much more suitable for him and so she almost didn't tell him the real reason she wanted to stop working at the Follies. The thought of losing him made it difficult to breathe, as if it could literally cause her to choke to death on her sorrow. But he'd given her so much; he'd told her he loved her. She had to be as honest with him as he had been with her. She had to believe that he would come back to her; that if he didn't, it would kill him too.

'I'm quitting because I can't bear the thought of performing for any man, not now that I have you,' she said. 'And because I love you.'

And then he said something that almost made her cry, because it was beautiful and perfect and she realised that she wished with all her heart that it would come true. 'I'll marry you when I get back, Evie Lockhart,' he said.

'But –'

He put a finger against her lips. 'Don't say anything now. Think about it while I'm away and you might come to realise it isn't impossible.'

She kissed him as hard as she could then, wanting to make the memory of it last for all of the long months ahead.

Chapter Twenty-Two

Evie was lying awake in her bed at the boarding house at five in the morning when Thomas's ship pulled out of the harbour. She'd been up until after midnight telling Lil all about her wonderful weekend, but she hadn't mentioned Thomas's proposal. It was too new and precious an idea to give voice to just yet. Because it was ridiculous to think of someone like Thomas marrying a woman like her, but Evie wanted to stay on the side of hope and believe that maybe it could happen.

And while she felt like this, more optimistic than she had in a long time, she'd do two things. Report to Dr Brewer as requested and face the inevitable music about the craniotomy. Then she'd talk to Charles about Mary.

～

When she arrived at the hospital promptly at nine, the first person she saw was Francis, walking downstairs towards the main doors. His tic had returned, his shirt was untucked and he was carrying a box.

'What are you doing?' Evie asked.

Francis didn't reply, just strode past her. Evie quickened her pace and ran up to the ward.

'What happened to Dr Sumner?' she asked a nurse.

'He was asked to leave,' the nurse whispered, her eyes wide.

'And go where?'

'Nowhere. He's been fired.'

Evie's stomach dropped to the floor. She wanted to sit down. They'd fired Francis. They'd run her out of town.

She knocked on the door of Dr Brewer's office.

'Miss Lockhart.' The dean of the medical school opened the door. They really must be throwing her out if they'd called him in too. But he only said, 'We hope you're feeling better?'

'What?' Evie blurted. His demeanour was so at odds with the supercilious man she'd encountered at her admissions interview that she entirely forgot both her manners and that she was supposed to have been sick on the weekend. 'Thank you, I'm fine.' She eyed both men warily. Dr Brewer avoided her gaze and the dean's face was impassive, giving nothing away. What was going on?

Dr Brewer cleared his throat and the dean looked at him expectantly. 'We apologise, Miss Lockhart, for Friday's . . . situation,' said Dr Brewer so coldly that Evie hoped his gums might freeze to his lips.

'You apologise?' she asked, stunned.

'We understand that you might find an apology difficult to accept,' the dean said. 'The college rules list a set of procedures that no student is to perform. And Dr Sumner ordered you to perform one of those procedures, which was in clear violation of the rules. We hope an apology will ensure that you won't feel the need to mention the situation again.'

In her shock, Evie almost laughed. It seemed the hospital and the college were in as much trouble as a naked President snapped by a press hound while in the company of his mistress. If anyone found out that a student had been ordered to perform a procedure she wasn't allowed to conduct, the college's reputation, and the hospital's, would be seriously harmed. The Sloane family, who funded the hospital and who were already baulking at requests to cover bigger and bigger deficits, would be horrified at any hint of impropriety.

Evie could now guess what had happened. Francis must have rushed in to see Dr Brewer, gleeful with the news that Evie Lockhart had killed another patient by performing a craniotomy. Francis was too stupid to have thought about the college rules. And Evie had handed over her notes to the hospital with the mother, so Dr Brewer couldn't pretend it had never happened. Evie would survive. Francis wouldn't. Who'd have thought things would turn out like this?

She could exult in this moment. But there was a certain strength in being magnanimous. In shutting her smart mouth. In making Dr Brewer see that there was another way to behave. 'Thank you, gentlemen,' was all she said.

That stunned them both. But not for long. 'I'm placing you on light duties,' Dr Brewer added, barely able to hide his fury at having to apologise to her.

'I'll stay on the ambulance service until we break for exams,' Evie replied.

'Why?'

'Because I'm learning more out there than I've ever been allowed to learn in here. You've given me a wonderful opportunity to thoroughly prepare for my examinations. Maybe I'll get top marks after all.' Evie smiled at Dr Brewer as she spoke, as if she was grateful to him. He looked as if he'd like to hurl the heart-shaped paperweight at her, just as she'd wanted to toss it at his framed certificates not long ago. How things had changed.

~

After she'd calmed herself, Evie went to the morgue – that place devoid of sensory detail; colourless, lifeless, silent, and strangely odourless once the bodies had been packed away. Today she wanted to find the baby she'd performed the craniotomy on. Someone else was already there, she saw, visiting the body of a mother: a mother who was now just a memory to a downtown family, another death to buttress the statistics.

It was Dr Kingsley. He didn't notice Evie enter, because he was studying the face of a dead woman. He tucked a piece of loose hair behind her ear. Evie was so shocked to see this small act of kindness that she gasped. Dr Kingsley looked around.

'I-I came to see the baby,' she stuttered, wanting to cover her eyes rather than see Dr Kingsley exposed.

'The first craniotomy is something you never recover from.'

Evie nodded, sensing the truth of this. It was why she'd come to the morgue. Because now there were three babies who would always be with her, one alive and two dead. The one from the river. The one with the broken neck. And now this one.

'It was the correct procedure in the circumstances,' Dr Kingsley said.

For the second time that morning, Evie nearly said, *What?* But then Dr Kingsley's face grew severe again and he snapped, 'You're due out on the ambulance in less than five minutes. You can't afford to be late.'

Well, I'll be damned, thought Evie. Perhaps that was what happened to you when you saw so much death. You had to hide the pain away behind something. Evie knew she wouldn't hide hers the same way Dr Kingsley did, behind a disagreeable exterior; she'd hide it here, in the morgue, visiting every patient who lost their life under her care.

No one asked you to do this, Evelyn Lockhart, she told herself. *You wanted to. So do it. And do it well.*

And perhaps Dr Kingsley was warning her not to be late because he was looking out for her, rather than scolding her.

~

After her shift, Evie changed into the glorious white dress from Bergdorf's that she'd brought with her in preparation. Then, on the way to see Charles, she stopped at the Foundling and found the door as resolutely barred against her as it had been the last time. Charles must be paying them a fortune to keep her out, but she knew he could afford it.

Evie slipped a note under the door, addressed to Mary, hoping that Sister Margaret would find it. Every time she thought of Mary in there, with no one to visit her, wondering why Evie had abandoned her, it broke her heart. But tears wouldn't serve her in her meeting with Charles. She needed something more like rage to get her through the next part of the day, to get under his skin, to provoke him into acknowledging and caring for his daughter. Surely, after this morning's victory, the meeting with Charles would go well too. She told herself this to cover the anxiousness she felt at the thought of confronting him.

She rang the bell and the butler asked her to wait in the hall, an instruction she chose to disregard. Following him into Charles's study, she noticed that the heads hung on the walls had been added to with a hyena and a zebra.

'Going for a touch of the exotic, are you?' she enquired, and Charles shot up from his seat, where he'd been talking on the telephone, dressed in a brocade smoking jacket with a velvet shawl collar. For once, Evie felt the advantage of being more suitably clothed for their meeting than he was.

'I'll telephone later.' He hung up and advanced on Evie as if she was a stray animal whose head he'd like to hang too.

'Trouble is, I don't think there's a lot you can do to add any class to this room,' Evie continued. 'Except, perhaps, remove yourself from it.' She smiled at him, walked over to the decanter on his desk and poured herself a drink. 'Cheers.'

'Always a pleasure, Evie,' said Charles. 'What do you want?' He nodded to the butler, who withdrew with one last baleful glance at Evie, as if to let her know he'd come to Charles's rescue if needed.

'For you to take responsibility for what's yours.' Evie held both hands around her glass to stop them from shaking as the memory of Charles's mouth on hers and Charles's hand down the front of her dress flashed in her mind.

'Viola has plenty of money to buy dresses. And, when the time comes, my child will be well cared for.'

'It's not Viola's child I'm talking about.'

'Don't tell me you've fallen prey to the men at Ziegfeld's and have a child on the way?' Charles stepped closer.

'No, Charles. I mean Mary. The child you abandoned at the Foundling.' Evie put down her glass, feeling stronger now.

Charles began to laugh. 'So you've put two and two together and come up with me? Which means you and Tommy must have had a reunion, if you know he's not the bastard child's father.'

'We were talking about Mary.'

Charles picked up Evie's glass and swallowed the contents. 'Yes, let's talk about this girl you've taken such a liking to. It's a good thing you have, because I think you'll find she's your sister.' He held up Evie's empty glass. 'Another drink?'

Evie frowned. 'What do you mean? If she's your daughter then that makes her the sister of the child Viola's carrying.'

'I think I'll have another.' Charles didn't bother to get a clean glass. He poured brandy straight into Evie's, speaking conversationally over his shoulder. 'It makes her your sister because your father is her father.'

Evie started to laugh but Charles talked right over her. 'Your father had a liking for, shall we say, demonstrating rather than theorising with the Radcliffe girls who came over to Harvard for the lectures he gave. The child in the Foundling probably isn't the only one. But it's the only one unlucky enough to have been born on your father's doorstep.'

Evie wiped away her tears of laughter; she'd underestimated Charles's talent for the farcical. 'Charlie, earlier you tried to make me believe Tommy was Mary's father. I'm not such a dumb Dora as you think.'

'Oh no, you're a real high hat, Evie. But think about it anyway. Your father asked me to pay off the nuns to keep you away, which I did, because I don't want my wife tainted by the association. But when I saw the girl for myself I couldn't understand how you hadn't figured it out. Don't you think she looks just a bit like you?'

A memory surfaced. The woman complimenting her on her daughter that afternoon near Central Park. Evie had thought the woman's assumption came from the way Evie and Mary were embracing, but perhaps it was more than that. There *was* a resemblance between them. Another memory: the bonnet from the hospital in Concord. Evie had thought it looked familiar. Now that she had a reason to fit the mahjong tiles in the wall, she suddenly remembered that a week or so before Mary's birth at the river, Evie and her mother had cleared out a chest of her and Viola's old baby things to give to the hospital fair. Her mother had put the box of unwanted items in her father's study, ready to be moved. That was why the bonnet the nurse had given Evie at the hospital was so familiar. It was one of Evie's old bonnets. And when Mary had pulled it down over her head, Evie had felt a jolt of recognition that she'd not understood at the time; now, though, it seemed so incredibly obvious. How could she not have seen it before?

She sat down in the nearest chair. How extraordinary. She'd been visiting her sister at the Foundling all along. 'Telephone the Foundling and tell them I can visit Mary again,' she said.

'Why should I?'

'Because you don't want me to tell Viola she has another sister.'

She saw Charles clench his jaw and knew she'd struck home. That he would do as she'd asked. But rather than respond, Charles turned the subject to something more disquieting.

'Will we be hearing any wedding bells in the near future?' he asked.

Evie held her head high. Why should she lie? 'Thomas has asked me to marry him.'

Charles laughed again, as if what Evie had said was the greatest joke. 'He's a lucky fella to have someone like you, isn't he? The one woman in New York no one else would marry. You're going to let him suffer the social embarrassment of having a showgirl obstetrician for a wife? That's true love. Always thinking of yourself.' He pointed at the copy of *The New Yorker* on his desk, with Thomas on the cover and the article inside with its mocking lines about Evie.

Charles kept going. 'You think it'll be good for Tommy's reputation if he marries you? That the wives of his rich clients will have you over for afternoon tea so long as you've washed the syphilis off your hands and exchanged your feathers for a gown? That the newspapers will ever stop printing his name so long as it's joined to yours? Especially now that you have an illegitimate half-sister to add to your charms.'

Evie wanted to press her hands over her ears to block out what Charles was saying. For he was giving voice to her own doubts, her fear that marrying Thomas would do him more harm than good, that she was selfish to even think it was possible – all the things she didn't want to think about, because all she wanted to say was *Yes, of course I'll marry you.*

'If Thomas loses the bank's money because of his attachment to you, then I lose my money too,' Charles continued. 'Which means Viola loses her money. And so will your nephew or niece.'

More things Evie hadn't thought about. More people she would hurt, including Vi. More difficulties that couldn't really be put off until Thomas returned. She shut her eyes and saw Mary's face behind her closed lids, as if the wraith of a child had entered the room and was standing before Evie, saying, *Look at me. See who I am.*

No matter what, Evie knew she could not, ever again, turn her back on Mary. She opened her eyes and fled. Charles didn't stop her. He sat back down in his chair and sipped his brandy, relishing his victory.

She was almost at the front door when she heard her name.

'Evie?' Viola was standing in the hall, a very pregnant Viola, who looked bone tired and so much older than Evie remembered.

Evie reacted instinctively; without even thinking about it she led her sister over to the stairs near the entry and said, 'You need to sit down, Vi. You look worn out. Are you feeling all right? Have you been seeing the doctor?' It was almost a relief to concentrate on something so practical, so ordinary, rather than trying to rethink her entire life to take into account the fact that Mary was her own flesh and blood.

Viola laughed and batted Evie's hands away. 'All expectant mothers are tired.'

'But you look exhausted. I'll call the butler to fetch some tea.' Evie could arrange tea, at least. That was much simpler than anything else that had happened today.

Viola shook her head. 'No. Sit down beside me.'

So Evie did. For a moment, neither spoke. Evie's mind was full of one simple fact. They had another sister. It was remarkable. It was so astonishing that Evie could no longer remember or care about why she had ever been cross with Viola. Should she tell her about Mary?

'You've been dating Thomas,' Viola said.

Evie blushed as she considered whether dating was the right euphemism for their weekend in Newport. 'Yes.'

'I heard the end of your conversation with Charles. I know you want to think that because he's Charlie, what he's saying isn't true. And I'm not saying this because I don't want to lose our money. I'm saying it because I watched you and Thomas walk away together after you were here for dinner. I saw you look up at him and I knew that nobody had ever looked at me like that before and that nobody ever would. I don't want you to get hurt. Heartbreak isn't easy to live with.'

Evie's eyes filled with tears. She put her arm around Viola. How easy it was to let go of petty resentments now that they both knew how cruel the world could really be. 'I'm so sorry, Vi. I'm sorry that Charles isn't who we wanted him to be. But I think Tommy is.'

'And that's the problem. Thomas is even more of an idealist than you are. Especially when it comes to you. But he might not always have that luxury, especially if the newspapers get involved. I know it might be hard to believe, given the way I've behaved, but I'm worried about you.'

Evie wiped her eyes. 'My behaviour hasn't exactly been perfect either. But let's not talk about that now. Tell me what I can do to help you.'

'Nothing. I'll soon have my child. That's all I need now.' Viola smiled, and Evie was glad that one good thing might come out of her sister's marriage.

'I'll come back and see you tomorrow. You should rest today.'

'I will,' said Viola, and the two sisters stood up and walked towards the door together.

Before they reached it, Evie thought of something. 'Did you hear what Charles said about Mary?'

'Mary?' Viola asked blankly.

'Never mind.' Evie hugged Viola, glad to have one sister back, and ready to work out what she had to do to rescue the other.

Chapter Twenty-Three

May 28th, 1925

Dear Evie,

I've hardly slept since I've been in London. Every time I close my eyes, I imagine you lying beside me and then I'm awake for the whole night.

I'm working on the deal with the English lords, as you call them. Everything is going well and I think I'll be able to pull it off. It feels good to have worked hard for something like this, to know that what I've done will make the bank even more successful.

I meant what I said at Newport. I want to marry you, if you'll have me. I know you think it's impossible because of your work. But think of how good it would be to come home from a long day at the hospital to our home, to me.

I love you and I want to spend all of my life with you.
Tommy

June 10th, 1925

Dear Tommy,
This morning Bea took me out to her favourite store because she thought I needed something to cheer me up. I had no idea where she was taking me, and as we made our way down a long flight of stairs into a very dingy basement, I began to think she'd lost her mind and was taking me to an opium den. It turned out there were other illicit pleasures to be found in the basement, all of which involved tiny amounts of sheer fabric and lace. The store sold French lingerie, the French obviously having a very different idea about the purpose of underwear than we Americans do, hence the need for such a place to be hidden away below ground. I left having purchased something that Bea said was the eel's hips and which I have no idea how to take off, as there are so many straps and fastenings, with very little in between. I'm counting on you to give me a hand to work out my new lingerie contraption when you return.

Otherwise, I've quit the Follies and done nothing other than study. It'd be so helpful if you were here; diagrams in Gray's Anatomy are all very well but I'm sure I'd learn more quickly if I had a life-size model to examine!

Love, Evie
PS I've been seeing Viola a bit. It's nice to have my sister back. I also spoke to Charles. We were wrong. He says he isn't Mary's father, and I believe him.

She knew the tone of her letter was flippant, that she was talking about lingerie to conceal the fact that she was again keeping something from him: the identity of Mary's real father, and her decision to get Mary out of the Foundling. Evie had realised that getting Mary out meant only one thing: adopting her. Was it even possible? And what would adopting her illegitimate half-sister mean for Evie and Tommy? No matter how she tried, she couldn't get Charles's words out of her head: *He's a lucky fella to have someone like you, isn't he? The one woman in New York no one else would marry.*

But it was as if the week that followed Tommy's letter conspired to show her that Charles might be right: that no matter how much she wanted to do it, marrying Tommy might be a selfish thing to do.

First there was Evie's grand finale at the Follies, which was a night to remember. Bea had convinced Ziegfeld to let the chorus girls sing a song just for Evie at the end of the show. Two of the male dancers held her aloft in the middle of the stage in her magnificent crown of stars, and Eddie Cantor led them all in singing 'Oh! Boy, What a Girl'. Evie was in tears by the end of it, as the firecrackers sparkled and everybody on the stage smiled up at her, and the audience gave her a standing ovation. After the curtain came down, Bea hugged her and they cried until Bea eventually said, 'You're ruining my face. You'd better scram.'

But it took hours for Evie to leave, because there were so many people to hug and to farewell: all of the girls who'd come to her with their gynaecological ailments over the past three years; Bob the stage manager, whose eyes were suspiciously shiny; Zalia the wardrobe mistress, who said she'd never be able to get the star headdress to fit on anyone's head the way it did on Evie's; and even Ziegfeld himself.

'You were worth the gamble,' he said as he kissed her cheeks.

After picking up the case containing her kimono and her makeup, Evie took one last look in the bulb-studded mirror. She had the strangest sense that even after she'd she walked away, her reflection would stay there, backstage at the New Amsterdam, forever lingering in the theatre. But she also felt as if Ziegfeld's would always be with her, reminding her that she was capable of doing whatever she had to in order to survive.

Two nights later, while Evie was furiously studying, Mrs Whitman called to say that Viola had gone into labour. Evie tossed and turned instead of sleeping, and woke to the news that she had a niece. She ignored her studies and went to visit Viola and the baby, accompanied by Mrs Whitman.

'I'm going to name her Emily, after Mother,' Viola said as she watched Evie cuddle the baby. She smiled at her mother-in-law. 'Emily Mabel Evelyn Whitman.'

'What does Charles think of that?'

'He thinks the name Mabel is lovely.'

Evie and Mrs Whitman laughed. Whoever would have thought that Viola could be so determined, in her own quiet way, to get what she wanted?

'Speaking of Mother, she wrote to me at last.' Evie pulled the letter out of her purse and showed it to her sister.

June 12th, 1925

Dear Evelyn,
Thank you for your letter. I find it hard to know what to say. You seem to do so much and I have very little news to provide in return. The garden looks lovely. The roses are blooming, and when I look out the window,

I'm reminded of you as a girl pulling off all the flowers
so you could rain rose petals down upon your head.
How I used to scold you for that.

I know you want me to wish you good luck for
your examinations, but I'm not sure I'm able to do
that yet. I still can't quite conceive of my daughter
being a doctor, but you know that and there is no point
saying it again.

Viola mentioned she'd seen you. I hope she is well
and not doing too much.

Affectionately yours,
Mother

'That's just the kind of letter she writes to me,' Viola said with a rueful grin. 'We'll have to remember not to be like that with our own daughters.'

Evie raised one eyebrow. 'You mean you'd welcome your daughter with open arms if she told you she wanted to be a doctor?'

'I'm not quite there yet. But with an aunt like you, she'd probably go straight to you before she told me anything.'

Evie felt a large tear roll down her cheek. She whispered to the baby, 'I hope the world is a different place when you're all grown up.'

'Being an obstetrician isn't the worst thing you could be,' Viola said, touching Evie's arm.

'No,' agreed Mrs Whitman. 'It's not the worst thing. Thomas wrote to me last week and his letter was full of talk about you, Evie.'

Despite Mrs Whitman's words, the unspoken truth was that there were so many more acceptable things Evie could be if she wanted to be Thomas Whitman's wife. And Mrs Whitman and Viola as yet knew nothing about Mary, nothing about Evie's desire to adopt her. Tommy's mother might be understanding of Evie's ambitions, but Evie was certain she would not want to see her son's name all over the newspapers connected to an illegitimate child.

Lil and Leo were the next to surprise her, when they were all walking home after seeing a show at the Cherry Lane Theatre. Evie thought they were both smiling even more than usual, and so their news wasn't a surprise, but it unsettled her all the same.

'We decided last night,' Lil said, blushing. 'Leo and I are getting married.' She beamed at her fiancé and then at Evie.

'Oh, that's wonderful!' Evie wrapped her arms around Lil and then around Leo, full of happiness for her friends. But seeing their faces lit up with uncomplicated joy made her mind whirl uncomfortably. Lil and Leo had discovered that loving one another was so simple in the end when there was nothing standing in your way. That was the way love should be: there should be no secrets, no doubts, no fear that by loving someone, and letting them love you in return, you could also be ruining them, destroying everything they had achieved.

~

There was nothing Evie could do about it the following day. She was cloistered in a room answering exam questions, which took up all her time and concentration. But when she'd finished it was not quite dusk so, instead of returning to the boarding house, she walked across and uptown. She knew she'd been putting off two things: the fact of her father's despicable behaviour, and seeing Mary.

The first of these she did not wish to face yet; it was too raw, too harrowing to contemplate. That her father's mistress had died on his doorstep while giving birth to his child, and that he had shown no grief, simply gone out to a dinner party that night as if Rose and Mary meant nothing, was distressing beyond belief. She would write to her father after her examinations. In the meantime, she would bury her distress beneath the thousands of anatomical facts and diagrams with which she had to fill her mind.

She'd been delaying visiting Mary because she understood that, once she'd seen her, Evie would no longer be able to prevaricate about Tommy and marriage. She would have to make a decision. The realisation she'd had at the news of Lil and Leo's engagement had made that clear.

When she arrived at the Foundling, Sister Mary let her in without a word and Evie was relieved that Charles had done what he'd been asked to. She followed Sister Mary's silent figure to the dining room, where rows of unloved children were sitting down to bowls of stew as if in a Dickens' novel.

'Evie!' A tiny girl leapt out of her seat, heedless of the nuns' admonitions to sit down and eat. She arrived safely in Evie's arms. 'You came back,' said Mary, with a look of wonder on her face. She slipped her hand into Evie's and Evie thought she looked thinner and paler than she remembered.

'I did,' said Evie. 'I missed you.' And it wasn't until she hugged Mary tightly to her that she understood just how much she had missed her. That she never wanted to go that long without seeing Mary again.

'I missed you too.' Mary said.

Sister Mary interrupted. 'Mary, you need to finish your dinner.'

'Off you go,' Evie said. 'You'll only grow as tall as me if you eat up. I'll wait over here until you've finished.'

Mary skipped back to her place and stuffed the rest of her stew into her mouth, eyes on Evie the entire time as though afraid she might disappear. When she was allowed to leave the table, she and Evie walked through to the bathroom, where lines of girls waited to wash their face and hands before bed. Back in the dormitory, Evie helped Mary change into her nightgown, noting the way it draped on the ground. 'This is a bit big for you.'

'I should eat more stew.'

Evie was caught by surprise at this attempt at humour. She laughed aloud and hugged Mary to her, delighted that in spite of the ill-fitting clothes and Dickensian dining room, flashes of spirit could still be found. 'Could I tuck you into bed?'

'Yes, please.' Mary climbed onto the bed and slipped beneath the covers. The sheets were grey from overuse and under-laundering, and as Evie pulled the thin blanket up to Mary's chin she thought that perhaps it was a good thing the nightgown was so large, as it wrapped snugly around Mary's feet. She bent down and kissed Mary's cheek, and the little girl threw her arms around Evie's neck. Evie imagined doing this every night, tucking Mary into bed and embracing her, bringing her up in a home full of love. She imagined Mary smiling all the time because she knew that Evie would always be there. She imagined Mary happy. And safe.

The most important thing to consider was Mary's — her sister's — future. Even thinking the word *sister* felt miraculous, that out of betrayal and tragedy could come this gift, this joyous bond. She would not leave her sister in an orphanage to grow up destitute, to be farmed out to a strange family when she was old enough, or to die from disease and under-nourishment before she was an adult.

'Mary, what if . . .' Evie stopped. She needed to speak to Sister Mary before she gave the little girl hopes that might be dashed. Instead she said, 'What if I come back, not tomorrow but the next day? We'll go to Central Park.'

Mary nodded, unable to speak in the face of this unexpected bounty of things to look forward to.

On her way out, Evie saw Sister Margaret. Perhaps she could advise Evie on how best to tackle Sister Mary. 'May I have a word?' Evie asked.

Sister Margaret nodded, pleased to see Evie, and led her into an alcove near the door. Before Evie could speak, Sister Margaret said, 'She's not been well, the child. Refusing to eat. Pining for you.'

The thought of Mary so sad as to refuse the meagre food on offer gave Evie the courage to finally say the words aloud.

'If I wanted to adopt Mary,' she said, 'what would I need to do?'

The question was enough to make Sister Margaret's mouth fall open in horror.

'What?' asked Evie, taken aback. 'I know Mary's background and I'm not concerned by it.'

'But you're not . . .' Sister Margaret lowered her voice to a whisper, evidently about to utter something so scandalous that Jesus himself, who'd seen every sin the world, would blush. 'You're not married.'

Of course. How foolish she was, not to have realised that marriage would be required. 'And if I was married . . . ?'

'I'm sure Sister Mary would be grateful to have one less mouth to feed.'

'Thank you.'

Evie walked out to the street. She knew two things. She had to adopt Mary. And in order to do that, she had to be married. There was just one thing she didn't know. And to find out the answer, she had to talk to somebody who would be honest. It couldn't be Mrs Whitman, because she was Tommy's mother, and it couldn't be Lil, because she was pals with Tommy. It couldn't be Viola, because she'd just had a baby and needed rest and peace, not unsolvable problems.

Evie needed to talk to someone who understood how the world worked.

As she hurried through the stage door of the New Amsterdam Theatre, Bob caught her arm. 'You're back!' he said, as if he'd missed her.

Evie kissed his cheek. 'For one night only,' she said, then raced into the dressing room, where Bea wrapped her in a hug and commanded the rest of the girls to scram.

'What's eating you?' Bea said.

'Is it that obvious?'

'You look like you've got the weight of the world on your shoulders. Missing that man of yours?'

'I am.' Evie sighed. 'He wants to marry me when he gets back from London.'

'Shouldn't you be shouting from the rooftops? If a man like him said that to me . . .' Bea trailed off, face suddenly sad. She didn't need to say it aloud. They both knew what she was thinking: if it hadn't happened to her after hoofing it at Ziegfeld's for six years, it probably never would.

'Bea –' Evie began, but her friend blinked and shook her head.

'I can take care of myself. Tell me what the problem is.'

Evie sighed. 'Tommy's a banker. No, Tommy owns a bank. He looks after people's money. They have to trust him. If he doesn't have a good name and a good reputation, he has nothing.'

'And you're a little controversial for a world where they make money between breakfast and lunch and go out dancing all night on the proceeds.'

'I want to adopt Mary too. Turns out she's my half-sister.'

At this news, even Bea was lost for words.

'You'll catch a fly,' Evie said. 'I'll tell you all about it another time. But it makes things worse. Now I'm not just an ex-Ziegfeld Girl wanting to be an obstetrician, I also have an illegitimate sister I want to adopt.'

'Story gets better all the time. Panther sweat?' Bea pulled out the flask of whiskey she kept in the dressing table.

Evie took a sip. God, she needed it. 'I have to adopt Mary. I can't leave my own sister at the Foundling. But adopting the illegitimate child of my father is one of the least conventional things I could do. I can't trap Tommy into a life with me and a child born on the wrong side of the blanket.'

'So you can have Mary or Thomas, but not both.'

Those were the words Evie hadn't wanted to say to herself. She looked at herself and Bea reflected side by side in the mirror. Bea's face was a yellowish hue beneath the makeup, which almost hid the finest of lines that were starting to scar her complexion. Bea, the oldest of Ziegfeld's Girls now, the one who'd been there the longest, who still had nothing – no man, no child, no family, and no job to turn to next year or the year after or whenever Flo decided to put her out to pasture like an exotic cow milked for the last time. Whereas Evie just about had everything she'd come to New York for. An obstetrics internship was in reach if she performed well enough in her exams. She'd found the baby from the river and in the process gained a sister. Trouble was, after she'd arrived in New York, she'd added something else to her list of wants: Thomas Whitman. She wanted to marry him, to have children with him, to grow old with him, to always be able to slip her hand into his and feel his lips against hers. But wanting it didn't mean it was the honourable thing to do.

'If you told him about Mary, he's the kind of man who'd do the right thing, no matter what,' Bea said.

'I know he would. But is it right to let him?'

As soon as she said it, Evie knew the answer. Of course it wasn't. Because Tommy had done everything for her. From the moment he understood that all she needed was a push in the right direction, he'd helped her believe she could go to university, become a doctor, *do something*, just like she'd said to him in the tree. He'd encouraged her; he'd had more faith in her than anyone had ever had. And he'd never once done anything to hold her back, he'd never encumbered her the way she would encumber him if they were to marry.

Evie held out *The New Yorker* for Bea to see. 'This is what he's worked for. Everything I am will ruin him. I love him too much to destroy his life.'

'It'll hurt like hell to set him free, Evie.'

'I know.'

Chapter Twenty-Four

June 22nd, 1925

Dear Evelyn,
I received your letter. I ask that you don't share the information you've learned about the child with Viola or your mother. There is little point disrupting their lives with this.

The child will continue to be accommodated at the New York Foundling until such time as she is old enough to be adopted by a family outside New York. I will concede to your visiting her until then.

Of course I don't have to say how much I wish you had left the situation alone and then nobody need be burdened by this knowledge.

Sincerely,
Your father

PS I had a high regard for the child's mother.

July 25th, 1925
Columbia College of Physicians and Surgeons

Dear Miss Lockhart,
I am writing to advise that you received the
highest grades in your year group for your final
examinations. As you are aware, this guarantees
your first choice of internship, thus bypassing
the usual competitive interview and selection
process. Please advise by return post which
position and at which hospital you would prefer.

Yours sincerely,
Dr F. Dunnett MD
Dean, Columbia College of Physicians and
Surgeons

August 19th, 1925
Sloane Hospital for Women

Dear Miss Lockhart,
It seems you have achieved your goal and
will be taking up a position as intern at the
Sloane Hospital for Women. You will commence
on January 4th, 1926. You will be paid a wage
of $25 per week. Please advise the hospital
immediately should you change your mind about
accepting this position, as we have received
several other very worthy applications.

Yours sincerely,
Dr Richard Brewer MD

Until she'd received those three letters and was sure of her future, Evie had forced herself not to think about Tommy. Because every time she did, she thought she might faint from the pain of what she had to do. She'd stopped writing to him and had made herself not read his increasingly worried letters. She'd avoided Mrs Whitman. She'd even managed to intercept the letters Tommy had written to Lil in an attempt to find out what had happened to Evie. All she'd done since her exams was plan and organise and visit Mary. Luckily Lil was distracted with wedding preparations, so Evie was able to pretend that everything was fine. She smiled and danced and was as happy as a best friend should be on the night of Lil and Leo's very informal wedding reception at Chumley's. She helped them move into their new apartment on Grove Street and tried not to think about their love because it made her wonder if she could go through with what she had to do.

Her father's letter angered her, but it also made her absolutely certain that she was doing the right thing. He wouldn't look after Mary, so Evie must. The news from the college and the hospital would once have delighted her, but now she didn't feel anything.

The day after she received Dr Brewer's letter, she invited Lil and Leo to lunch in the Village at the San Remo Cafe, where she explained everything. Her plans to adopt Mary and to take up the internship to support them both. Her decision not to see Thomas again.

Their initial reaction was silence. Then Lil began to plead. 'You can't do that! Tommy wouldn't care what anyone thinks about Mary. He loves you more than the bank. Tell her, Leo.'

Leo hesitated, and Evie saw in his eyes that he heard the truth of what she was saying. If he had told Evie that she was wrong, that none of it mattered, she might have faltered, because God she wanted to falter. But Leo was a lawyer. He worked in the world of men. He knew that New York would rip Thomas to shreds if Evie married him.

The three strikes against Evie were bad enough: obstetric intern, former showgirl, and hopefully the soon-to-be adoptive mother of the adulterine Mary. But there was something else, which Evie knew was the bullet in the gun, the final unarguable reason why she could never marry Thomas Whitman. 'I'm also pregnant,' she said.

She'd only realised this herself a couple of weeks ago. She'd been so busy sitting exams that she'd lost track of things. The precautions they'd taken had failed. She knew when it must have happened. It was when they were in the sitting room in Newport on their last evening there. They'd been too impatient to be naked and joined together, unable to slow down and check that the rubber was on properly, because how could you slow down when you knew what it was like to fall bodily and utterly into the person beside you?

'By the time Tommy gets back from London, I'll be six months along and obvious to all,' Evie continued. 'There'll be no shotgun wedding; I'll look more like I've swallowed a cannonball. Nobody in New York is foolish enough to believe a baby only takes three months to gestate. That's too tall, even for a New York story. So tell me, does the newspaper headline *Thomas Whitman marries hugely pregnant ex-showgirl, who has adopted the illegitimate daughter of her father, and who is also an obstetrician* sound like the kind of thing that will pull in a lot of new business for the Whitman bank?'

Lil was openly crying now. 'But you love him. And he loves you.'

Leo took Lil's hand. 'She's not doing it to hurt Tommy. She's doing it to save him from the ignominy of trial by newspaper, which every client of Whitman's bank would see as an utter humiliation that will taint them and their money. I don't like it but that's how it is. She's doing what has to be done, Lil.'

'There has to be another way.' Lil looked beseechingly at Leo, tears running down her face. But it was beyond anyone's power to make the wealthy men of New York stand by the president of a bank who was so embroiled in immoral behaviour that it surely wouldn't be long before the money in his hands began to stink too. Nobody wanted anything that whiffed of dirty money.

Evie shook her head, her eyes tired and sad, too old for her years. 'All I want is to rush in and tell Tommy about our child. But it's not right. So I'm calling in a favour.' She pushed on, knowing she had to, that it didn't matter if she felt like she was dying. 'You've both told me I'm the reason you're together. So I'm asking you to keep my secret. Tommy can never find out about any of this.'

'That's not fair,' Lil cried.

'I know,' said Evie. 'But I really need my best friend to help me. Please?'

Lil shook her head and dashed at her eyes with her hand. 'Goddamn you, Evie Lockhart. You know I hate crying in public.' She sniffed and took the hanky Leo was offering. 'But of course we'll help.'

'There's one more thing. Will you and Leo sign the adoption papers for Mary?'

'Of course we'll sign them,' said Lil. 'But what will you say to people?'

'I'm going to start talking to everyone around here about the wonderful man I've met, who I'm marrying in a few weeks' time. That I'm going on a vacation across America with my new husband so I won't be around for a while. Not till January. And I'll tell them how kind he is, that he's consented to me adopting a child left behind by a mother who died at the hospital. And when I show my face around here again in January, I'll have another child, too. My husband's child.' Evie paused. 'Do you think it'll work?'

'Maybe,' Lil said doubtfully.

'And I know I'm asking too much but . . .'

Lil reached across the table and took Evie's hand. 'You can't do this by yourself. I'll do whatever you need.'

'Can you tell Vi that you've helped me adopt two children and that I have to go away for a while? She won't believe the husband story and she'll ask too many questions and then she'll tell Mrs Whitman. I can't risk talking to either of them.'

'I'll handle Viola.'

'That's it then.' Evie shut her eyes. 'Now we won't ever talk about Tommy again.'

Lil and Leo moved around to Evie's side of the table. They slipped in beside her and hugged her and her baby close. Evie began to cry at last, to sob, because she knew she could never love any man again, not after she'd loved Thomas Whitman. Theirs was the once in a lifetime, the genuine miracle, the joining of soul to soul. To survive the loss of it, Evie thought she might have to cut out her heart. It was almost impossible to believe that in doing the right thing, she could hurt herself and the man she loved so much.

Three

Chapter Twenty-Five

Evie flicked through the newspaper with one hand while she alternated between sipping coffee and spooning food into the mouth of one-year-old Lucille with the other. Mary, now four, had finished her breakfast and was putting on her shoes.

A photograph in the newspaper made Evie stop. Thomas Whitman. The picture accompanied an article about his latest success, and the remarkable ascension of Whitman's bank under his presidency. Every time she saw such an article, which was often, Evie would smile a little. It reassured her that she'd done the right thing. The newspapers wouldn't be lauding him if he'd married her.

But she also knew she would dream about him that night, wanton reckless dreams from which she woke gasping, because it was as if he really was in her room, in her bed, kissing her, holding her body, hands caressing her skin. Sometimes, in weak moments, she allowed herself to wonder if he was having the same dreams — if they were, somehow, visiting each other in a nightlife that was beyond the realm of reason.

'Ma-ma-ma.' Lucille's babbling roused Evie and she looked at the clock. They'd be late if she didn't hurry.

'Let's clean you up, my darling,' she said to Lucille, pulling the baby out of her highchair. 'Well done, Mary,' she said, planting a kiss on the head of her older child, who'd appeared with her shoes on, ready to go. It took Evie just a few minutes to collect all the bags she'd packed the night before and leave the apartment on Grove Street. Their new home in the Village was small, as Evie's wages were much less than the men in her position were paid, but she was used to scrimping and saving and so they got by. Their life was simple and without any of the luxuries Evie had taken for granted when she was growing up. But the children didn't seem to notice what they didn't have.

They stopped to peep through the wrought-iron gates into the private enclave of Grove Court, with its grand white-shuttered homes of red brick, wreathed like Christmas trees with long ribbons of green ivy. Mary always liked to pause there, imagining the kind of people who lived in such fine houses.

It was the same thing they'd done every day since Evie had started her internship. Evie walked to Lil's in the morning, where she left the children for the day. Then she caught the El to the hospital, where she worked harder than ever, did what she was told, got through each day and kept her thoughts to herself. She was no longer the brash and back-talking Evie of eighteen months earlier; these days she had to think about Mary and Lucille and how much they needed the money Evie made. And she kept herself to herself because she didn't want any new friends who would ask awkward questions about her life. Luckily, in a way, the world hadn't changed and being a female obstetric intern and now resident guaranteed there would be no friends. She'd turned up on the first day of her internship with a wedding ring on her finger and the story she'd created of a tragically dead husband. She didn't talk about the children, because women didn't work and have children. It was unheard of.

Her life had shrunk to work, the children, and Greenwich Village; even there she did little more than make a trip twice a week for bread to Zito's, where the children were patted on the head and pitied for their poor dead father. The Village shopkeepers had long ago forgotten that Mary was adopted. Evie never went anywhere else, because the risk of discovery was too great. The only time she ever heard about life uptown was when Viola came for her clandestine visits with baby Emily, visits they all enjoyed, and Vi knew better than to mention either of the Whitman brothers. Evie wasn't sure what Viola really believed about Lucille, and Vi had, for once, been willing to swallow the adoption story without comment. More importantly, she hadn't mentioned Evie's children to anyone. And Evie no longer wrote to her mother, because it would be yet another person to lie to. She felt despicable for abruptly cutting off the fragile connection they had re-established, but she had no choice.

Mary finally drew her face away from the gates and they entered another building further down the street. 'Auntie Lil!' Mary called as Evie pushed open the door to Leo and Lil's apartment. The space was full of light, a little pot of gold at the end of the rainbow. Honey-coloured wood panels decorated the walls, and in the sitting room were two ebony wood and leather armchairs, a fading rose velvet sofa and, in the centre, a delightful U-shaped table, which always looked to Evie like a smile or a pair of arms ready to embrace.

'Hello, precious girls,' Lil cried, hugging Mary and Lucille and covering them with kisses.

'Where's Eleanor?' Mary asked.

'She's asleep, but when she wakes up you can play with her,' said Lil.

Lucille waddled back to Evie, holding her arms up in the air. Evie bent down to cuddle her and pressed her lips against the soft, warm cheek, hoping to keep the memory with her through the long day at the hospital.

'The menagerie's arrived!' Leo appeared from the bedroom with his briefcase and hat.

'The additions to the menagerie, you mean,' said Evie.

Leo smiled. 'The other day I was looking for my hat and discovered I'd put it in the diaper pail. The dirty diaper was on the coat hook.'

Evie laughed and kissed him on the cheek, then watched his mock-frantic attempts to get out the door while distributing kisses to Lucille, Mary and Lil. As her friends and her children laughed together, among the mess of shoes and umbrellas and bags filling the hallway, Evie reminded herself that she was blessed, as were her children. Blessed to have a second family in Lil, Leo and Eleanor, who gave them an abundance of warmth, and as much love as they needed. She couldn't help recalling the night she'd met them at Chumley's, when drinking and dancing and flirting had been uppermost in their minds, not love and marriage and children. She gave Lil an impulsive hug.

'What's that for?' asked Lil.

'Because I can never thank you enough for looking after the girls.'

'Like I keep saying, there's nothing to thank me for. You know I use them shamelessly for inspiration.'

'I didn't see yesterday's column. Do you have the paper?'

'Leo still keeps each one, no matter that I tell him there won't be room for us with all the newsprint filling this place.'

Lil tossed the newspaper to Evie, who flicked through until she came to Lil's by-line; her column was called 'Slapstick: Tales of Motherhood in the Village'.

Lil's dreams had all come true. She'd been lured away from advertising to write a regular column for the *New York Herald Tribune*, a role that allowed her to work from the comfort of home. She had a beautiful daughter Eleanor, and Leo.

'Remember when it was Lipstick's debauched exploits we were reading about?' Lil asked ruefully. 'Speaking of which, you should come to a party tonight.'

'I can't go to a party,' Evie said automatically.

'Why not?'

'Because.'

'Because it's more fun sitting home alone every night?'

'I have to look after the girls.'

'Bea's going to look after them all tonight. I already asked her. I'll bring Eleanor over when we pick you up in the taxi.'

'Lil,' Evie said, looking pleadingly at her friend.

'Do you want to be lonely for the rest of your life?'

Evie picked up her bag. 'I should go to work.'

'The train doesn't leave for ten minutes. Sit down. Girls,' Lil said to Mary and Lucille. 'Why don't you look through the toy chest while I talk to your mama?'

Mary took Lucille's hand and led her over to play with a tea set.

Evie sat down in one of the armchairs even though she didn't want to. 'Why do I feel like I'd rather face Dr Kingsley right now?'

Lil laughed. 'I'm not that bad! The *Tribune*'s Valentine's Day party is the talk of the town. One night out in eighteen months is all I'm asking of you. It's time.'

'Time for what?'

'To drink champagne. Dance with a man.'

Evie stiffened. 'I can't imagine dancing with anyone.'

'Seems a waste of a life to me.'

'You won't stop until I say yes, will you?'

Lil shook her head decidedly. 'No.'

Evie sighed. 'I'll come. Eleanor can stay the night at my place to save you waking her up in the middle of the night. I'll drink champagne. But I won't dance with anyone.'

'We'll see about that,' Lil said grimly.

~

When Evie reached the hospital, she took off her pretty home clothes, as Mary called them, and changed into her more robust work clothes. She put her wedding ring in her locker and walked out onto the ward.

'Dr Lockhart, a patient's asking for you.' It was one of the new medical students, a girl named Dolores, as green and keen as Evie had been when she started almost five years before.

'Does she have a name?' asked Evie.

'I didn't ask,' said Dolores. 'I'm sorry.'

'The first thing you find out is her name. She's a person as well as a patient.'

'Sorry, Dr Lockhart.'

'You've apologised once already. That's more than enough.'

'Sorr—' Dolores closed her mouth just in time.

Evie hid a smile. 'Are you coming? You can assist.'

'Thank you! I'd love to assist. I haven't had a chance yet; the other students are always asked instead of me. So thank you. I'll do my best –'

'Saying thank you once is also enough.'

'Sorr—' Dolores snapped her mouth shut and followed Evie, who knew that being too nice to a student like Dolores would never prepare her for life as an obstetrician.

'Gretel O'Rourke said to ask for you,' said the patient, Mrs Jones, when they arrived at her bedside. 'That you wouldn't knock me out and cut me up.'

'If you and the baby are happy and healthy, I'll only help as much or as little as you'd like,' Evie replied. 'How is Mrs O'Rourke? I haven't seen her for months. It must be about time for the next one.'

Mrs Jones laughed. 'She'll be back in two months.'

'What will that be? Baby number seven?' Evie asked.

'Sure will.'

The delivery that followed was simple and uncomplicated, a woman labouring, a baby making its way into the world alive and well, and Evie stepping in only when she was needed to ease out the head. No forceps were used, no scopolamine, and only a few stitches were required. At the end, the mother could hold and feed her baby and know that what she'd done was extraordinary. More and more this was how Evie's days unfolded as she quietly and carefully made a place for herself at the hospital. To her satisfaction, it was a place that Dr Kingsley and some of the nurses had begun to accept she had a right to occupy. This was an astonishing victory, and was the one good thing in her life besides her children. It made her feel, sometimes, as though all her hard work and sacrifice might have been worthwhile.

'I don't think obstetrics is for me,' Dolores said as they left the delivery room. 'I want something more exciting.'

Evie couldn't help laughing.

'What's funny?' Dolores asked.

'Nothing. Just don't pray for too much excitement too soon. You might get more than you wished for.'

At the end of her shift, Evie returned to the locker room to change her clothes, reluctant to go home to get ready for a party she didn't want to attend, but eager to see her children. Dolores came in, coat splattered with blood, a grin on her face. 'Find any excitement?' Evie asked.

'Did I ever!' said Dolores. 'Mrs Goldfinch haemorrhaged. I've seen more blood today than most people see in a lifetime.'

'So you're enjoying it?'

Dolores nodded emphatically, following Evie out into the hall. 'Say, do you want to get a drink? I haven't met many other women and . . .'

Before Evie could answer, a passing intern butted in. 'Dr Lockhart never goes out. She always rushes home to her husband.'

'He's dead,' Evie said.

The intern dropped his file in confusion. 'Sorry. I didn't know. You wear the ring, so we just thought . . .'

'He died not long after we married.'

'That's awful,' Dolores said, eyes big and round and showing too clearly that she knew nothing of how cruel life could be.

'Excuse me,' said Evie. She escaped outside and took a deep breath. See? she told herself. Every time she told the story, people believed her. No one ever suspected there was anything more in her past than the calamity of losing a husband. Perhaps she'd be able to get through a party tonight after all.

When she arrived back in the Village she found that Auntie Bea, as the girls called her, had already taken the girls back to the apartment and was bathing them.

'You get yourself ready!' Bea hollered from the bathroom. 'About time you went out.' Her head appeared around the doorframe and she whispered so the girls wouldn't hear, 'Treat yourself to a night of chin music with a fella.'

'I won't be doing that,' Evie said, shaking her head.

'You're allowed to, you know,' Bea yelled back as she disappeared into the bathroom.

But I don't want to, Evie thought. Even after so much time had passed, it was impossible to contemplate kissing anyone other than Thomas. Just as it was impossible to look at her old dancing dresses and not remember the times she'd worn them with him. She sat down on the bed and stared into her wardrobe, her eyes scanning through each of the outfits she could never wear again — because that was the dress she wore when she first went out with him to Chumley's, and that was the dress she wore to the ball the night she realised she loved him . . .

'I got you something to wear,' Bea said, coming into the room.

'Not lingerie, I hope,' Evie said, trying to smile.

Bea had quit the Follies six months ago with her dignity still intact: she'd been saving her nickels and had bought herself a business. It was a lingerie store, the same one she'd taken Evie to while Thomas was in London. Now renamed Bea's Secret, it was no longer quite so discreet. In true Bea style, she'd had big, bold signs made up and placed at the entrance. Customers now had to be prepared to dash across the street and hurtle down the stairs at a pace designed to avoid the damning looks from nearby businesses; they exited half an hour later, arms hung with bold red shopping bags that those in the know understood to contain the best-quality silk underwear in Manhattan, sold by a woman whose flapper garters could be seen adorning the legs of the beautiful and the damned all across the city. Bea was able to look Ziegfeld in the eye at last, when they met at parties, and know that she'd made good on her escape. She also cared for Mary and Lucille on Mondays, when the shop was closed, and the girls loved to play in the piles of satin, to dress up in slips and pretend to be princesses.

Now Bea laughed. 'No, I stopped at the theatre and called in a favour from Zalia. She lent me a floor-flushing number the likes of which you've never seen!'

'With sequins and feathers to boot?'

'Take a look.' Bea unfolded a package and Evie couldn't help but gasp. It was not at all what she was expecting. The dress had a scooped neckline, a fitted bodice and then a full skirt, gathered at the waist so that it billowed as if it had a dozen petticoats beneath it. And it was long, falling to just above Evie's ankles. The colour was exquisite, a bold blush pink that made Evie's cheeks glow to match.

'It's beautiful,' she said.

'If that doesn't do the trick, I don't know what will,' said Bea.

⁓

Mary and Lucille pronounced her a queen and Leo whistled when he saw her. And Evie had to admit that she felt the tiniest bit excited to be going out in the evening to a party, just as she used to.

Lil had been right about the *New York Herald Tribune*'s party being worth attending. It was held in a circus tent in a secret garden off Park Avenue and Sixty-Sixth. Trapeze artists flew overhead, an elephant trumpeted anxiously in one corner, and beautiful girls in sequined leotards rode horses bareback across a stage.

Evie held onto Lil's arm as they stepped inside. 'Stay with me for a while. Just until I find my feet.'

'Let's have champagne,' Lil said. 'Look, Leo's found some for us.'

After a while, Evie felt settled enough that she gave Lil permission to go and dance with her husband. As she sat watching the glamorous crowd, she was asked to dance more times than was comfortable, and to save herself from giving too many refusals, she decided to walk around and see the elephant and the girls on horseback. Laughter and snippets of conversation floated past her, none of which caught her attention, until the sight of a woman's face stopped her in her tracks. It wasn't until the woman opened her mouth that Evie realised where she'd seen her before. The woman spoke with a haughty English accent and her earrings had been described, once upon a time, as requiring talent to look so cheap. It was Winnie, flapping her gums at a group of people gathered around her as if she belonged in New York. Winnie, the woman who'd kidnapped Thomas at the Egyptian ball.

Evie could hear her say, 'He asked me this morning. I was thrilled, of course. He doesn't have the ring yet because he said he wanted the pleasure of taking me shopping for it. Tommy's like that.'

Evie's heart plummeted out of her chest. Surely Winnie wasn't talking about Thomas Whitman? And surely she wasn't talking about an engagement?

As if answering Evie's unspoken question, Winnie said, 'Mrs Thomas Whitman. Doesn't it sound splendid?'

Evie reeled. She felt as if she was suffocating, as if the long arm of the past had reached out and taken hold of her throat, reminding her that it wasn't done with her yet, that it wouldn't rest until she'd been wrung dry of every last piece of joy and affection she had left.

Evie spun around. She had to leave. But there in her path, with his back to her but his head turned to the side in conversation, was Thomas. There was the black hair that Evie had once been able to run her hands through, the lips she knew as well as her own. Evie gasped and moved back towards Winnie. She had to get away before Thomas saw her. Without a word of apology, she pushed blindly through the middle of Winnie and her coterie.

She heard Winnie's horrified 'How ill-mannered!', but she ploughed on, unable to bear seeing Thomas's face again or to hear Winnie repeat those words: *Mrs Thomas Whitman*.

She didn't try to find Lil and Leo and tell them she was going. Instead she hurried outside, forgetting her coat, and across town to the train. It didn't occur to her to hail a taxi; instead she needed something familiar and unchanging, something unlikely to bring her any more shocks. For the length of the ride home, Evie stared out the window, ticking off familiar landmarks in order to avoid thinking: the Times Building looking down upon Bryant Park; the grand Hotel McAlpin near Herald Square, with the Turkish baths on the top floor, where society ladies washed off the soot of the city; the beautiful Beaux Arts Siegel-Cooper 'Big Store', once the largest store in the world, now another New York casualty, its dreams proving too big for its pockets; the Fourteenth Street Station with the original Macy's store opposite, which Evie didn't look at, because she was staring at buildings in order to forget Tommy, not to remember him; and the Jefferson Market Courthouse, which tonight looked more like Rapunzel's prison than a fairytale palace. It was comforting, almost meditative, the snaking of the train, the blur of the commonplace.

She walked home from the station in the same state, mesmerised by the everyday, the mundane. She could almost believe she'd heard nothing. When she arrived home, she thanked Bea and said nothing about what had happened. She checked on the girls and found them sleeping soundly, smiling a little as if their dreams were the sweetest. Then she took off the magnificent dress and laid it carefully over a chair. She dropped the wedding ring from her left hand into a dish on the dressing table.

She stared at it as if seeing it for the first time. It was a plain gold band that she wore to keep herself safe, to keep her daughters safe. She tried to picture Thomas's hand wearing such a ring, and couldn't: hands like his deserved something finer, a special commission from Tiffany perhaps. Which Winnie could afford.

'Why?' she whispered, leaning her head against the door of her wardrobe. She knew the question was unfair. Of course Thomas would get married. But it had taken so long that she'd half hoped he was, inexplicably, still waiting for her.

Chapter Twenty-Six

She could tell from Lil and Leo's faces when she dropped all the girls off the next morning that they'd heard about Thomas's engagement.

'I tried to talk to him,' Lil said. 'But he had so many people around him that I didn't even have a chance to say hello.'

Mary interrupted. 'When can we go to a party, Mama?'

'I don't know, darling,' Evie equivocated.

'What are you going to do?' Lil asked.

Evie looked at her friend. 'There's nothing I can do. He's getting married.'

Lil met Evie's stare. 'He's not married yet.'

'I have to go.' Evie kissed the girls and left.

But once she was on the train she could no longer equivocate. Mary's question echoed in her mind. It was a fair one. When would Evie take her children out into the world? No matter how much the realisation hurt her, it was as clear as the shriek of the wheels on the El as it took the sharp corner at Fifty-Third that it was time to put Thomas behind her. To stop simply pretending she had. To live a real life, not one where she was always tiptoeing around, staying close to Greenwich Village, avoiding half the city in case she ran into Thomas. He was getting married, he had moved on. Despite what Lil said, there was nothing Evie could do about it.

After a year and a half of secrets and stories and lies, maybe it was time to let go.

~

When Evie left the hospital that afternoon, she decided to test her nerve. It was only four o'clock. She could take the girls to Central Park, somewhere Lucille had never been.

She picked them up from Lil's and they caught the train to the park. Mary threw the ball for Lucille, who tried to run, but tumbled and rolled after it, like a little ball herself. Evie sat on a bench and watched, then she joined in the fun, chasing the girls and catching and tickling them until they were giggling and gasping for air. Soon it was time to pick up the ball, pick up Lucille, hold Mary's hand and walk back to the station. On a whim, Evie decided to exit the park at the Arsenal and walk down Fifth to the corner opposite the Plaza Hotel. When she saw its elegant facade, she touched her lips and could almost feel, across the years, Thomas's lips on hers the first time they'd kissed, inside the Plaza.

Why was she doing this to herself, picking the scabs off unhealed wounds and watching them bleed like the tears that were dripping unchecked down her cheeks?

'Evie?'

Evie wiped her face, whirled around and blanched. 'Mrs Whitman.' Oh God.

'How are you?' Mrs Whitman asked politely, the way she used to speak to Evie's parents, as if the conversation would be tolerated, but was not welcome.

'Well. And you?' Evie stammered, feeling so guilty for the way she'd cut Mrs Whitman out of her life, knowing she didn't even deserve the formalities they were exchanging.

'I'm well also.'

Mrs Whitman's eyes swept over Lucille in Evie's arms and Mary at her side, and Evie began to babble, anything to fend off the questions that would be sure to come. 'I'm sorry I haven't replied to your letters. And sorry not to have made time to see you. The internship and then the residency took up all of my time and by evening I'm exhausted . . .'

'Who are these delightful children?' Mrs Whitman's question came at the same time as Mary said, 'Mama, I'm tired,' leaving Evie no option to pass them off as Lil's, whether she wanted to or not.

'I adopted them,' Evie said. That was true of Mary, but what of Lucille? She floundered on. 'Their mother was one of my patients. She died in childbirth. I wanted to help.'

Mrs Whitman frowned. 'I thought one had to be married in order to adopt a child.'

Evie looked away. She was ashamed, more ashamed than she'd ever felt at Ziegfeld's when most of her body was on show but everything about her was honest. She couldn't tell her story of a dead husband to Mrs Whitman, couldn't tell that last terrible lie to someone who'd been like a mother to Evie when she'd most needed it. Then she remembered. 'Congratulations,' she said.

'Congratulations?'

'For Thomas and Winnie.' She forced out the words. 'I understand congratulations are in order.'

'Perhaps they are.' Mrs Whitman reached out a hand slowly, as if she was afraid of how it might feel, to tuck one of Lucille's spirited blonde curls behind her ear. 'It's astonishing how much an adopted child can look like you,' she whispered.

'It's just because we both have blonde hair. That's all. If she was dark —' Evie could have bitten off her tongue. Why did she say that? Thomas was dark. 'People see what they want to see,' she added formally, hating herself for the way she sounded.

'Or what they're forced to see. I won't keep you any longer.' Mrs Whitman's eyes glimmered suspiciously but she kept her gaze fixed on Lucille.

Evie almost ran, she was so eager to get away. But she could only go as fast as Mary's short legs would allow. She didn't even know what she was running from, other than the thought: would Mrs Whitman tell Thomas about the children? And what would he think of Evie if she did?

~

When they got home, Evie lit the fire. She let the girls sit on the hearthrug and watch the flames while they ate steaming bowls of soup. Then they asked for a story and Evie began to recite 'The Steadfast Tin Soldier'. But as she neared the end, she remembered that both the soldier and the ballerina were burned in a fire, dying together, with only a spangle and a tin heart left behind in the ashes. She decided that the girls were too young to learn that love always ended in disaster, so instead she told them that the soldier and ballerina were eventually found by a little girl, who took them home.

After the story, Evie scooped up both girls and jumped in the bathtub with them; Lucille usually splashed around so much water that Evie ended up soaked anyway. The two girls raced their rubber ducks up and down until it was time to be rubbed dry, cuddled into warm pyjamas and tucked into bed.

Mary always liked to stroke Lucille's hand between the bars of the cot before she hopped into her own bed right beside it. Evie watched the little ritual, smiling at the fierce affection Mary always showed for her baby sister. She kissed them both. 'I love you,' she said.

'I love you too, Mama,' said Mary.

'Ma-ma-bub-bub-mar-mar,' came from Lucille.

Evie turned off their bedroom light. She tidied away the remains of dinner, ensuring every crumb was swept from the hearthrug, every speck of chicken broth scrubbed from the bowls, that the glasses were dry and sparkling. She ironed the girls' dresses for the morning, got out everything she'd need for breakfast, and brushed the dirt off Mary and Lucille's matching black patent Mary Janes. She swept up the mud from the step in the hallway. She took out her clothes for the next day. She peeked into the girls' bedroom to make sure they were asleep.

There were no more jobs to do. Evie poured herself a brandy, in the one glass she had that was up to the task. It was from a Karl Palda set that Mr Childers had given her as a congratulatory gift at her commencement ceremony, and it had striking black triangles of enamel etched into the glass. As she drank, it no longer seemed possible that she was old enough to have two children or that she was alone and raising them by herself; instead she dreamed that she was wearing a backless black dress of silk jersey and one long strand of jet beads, holding her glass and dancing with Tommy, lips nearly touching, united in the erotic delight of the tango. But one look in the mirror told her otherwise.

She telephoned Bea. 'I need somebody to drink with.'

'Gimme ten.'

True to her word, Bea arrived ten minutes later, bearing more brandy and a package for Evie. 'Thought that might cheer you up. It's from the store,' Bea said, nodding at the parcel, which contained a pair of black silk chiffon knickers trimmed with alternating bands of ivory lace, and a matching slip.

Evie couldn't help laughing as she sank into a chair. 'What am I going to do with these?'

'See, that's a question someone as young and pretty as you shouldn't be asking.' Bea lit a cigarette and offered one to Evie, who shook her head.

'I saw in the paper that your fella's going to be taking a stroll down the middle aisle,' Bea said, filling up Evie's glass, as if brandy was the only way to medicate a broken heart.

'He's not my fella. He's Winnie's fella, apparently.' Evie's voice was wooden.

'You know, the worst is over. You got away with it. Half the shopkeepers in the Village could probably describe your make-believe dead husband because they think they met him sometime. That's how stories work. People hear them and they become real. All you are now is another Village eccentric. You're the crazy obstetrician lady who the fella at Zito's gives an extra loaf of bread to because your poor children must miss their father.'

Evie shook her head. 'So?'

'So if Thomas still loves you and you still love him you could just about make it work. You're not pregnant. You're a saint for adopting Mary. Maybe Lucille's adopted too. You're a widow. Okay, so you're still a crazy obstetrician, but that's the worst of it. Maybe he could weather that.'

'I could never lie to him about Lucille.'

'So tell him the goddamn truth,' Bea said with irritation. 'Doesn't he deserve to know, before he marries someone else, that he has a child?'

'He told me once that he would never abandon a mother and child. I don't want him to be with me just because we have a daughter. I want him to be with me because he loves me. And I don't know if he does. He never came looking for me when he got back from London.'

'You can't expect him to chase after you every time you decide to run away,' Bea chastised. 'You took off after the ball with no explanation but he didn't stop searching until he found you. Maybe he wanted to see how hard you were willing to fight to make it work this time. And you'll never know how he feels unless you go see him. Are you brave enough?'

Evie stared down at her glass. 'I don't know. I used to be. But now –'

'This is it, kiddo. Last chance. Once he's married it's finished. Isn't the chance to be with him worth the risk?'

Evie finally looked up at her friend. 'But if he turned me away, I don't think I could survive losing him all over again.'

⁓

Evie's dreams that night were more vivid than usual, as if every memory was lit up in Broadway neon. Thomas and Evie sipping whiskey in an apple tree while he helped her to see that she could do more than fritter her life away on embroidery. Thomas and Evie walking arm in arm into the Vanderbilt mansion to see a woman wearing a chandelier. Thomas and Evie eating pretzels one night, running hand in hand to catch the late show at the movies, kissing for the first time at the Plaza Hotel. Evie undoing the buttons of his shirt so she could place her palms on his chest. Thomas drying her hair after a bath in Newport, Thomas saying those words that hadn't come true: *I'll marry you when I get back, Evie Lockhart.* Then Lucille's face, so like Thomas's, pressed against his, cheek to cheek, the child held in her father's arms. A memory that hadn't happened. A memory that might never happen unless she did something, now.

Evie woke with a start. The images fell away but the urgency she'd felt in her dream stayed with her, forcing her to get out of bed even though it was only five o'clock in the morning. She bathed and dressed as quietly as she could so as not to wake the children. Then she drank three cups of coffee while she waited for Mary and Lucille to stir.

It seemed to take forever to feed them breakfast and help them dress, but Evie smiled and chatted throughout, telling herself to remain patient; it wasn't their fault she was so jittery. Finally they were ready and they walked to Lil's, with the inevitable stop outside Grove Court, even though she tried to hurry them along.

When they reached Lil's at last, Evie raced through the door and kissed Lil on both cheeks. 'I might be a bit later tonight. I'm going to see Thomas after work,' she blurted. 'I can't talk about it, because I can hardly dare to even think about it. So don't ask me any questions. I have to go.' She kissed the girls and fled for the train.

Chapter Twenty-Seven

*I*t was the longest day of Evie's life. Every pregnant woman, it seemed, had decided to have her baby, and Evie went from delivery to delivery, stopping only to take her orders from Dr Kingsley, who even let her handle a case of placenta praevia all on her own. Ordinarily she would have rejoiced at the victory. Today she just wanted to get it done so she could go and see Thomas. She didn't finish until well after six o'clock, and as she hurried back to her locker to change, she hoped that Thomas still had a habit of working late and that he hadn't dashed off to spend the evening with Winnie.

Then she realised that all of the clothes she had with her were stained, even her home clothes. It was as common a problem for her as chalk marks were for teachers, but decidedly more wearing. She rummaged around in her locker for anything else to wear and her hand touched a bag right down the back. She reached into the bag and pulled out a dress.

It was Lil's black Chanel dress, the one Evie had worn to dinner at Charles and Viola's house on the night Charles had tried to blackmail her. Evie had found it among her things when she'd moved out of the boarding house, and had taken it to be laundered; then she'd evidently forgotten about it, and it had sat in her locker at the hospital ever since. Now she slipped it on and felt the silk chiffon trail lightly down over her skin like Thomas's hand used to. She combed her hair and re-applied her lipstick, then hurried for the train.

The bottom of town had never seemed so far away. Evie counted down every stop until Rector Street, where she jumped off and turned onto Wall Street.

A building on her right bore a familiar name: WHITMAN's. It was spelled out in bronze letters above the door, elegant but not flashy. The door was wooden, large and solid, implying that once you'd invested your money behind it, there it would stay, doubling, quadrupling, increasing one hundredfold as money seemed to do in these crazy times.

The doorman was still there. So Thomas might be too. Evie stepped inside, glad of the Chanel, her ticket to entry to a place like this.

'I'm here to see Thomas Whitman,' Evie found herself saying to the secretary, who was packing up her bag to leave.

The secretary looked at her watch, doubt written all over her face. 'Do you have an appointment?'

'No. But tell him that Evie . . .' she hesitated, 'that Evie Lockhart is here.'

'Please take a seat.'

Evie sat in an armchair, antique of course. The clock in the corner ticked away the minutes of waiting like a bored pair of heels in a dance hall. In the end, Evie stood and walked over to it, just to have something to do. A seashell was carved into the wood below the face. She reached out a hand to touch it, to feel the wood smoothed by polish in the same way that a shell might be smoothed by the sea.

'It's a Newport tall clock.' Thomas's voice spoke behind her.

'Oh.' An insignificant word, but it seemed to shout out the differences between them – that Thomas Whitman could identify a Newport tall clock whereas Evelyn Lockhart just wanted to reach out and touch the shell. She almost lost her courage, but then she turned and her breath caught at the sight of him. He was improved, if that was possible, by the previous eighteen months, and he now looked even better than he did in her dreams. Thomas's face registered nothing at the sight of her. She might have been any client coming to him for help with a business transaction.

'This way,' he said, and he led her to an elevator, where neither said a word, and then into a large room with a window looking out onto the street. In fact, the view stretched all the way to the harbour, and Evie couldn't help but walk across to the window, to see the vast comings and goings of the city, as well as to hide her face, which she thought must plainly show how flustered she felt.

'You've been busy?' Thomas finally spoke and she couldn't tell if he was being sarcastic, referring to the fact that she'd stopped writing to him with no explanation, or if he was asking a genuine question. She chose to believe the latter.

'The boom's good for business,' she said. 'I hate to think what will happen to the children when the money stops coming.'

'Which it will. Tea?'

'No. Thank you.'

'So you're a doctor now?'

'Yes. A resident at the Sloane.'

'You got what you wanted. Congratulations.'

'Thank you.'

Evie was still standing beside the window and Thomas was standing behind his desk. The physical distance was several feet, but the emotional distance Evie heard in the word *congratulations* was immense. It was the same tone he'd used years ago in Concord when he'd said that Alberta was lovely, and Evie had hoped that a man in love with her would speak with more passion.

But she'd come all this way and she was in the part of town where deals were made, so she offered up her own promise to the city of New York, which was the only God she believed in: that if Thomas Whitman forgave her, she would . . . what? Cry, at the very least. But the city had had enough tears given to it over the years, and it sure didn't need any more of hers.

She turned her back on the view, on the drift back and forth of the water and the ships and the people. 'I saw your mother yesterday.'

'She said she'd seen you.'

'I had two children with me.'

'She mentioned that too.'

'She thought I must have married someone. You have to be married to adopt children.'

Thomas bent down to pick up a pen, eyes shielded from her so she couldn't tell what he was thinking.

'I'm not married. Lil and Leo are officially the adoptive parents.' Evie chose her words carefully. 'They knew how much I wanted Mary. She's the child from Concord. So they signed the papers for me, but the children live with me, as my daughters.'

'Why are you here, Evie?' He still said her name like nobody else in the world, like a caress. But he was studying the pen, rather than her.

'I didn't want you to think I'd gone off and married somebody else,' she said.

'It's no concern of mine.'

'I hoped it might be.' Evie summoned up every bit of fortitude she could muster to help her say the next words. 'I was . . . shocked . . . when I heard about your engagement.'

'Why?'

'Because I love you.'

'Any other reason?'

He looked at her, at last, but it might have been better if he hadn't. His expression was perfectly composed, as if neither her presence nor anything she'd said had affected him at all. Whereas everything about being in a room with Thomas was making her hands and her voice shake. What he'd asked – *any other reason?* – was such a short and simple sentence, but the hurt it inflicted was immense. Evie knew she had to keep going, to take the blows that were her due.

She took a step towards Thomas. 'What better reason is there?'

Thomas remained behind his desk. 'What's changed, Evie? Evidently you discovered that you didn't love me when I was in London, because you returned all my letters and disappeared. And yet now you say you do? I want to love someone who'll stay true to me, no matter what. Someone who trusts me as much as I trusted you.'

'It wasn't that I didn't love you.'

'Then what was it?' Thomas stared at her, waiting.

Evie couldn't risk it. If she told him he was Lucille's father before he said he loved her then she would never know what his feelings really were, and what was obligation. She remained by the window; the sky had shifted from day to night behind her, passing through its gloomiest phase in that sliver of time when the sun had almost gone but the lights of Manhattan hadn't yet turned on. New York was now incandescent, its sequined dress on, beads lustrous, smile resplendent. But the brilliance faded at Thomas's office, which was lit only by a desk lamp, so that darkness and shadow tapestried the walls, carpeted the floors and seeped into every space between. Evie was silent.

'So it was nothing,' Thomas said.

'I shouldn't have come.' Evie walked over to the door, knowing he wouldn't reach out and stop her.

In the train on the way home, Evie didn't cry. When she collected the girls, she simply shook her head at Lil but did not speak. Back at the apartment, she bathed the girls, kissed them and put them to bed. At last they were asleep and she could take her phony smile off, be the blank and empty thing she really was now that she knew she'd squandered her beloved.

~

When Evie woke the next day her limbs were heavy and it was so hard to shift her body out of bed. She tried to convince herself she was falling ill, but she knew that her body was immured in the sadness she'd told her heart not to feel.

It was over. Brutally and finally over. Thomas was marrying Winnie.

She sat on the edge of the bed until the ache lessened. Until she could stand up and open her arms to Mary and Lucille, who were excited that their mother had a rare two days off work and could spend time with them. Evie would let their smiles wash over her and scour away her grief so that she could face the world again as if nothing had happened.

The girls wanted to make waffles, and Evie sat with them at the table and helped stir the mixture, trying to concentrate through the clouds in her head.

Then the door buzzed, and Evie was surprised to find her sister on the doorstep. Unusually, she was by herself. 'Vi. What are you doing here? Where's Emily?'

'Auntie Vi!' called the girls, rushing over to hug their aunt as she came into the kitchen.

Viola kissed them both. 'Emily's with her Grandma Mabel. And I've brought you girls a beautiful puzzle.' She pulled a parcel out from behind her back. 'Why don't you two go into the other room while I talk to your mama.'

The girls toddled off, excited to open their present.

'Now everyone knows you have two adopted children,' Viola said.

Evie sank into a chair at the kitchen table. 'Mrs Whitman told you.'

'She told Thomas as well.'

'I know.'

'You've seen him?'

'Yes.'

'And?'

Evie felt her damn eyes fill again with tears. She didn't answer because she couldn't, not without howling.

'Oh, Evie.' Viola sat down opposite. 'Did you tell him?'

'What?'

Viola looked at her steadily. 'About Lucille.'

Evie moved away from her sister and stood at the small window that looked out onto the street. It was quiet outside; most people were probably still abed, enjoying the lazy Saturday morning. Evie wished she was still asleep as well, blissfully oblivious to yesterday's conversation with Thomas. 'You know Mary's the baby from Concord?' she fudged.

'I thought as much. Thomas did too. That's what he said to Mabel.'

'But do you know who Mary really is, Vi?'

'What do you mean?'

'She's our half-sister. Father is her father too.'

Evie succeeded in silencing Viola for almost a minute. Eventually she said, 'I think I need coffee.'

'Me too.' Evie busied herself with the cups and added, unsure if Viola's silence had been from shock or disapproval, 'It's not Mary's fault.'

'Oh, I know! It's just . . . unimaginable. Why didn't you tell me?'

'Father asked me not to. You were pregnant and I didn't want to upset you. I wasn't sure how you'd take it.'

'So that's why you adopted her.'

'I had to.'

Viola stood up and hugged her sister. 'I can't believe you did everything for Mary by yourself,' she said in awe, eyes wet with tears. 'I could have helped.'

'Charles would have made all our lives miserable if I'd involved you. It was easier this way.'

'You know I saw Father with a woman once? It was years ago, before we both left Concord. I was in Boston with Mother. She'd gone to meet a friend and I was shopping for clothes. Father and the woman were in a restaurant, an out-of-the-way place along a lane, and I'd gone down there to retie my bootlace. She was young. And Father looked young too. He seemed attentive, as if whatever she was saying to him was captivating. I'd never seen him look like that and it frightened me. I put it out of my mind. Until now.'

'What did the woman look like?'

'She had red hair. That's all I remember.'

'Mary's mother had red hair too. But if he was so captivated, why did he let her die?'

'I don't know.'

Evie put two cups of coffee on the table and sat down in her chair. They'd never know, she supposed, whether her father had just been taking what he could get from Rose or whether he'd felt true affection for her. Evie had always supposed it to be the former, because if he'd ever had a shred of feeling for Rose, he'd made a mockery of it by everything that came after.

Viola sat down too. The sisters were silent for a time until Viola said, 'I came here to say that, now everyone knows you have two adopted children, you should come out with us tomorrow. I'm having a little celebration for my birthday. No more secret visits. One doesn't turn thirty every day.'

'I can't do that —'

But Viola continued talking, the hint of a smile on her face. 'You should have heard Charles when he discovered you had two children and that I'd known about it all along.'

'How did you explain my being able to adopt them to the Whitmans?'

'I said that, not being content to stop up your bleeding heart by being a doctor, you'd asked some married friends to help you adopt Mary and another stray. That's what you'd always told me. Isn't it the truth?'

Evie heard the question Viola was asking, and prevaricated again. 'I can't come to the party. Not with everyone there.'

'It'll be me, Emily and Charles, plus you and the girls. No one to worry about. And it's not at home. It's at the Plaza. Afternoon tea.'

'What about Charles?'

'He'll be on his best behaviour – because if he isn't, I'll make sure his mother and father find out about his latest mistress.'

Evie smiled. An afternoon tea party at the Plaza was exactly the sort of thing she thought Mary and Lucille would love. 'Lucille's table manners mightn't be up to the Plaza's standard, but we'll come.'

Viola actually squealed with pleasure, and Evie laughed to see her sister so happy.

'See you tomorrow at one,' Vi said as she slipped out the door.

I hope I'm not doing the wrong thing, Evie thought. Going out so publicly with the girls to meet people so closely connected to Thomas. But the girls loved their cousin and deserved to spend time with her. Rather than worrying, she decided she would try to turn it into a celebration. Something to look forward to.

She went to find the girls. 'Let's make those waffles. Then we're going shopping for new dresses to wear to Auntie Viola's party.'

The girls' cries of delight made Evie feel better. Her children would get her through this; they would help her to forget, show her there was still joy to be found even in the midst of such anguish. After breakfast they got dressed and Evie took them to Macy's, where they chose party dresses in frilly, flouncy white. When they put them on, they looked up at Evie with smiles almost bigger than their faces could hold.

'Thank you, Mama,' Mary said.

Evie sank to her knees and wrapped her arms around her children. Her cheeks were wet and Mary looked at her with concern, but Evie said, 'They're happy tears.' It was half true. Some of the tears were from happiness, and some were for the other pair of arms that should have been wrapped around the three of them. Thomas's arms.

Chapter Twenty-Eight

'*W*e're going to that nice hotel opposite Central Park. The one you said looked like a palace,' Evie said to Mary the next day as she hailed a cab.

'Will there be cake?' asked Mary, while Lucille mumbled, 'Yum, yum, yum,' and tried to run off after a pigeon just as Evie had succeeded in flagging down the taxi.

'Yes, there'll be cake. And probably lots of it,' said Evie. She picked up Lucille and stuffed the little white ball of froth securely into the taxi between her and Mary.

The taxi swept them down Fifth Avenue, past Tiffany & Co., Lord & Taylor, B. Altman and Company, Saks, Bergdorf Goodman, Best & Co., Gorham, and Arnold Constable. Everyone on the sidewalks seemed festive that afternoon, hung with shopping bags and smiles and with a skip in their step. Crowds of ordinary people, high on the boom-time promise of living in the city that housed the tallest building in the world, an accomplishment that made them feel as if everyone in New York could have their feet on the ground and their head in the sky all at the same time. Evie watched a young couple walk out of Tiffany & Co., faces aglow like the diamonds they might have bought. No shattered hearts there.

By the time they reached Fifty-Ninth and the taxi swung around the Grand Army Plaza, Evie had fixed her smile back on.

'I'm going to walk up the steps like a princess,' said Mary.

Evie laughed. 'You do that.'

She stood back and watched as Mary took her skirt in her hands, held it out like a ballerina's tutu and slowly ascended the stairs with perfect posture and grace. She noticed that an elderly man had stopped still on the steps and the woman at his side was urging him on. 'What's wrong with you?' she was saying. 'We look like a pair of tourists stopped out here.'

The voice was as familiar as Evie's own skin. Her mother's voice. And then she looked properly and saw that the man staring at Mary was her father.

'The little girl reminded me of . . . Evelyn,' he said, at which point Evie thought it'd be best to show her hand.

'Hello, Father. Mother.'

Her father looked as if he was about to cast a kitten right on the front steps of the Plaza.

'I think we'd be more comfortable catching up inside, which is obviously what Viola intends for us to do,' Evie said. She wanted to kill her sister for springing such a surprise on all of them, but wasn't that so like the Viola she'd grown up with. Anything to put Evie at a disadvantage. And here was Evie thinking Viola was mellowing, that she wanted them to be real sisters. Real sisters would not do something like this!

Evie strode on ahead, furious, with Lucille in her arms, following Mary through the doors. She could sense her mother and father trailing several feet behind. When they reached the Palm Court and Viola stood up to wave, Evie glared at her sister.

Then she turned to her parents. 'These are my daughters, Mary and Lucille. Adopted from the Foundling.'

She directed the last sentence at her father, to make sure he knew. He lifted his eyes to her and Evie almost took a step back. Because she saw that her father was now an old man. The past two years had not been kind to him, and his back was stooped, his face whiskered with grey, and his hair had vanished from his head. More than that though, his eyes were receding, settling back into his skull as if they couldn't bear to look upon the world in which he'd cast aside so many dear things.

Mary was lucky, Evie thought, that her father had given her away to live a better life than the one she would have had with him. And Evie was so blessed to have Mary as her daughter. She could not regret for a moment what her father had done.

'I thought Mary needed a family,' Evie said. 'And we're all very happy.'

Her father nodded and Evie knew he understood. He'd get away with what he'd done because Evie had taken responsibility for it. But while Evie could sleep at night with a clear conscience over Mary, he would always be haunted by the child he'd never know. Mary was his penance and Evie's godsend. Her anger at her father disappeared; how could anyone be angry with a man who deserved only pity?

'This is Mr and Mrs Lockhart,' Evie said to her daughters. 'Say hello, girls.'

'They have the same name we do,' Mary marvelled.

'They do.' Evie looked at her mother and said, 'I couldn't write to you any more, because it was impossible not to write about them. I knew you'd disapprove.'

But her mother surprised her. She held out her hands to the girls, face soft with folded skin and with an expression that looked a lot like affection. 'Perhaps you'd like to sit beside me for a moment.'

Mr Lockhart shook his head slightly at his wife, but Mrs Lockhart said, 'I think we've let this go on long enough.' She sat down with Mary and Lucille and began to ask them the kinds of questions one didn't really ask a child, such as *did they enjoy visiting the Plaza?*, but Evie knew her mother was trying and that was better than anything.

She was about to give her niece a kiss and find somewhere to sit that was not too close to Viola, who she was still cross with, when somebody said her name. 'Evie.'

She turned around. 'Charles,' she said, and they regarded each other like boxers before a fight. But she realised that Charles, too, no longer warranted her hatred. He was another man whose choices had left him with nothing, even if he didn't know that yet. 'I think the idea is for us to pretend to be nice.' She held out her hand.

'You still think that all I want is to shake your hand?' he said under his breath, staring at the cup and saucer in his hand as if wishing it contained something stronger than tea. He turned away and strode to the bar, which was serving nothing other than lemonade, and shouted at the bartender as if Prohibition was all his fault. Evie sighed. It seemed that neither of the Whitman brothers would ever forgive her.

The pianist began to play 'I'm Nobody's Baby'. Evie tried to ignore the words and was thankful for the tap on the shoulder from none other than William Dunning, not a bell-boy any more, but wearing a badge that proclaimed him the Assistant Manager.

She kissed his cheek. 'You got what you deserved,' she said, nodding at his badge. 'I still have that white dress you know.'

He blushed to the tips of his ears when she kissed him. 'I'd hoped you would have what you deserved too, but you look as sad as you did the last time you were here.'

'Perhaps I did get what I deserved,' she said, squeezing his hand. 'I have another favour to ask.' She pointed to Charles. 'Can you make sure he doesn't spoil our party?' she asked, anxious for William to move away before the memories attached to him – being lost in a kiss with Thomas in this very room – made her feel more overwrought than she already did.

'Of course,' he said, and she watched as he expertly led Charles to a far away table and distracted him with a box of cigars.

Evie relaxed a little. Everything would be all right. These were all things she would have had to face eventually. Perhaps Viola was right to make her deal with them at last. She walked over to her sister. 'Haven't you been busy organising this?' she said to Viola.

Viola grinned the same way Evie used to smile at Viola when they were younger and Evie had outwitted her sister yet again. Evie was bemused to see the tables so turned. 'We have Emily and Mary and Lucille now,' Viola said. 'Time to stop thinking of ourselves and think of what's best for them.'

'When did you get so wise?' Evie sat down beside Viola, determined to hold onto the wonder of being close to her, the joy of having two children, and the pleasure of being able to freely visit her niece.

'We have to let some cats out of their bags before they run out of air. Emily needs her cousins.' Viola waved at two people coming in through the doors. The waiter placed a teapot and a plate of sandwiches on the table in front of them.

At the same time, Lucille pulled on Evie's skirt. 'Mama?'

'Yes, darling?' Evie lifted Lucille onto her lap. Mary climbed up on the other side.

When Evie looked up and recognised the two people Viola had waved to, she had her children arranged around her in a delightful tableau from which she could not escape. The people walking towards the table were Mabel Whitman and Thomas.

Chapter Twenty-Nine

'*V*iola!' Evie hissed. 'What are you doing?' What was her sister thinking inviting Thomas? How awkward for everyone, and how unbelievably awful for her. Evie picked up her purse. She could not stay. Could not bear to look at Thomas and know she could never, ever have him. That he was Winnie's now. But she was stopped by her sister's hand.

'Stay.' Viola was silent a moment, and when Evie saw the sadness in her sister's eyes her anger melted away. 'This is my thank you. For looking after Mary,' Viola said as she moved away.

Mrs Whitman and Thomas were standing in front of her now. She tried to compose herself. She would let the girls eat some cake and then they would go, she decided quickly. For safety, she'd sit near Viola. Thomas wouldn't have to speak to her once he'd said hello. She gently moved Lucille off her lap and stood, hoping to get the uncomfortable greetings over with, gripping her purse so that she wouldn't have to shake Thomas's hand. Touching him would discompose her utterly.

'Evie. Lovely to see you again,' said Mrs Whitman. She looked friendly, at least, and Evie was grateful for the politeness, even if perhaps it was forced. 'And Mary and Lucille, if I remember correctly,' Mrs Whitman continued.

Mary nodded solemnly and Lucille copied her sister.

'I'll go and speak to your parents, Evie. They look a little lost.' Mrs Whitman rustled away before Evie could stop her.

That left Thomas and Evie in the Palm Court at the Plaza Hotel once again, but this time with two children watching on. And with no chance of repeating that glorious kiss. She wondered for a moment if he was remembering it too, then dismissed the thought. The only kisses he would think about now were Winnie's, a thought that cut Evie to the quick.

'Who are you?' Mary asked before Evie could say anything.

'I'm Thomas,' he said gently, and Evie's hand just about strangled her purse at his tone, which only made her see more clearly what a wonderful father he would have been.

'Nice to meet you, Thomas.' Mary held out her hand to be shaken, and Evie couldn't believe that at such a moment the usually reticent Mary would be so talkative.

'What's your sister's name?' Thomas asked.

'Lucille,' Mary offered eagerly.

Lucille, ever the imitator, held out her hand too. To Evie's consternation, Thomas took it in his and bent down playfully to kiss it. Mary and Lucille dissolved into giggles.

Evie had to sit down. She willed herself to get through the next hour, to appear as if she was enjoying herself, and to not look at Thomas, not even for one second.

'Are you a friend of Mama's?' Mary asked, clearly delighted at this new acquaintance who seemed so much like a prince from a storybook.

'I've known your mama for a very long time. Since she was about as old as you.' His voice was still warm, and Evie almost wished he would revert to the coldness of their last encounter, anything other than remind her so accutely of what she'd given up.

'Really?' Mary looked at Evie as if unable to believe that Evie could ever have been so small. 'What did she look like then?'

'Much the same. Beautiful. And fearless. Except I think she's more careful now than she used to be. Because she has you and your sister to think about.' Thomas looked at her then and Evie felt her heart cleave.

She fixed her gaze on the teacup. Something wet landed on the saucer. A single teardrop.

Lucille tugged on Thomas's trouser leg. Mary interpreted. 'She wants you to pick her up.'

'No,' whispered Evie, looking up. But it was too late.

Thomas bent down and gathered up the little girl in the frilly white dress. He held her in his arms, all blonde curls and big dark eyes. Lucille clapped her palms against Thomas's cheeks, marking each of them with a red spot the size of her hand. Then Thomas and Lucille both turned to look at Evie with eyes that were exactly the same. It was bittersweet and beautiful and Evie wished they would stay like that forever.

She found herself telling the truth for the first time in so long. 'You said I didn't trust you, but I did what I did *because* I trusted you. I knew what you'd do if you found out the truth. And I *was* fighting. For you to be free to be the person you were meant to be.'

Before Thomas could reply, Mary asked, 'Where's your wife?' She looked around for another person to complete the princely picture.

'I'm not married,' Thomas replied, at the same time as Evie said, 'Thomas will be married soon.'

Thomas sat down beside Evie with Lucille still in his arms. 'Winnie's parents placed the engagement announcement in the newspaper. But I'm not marrying Winnie.'

'Don't marry me for our child, if that's what's holding you back.'

'I won't marry you for our child.'

That was it then. The end. It was the first and last time Evie would ever see Thomas with their child in his arms.

But then came the most surprising words of all. 'When you were standing in my office, I had to hold onto my desk to stop myself reaching out to you. I'll never feel for anyone what I feel for you. But I didn't know or understand then what you'd done. Viola explained everything yesterday. That it was all for me. And for Lucille. So, I won't marry you for our child,' he repeated. 'I'll marry you because I love you.'

Thomas leaned forward, reaching over Lucille's head, and kissed Evie in the Plaza Hotel for the second time in their lives and once again without regard for who might be watching. As his lips touched hers, Evie knew that what she'd once dreamed of, a kiss from Mr Fitzgerald, the casual kiss so sought after in one of his novels, was a hollow thing. What she had now with Thomas was a kiss she would never tire of, a kiss she wanted to lose herself in every day of her life.

Thomas pulled back a little to let Lucille in, to let Mary in. He said to Evie, 'It was always you.'

The New Yorker, **June 20th, 1927**

NEW YORK society was agog today as one of the city's most eligible bachelors, bank president Mr Thomas Whitman, married obstetrician Miss Evelyn Lockhart. The bride wore a sleeveless black and white Lanvin gown covered in sequins to a point just above her knee, where the dress fluttered away like two long and dazzling butterfly wings to trail along the ground. I declare the gown will become the most copied dress of the season, despite Miss Lockhart's scandalous profession. Fashion always trumps scruples, in my opinion.

Miss Lockhart's two adopted daughters sprinkled the church with white rose petals for the bride to swing her heels through on the way to the altar. The two blonde cherubs made a beautiful picture with their adoptive mother, although I suspect a few gasps could be heard from the Victorian antiques in the back when the little girls preceded Miss Lockhart down the aisle. But this is 1927 and who cares for antiques these days?

In spite of the gasps, the sky didn't fall down and banking stocks continued to rise. Perhaps Mrs Evelyn Whitman has demonstrated that you can be a successful woman whose vocation it is to help others and still marry your Prince Charming – and if he truly is charming, he will not mind a jot if his wife continues to work as a doctor, thus helping to make the world a better place to be. And that one can adopt and raise two orphaned children who are now heirs to a whopping fortune, in true Dickensian style. I believe it's called philanthropy – thinking about the good of others, rather than always worrying about what others think of us.

As the car left the Plaza Hotel, bound for Newport, the newly wed Mr and Mrs Thomas Whitman could be seen necking in the back with such passion that I wouldn't mind betting theirs is the kind of love that will well and truly last a lifetime.

– LIPSTICK

$\mathcal{A}$cknowledgements

$\mathcal{T}$hank you to those institutions who keep archival material, without which this book would be much the poorer. To Stephen Novak, Head of Archives and Special Collections at the Columbia University Medical Center, thank you for your assistance. In these archives I found the invaluable papers of Leoni Neumann Claman, comprising notes recorded by Claman in 1923 as she sat, one of a handful of women, in the lecture halls of the Columbia College of Physicians and Surgeons.

Many divisions of the New York Public Library provided assistance and archival materials, especially the Lionel Pincus and Princess Firyal Map Division, the Theatre on Film and Tape Archive, the NYPL Digital Gallery, and the Billy Rose Theatre Division, which gave me access to the papers of Billie Burke, Florenz Ziegfeld's wife. These provided me with a huge amount of information about the Ziegfeld Follies in the 1920s. The archives of *The New Yorker*, especially the advertisements of the time and Lipstick's columns, were a terrific source of information about daily life in the city.

Many books have also proved useful. For information about New York in the 1920s, I used *The Encyclopedia of New York* edited by Kenneth Jackson; *Daily Life in the United States, 1920–1940* by David E. Kyvig; *Flapper: A madcap story of sex, style, celebrity, and the women who made America modern* by Joshua Zeitz; *The Historical Atlas of New York City* by Eric Homberger; and the wonderful catalogue of Berenice Abbott's photographs, *Changing New York*. For information about the Sloane Hospital for Women, Harold Speert's *The Sloane Hospital Chronicle* was invaluable. For information about obstetric practices at the time, I referred to *Brought to*

Bed: Childbearing in America, 1750–1950 by Judith Walzer Leavitt; *Lying-In: A history of childbirth in America* by Richard and Dorothy Wertz; *The Management of Obstetric Difficulties* by Paul Titus; and Dr Joseph DeLee's controversial article 'The Prophylactic Forceps Operation' first published in the *American Journal of Obstetrics and Gynecology* in 1920. For information about the Ziegfeld Follies, *The Ziegfeld Touch: The life and times of Florenz Ziegfeld, Jr.* by Richard and Paulette Ziegfeld and *Ziegfeld* by Charles Higham were useful. Finally, Emily Dunning Barringer's account, *Bowery to Bellevue: The story of New York's first woman ambulance surgeon*, was fascinating. The 1925–26 Columbia University catalogue provided me with information about the requirements for entry into the College of Physicians and Surgeons at the time.

To my wonderful writing group, Dawn Barker, Amanda Curtin, Sara Foster and Annabel Smith: thank you, not just for providing much-needed feedback on my first draft, but also for being there throughout the highs and lows of getting this book published. Thanks also to Liz Byrski and Vanessa Carnevale for your feedback on an early draft.

Biggest thanks of all to my amazing agent Jacinta di Mase for being the first person to make me believe in this book and for all her invaluable advice. To Rebecca Saunders, thank you for being the best publisher a writer could wish for, and to everyone else at Hachette, where I feel very lucky to have found a home.

And to all of the wonderful readers who talk to me every day on my blog and on social media, thank you for being a part of this journey, for making me feel that writing isn't a lonely business, for making me want to keep writing more books to share with you.

Finally, as always, to Russell, Ruby, Audrey and Darcy, all my love and thanks.

Author's Note

A Kiss from Mr Fitzgerald is a work of fiction. However, many of the events and circumstances described in the novel are based on fact.

First and foremost, Dr Joseph DeLee's ideas about birth as a pathological process which damaged women, and his prescription of sedation, ether, episiotomies and forceps as necessary for every birth, were fundamental in governing the way obstetrics was practised at the time. For more information about his philosophies, please see his article 'The Prophylactic Forceps Operation', first published in 1920 in the *American Journal of Obstetrics and Gynecology*.

The Sloane Hospital for Women and the Columbia College of Physicians and Surgeons are both real institutions. The first group of women to graduate from the college did so in 1922. None of the characters in this book from the college or hospital, including Evie, are based on real people. Virginia Kneeland Frantz is mentioned as the first woman from the College of Physicians and Surgeons to gain a surgical internship, and this is fact.

Chumley's did exist, and as there is some debate about when it actually opened its doors, I have used the creative licence of the fiction writer to have it open by 1922. The Ziegfeld Follies were an essential part of Broadway life for many years, from 1907 to 1931. The column published in *The New Yorker* under the pseudonym Lipstick on page 184 is genuine, as is the quote from the *Ladies' Home Journal* on page 3. And Mrs Vanderbilt was said to have greeted guests at her parties wearing a dress covered in hundreds of electric bulbs, although probably at a slightly earlier time than I have used this incident in the book.

A Playlist

Here is a list of the songs from the 1920s that are referred to in the book. Look them up, load them up and listen while you read!

'A Good Man Is Hard to Find', Marion Harris

'April Showers', Al Jolson

'Bugle Call Rag', New Orleans Rhythm Kings

'Charleston', Paul Whiteman and his Orchestra

'Hot Lips', Paul Whiteman and his Orchestra

'I Love You Truly', Elsie Baker

'I'll See You in My Dreams', Isham Jones with the Ray Miller Orchestra

'I'm Nobody's Baby', Ruth Etting

'Let Me Call You Sweetheart', The Peerless Quartet

'Oh! Boy, What a Girl', Eddie Cantor

'Oh, Lady Be Good', Cliff Edwards

'Somebody Stole My Gal', Ted Weems and His Orchestra

'Sweet Adeline', Haydn Quartet

'Tain't Nobody's Biz-ness if I Do', Sara Martin (with Fats Waller on piano)

'The New York Glide', Ethel Waters

'Toot, Toot, Tootsie (Good bye)', Al Jolson

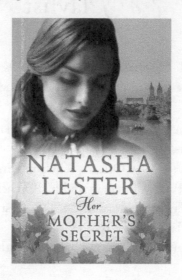

1918, England. Armistice Day should bring peace into Leonora's life. Rather than secretly making cosmetics in her father's chemist shop to sell to army nurses, Leo hopes to now display her wares openly. Instead, Spanish flu arrives in the village, claiming her father's life. Determined to start over, she boards a ship to New York City. On the way she meets debonair department store heir Everett Forsyth . . .

1949, New York City. Everett's daughter, Alice, a promising ballerina, receives a mysterious letter inviting her to star in a series of advertisements for a cosmetics line. If she accepts she will be immortalised like dancers such as Zelda Fitzgerald, Josephine Baker and Ginger Rogers. Why, then, are her parents so quick to forbid it?

Her Mother's Secret is the story of a brave young woman chasing a dream in the face of society's disapproval.

Chapter One

*T*he jar in Leonora's hand contained a substance as black as the sky on a new moon night. She unscrewed the lid, her friend Joan watching eagerly over her shoulder.

'It worked,' Leonora said.

'Try it on!' Joan said.

Leonora dampened her finger and rubbed it over the mascara she'd made the day before, creating a film of black liquid. She applied it to the curve of her lashes, cautiously at first, before dipping her finger back into the jar and adding some more. 'How does it look?'

'Wait.' Joan picked up a hand mirror and the copy of *Picture Show* magazine that was lying open on the workbench in front of them. She held the mirror in front of Leo and the magazine, opened to a photograph of Theda Bara as Cleopatra, beside Leo's face.

Leo smiled at her reflection, green eyes made larger and brighter by the mascara. 'It's better than I hoped it would be. Here.'

391

She passed the jar to Joan, who coloured her lashes as Leo had done.

'I think next time I'll add some oil to make it shinier,' Leo said as she studied her face. 'Cleopatra's lashes definitely have more gloss.'

'Given it's the only mascara available for hundreds of miles around, I think it's a very good first effort.'

'Would you believe it's just soap flakes and lampblack? I tried Vaseline and lampblack, but it was too gooey. This is easier to put on, but I think I can make it even better.' Leo sighed, looking around the mess of the stillroom, workbench cluttered with salves and ointments and her cosmetic experiments. 'That's if I can find the time in between making medications for venereal disease.'

'I can understand why the boys do it though,' Joan said sadly. 'The ones I've nursed told me they were prepared to do anything to feel a bit of love in the midst of what they've had to face.'

Leo shivered imagining Joan in the hospital of the army camp situated about a mile out of Sutton Verny, listening to such admissions while she bandaged wounded men. 'Are we awful, do you think? To stand here talking about the movies and mascara while . . .'

'Of course not!' Joan was emphatic, her Australian accent always more pronounced in moments of fervour. 'I spend twelve hours a day trying to keep men from dying and you spend just as long making medicines for the same purpose. Not to mention keeping up their morale; making the run to the chemist to collect supplies is the most popular job at camp.'

Leo blushed. 'Are we going to the cinema or not?' she asked.

'I just need some lipstick to go with my lashes.'

Leo passed Joan a jar filled with a glossy red cream.

'You're a treasure. I'm sure you keep the nurses here better supplied than the ladies of London are.' Joan dabbed some colour onto her lips, smoothed her hands over her brown hair, put a navy cloche hat on her head and nodded with satisfaction.

'What if Mrs Hodgkins sees us?'

Joan shrugged. 'What if she does? It's not illegal to wear mascara.'

'Not yet. But probably only because nobody understands quite how much we all want to.' Leo pointed at the magazine. 'Do you think "Theda Bara made me do it" is a reasonable excuse?'

Joan laughed. 'Let's go. I have news to share on the way.'

'I'll check on Daddy first.' Leo flipped the closed sign on the door labelled *Harold East, Dispensing Chemist and Apothecary* and ran up the stairs to the flat where she and her father lived.

Harold East was sitting at the table, supposedly reading the newspaper, but he had taken off his glasses and his eyes were closed. He looked thin and even paler than usual and Leo wished for the thousandth time that she could get him the food he needed; rationing was fine for someone young like her, but not for her father, whose health had floundered from the effects of grief since his wife had died in childbirth, the strain and deprivation of war making him age all the quicker.

'Daddy,' she whispered, putting a hand on his arm.

He jumped, eyes flying open. 'What's happened?' he said, searching for his glasses.

Leonora found them beneath the newspaper and passed them to him, but he only held them in his hand and looked at her through eyes she knew were too foggy to see her properly. 'I'm sorry I scared you,' she said softly. 'Nothing's happened.

I came up to say goodbye. I'm going to see a film with Joan, remember?'

'Of course you are.' Her father beamed and held out his arms.

Leo kissed the top of his head. 'You had some bread?'

'I even licked the plate clean of crumbs,' he said. 'You go off and have a good time. You spend too much of your life here with me.'

'How did things go in the shop this morning?'

'Fine. Some soldiers came in and were most disappointed to hear you were out tending to a luckier bunch of soldiers at Sutton Veny House. And you'll have to make another batch of Leo's Cold Cream. We've sold out again. Mrs Kidd told me it was even better than Pond's.'

'I knew they'd love it. Maybe now you'll let me sell lip colour too.'

Her father shook his head, but he was still smiling. 'Imagine what Mrs Hodgkins would say about that!'

Leo knew all too well what Mrs Hodgkins, who'd appointed herself responsible for Leo's moral upbringing, would say. She thanked God that her father hadn't put his glasses on and couldn't see her lashes. 'I don't need mothering from anyone except you,' she said.

Her father's eyes filled with tears, and Leonora knew he was thinking of her mother, who'd never even had the chance to hold her daughter. 'Well,' he said, voice quavering a little, 'it's your shop really. I'm hardly in it any more. You should do what you like in there. I might head off to bed, my love. I'm tuckered out.'

Leo watched him shuffle away, touching the wall once or twice for balance. Then she hurried downstairs to Joan. 'Sorry that took so long.'

'Is he all right?' Joan asked.

Leo shook her head. 'I don't know. It's like the war is draining the life out of him, making him frailer than ever.'

'Can I do anything?' Joan squeezed Leo's hand.

'No.' Leo dabbed at the dampness in the corner of her eye. 'Let's go.'

They set off along the high street, Leo waving to her neighbour, Mr Banks, who did a slight double-take when he saw them, though he waved back nonetheless. Leo felt her shoulders relax. It was nice to go out for the night and forget, for a short time, what the world had become. It was nice to add a little colour to her face to compensate for the fact that her dress was four years old, faded to a dirty grey, and had been mended so many times it felt almost as if it was made from thread rather than fabric. It was nice to laugh with Joan, rather than being always on edge, waiting to hear who was the latest of the boys from the village to die.

As they walked, their feet crunched through the elm leaves on the road, leaves that appeared in autumn as quickly as the new gravestones in the cemetery. Leo opened her mouth to ask Joan for her news when a group of soldiers from the army camp came streaming towards them. The presence of soldiers, Australian nurses like Joan, and an army camp was so familiar to Leo now that she could hardly remember what the village had looked like before the neat rows of identical huts, and the hospital where Joan worked had been erected. In the distance, she could see the butts on the shooting range, rectangles of white, like hankies set out to dry. A biplane flew overhead, preparing to land in the grass near the camp but Leo still ducked, still unwilling to trust anything that fell from the sky.

All of a sudden, Joan grabbed Leo's hand. 'Quick,' she hissed. 'Mrs Hodgkins is over there and if we don't move, she'll see you.'

The crowd of soldiers, so many that the villagers going in the opposite direction had to stand aside to let them pass, gave Leo and Joan a good place to hide.

'Leonora!'

Leo smiled up at the familiar face of the boy – well, he was a man now – in army uniform who she'd known all her life as Albert from Gray's Farm. He'd taken her for a walk the last time he was on leave, and also to a film. When he'd escorted her home, he'd kissed her hand and Leonora had closed her eyes and willed herself to feel it, the bolt of lightning that always struck lovers in books when they touched. But all she'd felt was a wish to be elsewhere – back in London, perhaps, where she had spent three years at school before the war had started and she'd returned home, bringing with her a yearning for more that was hardly satisified by running a black market in lipstick between the chemist shop and the nurses at the hospital.

Albert didn't reach for her hand this time. 'What have you done to yourself?' he asked, eyes wide with bafflement at the sight of her darkened lashes.

Leo felt the joy she'd painted on her face fade away.

What *had* she done? Making mascara while men were fighting to save her country. She stared down at the pavement, shame at her own frivolity flooding through her.

'You look like a . . .' He stopped himself just in time. 'You'll make yourself a laughing-stock, Leonora. What will your father think?'

What will your father think? Of all the things Albert could have said, that was the worst. Her own shame she could bear, but not her father's.

'Excuse us,' Joan said crisply. Taking Leo's arm, she led her into the Palace Cinema, where she chose seats right up the front, a safe distance from the soldiers who tended to occupy the back rows.

As Leo sat down, her spirit reasserted itself. 'Honestly, why is there such a fuss made about a little bit of make-up?' she said, vexed that she'd been so affected by Albert's judgement. 'It's all right for a man to contract VD from a French prostitute – who's probably wearing lipstick, I might add – but a woman isn't allowed to do something as innocuous as make her lashes darker?'

'Don't pay any attention to him.' Joan lit a cigarette and offered one to Leo, who shook her head. 'You look beautiful and he's scared of that.'

'Do you think, one day, everyone will stop being scared?' Leo asked. 'That Mrs Hodgkins will ever stop bleating about the horror of so many ankles on display beneath the nurses' uniforms, that Mr Ellis won't ask me to *turn off that rubbish!* when he comes into the shop and hears Marion Harris playing on the Victrola instead of "Oh! It's a Lovely War!"?'

'Probably not any time soon,' Joan admitted.

The newsreel flickered onto the screen and the lights dimmed. Leo had just settled back in her seat when she had a sudden thought. 'Why is Albert back?' she whispered. 'And so many other soldiers?'

'They shipped an entire regiment back this morning,' Joan said, ignoring the reproving stares of their neighbours. 'That's what I wanted to tell you. Pete wrote that he'd be here in a few days.'

'Really?' Leo asked.

She was reprimanded with a loud 'Shhhh!'

'Maybe the war is nearly over,' she whispered.

'Maybe.'

Leo grinned. 'If that was true, I'd cartwheel around the theatre.'

'Pete asked me to move to New York with him when he's discharged. That made me feel like cartwheeling to the moon.'

'New York! But what about Sydney?'

'Shhhhhh!' Even more people turned to shush them now.

'I'll tell you after the show's over,' Joan said.

They turned their attention to the screen, but Leo couldn't concentrate. She could see New York in her mind, the legendary city, a place filled with love and hope and skyscrapers-in-the-air; buildings that reached into the solid foundation of the ground so that the dreams they flung into the air must surely become real, as they had both bedrock and backbone to support them. If the war was nearly over, then the future might come after all; life would begin again, rather than being stalled as it had for so long. Then what might she do?

Her smile remained on her face throughout the shorts, the feature and back out onto the street, where a soldier whistled. Even then, Leo couldn't stop smiling. Who cared if it looked like she was flirting? Wasn't it wonderful that she was here and that the soldier was still alive and that they *could* do something as simple as flirting?

'Did you say yes?' Leo asked, threading her arm through Joan's as they stepped onto the pavement, walking fast to escape the November wind biting viciously through their cloaks and mittens. 'To New York?'

'I did and you should come with me.'

'I can't,' Leo said. 'Daddy wouldn't survive a journey to New York and he certainly wouldn't survive if I upped and left him.'

'Joan!' A shout from behind made Joan and Leo whirl around, straight into the wind that had swept up like a cavalry charge, pounding their cheeks.

'You have to come back,' a nurse panted as she caught up to them.

'What is it?' Joan asked.

'Spanish flu,' the nurse said sombrely.

With those dreadful words sounding like a requiem in the night, Joan was off into the darkness and the wind, leaving Leo shivering.

Influenza. Not again. Not now, not when the boys were coming home, when the war was so close to ending. They'd been through it once already, back in the spring, and Leo and Joan had both been laid low for a fortnight with it. But she'd heard whispers from the towns and villages it had already struck that this one was worse.

She hurried the rest of the way home, unable to shake off the worry that fluttered relentlessly in her stomach. The first thing she did when she arrived, even before she took off her cloak, hat and gloves, was to creep along the hall to her father's room. She opened the door a crack and could see his huddled shape in the bed, could hear him snoring loudly, lost in a deep and lovely sleep. She smiled, throwing off her cloak and her fears.

The next morning, Leo woke early and went downstairs to the stillroom at the back of the shop. If influenza had come to the army camp, she'd be in for a busy day. She made certain she had enough liniments for chests and tinctures for coughs before she took advantage of the quiet dawn hour to pull out the stepladder and reach up to the highest shelf, which held her father's books. Chemistry books, science books – books filled with long and seemingly obscure words, but Leo had found that, if you spent time getting to know those words, they were among the most enchanting in the English language. Petrolatum was both an unctuous and hydrophobic mixture of hydrocarbons, but add some lampblack and you had mascara. She ran her hand along the spines and stopped when she reached her treasures: an enamelled Fabergé powder compact in which was nestled a swansdown puff, and a Coty perfume bottle, made by Lalique in the shape of a dragonfly. They were the most precious things Leo owned, both because they had belonged to her mother, and because Leo wished her cosmetics could be placed inside something just as lovely, lined up in rows on the shelves of a shop. Then she climbed down the ladder. Provided this influenza wasn't too bad – and in the pale gold light of an autumn morning it didn't seem possible that it would be – she really would put some lip colour in the shop rather than just joking with her father about it, and who cared what Mrs Hodgkins had to say about that!

She took out a saucepan and wooden spoon – her crude version of a mixing kettle – and heated and stirred beeswax, carmine, almond oil, blood beet and oil of roses until it was the perfect shade of red. She poured the mixture into several small jars to set – soupçons of beauty in the midst of the horror in which they lived.

Then she went back upstairs. 'Daddy?' she called.

'I've slept in a bit today, love.' Her father's voice came from his room. 'Be there in a minute.'

Leo boiled two eggs, put out a slice of bread for each of them, then made the tea, with just half a scoop of leaves rather than the three her father liked; tea had become as rare as good news these last few years.

When her father appeared, he sat down heavily in his chair, body shaking.

'You're cold!' Leo cried. 'Let me get you a blanket for your lap.'

'Don't fuss. I'll be fine after my tea.'

Leo passed him his cup. 'Drink up then,' she said mock sternly. 'And I'll make you another.'

'You're a good girl, Leo. How was your night?'

'I saw Albert. His regiment's been shipped back.'

'I'll wager he was glad to see you,' her father said in a tone Leo couldn't quite decipher.

'I don't know. Maybe I shouldn't have but I wore mascara. He was a little shocked.'

'Pffft!' her father scoffed. 'He's been in a trench at war but he gets shocked by black stuff on your lashes? He's not the man for you. None of them are.'

'You're just being a protective father,' she teased.

'I'm not,' he said decidedly. 'He'll ask you to marry him, mark my words. And you're to say no. Don't let yourself get stuck here. As soon as the war is over, I'll find a way to get you back to London, you see if I don't.'

'I won't leave you, no matter what you say.'

The sound of church bells sang through the window, interrupting them. 'It's not Sunday,' Leo said.

She ran to the window and threw it open, heedless of the cold air that streamed in.

The bells rang on and on, and people thronged the street. The sound they were making was unfamiliar to Leo's ears at first. Then she realised – they were laughing.

'What is it?' she called down to Mr Banks, who was standing outside his solicitor's office next door, beaming.

'The war is over!' he shouted back.

Leo flew to her father and squeezed him so tightly he began to cough. 'It's over!' she cried.

He clapped his hands over his ears and laughed. 'Well, don't stand around here,' he said. 'Off you go!'

Leo pulled out her handkerchief and wiped the tears of relief off her father's face. 'I love you,' she said.

Then she tore down the stairs and outside, hoping to find Joan and dance with her in the streets. But it was almost impossible to move, as with every step she met a soldier who wanted to take her hands to twirl her around or lift her high in the air. One even tried to kiss her and she let him because it was a day when proprieties had ceased to matter.

'Thanks,' he shouted, grinning at her before running off.

The town went mad that morning: shops were left unmanned, cows unmilked, breakfasts uneaten. The church was full of people giving thanks, the Woolpack Hotel proprietor passed mugs of frothing beer out to anyone who waltzed by, the policemen ignored such flagrant violations of the rules and even the trees seemed to join in the celebrations, dropping leaves like blessings onto Leo's red-gold hair and the heads of all the villagers gathered together in an impromptu celebration on the high street.

Leo was sipping a beer and joining in an improvised circle dance when someone tapped her shoulder. 'Miss, my mum needs something for her cough.'

The words were like a slap on the cheek and Leo realised that she hadn't seen Joan, that very few nurses were out enjoying the revelry. But look how many soldiers had come into town. The influenza couldn't be too serious. Still, unease made her sober. 'I'm coming,' she said to the lad in front of her.

As she turned towards the shop, it began to rain. Her skirt was quickly muddied, hems weighed down with clay and water. Back at the shop, she gave the boy some medicine for his mother, asking him about symptoms, frowning as he described fevers and coughs and headaches. After he left, she ran upstairs to see her father, who was still sitting at the table where she'd left him.

'The influenza's come,' she said without preamble. 'You're to stay up here. I couldn't bear it if you caught it.'

'Don't be a goose,' her father said fondly. 'I'll be right as rain. But I might lie down for a bit till that cup of tea oils my joints.'

Her father safely in his room, Leo returned to the shop. The flow of customers that afternoon was steady, but not overwhelming. A few coughs and fevers, but it *was* autumn. She closed the shop at six, made her father eggs and toast again for supper and went to bed, only to be awoken at five by a loud knocking on the shop door. Dread made her dress hurriedly, knowing that only those caring for the very ill would seek help so early.

'What is it?' her father called from his room.

'Just a customer whose clock mustn't be working.' She made her voice sound light, as if it was a minor inconvenience having to get up at dawn, nothing more.

But there wasn't just one customer; there were many. Their faces were dazed with the bewilderment that they'd beaten one merciless opponent – the war – only to have another that might be just as brutal land on their doorstep. They all wanted something Leo didn't have: a cure. A miracle. A way out of the hell this world had become.

In the space between yesterday and today, influenza had reached out its hand and gripped as many as it could by the throat, and it wasn't letting go.

Leo did her best all that long, long day, frantically making up more liniments to ease coughs. She gave away all the muslin masks she had left, not charging a penny for anything. She'd thought the worst moment was when the baker's wife ran in, eyes wild, shouting that her husband had turned purple. Leo knew it meant the end was nigh; the cyanosis that was such a distinctive feature of this flu had set in. There was nothing Leo could do.

'Be with him,' Leo whispered, hugging her.

But then the news came in that Albert – Albert, who'd never done anything wrong – had succumbed too.

After that, Leo turned off her thoughts. She concentrated on helping those she could, advising everyone to keep their hands washed, to thoroughly clean all bedding and handkerchieves, to stay off the streets. By mid-afternoon, there was nowhere to go anyway. Most shops had closed. The church was closed. The Palace Cinema. The Woolpack Hotel. There would be no more celebrations of the armistice. Instead, their village of five hundred people, already decimated by war, would start to bury more dead, until the dead almost outnumbered the living.

When night fell, she hurried upstairs to her father. She expected to find him at the table with a pot of tea for a companion but the flat was in darkness. Surely he wasn't in bed already?

Then a sound reached her ears. A wet, hacking cough. Dear God. Leo threw open the door to his room. 'Are you all right? I thought I heard . . .' She couldn't bring herself to say it.

'I have a fever,' her father rasped.

Black fear clogged Leonora's heart. 'You'll be fine,' she said, aiming for cheeriness but falling a million miles short. 'I'll make you some broth.'

'No. I'll sleep it off.' His eyes closed, but rather than finding peace in sleep, his lungs rattled with every hard breath in and out.

Leo fetched a cloth and basin then sat down beside his bed. She laid the damp cloth on his forehead. She rubbed his back when he coughed so hard he seemed almost to lift off the bed, holding a basin to catch the sputum, washing it out and returning just in time for the next spasm. She changed his sheets when they became soaked through with sweat. Occasionally he quietened and she perched on the edge of her chair, fingers worrying a hole the size of a handkerchief into her skirt. Then another violent paroxysm of coughing racked him, not stopping for what felt like hours. For its long duration, Leo's father clung to her, as if he was her child, and she held his hand and tried to sing him into sleep, just as a mother would.

It was dawn when she realised the only sounds she could hear were roosters and the delivery boys' carts. The relief that her father's coughing had settled made her woozy; the room tipped a little at the edges and she breathed in deeply and slowly to set it to rights. Through the first sliver of morning light creeping under the curtains, she could just make out his shape, curled on his side, resting peacefully.

She tiptoed from the room. She'd make him some porridge while he slept; it would warm him, give him strength. She even tipped in a little precious sugar. When it was steaming hot, she carried it down the hall, sure he would have smelled it cooking, that he'd be waiting with a hungry stomach for this unexpected feast.

But he hadn't moved.

'Daddy? I have some porridge for you.'

No response.

'Daddy!' The word cracked in two.

She knew she could move to the bed, touch his shoulder, watch him jump awake and flounder for his glasses. Or she could remain where she was, in a space that existed out of time. She could stop the future from coming, if only she waited there long enough. A tear fell into her father's porridge. Then another.

She shook her head. It was her silly imagination, an imagination that Mrs Hodgkins had often said should be kept in check. Well, check it she would. She marched down the stairs, out the front door and knocked at Mr Banks's house.

But when Mr Banks answered, she found that the bravado she'd mustered had deserted her. She stood mute, eyes damp, hands clenched into fists.

'What is it?' Mr Banks asked.

'Father,' she said. 'Influenza.'

'Oh, Leo.' Mr Banks embraced her and she stood stiffly in his arms, wanting nothing more than to break down. But that would only make it true.

'I'll go and see,' Mr Banks said.

Leo nodded. She followed him into the flat and waited in the kitchen while he went to her father's room. She'd left the cooker on, she realised, and the kettle was still whistling. But her father hadn't come out to turn it off. The minutes scraped past.

Then Mr Banks appeared. He shook his head.

It felt like a knife had been plunged into her very core, shearing off everything that had ever made her Leonora East.

She hurried into the bedroom, pulling back the sheet that Mr Banks had drawn up over her father's face. That precious face, a face that was more familiar to her than her own, had vanished in the night, leaving behind something cold and livid. And his mouth — it was stretched open as if he'd been calling for her when he'd passed. But she hadn't heard him, would never know what he had wanted to say.

She sat by her father's side all day, wordless, tearless, holding his cold, cold hand. From all over the village, she thought she could hear coughing, people choking on the crimson fluid that filled their lungs, fluid that had suffocated her father. She pushed away the Bible someone tried to put in her hands. Who wanted God? Instead she raged at God, that He would do this to her, to Daddy, to everyone. She called God every bad name she could think of, including words she'd never said before.

Then they came to take her father's body away. 'No!' she hissed, jumping up from the chair. 'You can't have him.'

'Hush,' Mr Banks soothed her, holding her tightly in his arms so she couldn't stop the people lifting her father out of bed. 'You have to let him go.'

'How?' Leo whispered. 'How can I ever do that?'

Only when her father had gone did the tears start to fall, hard and fast, like iron bullets shooting into her father's now, and forever, empty bed.

NATASHA LESTER worked as a marketing executive for ten years, including stints at cosmetic company L'Oréal, managing the Maybelline brand, before returning to university to study creative writing. She completed a Master of Creative Arts as well as her first novel, *What Is Left Over, After*, which won the T.A.G. Hungerford Award for Fiction. Her second novel, *If I Should Lose You*, was published by Fremantle Press in 2012, followed by *A Kiss from Mr Fitzgerald* in 2016. *The Age* described Natasha as 'a remarkable Australian talent', and her work has appeared in the *Review of Australian Fiction* and *Overland*, and the anthologies *Australian Love Stories*, *The Kid on the Karaoke Stage* and *Purple Prose*. In her spare time Natasha loves to teach writing, is a sought after public speaker and can often be found playing dress-ups with her three children. She lives in Perth.

natashalester.com.au

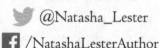

@Natasha_Lester

/NatashaLesterAuthor

#KissFitz